DOWN AND DEAD IN DALLAS

Down and Dead, Inc.

VICKI HINZE

MAGNOLIA LEAF PRESS

Down and Dead in Dallas

Print Edition 2018. ISBN: 978-1-939016-20-1
Electronic Edition 2017. ISBN: 978-1-939016-18-8

Cover Design by VK Hinze
Published in the United States by Magnolia Leaf Press
Related Works:
Down and Dead in Even
Down and Dead in Dallas

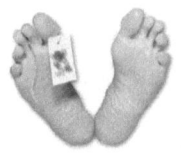

Dedication

For Readers Who Dare to Dream,
To Hope, To Seek the Best in Others.
For All Who Walk and Are the Bridge...
And For
The Bridge-Walker Team
With Admiration and Boundless Gratitude
Blessings,

Vicki Hinze

Contents

Chapter 1

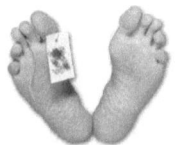

*March 21*st
Even, Georgia

What was she doing here?

Good grief, she couldn't be here. Yet, there she stood, plain as day. Why, of all places, was the woman in Even? Was she *trying* to get them killed?

Fear and dread collided and pumped a massive dose of adrenaline through Rose Green. Her fingers tingling, her heart thumping against her ribs, she pulled her phone from her pocket, speed-dialed her brother, then whispered to avoid being overheard by the other diners in the busy Main Street café. "Jackson?" Rose's gaze never strayed from the beautiful blonde woman she'd met as a redhead not three months ago.

"Hey, sis. How are you?"

"At the moment, I'm at Danny's Diner having a heart attack." One more shock would do it. Her heart would crack her ribs and bust her chest wide open.

"You and Matthew at odds over having a baby again?"

Of course, Jackson would go there. It was barely seven in the morning and she was having coffee at the diner instead of at home in her kitchen. "We are, but that's not why I'm calling."

Two men entered and headed to a table near the front window. Both were in their sixties and a little slump-shouldered. The shorter of the two shuffled his steps. No threat there, yet Rose remained hyper-vigilant.

"This time, are we for or against you having one now?" Jackson asked.

Rose frowned, a little miffed he wouldn't see it. "This time, he's for, I'm against, but that's beside the point." Couldn't her brother hear her anxiety? Evidently not, but he had been driving all night. Safer to travel under the cover of darkness...

"Switched sides again, huh?"

"We both did." Her patience snapped. "Jackson, would you forget the baby debate? I said, I'm having a heart attack."

"I heard you," he barked back, then hesitated. "Oh, that isn't over whether or not to have a baby?"

She couldn't blame him for his confusion. The debate had been raging back and forth between Matthew and she for the last six months. It had almost become a friendly war with all their switching sides and everyone they knew weighing in. "No, a baby has nothing to do with this heart attack." Though the debate likely would incite one of its very own.

"Well, what's wrong then?" Jackson asked, then before she had time to answer ran another question to her on its heels. "You haven't been spotted...?"

"Not yet but, as we speak, we've got a disaster in the making."

His tone dropped low, hushed and simmering. "What's wrong, Rose?"

Finally, her baby brother had tuned in. "You remember that woman you brought to the house last Christmas?"

"Caroline?"

"That's the one."

"Sure, I remember her—"

Rose cut him off. She needed verification—the sooner, the better. "Did you really take her to Dixie and then to…" Rose dropped her voice even more, cupped her hand over the phone and then whispered, "Sampson Park?"

"You know I did. I told you so myself. Why?"

Rose's stomach dropped to her knees. She skimmed the diner, gauging to be sure the senior men seated at the next table for their daily prayer meeting were talking to each other loudly enough to cover her voice. This morning, they were debating signs of the Second Coming. "Well, apparently she's missed a step in her instructions on staying dead."

"What?"

"She's here, Jackson—alive and well and above ground."

"No way."

"I'm looking right at her." The object of Rose's worry smiled and filled coffee mugs for the two men seated near the front window. How could she be so cheerful? It wasn't natural anytime, but under the circumstances…

"What's she doing there?" Jackson asked.

He had to be kidding. "Well, aside from waitressing at the diner, I do not know. Since you brought her into our world, I hoped maybe you could tell me—"

"You're sure it's her. Caroline Branch Easton is waitressing at Danny's Diner in Even?"

"Uh-huh."

He muttered, "Holy—"

"There's nothing holy about it. The idiot woman is going to ruin everything."

Beneath the table, Rose rubbed her Grant half-dollar so hard its ridges felt almost smooth. "Between learning the funeral home business, making connections and getting all the licenses and everything in order, I just last week got my garden planted, and Matthew finally had time to paint the kitchen, which is why I'm at the diner this morning having coffee instead of at home." Rose again cupped the phone and dropped her voice another decibel. "If I have to die again and move already, I'm going to be seriously ticked-off, Jackson Lee Grant."

His whole life, she'd reserved that middle-name warning for only his most serious offenses, and she meant for him to know this woman's sudden appearance on Rose's turf was deadly serious.

"Did you talk to her?"

"I said hi." Rose sipped from her steaming coffee cup and watched Caroline wait on two of the regulars from the auto shop down the block. Billy Joe Baker and Dean Hester sat grinning, clearly enjoying their conversation with her. Considering Billy Joe never smiled much less grinned, she obviously had a knack for engaging conversation.

"Something's bad wrong, Jackson," Rose said. "When she poured my coffee, she looked right through me. The woman didn't have a clue who I was."

The worry Rose felt penetrated, and her brother's tone sobered. "Did you call Miss Emily?"

That very thought had crossed Rose's mind. "I'm not exactly able to do that, being in a public place with the wrong phone." He knew as well as Rose one only called the Sampson Park matriarch using one's dedicated phone. "I didn't expect to walk in here for coffee and see a ghost, you know?" Rose let her exasperation show. "You brought her here and now she's going to fool around and get us all killed again."

"Calm down, and don't borrow more trouble than we've already got," he said. "There's likely a reasonable explanation. Let me call Miss Emily and see what's up."

"There's nothing reasonable in *her* risking *our* futures. She's got to get out of here before—"

"Don't jump the gun, sis. We don't know what's at risk yet," he cut in. "I'm only about ten minutes out. Hang tight, and don't let Caroline out of your sight."

"You need not worry about that." Rose wouldn't shoot her, but if she had to hold her at gunpoint, she wasn't above it. "Whatever brought her back here, we've got to resolve it fast. Our first funeral is in a few hours."

"It's not yours or Matthew's, is it?"

Hadn't she just told Jackson if they had to die again and move so fast she'd be ticked? Rose's temper spiked but, lucky for her brother, empathy also did a slow roll through her. He was upset about this news, too, and rightly so. Rose tempered her response. "Not this time. Carl Wooten's heart gave out. But with your friend here, we could be next. Or you."

Jackson's tone soured, went deadpan flat. "I'll call you right back."

Rose ended the call then dropped her phone into her shirt pocket. The object of her anxiety, wearing jeans, sneakers and a *Dixie Darling* t-shirt, came up to the table, carrying the coffeepot. "Refill?" She smiled.

"Please." Rose looked her right in the eye. She might be a blonde now instead of a redhead, but she was definitely the same beautiful woman Jackson had transported from Dallas and brought home to Christmas dinner. Testing the waters, Rose said, "You look so familiar to me."

"I do?"

There was a hope and eagerness in her voice that sent cold chills up Rose's spine. She swiped her auburn hair back over her shoulder and nodded. "What brings you to Even?"

Caroline glanced around then bent low and whispered a warning. "Another time. I have to tell you something."

"What?"

"Expect a little trouble at Carl Wooten's funeral. The locals are bent out of shape and plan on showing you they're not pleased."

"About what?" Rose asked.

"Carl selling the funeral home to you instead of to a local then dying as soon as your training was done." Her gaze shifted uneasily. "Just thought you'd want to know. It's ironic that Carl's would be your first solo funeral."

It was. "Surely they don't think we wanted Carl dead." He had been and would have remained a tremendous asset to them, particularly when their mentor, Paul Perini down in Dixie began sending them special clients.

"They haven't gone that far. At least, not that I've heard. They're just saying letting outsiders in brings Even bad luck."

Rose had expected a little of that kind of thing. Change always upset some. But to stir up trouble at a lifelong resident's funeral? She couldn't see that. Carl had been a pillar of the Even community his whole life. "I appreciate you letting me know."

"We outsiders have to stick together."

Rose didn't know what to do with that. Did the woman remember Rose, then? Probably not. Yet her call had been accurate. Unless your kin have been in Even for three generations, you are an outsider. At least, you are unless an outsider who didn't live in Even at all messes with you. Then you are a local. That mentality might seem a little twisted on the surface, but it had been one of the reasons Matthew and she had chosen to settle in the one-street, two-traffic-light town. It shielded its own. In their new enterprise, that shielding was vital for them.

"Caroline." Danny, the owner and cook, yelled from the kitchen. His apron had grease splatters across the chest that gave his wife, Hazel, fits. Hazel liked things nice and neat and her whites spotless. Everyone in the county with a stubborn stain called Hazel for a remedy to remove it. "Order's up."

Rose's insides froze to ice. *Caroline.* Same name. Yet zero recognition. What had happened to her? And why had she come back here?

"Coming," Caroline called out over her shoulder then turned back to Rose. "Excuse me. Can't serve the prayer breakfast group cold food." Her eyes twinkled. "They've got consequential connections." Turning on her sneaker-clad heel, she rushed to the kitchen pick-up window.

A guest in Rose's home three months ago and today the woman truly didn't know her from Adam? How could that be? Something had to have happened to her. Something bad.

Figure this out and do something, Jackson. Fast.

Rose sipped from her freshly filled cup, inhaled the steam and hoped it soothed her, though, truth be told, anything soothing her right now seemed impossible. Whatever this sudden appearance was about, it was suck-lemon-bad trouble. Only a fool wouldn't know Caroline's presence in Even could wreck a lot of lives—and deaths.

In Dallas, in Dixie, at Sampson Park, and in Even.

Why hadn't the woman had the good sense, or the mercy, to stay down and dead?

Chapter 2

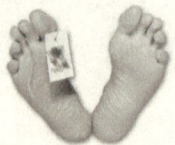

Ten Days Earlier
Dallas, Texas

Seated at the desk in her upscale office, Dr. Nell Richmond finished a few notes from her last patient session with Mr. Kendrick, then sat back in her chair.

Her neck felt stiff. Rubbing at it, she sat back and gazed out the wide window onto a bustling downtown Dallas. It'd been a long day and she'd been booked solid, which was both a blessing and a curse, and normal. Requests for her appointments generated a waiting list longer than most counselors' patient lists.

Her receptionist lightly tapped on her door. "Dr. Nell?"

Nell responded. "Come in, Belinda."

Dressed in green scrubs for reasons only she understood, Belinda walked straight over to Nell's desk, carrying a large white Tyvek envelope. "While you were in with Mr. Kendrick, Miss Branch dropped this off. Must be important. She said to put it straight in your hands, so here you go."

"Thank you." Nell took the package. "We are officially done for the day, yes?"

"Yes, ma'am. The front desk just called. Mr. Kendrick has cleared the exit door."

Last visit, when leaving the office, he'd had a flashback, crouched down in the corner of the waiting room, and barked orders to bug out into an imaginary radio. It'd taken hours to talk him around. Poor guy thought he was back in the desert. Nell stroked her ebony cheek. "Good." She was weary tonight and had held her breath, hoping this session he would make a clean exit. "PTSD takes all forms."

"Don't we know it? And he's such a nice guy—when he isn't fighting the demons."

"Not demons, Belinda." Hadn't they had this discussion a dozen times? Maybe more.

"They are to him," she countered, tilting her head. "I'm headed home. You want the alarm on?"

Considering Caroline Branch had just left the office, Nell didn't think twice. "Definitely. And watch yourself going to your car."

"Don't worry about me. I stay locked and loaded," Belinda said. "Though, if I had to shoot through my purse today, I'd be madder than a hornet." She wrinkled her nose and untucked it from the pit of her arm. "It's new."

A hunter orange clutch with a leather bow over the clasp. Not exactly Nell's style, but closer than Belinda's usual. "Cute."

"I love it. Had my nails done to match." Belinda wiggled her acrylic-tipped fingers then left the office without a backward glance.

She was one of two women Nell knew who didn't give a flying fig what anyone else thought about anything. If she liked something, she liked it. Appropriate or not, Belinda could care less. She also had a loyalty streak a mile wide and was unflappable, which came in handy with some of Nell's more problematic patients and more than compensated for a multitude of sins, especially with fragile patients like Caroline Branch.

Rattled, Nell stared at the package. Caroline was supposed to be safely hidden away in parts unknown. What in the world was she doing back in Dallas? At Nell's office, no less? Was she determined to let her crazy ex-husband kill her?

Nell ripped open one end of the envelope with an unsteady hand. Spotting a CD, she pulled it out and a note came with it. She read:

NELL,

There's a video and a letter on the enclosed CD. For your own protection, do NOT watch the video or read the letter now. If you don't hear from me on or before March 31ˢᵗ, then watch the video, print out the letter and deliver both for me on April 1st. I hate to assume you'll do me this favor, but if I don't get in touch by then, odds are good I'm dead. That leaves me little choice but to impose.

Between the video and letter, you'll know what to do.

Thanks for everything, Nell. You've been a wonderful friend.

C. Branch

CAROLINE PROTECTING NELL? Now, that scared her to death. Hiding out had never been Nell's style. She was a well-heeled, successful African-American woman. A respected psychologist specializing in PTSD and domestic abuse. Little happened in anyone's life she hadn't run across at some point in her practice. Caroline knew all that, and yet she still felt compelled to protect Nell? That was downright terrifying.

As terrifying as looking at the CD and having no idea what was on it.

Did she dare to wait until April 1ˢᵗ to view it?

Nell vacillated between watching and reading, and not watching or reading. She shouldn't do it; Caroline trusted her. But, in Nell's experience, knowing what was coming could make all the difference in surviving what came. *Forewarned is forearmed.* Bearing Caroline's precarious position in mind...

Nell pulled open the CD case and popped the disc into her computer.

Chapter 3

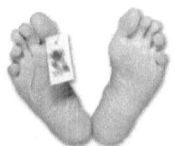

The video loaded.

An image of Caroline appeared on Nell's computer screen. No longer was her hair short and red. The video background was blacked out, giving no clue to her whereabouts at the time of filming. Just the woman seated in an armless chair, her long blonde hair pulled back at her nape, resting below the shoulders of her blood-red blouse. A haunted expression Nell hadn't seen on her in months marred her beautiful, oval face.

Anxiety tumbled into worry. Nell's mouth went dry. She adjusted the volume and braced, instinctively knowing whatever had forced Caroline out of hiding and into making the video had to be significant. The question was how bad it was, and how many would pay the price. The costs would be heavy. No skirting that truth.

She pushed play to start the video.

On the screen, Caroline drew in a deep breath, then began to speak...

TODAY IS MARCH TENTH, but for you to understand what I'm

about to tell you, I need to give you a little history and start at the beginning. Well, at the beginning of the trouble.

This whole mess started just over seven months ago. My sister, Caroline, and I were on the telephone—her, in her penthouse in New York, and me, on my ranchette in Dallas.

You see, we had to keep our conversations secret because her husband, Martin Easton, would give birth to a live cow if he knew we were talking at all. He's forbidden Caro—I've always called Caroline, Caro—from talking to me for years. Actually, since early on in their marriage, he's forbidden her to have any contact with anyone other than him.

The truth is, Martin Easton is an abusive control freak of the worst kind. Physically and emotionally. Caro once tried to leave him, but he forced her to return. How? I don't know. But she says she had no choice. Since she's all the family I have left in the world —our parents died in a train derailment the year we turned sixteen —and since I'm grateful we're talking again these past two years, I don't ask her questions. I'm afraid to rock the boat. The last thing I want is for her to clam up and disappear from my life again.

I know she didn't go back to the jerk because of money. We both inherited enough from our parents to live well forever. It's...something else. Honestly, I have no idea what he's holding over her head, but whatever it is, it's strong and powerful and evil.

Caro is meek, the timid one. Me, I'm bold and blunt. I'm not sure why we're so different, but we are and we always have been.

Anyway, out of the blue one morning last August, she phones me and says she's arriving in Dallas that day on a late-afternoon flight. She's done with Martin. I asked if he'd hit her—he has before, I suspect, many times—and she told me she'd asked herself the question and answered it.

I knew what question she meant. It was one I'd put to her. *How long are you going to live like this?* That she was coming to Dallas confirmed she'd answered it. When I asked for her specific response, she said, "I'd rather be dead than live like this one more day."

Hearing that shattered my heart, but it also frayed every nerve in my body. What Martin the Miserable had done to make her finally fear staying more than leaving him, I can't tell you, but with his record, it had to be wicked. Frankly, I didn't think about the reason much then. Instead, I rushed to plan for Caro's arrival.

I hired a crew of bodyguards to protect her around the clock and the best abuse counselor in the state, Dr. Nell Richmond. You can't be a long-suffering victim of something like Martin put Caro through and not need help working through it. Whether or not Caro would agree to talk to Nell, well, that was another matter, but Nell was there waiting for her, and we both hoped Caro would accept her help.

And so Caro came to Dallas. As soon as I saw the bruises she'd tried to hide—her makeup was so thick it looked like she'd applied it with a trowel—I knew what had happened, if not why, and, when I looked in her eyes, I knew she meant what she'd said—she was finished with Martin the Miserable Easton. There would be no going back to him this time. Not ever again.

I have to tell you, I'm not normally the violent type, but that day, knowing Caro had finally broken his hold on her and had left him for good was the only thing that kept me from finding and killing that man for what he'd done to her. How bad was it? Ask Nell. She took pictures in case Caro needed them for, um, legal reasons.

Back when we first started talking again, I had a courier deliver Caro a few necessities while she was in the grocery store shopping. A phone, credit card, and a duplicate copy of my driver's license. I'd specifically sent them so I knew she had the means to escape from Martin. Grocery shopping was one of the few things Martin permitted her to do on her own. Having the delivery made to her there might seem like overkill paranoia, but it wasn't. Her doorman was a snitch. If I'd sent the courier to her there, he would have reported the delivery to Martin immediately.

Oh, Martin tried to make it impossible for Caro to escape, taking the house phones and Caro's purse and money with him every time he left their apartment. Her home might have been opulent, overlooking Central Park in Manhattan, but that place was her prison. I would have moved heaven and earth to get her out of there. If she hadn't sworn she wouldn't come with me, I'd have gone up there and pulled her out. Since she had refused, I provided the means for use when she was ready, and finally—*dear God, finally*—she had been.

Even today I don't know the details of that final straw. All I can say is imagining is the stuff of my nightmares.

Once Caro was tucked away at my ranchette in Dallas and protected by the bodyguards and me, she faced a different problem: Surviving. I mean that literally.

Martin had threatened to kill Caro if she ever left him again, and he'd convinced her he meant it. She'd left him anyway, so we both expected trouble. But looking at her in the airport, I saw the shell of the woman I knew as my sister. Battered. Beaten down physically and emotionally…I don't think I've ever seen anyone so weary.

It was clear that more than anything, she needed time to heal. Only when she remembered who she was would she be ready to take Martin the Miserable on in court and divorce his sorry backside.

The day after she arrived in Dallas, it became clear he had no intention of giving her time and every intention of giving her trouble. Alex, the head bodyguard I'd hired, reported two private investigators at the gate asking for her. They took to parking on the street and watching the gate. We all knew they were Martin's thugs, and their presence really unnerved Caro. She was brave but so fragile. Something had to be done, so I did what sisters do. I planned and arranged *Operation Switch and Bait.*

Caro and I would switch lives and I'd bait Martin's goons away from Caro while she healed and divorced Martin. It was a simple plan. Effective, I thought, but simple.

Caro opposed it from the start. She was afraid of me drawing Martin's fire. He was ruthless, she said, and he'd do anything to force her to bend to his will. I assured her I was equally determined she would not. She would assert her own will. Martin Easton, I vowed, would not break me. I hoped I wouldn't have to kill him to keep that promise but, after what he'd done to Caro, truth be told, I'd sleep nights fine either way.

Finally, Caro agreed to the plan, and so, with the help of my trusted hairdresser, Dawn, we pulled off the switch and bait. Going into the salon, I was myself, the redheaded Christine Branch, a single and successful software developer. Coming out, my sister was me and I was the blonde Caroline Branch Easton, estranged battered wife of Martin Easton.

Our careful planning worked. Martin and his hired thugs believed I was his Caroline and they followed me. Caro, as me, went home to my Dallas ranchette.

The new Christine was motivated to reclaim herself, and Nell stood by her every step of the way. That helped me to do what I had to do in ways I can't even express, which included staying away from my sister and the ranchette, though we did talk by phone—untraceable ones we used only to talk to each other—every Saturday morning at ten.

For me, the next six months were, to say the least, interesting. Martin's thugs threatened me often and kept me hopping, but I eluded, evaded and ran the marathon race, trying to stay a step ahead of them.

I got a fistful of restraining orders across more counties than I care to recall, too, but I learned quickly that words on paper don't change what's in a man's heart—or the determination of thugs getting a paycheck to keep getting a paycheck. Martin the Miserable was spending a fortune on the thugs, and I did my level best to make them earn every single penny—twice.

Four states later, something changed. Martin lost patience with being *inconvenienced*. He has a thing about that. Caro says it brings out the worst in him, which is saying something. If the man's got good in him, I've never seen it.

Anyway, he fired the old thugs and hired a new crew that began tracking me. They weren't as ethical, and they sure didn't toe the line on the law. These jerks loosened the lug nuts on my tires. They tampered with my brakes. And they put a rock the size of a head of cabbage through the front window of my motel room at three in the morning.

Fearing they'd do even worse kept me far, far from Dallas and my sister. She sounded better on the phone, stronger, but something like that rock incident could have had her hiding under the bed or sleeping in the closet for months. I couldn't risk that.

While I've been undercover as Caroline, I've done my software developing on the side and worked as a waitress at dives across the South because that's what Caro did before marrying Martin. Our parents insisted we work from sixteen on, so we appreciated the value of a dollar. I preferred solitude and computers. Caro loved being around people. Waitressing was made for her, and people just seemed drawn to her to share their troubles. She's a nurturer and empathetic.

The job and she were well suited. I endured it, and looked forward to us spending Christmas together. But a couple weeks before, an event occurred that proved we couldn't celebrate the holiday together. One of Martin's new thugs ate at the restaurant I was working in at the time. On his way out, he slipped me a message scrawled on a napkin. "Go home now and he'll let you live. If you don't, he's coming for you."

That was in Grady, Louisiana. I called the police, but they said not to take the threat literally. Tense people tended to jack up emotionally around the holidays.

I knew the message was a warning, and I'd be crazy not to take it literally. Martin stayed jacked up. In giving me the note, the thug was putting me on notice. He either had a conscience or a heart. Anyway, he didn't want to kill me, but if Martin issued the order, he would do it. I think the thug was trying to give me a fighting chance.

Then a few days before Christmas, Martin showed up at the ranchette and confronted my sister. Thank heaven, he believed she was me. Otherwise that visit would have ended even worse than it did. He told her to get a message to his wife. "Be home by Valentine's Day or else."

No further explanation was needed. By then, Caro had divorced Martin, but he refused to accept it. Caro was livid. She told Nell, who happened to be at the ranchette during the confrontation, it was time we both got our lives back. Nell recorded the whole ordeal, should you care to hear it. She assured me Caro was leaving Dallas and the ranchette—destination unknown—in a good place mentally and emotionally and she would soon be in touch.

Nell was right about that. I heard from Caro on Christmas Day. She said a Dallas chef was helping her get away and Operation Switch and Bait was officially over. It was past time she put a stop to Martin threatening me. She also said she'd resumed her true identity and was traveling as herself.

At the time of the call, Caro said she was in Even, Georgia, but within the hour, she would be leaving for Sampson Park. She promised to call me as soon as she settled in there and had a minute.

I haven't heard a word from her since then and it is now March. Was the chef a chef or a serial killer? Did he work for Martin the Miserable? Had Caro been lured away from Dallas? Kidnapped or murdered? I have no idea.

I don't think Martin has her. His henchmen haven't eased up on me. If anything, since Valentine's Day, they've been more aggressive and persistent. Once his "get home" deadline passed without Caro returning to New York... well, let's just say his thugs have been ruthless and relentless. They've also been harder to shake and evade. My guess is he's offered them a whale of a bonus and put them on a short deadline to get Caro to him and collect it.

Because he hasn't called them off, I've stuck with my Caro identity. Whether or not Martin has her, there being two of her creates a confusion factor and uncertainty. Martin's doubt about whether she's his wife or me might be Caro's only protection.

While I've been getting restraining orders and a conceal carry permit and learning to shoot, she's been doing only heaven knows what to shore up the tools in her self-defense arsenal. Actually, she's probably been cooking. When she's stressed, Caro always cooks.

It's possible, of course, Martin knows exactly where she is and he's yanking my chain to keep me from going to rescue her. He'd love to torment me for sport. According to Caro, it really needled him that he couldn't control a woman who looks like his wife.

The bottom line is I don't know if he has her or not. He could, or he could know she's running and is hoping to locate her through me. Believe me, I wish I did know. I haven't had a good night's sleep since she went missing. Martin is sadistic and totally obsessed with getting her back, so the truth could be just about anything.

I do know for fact I'm terrified. Terrified in a way dealing with Martin and his jerk thugs has never terrified me. I always knew, if he could get away with it, he'd kill me. And I knew he'd kill Caro without a second blink. Those were givens. What keeps me in a cold sweat is, I have no idea where Caro is or who she's with or if she's even still alive.

Martin could have found and killed her. He could be letting me keep Operation Switch and Bait active to shore up his alibi. Give people enough time and they'll forget anything.

It makes me sick to say it, but her death could be behind her disappearance. If Caro could have called me, she would have. She'd have kept calling Saturdays at ten on her special phone. If she had an interim emergency, she would have called then. Something has happened to her, and whatever it is, I fear she never saw it coming.

Her not calling at all leaves me between the rock and the hard place. I have no choice but to stop misdirecting the thugs and do all I can to find her. I have to know what's happened to my sister. Which means, I have to ignore my instinctive inclinations to stay away from her and go to Even, Georgia.

The risks in that should now be abundantly clear to you. If Caro is still there and I'm followed, Martin's thugs will nail us both. If she's not there, maybe someone who is can lead me to Sampson Park. So far, I haven't been able to locate even what state it is in, provided it's in the States. None of my techie friends have had any luck, either. Sampson Park seems to be a phantom park that doesn't exist. That's what has me worried about the chef supposedly helping her and his motives.

Now that's what's happened to get us to this point. I've asked Nell to hold this video until the end of March. She has no idea what's in it yet, but if I fail to contact her on or before March 31st, on April 1st, she will view it and hand deliver the video to you with the following note:

To: Hon. Dexter Devlin

Attorney-at-Law
Dallas, Texas

Mr. Devlin,

I'm enclosing double your usual retainer fee of $1,000,000 and asking you to view the enclosed video. Once you do, it is my hope you will search for my sister and me.

I realize you handpick your clients and you don't know me from Adam, but you're reputed to be the best legal mind maybe ever, and my sister and I need all you have and maybe more to survive… or for those guilty of killing us to be held accountable.

If my sister and/or I are dead, look first to Martin Easton. The video will explain. And please start looking for us in Even, Georgia.

Sincerely,

Christine Branch

NELL CRINGED IN HER SEAT, her mind whirling. So Christine—the real Christine—had made the video and delivered it. Not Caroline. Shaking the envelope, a check fluttered out and landed on Nell's desktop. It was made out to Dexter Devlin for $2 million and signed by Christine Branch. "Oh, my word."

Nell ejected the CD and put it and the check back into the envelope, then grabbed and dialed her mobile phone with her free hand.

The man whose neck lay as exposed as her own didn't answer. His voice mail picked up…

And it kept picking up for the next eleven days.

Had Martin Easton found him?

That thought horrified Nell. The implications for him, her and so many more had her breathless and mentally staggering.

On March 21st, someone picked up. Nell held the phone in a death grip and said, "Jackson, finally! Thank goodness—"

The call then rolled over to voice mail. "Sorry, I can't take your call right now. If you'll leave a message after the tone, I'll get back with you as soon…"

Why wouldn't he talk to her? Had their parts in this been exposed?

Nell let her head loll back against her neck, closed her eyes and prayed for intercession. The man either couldn't or wouldn't take her calls. That was troubling news. Daring to hope he hadn't been compromised, she paced a short path between her desk and the back of a cream leather sofa, waiting for the beep, then left the same message she'd left every day since Christine had left the package with her on March 10th.

Any guilt Nell had felt about violating Christine's wishes and viewing the video and reading the note to Dexter Devlin before the appointed time had long since fallen under the weight of fear.

Considering the circumstances and her own part in them, by the end of her first view of the video, Nell had been hyperventilating, horrified, and calling Jackson. Every day, she had the same reaction. Every time any of this sordid mess so much as crossed her mind, she had that same reaction.

In all her years of counseling, Nell never had faced an issue like this. One that could cost her everything. *Dexter Devlin, for pity's sake.* The man was notorious for never giving up and for going toe-to-toe with anyone short of God. He'd bury Nell and Jackson and everyone else involved.

In this case, there was a lot buried in Dallas that needed to stay buried.

The name of the patient whose records Nell had made disappear, whose appointments had been erased from her calendar. Whose every connection to her had been not only severed but obliterated. Those things topped the list but they weren't the only things on it, and Caroline wasn't the only patient. If Nell and Jackson weren't careful, their whole group could wind up down and dead in Dallas.

With a shaky ebony hand, Nell poured herself a stiff drink then downed it in a single gulp. It burned going down her throat. Of all times for Jackson to pull a disappearing act, he had to choose now?

Her hands sweat, making the phone slick and hard to hold. She shook all over. Her stomach knotted, and a bitter taste filled her mouth. *Check your messages and do something, Jackson. Please!*

Finally, she heard the droning beep. "It's Nell again," she said. "Call me as soon as you get this. I don't care what time it is, as soon as you get in, call me, Jackson."

She hesitated hanging up, then said aloud the name she'd avoided mentioning to anyone, including in her previous messages to Jackson. "It's about Caroline." Nell's voice thinned. "We have an emergency..."

Chapter 4

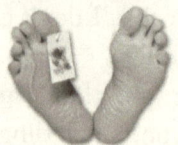

March 21st
Even, Georgia

Danny's Diner brimmed with regulars. Not a single table stood empty.

Jackson spotted Rose sitting alone against the back wall. It was covered with business cards and pictures kids had colored and taped up. Rose looked tense enough to jump out of her skin. That had dread dragging at his belly. He walked over and dropped onto a chair. "Hey," he said.

"Hey." Relief and fear waged a war on her face. "What did Miss Emily say?"

Rose wouldn't like this. "I got a recorded message about the associates' meeting." That was the reason he had headed out from Dallas in the first place, for the coming associates' meeting at Sampson Park. He'd planned to spend a couple days with Rose and Matthew, then head down to Florida for it. "I couldn't get Lester either, so I figure they're off on a jaunt somewhere."

"Great." Rose's disappointment hid in her sarcasm. "What about Darby? Did you try her?"

"I did," he told Rose. Miss Emily's surrogate daughter, Darby, managed the Park. If Jackson could have gotten her, she would have known what was up with Caroline and why she'd left there and come to Even. Darby made it her business to know everything going on with everyone in Sampson Park. "She's in the village," Jackson said. "No phones there, of course. But I left her a message to call."

"Heads up." Rose twisted in her seat. "Your friend is on her way over."

Caroline stopped at their table and smiled at Jackson. "Coffee?"

Jackson looked her right in the eye—and saw no indication that she recognized him. Until that moment, he hadn't believed it possible. Rose, he'd felt sure, had to be mistaken, but she hadn't been. Now what was he to make of that? He'd driven Caroline Branch from Dallas to Even, then to Dixie, Florida, and finally to Sampson Park on Christmas Day and now, three months later, she doesn't recognize him?

"Please," he told Caroline. Feeling his heart pumping like a wild beast's, he added, "Better make it decaf."

"Sure thing." She grabbed a cup, switched pots, then placed a steaming one on the table before him. "There you go." She glanced over at Rose. "Would you like another cup?"

"Please." Rose waited for her to refill her cup, then leave the table. When she had, Rose locked gazes with Jackson. "She doesn't know you, either."

"Picked up on that," he said, decidedly uneasy.

"You spent days traveling together," Rose said. "With all your charm, it's hard to believe she'd forget you so fast, Jackson."

Rose wasn't being sarcastic now, she was scared. And her being scared put him on edge, too. "It's a blow to the ego, for sure. But back then, she was in pretty bad shape."

"Not that bad," Rose insisted. "She seemed fine enough at the house."

They both read people too well to believe for a minute Caroline was pretending not to know them. And she had seemed fine during the trips and at the house. Scared, of course, but fine. "Something's happened." To cause this kind of reaction, something traumatic. He asked the question on his mind aloud. "What could Darby's bunch at the Park do to her to wipe out her memory?"

"Isn't that the million-dollar question?" Perplexed, Rose frowned and held it.

Jackson followed Caroline's movements from table to table. She seemed comfortable enough and busy but not at all distressed. "She's definitely not faking or playing games." The truth had been in her eyes. "She doesn't know us."

"I appreciate the confirmation. I didn't think so, either."

Jackson would bet on it. When he'd looked into Caroline's eyes, she'd looked back, bold and direct. Caroline didn't normally do that. She seemed almost amused, and the Caroline he knew didn't do that, either. But most telling, during their travels, Jackson had never physically reacted to her at all. Not once. He did now. "Who are those two guys chatting her up?" he asked Rose.

"Auto mechanics. Billy Joe Baker and Dean Hester. Don't be rude to them, I'm recruiting them for my team."

"I wasn't going to be rude. I just wondered why they were so friendly to Caroline. How long has she been here, anyway?"

"Today's the first day I've seen her, but I haven't been in for a couple weeks. Been tied up in classes. When Carl finished training us, Mr. Perini started. We're finally finished and ready to start receiving some of his special clients."

Carl was the previous owner of the Even funeral home. Mr. Perini, their associate contact at Down and Dead, Inc. in Dixie, Florida.

Caroline stopped suddenly. The coffeepot in her hand dropped, crashed to the floor and shattered.

"Yeow!" Dean Hester jumped to his feet and hustled to back up. "Nearly got me, girl."

Caroline stared through the window, across the street.

"What's wrong?" Billy Joe Baker asked her.

"Hey," Hester said. "It's okay, Caroline. No harm, no foul."

She didn't respond.

Jackson followed her line of vision to the other side of Main Street. On the sidewalk, under a canopy at the drug store, stood a tall, muscular man with features Jackson readily recognized. "Oh, man."

"He gives me the creeps," Rose said. "Who is he?"

"Martin Easton—Caroline's ex." Jackson warned Rose, coming up off his seat. "Get her out of here while I block him."

"No, wait," Rose said. "If you recognize him, odds are, he'll recognize you." She rushed over to Caroline, looked at Billy Joe and Dean. "Caroline needs some help. See that guy across the street?"

"Which one?"

"The one you don't know, Hester," Billy Joe said, eyeing Easton. "Who is he, Rose?"

"Caroline's ex. He nearly beat her to death and she's been running from him a long time."

Caroline swiveled her head to look at Rose, but kept her mouth closed. Unshed tears swam in her eyes.

Clearly, Caroline remembered Martin. Speaking to Billy Joe and Hester, Rose went on. "You guys intercept him and keep him busy long enough for me and my brother to get Caroline out of here."

"Where you taking her, Rose?"

To Jackson's surprise, the question didn't come from Billy Joe or Dean. It came from one in a group of old men eating their breakfast.

"Away before he kills her, Harold," Rose said, sparing the group a glance. "All of you, pray."

"You got it, Rose," Harold said. Everyone at the table dropped their forks and folded their hands.

"Prayer Warriors. They meet here for breakfast every day," Rose told Jackson. "Billy Joe, Dean, move it. Do not let that man follow us."

Billy Joe was the size of a small mountain. He tugged his ball cap down on his ears, reassured Caroline. "That ain't happening."

They headed out the door and Billy Joe and Dean crossed the street. As soon as they had Martin's attention, Rose motioned to Jackson.

"Caroline, come with me," Jackson told her. "My sister and I will protect you."

She looked torn. Afraid to go, and afraid not to go with them.

"We protected you before," he whispered. "We will again."

"Over here. Take her out the back way," Danny shouted from the kitchen, motioning them to him.

Caroline moved, following Rose. "I'm so sorry, Danny," she said.

"Just stay safe, hon. We'll be here." Danny hustled them through the kitchen to the back door. He stopped and spoke into his phone. "We clear?" He nodded to Rose, then unlocked the door. "Hazel's upstairs at the parking lot window. All's clear out back. She's got you covered."

Jackson looked over his shoulder, checked the street. Billy Joe blocked Martin's view. The Prayer Warriors' voices filled the diner and overflowed into the kitchen. Jackson figured they could use all the prayers they could get. If Martin Easton was here, his thugs couldn't be far behind.

In the rear parking lot at Rose's black hearse, Jackson told Caroline, "You ride with Rose. I'll follow, in case I need to run interference."

Caroline's eyes stretched wide. "You want me to ride in a hearse?"

"Go, Caroline," Jackson urged her, opening the door and waving his thanks to Hazel. She stood in the window, her hair in curlers, holding a rifle and scope. It would have made him uneasy, seeing a tiny old woman with a weapon like that, but she held it like she knew how to use it. He turned to Rose. "Get out of here before Martin outwits Billy Joe and Dean."

Caroline slid into the passenger's seat, and Jackson shut the door. "Hit it, Rose!"

Rose left half her tires on the pavement. The backend of her new hearse fishtailing, she turned right out of the parking lot onto a back street, avoiding the front of the diner, Main Street, and Martin Easton's prying eyes.

Chapter 5

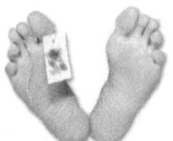

Christine had serious misgivings about getting into a hearse with Rose, but she had more misgivings about tangling with Martin in broad daylight, where innocent bystanders could be drawn into the fight. Rose was smaller and she didn't have as much to lose which meant, if push came to shove, Christine could take her in a fight. And while Rose had watched Christine's every move in the diner, she didn't seem at all threatening.

It wasn't until Christine had dropped the coffeepot—seeing Martin standing there had stunned her—and Rose got Billy Joe and Dean to intercept Martin then revealed she and her brother, Jackson, had protected Caroline that Christine had gotten her first link to anyone in Even knowing Caroline. To learn the details, Christine would follow Rose or Jackson or both of them anywhere.

"Your hearse has that new car smell," Christine said, seeking a safe topic. Rose drove it like a maniac, which proved she knew how dangerous Martin Easton was, and she was determined to avoid him. "Um, where are you taking me?"

"I just picked it up a week ago in Atlanta," Rose said, making a hard right and nearly clipping a row of azaleas with the backend. "I'm still getting used to driving it."

"Kind of figured that." Christine stated the obvious, then waited to see if her other question would be answered. When it wasn't, she asked again. "And we're going… where?"

"To my house. It's just a few more blocks."

"Good. If Christine had to run, at least it wouldn't be from out in the sticks somewhere. She could find her way back to the diner and her car from here. "Thanks for helping me out."

"Sure thing." Rose spared her a glance. "I don't mean to be rude, but can we chat after we get there instead of right now? I'm still not used to all the stuff on this puppy, and I'm scared to death of wrecking it. Today would be a really bad day to do it."

Wouldn't any day be a bad day to wreck your new vehicle? Christine wondered, but she didn't utter a word. Rose was nervous about Carl Wooten's funeral. "Mailbox. Two o'clock!" Christine winced.

Rose whipped the wheel and over-corrected, taking out a trash can on the far side of the street. "Oops."

Christine double-checked her seatbelt and closed her eyes. Might be cowardly, but she needed a few minutes to recover from the shock of seeing Martin standing on the sidewalk in Even with no warning.

Rose hit the brakes hard. Christine's eyes opened in time to see a last-second turn into a concrete driveway that ran alongside Even Funeral Home. She pulled around back, behind the two-story brick building, and then parked.

"You live in a funeral home?" Christine asked.

Rose had seen this kind of reaction before. "Sort of. Actually, the funeral home is attached to our house. It faces the acreage on the other side."

"Oh."

"We own both."

Caroline knew about the funeral home from the regulars at the diner. Not about the house. It struck her as kind of creepy. "I see." Her heart beat hard and fast. Maybe Martin had arranged this. Maybe they meant to kill her. It'd be convenient to already have her at the funeral home. "Do you work for Martin?"

"Good grief, no." Rose opened the door. "Let's get inside."

Gravel crunched behind them. Christine looked back down the drive and saw Jackson pulling in, driving a white truck. His license plate was from Texas. That made her feel a little better. She waited while he parked to the left of the hearse, blocking view of it from the road, though seeing a hearse at a funeral home shouldn't arouse suspicion in Martin or his goons.

A big guy with dark hair and bright eyes stepped out of the house onto a long porch littered with white-slatted rocking chairs. Good looking man. Likely Rose's husband, Matthew. Some of the female diners called him Matthew the Marvelous, though not in front of Rose.

"Caroline?" he said, clearly surprised to see her. His gaze shot to Rose.

He definitely knew her sister. Thrilled, Christine nodded at him.

"What are you doing here?" He went from surprised to worried in a flash, and slid an uneasy glance from Christine back to Rose. "What is she doing here?"

Rose shrugged that she didn't know.

Jackson joined them. "Rose, you and Matthew go catch up. I'm sure you're behind on what you need to do for the funeral."

Every instinct in Christine's body went on alert.

Jackson clearly noticed. "Carl Wooten," Jackson said, patting his chest. "His heart gave out. The funeral is this morning." Rose hadn't moved and Jackson walked toward the front porch. "Let's sit out here, Caroline, and have something cold to drink."

Rose looked relieved to have a minute alone with her husband, and didn't mention a word about Carl Wooten's funeral warning. "Remember," Christine said. "There could be trouble with the locals, Rose."

"I haven't forgotten. Thanks." Rose joined Matthew on the front porch. "Jackson, try giving our friend a call again."

He nodded.

Christine wasn't sure what to make of anything. These people obviously knew Caro and her situation. Jackson had recognized Martin on sight and Rose had known he was Caro's abusive ex.

Unfortunately, Christine didn't know them. But they had protected Caro. If Christine admitted she wasn't Caro, would they still help her? Or would she be blowing her only chance of finding out what had happened to her sister?

One question in her mind had been answered. Martin didn't have Caro or he wouldn't be here.

Mitigating her risks, Christine held her silence. The less said, the better. One slip, and her cover as Caro could be blown wide open. If that happened, she'd lose her only connection to Caro.

Chapter 6

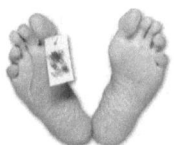

Having a funeral home attached to your house wasn't all bad, Christine decided. The view from the front porch of rolling green hills, huge oaks and, closer to the structure, islands of azaleas and white irises made for a lovely front-porch view. Looking away from the street, a sizable garden shone in the sun, freshly tilled and planted. New growth sprouted up in neat rows.

Jackson returned to the front porch. "Sorry for the delay," he said, passing her a tall chilled glass of iced-tea.

"Thanks." She smiled. "We were so busy this morning, I haven't had a chance to get anything to drink."

"Seeing Martin like that probably dried out your throat even more." Jackson sipped from his own glass. "What's he doing here?"

"I wish I knew." Truer words had never been spoken.

He nodded. "How long have you been in Even?"

"Just over a week." A simple question, and already she was treading into dangerous territory. She resisted the urge to shift on her seat.

Silence fell between them. If she had been Caro, it would have been comfortable. Jackson was a big man—tall, lean and incredibly good looking, which struck Christine a little odd. All her adult life, she'd thought she wasn't drawn to men who were blond, and she wished she weren't now. Jackson would be the exception. His hair hung long on his neck and low on his forehead, swept back, as if by an impatient hand. But his face was kind, his eyes intensely blue and incredibly gentle. And though she'd have to be blind or dim-witted not to know he and Rose and her husband had plenty of questions, at least Jackson didn't seem in any hurry to push hard for answers.

To keep him from deciding to push, she made an observation. "I know your sister is new to the funeral home business here, but as nervous as she is about the Wooten funeral, she must be new to the business altogether."

"She's been in training well over a year."

Christine hiked her brows. "Can't tell it by her driving."

"I saw she clipped the bushes. It's a new vehicle."

"She had a near miss with a mailbox, too."

"And took out a trashcan," he said as though it were no big deal. "I stopped and cleared up the mess."

Christine smiled. "You're a devoted brother."

"The delay gave me a chance to watch for Martin, which is why Rose it. We wanted to be sure he didn't follow us here."

"Are you saying she deliberately took out the trashcan?" Christine stopped rocking to reassess her assumptions on Rose.

"Definitely." The corner of Jackson's mouth lifted.

"She said the hearse was new and she wasn't used to driving it yet."

"It is, but Rose was born driving anything with wheels. If she hit the can, it was intentional."

Interesting. So she hadn't needed to focus, she just hadn't wanted to talk on the way to her house. Now why was that? "I see."

"She is nervous about the funeral this morning," Jackson said. "Carl Wooten used to own this funeral home. He trained Rose and Matthew and she doesn't want to disappoint his family."

So the man on the porch Christine had assumed was Matthew, was Matthew, Rose's husband. "Can't blame her for that. Handling my mentor's service would have me nervous." Any funeral would have Christine nervous. Since her parents' deaths, she had avoided them like the plague.

"Rose is worried the locals and Carl's family will pick apart everything she says or does. You know what I mean. People don't like being reminded that someone they were close to can be replaced."

"Change." Christine slid her fingertip down the chilled, sweating glass. "They fear change."

"And having someone come along and maybe do their life's work better." Jackson bent his knees so his legs weren't stretched out halfway across the porch. "Caroline, are you okay now?"

Uh-oh. The reprieve had passed and questions were coming. "I'm better. Seeing Martin standing there… Well, my heart rate is still hovering in the stratosphere, but sitting here has slowed it down a bit. It's surprisingly peaceful here."

"Glad to hear it. I think that's what made Rose and Matthew want the place." Jackson downed a long swallow of tea, then set his glass back onto the little table placed between their rockers. "When you're recovered, let me know, okay?"

He didn't want to push her, and he knew he might be. Considering Caro's usual fragile state, Christine understood his misgivings and apprehension. Thoughtful of him, though it grated at Christine to have Caro's fragility tagged as her own. Not that she was above using it to stretch out her thinking time, because she surely wasn't.

Jackson's phone rang. He checked caller ID and glanced her way. "Sorry for the interruption, but I have to take this."

"No problem." It'd give her another couple minutes to figure out how to handle the coming inquisition that could reveal her secret and blow her cover.

Jackson stood then stepped off the porch and walked over to the shade of a big twisted oak. A deliberate move, of course, that gave Christine zero chance of overhearing anything, or even trying to read his body language.

Every instinct in her told her to seize the upper hand and quiz him, Matthew and Rose about Caro. But those same instincts also warned her they wouldn't welcome quizzing and likely would shut down. Seemed they had secrets of their own they wanted to stay secret. Otherwise, at the diner, Rose would have greeted Caroline like someone she knew instead of a stranger. Jackson, too. But neither had. Only Matthew had called her by name on sight. Of course, he'd also been shocked to see her, and it wasn't a pleasant kind of shock. More like a stunned kind of shock that incited heaps of worry.

What did it all mean? Who were these people to Caro?

Christine prayed she found out…before they found her out.

You'd better, she told herself. *Or things could get really messy…*

Chapter 7

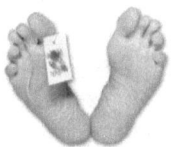

Jackson leaned back against the trunk of the oak, keeping one eye focused on Caroline and one on the street, half-expecting Martin Easton to be brazen enough to drive right up and start making demands.

"I'm good, Miss Emily," Jackson said into the phone. "You and Lester doing okay?"

"We're looking forward to seeing you. It's been too long, Jackson. Dallas isn't so far away that you can't get home to see us a wee bit more often."

"You know I'd love to be there, but I had to be careful. The last thing I want is to bring Martin Easton to your door."

"We're ready for him. Have been for months."

Jackson didn't doubt that for a second. The Park had a top-notch security team and the latest equipment. Everyone there, for one reason or another, relied on it, including Miss Emily. "Um, Rose and I were at the diner in Even this morning, and we were pretty surprised to see Caroline Branch here waitressing. When did she leave the Park?"

"Until I heard your message, I wasn't aware she had." Miss

Emily's displeasure about that came across loud and clear. "Darby hasn't said a word."

Miss Emily's adopted daughter, Darby, had been abandoned at an Interstate 10 rest stop. Poor kid was only nine years old at the time. Since Jackson's mom had done the same thing to Rose and he —dumping them out front at the Piggly Wiggly under the auspices of going to park the car and never coming back—he could empathize.

On learning Darby's folks had long rap sheets for running drugs, Miss Emily vowed that bit of business was done. Darby wasn't devastated, she feared her birth parents would come back, since she did all the cooking and cleaning and everything else that got done, drugs aside. Miss Emily nixed those fears in short order. She brought in her legal beagles and got Darby emancipated from her folks, then raised Darby herself. Before she went off to college, Miss Emily adopted her and, when Darby graduated, she headed right back to Sampson Park. Miss Emily had taken care of Darby. Now it was her turn to take care of Miss Emily. She doted on Miss Emily something fierce, and even went toe-to-toe with mobster kingpin Vincent Marcello, who had been Miss Emily's spouse in another life. She'd had to die twice to get away from him for good.

Everyone said, getting dumped and rescued by Miss Emily was the best thing that ever happened to Darby, and Jackson agreed. Things hadn't worked out so story-book perfect for Rose and he. They'd been separated in a long string of foster homes, but they'd still had each other. Until fate stepped in for Miss Emily and Darby, for all intents and purposes, they had been alone.

Sometimes the heart chooses the family the gene pool doesn't. Usually, the heart chooses more wisely.

Jackson turned back to the conversation. "I tried to call Darby but she was in the village."

"She is, and unfortunately Dr. Goodman isn't available, either. He's in Sweden at a symposium for the next two weeks. But I left a message for him to call. I'm sure he will as soon as he gets it."

Goodman was Caroline's counselor as well as Park Chaplain. "Shouldn't be long then."

"Longer than either of us would like. He's communing, they said. I'm sure that makes sense to them, but I'm not clear on exactly what it means," she said. "Probably that he's taking communion. In that case, it shouldn't be too long. Dr. Goodman is, of course, a very spiritual person."

That was an understatement. Jackson had witnessed some robust debates between the spiritual Goodman, who'd been excommunicated from his church and divorced by his wife for an indiscretion, and the scientific Dr. Laura Rossi, the Park's medical doctor who looked for all answers in science. "The delay puts us in a bit of a bind, at least for the short-term."

"What kind of bind?" Miss Emily asked.

"We don't know how to treat Caroline. She doesn't recognize Rose or me, and we're scared to ask her anything. We don't want to mess her up." Recalling her reaction to seeing Martin, Jackson worried that already had happened.

"Caroline's been going through the stages to get back to normal and come to terms with years of abuse, but coping well. I've talked to her myself every couple of days."

"Well, maybe she was fine, but if she was fine now, she'd know us. Something's happened to her." He glanced over to where the object of their discussion sat sipping sweet tea and rocking. *Calm. Relaxed. At ease.* Why wasn't she worried about Martin showing up here? Three months ago, she'd have been frantic—and she had recognized Martin. The shattered coffeepot proved it. "She's not acting strange or anything, she just doesn't know us."

"How odd."

"It gets odder," Jackson said, swatting at a mosquito buzzing his ears. "Martin Easton also showed up here this morning."

"Oh, no." Miss Emily's tone turned fierce. "Did he do something to Caroline?"

"No, but seeing him startled her."

"Was he watching her?"

"From across the street. No doubt about it." Jackson squinted through the sunlight and scanned, looking for movement. He spotted none. "A couple of Rose's recruits kept him busy while we got out Caroline out of the diner."

"So she's there with you now?"

"Yes, ma'am." He worried his lower lip. "I thought maybe when we got to Rose's she'd recall being here at Christmas. But she didn't."

"That doesn't sound good. But she came with you willingly, right? You didn't have to—"

"No, ma'am. Though, I think she'd have left with anyone to get away from Martin." Jackson sighed, scratched his shoulder against the rough tree bark. "Rose is a nervous wreck about it."

"Understandable. She's just finished her training and assembled her team. The last thing she wants is to have to die and start over again."

She was still working on her team, but that wasn't his business to tell. "So what do we do about Caroline?"

"Let me see what I can find out about her on this end and get back to you."

"It probably wouldn't hurt to brief Lester." Lester had been like a father to Jackson and Rose. Jackson trusted him—even when he thought Lester was a brick short of a full load and Rose was having to bail the man out of jail once a week. He kept forgetting his pants. The Biloxi police weren't impressed that he remembered his briefs, and hauled him in on a regular basis.

"Definitely. Lester happens to be here, so I'll speak with him right away."

"He's already at the Park?" The associates' meeting wasn't for another two days.

"He arrived last night," she said. "I think he was just lonesome. With Rose and you gone and me mostly at the Park now that I've died again, Biloxi just isn't the same for him."

"Why doesn't he move to the Park permanently?" Lester and Miss Emily were close and had been for many years. It seemed kind of sad for them to spend their golden years apart.

"If and when he's of a mind to, I expect he will. Until then, he comes and goes as he pleases. You know Lester. He's bent on living his way."

As much as any of them could, he was. Couldn't blame the man for that. Her gentle rebuke was Miss Emily in her protector-mode. Jackson smiled. She topped out at five-two, if she stretched hard, and she hovered somewhere in her mid-seventies. Jackson wasn't worried about retribution. But neither was he stupid enough to provoke or underestimate her. Miss Emily had proven extremely resourceful, and her protection extended to Rose and him. He owed her for the life he was living. He owed all of them.

"Jackson, are you listening or wool-gathering?"

"Sorry. I was just thinking."

"Well, think later. Right now, you need to keep a sharp eye on Caroline. If something's happened and she isn't quite right, we need to be prepared. Not that she'd ever intend to hurt us, mind you. But the woman could slip and do us all a lot of damage."

"Rest easy, Miss Emily. I won't let her out of my sight." Jackson twisted to look over at Caroline again. *Beautiful woman.* His stomach clenched. *Dangerous woman.*

"We need information to do no harm," he warned. "I'm tiptoe-ing, trying not to cross any lines with her. But it'd sure help to know there are lines, where they are, and what'll trigger them."

"I understand the situation clearly, my boy. I'll get back to you as quickly as possible."

Jackson ended the call, hoping Miss Emily responded with guid-ance sooner rather than later.

Chapter 8

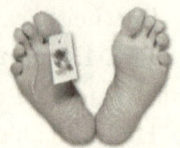

The front door swung open and an agitated Rose came flying out onto the porch, looking rattled to the core. "Jackson, Caroline, come. I've got an emergency."

"What's the matter, sis?" Jackson jumped to his feet. His foot landed on the tip end of the rocker, and he waved wildly to catch his balance. The glass tipped and the tea and ice splashed Christine right in the face.

Everyone stopped.

Christine swiped at her eyes with a fingertip. "Well, that was refreshing." The front of her t-shirt was soaked and clinging to her skin. She ruffled it to shake it loose.

"Caroline, I am so sorry." Jackson looked mortified.

"No problem. It's just tea, not blood, Jackson." Christine focused on Rose. "What's the emergency?"

"It's the flowers," Rose said on a rush, her mouth drawing tight with tension. "The florists just dropped them off, and they're not arranged. Half the people in the county have sent flowers, and they're all loose. What am I supposed to do with them? I don't know how to arrange flowers. Carl Wooten's family is going to have a conniption fit." Rose swiped a lock of damp hair from her forehead. "This is the trouble you warned me about," she told Christine. "Frankie and Myrtle did it deliberately. You know they did. To make me a laughingstock around here."

"Who are Frankie and Myrtle?" Jackson asked.

"The two florists in town." Rose's face was flushed.

"I did warn you there would be trouble," Christine said. "I had no idea what kind of trouble."

Rose frowned. "Frankie said they were going to bring the flowers directly to the cemetery, but since I helped you at the diner, they thought one good turn deserved another. So they brought them here."

"But they're not arranged. What are they going to do about that?"

"Nothing, Jackson." Rose shrugged.

"What are we going to do?" Jackson looked ready to pounce, and lost. "I don't know how to fix this."

"How much time do we have?" Christine asked. If she could help out, she would. Seeing anyone as worried as Rose grated. It couldn't hurt to have a favor on her side. Might make them more open to helping her find Caro.

"A little over an hour."

"Okay. Settle down, Rose." Christine headed toward her. "We've got this."

Rose frowned. "You know how to arrange flowers?"

"Not really, but it can't be that hard." Christine hiked her chin and silently apologized to every floral arranger in the world. She had to get Rose calmed down. "Do you have a computer?"

"A computer?" Rose went still, her hand on the doorknob.

"So I can look it up. You can learn anything on the Internet."

Rose looked skeptical. Her forehead furrowed between her eyebrows. "At this point, I'll try anything."

Christine followed Rose, and Jackson brought up the rear. They walked through the open living and dining room, passed the kitchen, which smelled of fresh paint, and took a second hallway to the funeral home. Christine revised her opinion. What had struck her as creepy initially now seemed convenient, having the funeral home and house all under one roof.

When they made the corner from the reception area and headed down a secondary hallway, she spotted three doors. The first room held a gurney and equipment. They prepared the bodies there, she figured. The second room was blocked by heavy blue drapes. On the other side of them, she supposed was the chapel and viewing area where the service would be held.

"Back here." At the end of the hall, Rose motioned for them to hurry, then stepped inside.

Flowers covered every possible surface—the long row of cabinets, the broad table dead center, the floor, and both desks. "There have to be a thousand flowers in here."

"I know!" Rose threw up her hands. "Matthew's calling Frankie's and Myrtle's, but of course, neither of them are answering."

Jackson frowned. "You've been set up, all right."

"Carl Wooten," Christine said, "must have been a good client who gave them a lot of business over the years or they wouldn't risk doing this. His widow had to have sanctioned it." Christine made her way to the computer and sat down, hit the keys.

"You'll need the password to get—"

"Got it, Rose," Christine said. "Jackson, come watch this with me. It's going to take us both to get these flowers ready." She swerved her focus to Rose. "We need something to put them in—vases, jars, glasses or whatever you've got."

Rose went running.

Jackson bent down beside Christine, narrowly avoiding a peace plant in a black pot. "We need fabric to cover those ugly things." Christine said.

"I'll tell Rose." He hooked a thumb toward the door. "Or do you want me to watch?"

"Go," she said. "I'll relay for you—and Jackson, quit freaking out. If we're going to pull Rose and Matthew's fat from the fire, we have too much to do."

"I don't want Rose upset. If they make her look like an unqualified fool, she'll be crushed. She's worked hard for this, Caroline. Matthew, too."

He was worried about them. She liked that. A lot. She hated and feared liking it, and should until she knew more about them, but she did. "I told you, we've got this," she said. "I promise."

He went in search of Rose and fabric and ran into her near the door. Her arms were full of vases and tall stacks of glasses. "Will this be enough?"

"I don't know." Jackson shrugged. "But we need fabric—to cover the pots in all the plants."

Christine looked over. "Ribbon, too."

Rose looked perplexed but didn't say a word. "There's at least fifty cards. The florists put them in a little box."

Christine spotted the box on the desk. "Got it."

"You ready?" Jackson asked her.

"Just about. Let me cruise through one more video to figure this out." She threw him the box. "You count the cards. We need an exact number."

He caught it, opened the box, and began counting.

"Okay." Christine stood up and turned toward the chaotic mess of flowers and greenery, swiped an arm across the center worktable and swept the whole mess onto the floor. She grabbed a vase. "Let's do this."

Rose returned with two bolts of blue fabric and a huge spindle wrapped with white ribbon. "Will this do?"

Christine gave both the once over. "Perfect." She glanced at Rose. "Where did you get this on such short notice?"

"It was supposed to be the new curtains in the guest room." She shot Christine a wistful look. "I saw it in a magazine."

"Good thing you did, or we wouldn't have them now." Christine slid her a sympathetic smile. "You're sacrificing them for a greater cause."

"I hope, I am." Rose cocked an ear. "Matthew's bellowing. He doesn't often bellow. I'd better see what's wrong. Thanks for helping."

"Not a problem." Christine said, snagging two white lilies and an orange tiger-lily and putting them in the vase. "Jackson, find me some Styrofoam blocks or something, so these stay where we put them."

"I doubt Rose has those green chunks of stuff or that special tape, Caroline."

"Improvise! Look for duct tape."

"Are you serious?"

"Every respectable Southern woman keeps a stock of duct tape, Jackson. It's versatile." She checked her watch. "Hurry now. We've got a little over an hour until people start showing up here."

"Don't remind me." He tiptoed through the flowers and plants then headed out the door and down the hall.

"There's got to be something useful around here." Christine went in search and in the mini-kitchen off the chapel found tall stacks of Styrofoam cups. There were at least a thousand of them in the pantry. Surely that many people wouldn't be at Carl Wooten's funeral. The whole population of Even was only about five-hundred people.

She scooped up two plastic bags that held fifty each, then took the cups back to the workroom.

Jackson returned carrying a bucket. Safety goggles dangled from a strap, looping his neck. "Matthew had a sheet of this stuff in the garage. I commandeered it and Rose's electric knife and cut it into blocks." He set the bucketful at her feet.

"Great work." Christine smiled at him. "Do I dare ask what the emergency was with Matthew?"

"You don't want to know," he said. "Best just deal with this crisis before Rose has a heart attack."

Christine stilled. "Does she have a bad heart?"

"No, but I've never seen her this rattled. Not even when Mom deserted us."

"Understandable," Christine said, adding splashes of greenery between the lilies. "She wants to make a good impression. Her business depends on it."

"With Rose, nothing is ever that simple."

"What do you mean?"

"Oh, she wants to make a good impression, but it's to prove to herself she's good enough. Not for them, though I think she liked Carl Wooten. She talked him into selling her this place. His family was against it."

"Why?"

"He wanted to retire. His wife—I guess, she's his widow now, Clara, didn't want him to retire. Having a man used to being busy underfoot all day would get on her nerves."

"It'd be an adjustment." Christine slid the arrangement back and eyeballed it. "Not bad."

"Actually, it looks good." Jackson grunted. "And you picked that up just watching a couple videos?"

"You'd be amazed what you can learn watching videos, Jackson."

For the next twenty minutes they worked in silence. Jackson putting flowers and supplies into Christine's hands, her doing her magic then setting them aside.

"This is it on the flowers," Jackson finally said.

Rose popped in and gave them her every five-minute update. "Fifteen minutes."

"We know, Rose." Jackson said, rolling his eyes back in his head. "Added pressure we do not need."

"Be nice. She's frazzled." Christine finished up the last arrangement, then eyed the body of work. "Well, I doubt we'd win any awards, but Rose shouldn't be ashamed. Frankie and Myrtle should be, though."

"They're just supporting the Wooten family," Jackson said. "Their families were all with the original Even founders, Matthew said. We're the outsiders. He's hoping this is the worst of the trouble today."

"I get the point, but the bottom line is they messed with the final farewell of one of their own." Christine punched the final stem into the foam block. "Carl Wooten deserved better."

"I doubt he cares much, being dead."

Hard to argue that logic. "I doubt he does." Christine moved the last arrangement to the lines of the others. "But they should."

"Now the plants." Jackson checked his watch. "Can we make it, Caroline?"

"Absolutely."

"We've got to get them into the chapel, too."

"Get Rose and Matthew to move the flowers. We'll snazzy up the plants, then move them over."

Jackson headed out while Christine ran a quick Internet search on how to make bows. Her arms felt like lead and a spot between her shoulder blades burned like fire. She rolled her shoulders, rubbed the sore spot, and watched a video.

By the time Jackson returned she had most of the plants wrapped.

"Wow, those look great."

"Thanks." The black pot was concealed by puffy blue fabric and a tasteful white bow.

They finished the last of them and carried them to the chapel.

"Last one," Christine said. Two steps from its designated spot, she tripped. Her hip and elbow banged against the tile floor. The plant tumbled and dirt flew out of the pot. The back half of the plant snapped off and landed awfully close to Carl Wooten's casket.

"I'll just, um, grab the vac." Rose scooted past, snatching up the broken stem and leaves, then disappearing down the hall.

"You okay?" Jackson helped Christine up and held on a long minute to make sure she was steady on her feet.

"I'm fine." She eyed the damage. "I think the plant's history, though."

"Only half of it. The rest seems all right." He switched its place with another plant and twisted the pot, then adjusted the bow. "Broken part to the back. No one will ever see the damage."

No upset. No haughty looks. Not a single snide comment. Impressed with his reaction, she smiled. "You're a gracious man, Jackson."

"What?"

At first, she thought he'd been fishing for more of a compliment. Now, she saw he clearly had no idea why she'd thought him gracious. "To not call me a klutz."

"I've dropped a thing or two myself. Pretty much everyone has. Besides, after all you've done to help Rose, me calling you anything like that... Well, it'll never happen, Caroline."

Christine looked into his eyes and believed him. The cool and distant reserve had melted away and warmth and a friendly twinkle that really got to her replaced it.

Of course, it'd disappear in a *poof* as soon as he learned the truth.

She backed away from him, reminding herself to not let anyone get too close. Her finding Caro depended on it...

Rose vacuumed up the last of the spilled dirt, then inspected the chapel. "I can't believe you pulled this off." She looked over her shoulder at Christine. "The flowers look lovely, and all the bows and blue fabric matching makes it look intentional—like you went the extra mile to make Carl's service beautiful. I love it, Caroline."

Her face heated. She wasn't used to getting such praise. Her clients expected perfection and no one was ever close enough to her to know anything about her. She liked it, and hated liking it. If nothing else, Christine had learned the hard way to be completely self-reliant. "I'm glad I could help." She said and meant it.

"Me, too." Rose grinned. "I'm in no mood today to be the brunt of bad jokes or ridden out of town on a rail."

Matthew, wearing a black suit and white shirt and tie, appeared at the door. He looked very distinguished, until you glimpsed into his eyes. They were deadly serious. "We've got a problem."

"Another one?" Rose slumped. "Can you handle it, honey? I've got to change clothes."

"I can handle it, but it could involve doing something you don't want me to do."

Exasperated, Rose huffed and held it so he couldn't miss it. "Right this second, I don't care how you handle the problem, Matthew. Just do it, okay? I have seven minutes to shower and change."

He let his gaze move to Caroline and then to Jackson, who asked, "What is the problem?"

"Martin Easton's car is in the driveway. I expect he's going to come in under the guise of being Carl's guest at the funeral."

"He's packing," Jackson said.

Christine felt the blood drain from her face and neck. Her body tensed everywhere at once. Unarmed, the man was dangerous. Armed, he was bent on murder.

"Don't worry," Matthew told her. "Just stay in the house and we'll take care of him."

"What else is going to happen today?" Rose slumped back against the wall, then squeezed her eyes shut.

"I'm sorry, Rose." Christine didn't know what else to say. "I shouldn't be here."

"Of course, you should. This isn't your fault. You've been a blessing, warning me about the locals and fixing all the flowers." Rose seemingly recovered, turned her gaze to her husband. "I am going to shower. Christine, stay put and out of sight. Under no circumstances are you to go anywhere Martin might see you." She looked back to Matthew. "And, darling, I don't care what Martin Easton says or tries to do, there will be no gunfire at Carl Wooten's funeral—and I mean it."

Christine's jaw fell open. She quickly snapped it shut and kept her mouth shut, watching Rose rush up the stairs to shower and change.

"Well." Matthew rubbed his neck. "Since I can't shoot Martin, Caroline, you'd best listen to Rose and stay out of sight." He winced. "Of course, I will if I have to, but then Rose will be in a foul mood for a week."

"Maybe two." Jackson worried his lower lip. "If shooting is necessary, best let me do it—for the sake of your marriage and peace in your home."

Christine twisted back and forth between the men. "You two are serious?" They just looked at her. "But—but you can't just shoot him." If she could have, she would have done it herself a long time ago.

"Course not," Jackson told her. "But self-defense is still self-defense."

"If you do shoot him, it better be in self-defense according to Rose," Matthew said.

Who were these people, talking like this? Did they really think they could just kill Martin? It wasn't that she objected exactly, but good grief. Maybe if she offered them a little reassurance, they'd get their minds off murder. "I'll stay out of sight." Christine said and meant it. "If he asks, just tell him I'm not here."

"You want us to lie to him?"

"Yes, Jackson." She hiked her chin. "It's better than killing him and having Rose all upset."

"Depends on the circumstances," he said, unveiling a hidden stubborn streak.

Christine propped a hand on her hip. "Look, I've managed to avoid killing the jerk since last August. If I managed that, you can at least avoid killing him for one day."

Jackson and Matthew shared a look, and what they were doing came through loud and clear. Their conversation had been to assure she stayed put, out of sight, and to minimize her fear. "You two played me."

"We don't want you afraid or upset," Jackson said. "Of course, we will protect you, but we'd prefer not to tick-off Rose or create a stir at Carl Wooten's funeral doing it."

They'd played her, all right. And it had worked. While they leaned heavy on murdering Martin for her benefit, she couldn't say she didn't have the smallest seed of doubt they meant every word. "I'm going to have to watch you two." And Rose. She had started this with forbidding gunfire. That had been intentional, like her hitting the mailbox with the hearse. Christine frowned at the men. "I will do my part to avoid Martin." Easiest promise she'd ever made.

Jackson rewarded her with a killer smile that weakened her knees. "Appreciate the consideration. Rose gets on a tear and she stays there, and that's the truth."

Rose was nervous not nuts. But maybe she did get ticked off and stay angry. Didn't everyone do that now and then? "The way you two connive, I suppose she does. Survival instincts being what they are."

They grinned at her. Both of them. She rolled her gaze. "Martin probably won't even come inside."

Gravel crunched. Jackson moved to the window and looked outside. "First cluster of mourners has arrived." He swerved to look at Christine. "And Martin is coming inside. He just opened his car door."

"Great." Good grief, the man had no boundaries, crashing a funeral. Well, if Jackson or Matthew shot him, it was his own fault. She'd done what she could. The next move was his—and she hoped to heaven he had the sense not to make it.

"I'd better get down there." Matthew tensed, then headed toward the hall. He was showing signs of being nervous, too.

Christine couldn't resist a last-second warning just before he cleared the door. "Don't shoot him unless you absolutely have to, okay? With Frankie and Myrtle's antics, Rose has been worried enough about this funeral. She really doesn't need the added upset."

Matthew nodded, then walked on.

That was thoughtful of you, Caroline." Jackson scrutinized her carefully. "I'd think after all Martin has done to you, you'd jump at the chance to see him dead."

"Not today." She refused to explain what she didn't understand. She owed these people. They'd helped her escape at the diner and they had helped Caro at some point in the past. "And not here. Rose has already sacrificed her guest room drapes for this funeral. That's more than enough."

Jackson gave her a lazy smile. "I like the person you're becoming."

She was the same person she'd always been. But she couldn't tell him that, so she just stood there, feeling an attraction to him unlike any she'd felt for a man. Far stronger than anything felt in her previous one serious relationship.

The attraction couldn't be real, of course. The timing was lousy, and it made no sense. She knew too little about him. Had to be all the upset. *High anxiety.* She wasn't herself. Tagging her emotional riot to attraction when it was fear and doubt masquerading.

Looking up at him, Christine checked again, suffered that magnetic pull and accepted defeat.

Oh, man. It was him.

That's it. You're certifiable.

They all thought she was nuts, unable to remember them. Being overly attracted to Jackson proved them right. And, from the look in his eyes, Jackson felt the same way about her, which made him as wacky as her and as dangerous to her as Martin.

After being married to that man, the last thing Caroline would feel right now is attracted to any man. Even a gorgeous hunk like Jackson.

Her brain back in gear, Christine looked at him again and her stomach fluttered.

Definitely him…and nuts.

Chapter 9

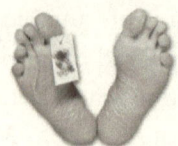

An exhausted Christine sat alone at the kitchen table, debating the merits of insanity.

Rose came down the stairs. Dressed in an appropriate and discreet black sheath and jacket with her long auburn hair knotted at her crown, she appeared elegant and surprisingly calm. "You look great."

"Thanks." Rose smiled. "I'm as dry as a camel. It's nerves, I think," she said, snagging a glass from the cabinet. "Thanks again for the help with the flowers. I don't know what we would have done without you."

"My pleasure." Christine bit into a cracker. "Jackson and I are having a snack. Well, we were. He's gone to backup Matthew in case Martin decides to…, well, be Martin."

"I'm surprised you can swallow with him so close." Rose filled the glass with ice from the fridge. "Not that he'll ever get near you. Neither Matthew nor Jackson would allow it. So don't you worry about that."

"I'm not worried." Maybe Christine should be, but even if the guys couldn't shoot him, she could. She hated that it would upset Rose and get Carl Wooten's mourners in an uproar, but no way was

Christine going to just stand there and let Martin Easton blow her brains out.

"Keep your weapon where it is, Caroline." Calm and collected, Rose paused to take a long drink of water from her glass. "Jackson and Matthew will disabuse Martin of any inkling to cause trouble here."

She hoped Rose was right about that. Chewing a crunchy cracker, Christine swallowed and stilled. "How did you know I was armed?"

"I saw the print in your t-shirt." Rose drained her glass and immediately refilled it.

"The iced-tea incident on the front porch?" Christine thought she'd pulled the wet t-shirt loose from her body in time to prevent printing. But apparently not.

"Before then," Rose said. "When we were in the hearse."

Christine nodded, not bothering to deny it. "Is that why you nearly took out the mailbox?"

"No, it was before then. The azaleas, I think." Rose shrugged. "I'm not sure."

She knew exactly. "Testing something?"

Rose didn't lose her affable manner, or pull any punches. "Just making sure you weren't of a mind to shoot me."

She was speaking the truth, but not the whole truth. Rose apparently still felt the need to keep her secrets. Since Christine had plenty of her own to keep, she let her questions go.

Parking the glass on the counter, Rose said, "Come with me."

She led Christine upstairs, through the master bedroom suite to the far wall. Rose dragged her fingertips under the baseboard. A section of wall slid inward, leaving a sizable gap and revealing a secret room.

Stepping inside, Christine scanned the space from one end to the other and recorded details. The eight-by-ten was filled with wall-to-wall security cameras.

"From here, you can watch what's going on anywhere inside or out without any risk of detection."

"Wow." Christine looked at Rose. "This is a pretty sophisticated setup."

"It's the best." Rose stepped back to the opening. "No matter what, you stay put in here until one of us comes for you."

Christine nodded.

"I'm trusting you, Caroline. Don't make me sorry. You have no idea how much we have riding on this."

Her trust increased Christine's guilt. If it were just her, she might have told Rose the truth right then. But it wasn't. And Caro's life wasn't Christine's to risk, only to protect. "You won't be sorry," she promised.

Rose gave her a long, steady look, then left the secret room. The wall slid shut.

Two chairs stood in front of a long, sleek desktop below the monitors. Christine dropped into the nearest seat and studied the screens. On the third one, her focus stuck. Jackson stood at the back of the chapel talking to the sheriff.

Christine recognized him on sight. She had served Harry a to-go cup of coffee—*Leaded. No sugar. No cream*—every morning since she had been in Even, working at Danny's Diner. The sheriff and Jackson seemed intense and on-alert.

She studied the mourners. Many of their faces were familiar, if not their names. All the men from the Prayer Breakfast Seniors Club filled the last pew on the right. Carl Wooten's widow, Clara, sat in the first row, in front of the men, already dabbing at her eyes with a white hanky.

Two women in their mid-forties entered the chapel and paid their respects, pausing at Carl's coffin, then moved on to examine all the flowers. No doubt, those two were the florists, Frankie and Myrtle. Christine hadn't yet met either of them.

Screening on to the right side of the chapel, Christine spotted Martin seated in the back row. Her stomach muscles clenched. He expected her to be there, and she would've been, out of respect for the people in Even, if he hadn't shown up. She'd be a piranha for not showing her face, but at least she wouldn't be a corpse.

Billy Joe Baker and Dean Hester walked up to the coffin,

54

paused, then walked all the back to the last row near the entrance door. They plopped down on either side of Martin.

Whatever Jackson and the sheriff had been discussing ended. The sheriff walked up, then back to that same last row and motioned Dean Hester to make room. He sat down on the end of the pew, one person from Martin, which frosted Martin, gauging by his expression. His mouth flat-lined. But it was seeing Jackson that had Martin's expression turning ice-cold. He'd recognized him. Why would Martin recognize Jackson? He had aided Caro, but Martin couldn't know that. Christine had kept his thugs too busy to dare to shift focus to her sister.

Circumstances aside, the two men clearly weren't friendly. Martin looked ticked to the nines, and Jackson looked ready for anything and willing to do it. She hadn't seen him appear so formidable. Gauging by his reactions, Martin had, and he grudgingly respected Jackson's ability to carry out his intentions. As if angry with himself for showing weakness, Martin glared at Jackson. Jackson moved away from the door, headed right toward Martin, and stood against the wall, directly behind him.

No intimidating that one. Christine almost laughed. "Well done, Jackson. Make him squirm." Martin couldn't see Jackson or what he was doing unless he turned backward in his seat. She regretted not opting for volume and hearing what they were saying, but she needed the quiet to conceal herself and to listen for sounds of any intruders, especially since Martin's thugs hadn't yet shown their faces.

Whatever Martin's plans had been when he had come into the chapel, she couldn't guess. But Jackson, the sheriff, and the locals putting the evil eye on him—all the breakfast prayer group seniors, and everyone else—surely had him thinking again. The man was a miserable jerk, but he was not stupid. He couldn't take them all on at once.

Word traveled fast in a small town. Christine shouldn't have been surprised the locals had banned together against an outsider. But they'd done it for her, and that touched her. Deeply.

Since her parents' deaths, no one else had stood up for her.

These locals doing so got to her. Exactly what she was supposed to do with these rioting emotions, she didn't know. But when others claimed you as one of their own, it sure gave you a good feeling inside.

This is what it feels like to belong…

She'd lost the opportunity to experience belonging, choosing computers and an isolated lifestyle. Feeling it now, she questioned her decision. What else had she intentionally and unconsciously forfeited?

The service began, progressed, and ended.

Matthew escorted Carl's widow, two kids and five grandkids to two limos. Billy Joe Baker had been hired to drive one; Dean Hester, the other. They followed the family. And Jackson… where had he gone? She scanned the other monitors but caught no sight of him.

Christine sat straighter in the chair. This was the most dangerous time. People were pouring out of the chapel and if Martin still intended to move, now would be the time he'd do it.

While his pew emptied, he inched down to its far end. "Here it comes," Christine mumbled to herself.

Sure enough, Martin looked around then headed for a little alcove, his intentions clear. He'd hide out until the chapel emptied.

Jackson stepped out of the alcove just before Martin could step into it. Christine gasped, as surprised as Martin. How had Jackson known?

And up behind Martin walked the sheriff.

Christine's lurching stomach settled. Martin Easton would be causing no problems here today.

Looking frustrated enough to spit nails, he exited the chapel and got into his car. Apparently, he was too impatient or inconvenienced to wait in line for the cars behind him to clear out. He hit the gas, slipped past the hearse—and cut right across Rose and Matthew's lawn.

Christine tapped the keyboard for sound.

"My garden!" Rose, who'd been talking with Frankie and Myrtle, stared in horror then snagged the sheriff's sleeve. "Harry, give me your gun. I'm going to shoot that sorry beggar myself."

"Now, Rose, you can't go shooting a man for taking out your cucumbers."

Frankie took objection. "He got her yellow squash, too."

"And her blueberry bushes," Myrtle added, wincing.

"The whole row. Rotten beggar has no respect or manners, misbehaving that way at Carl's funeral." An appalled Frankie reached into her purse. "Use my gun, Rose."

The sheriff intercepted the transfer of the weapon, shoved it back into Frankie's purse, then snapped it closed. "Now, ladies. You just stop it right there. There'll be no gunfire at Carl Wooten's funeral. It ain't seemly." He shot Rose a pointed look. "I heard you insisted on that, out of respect for Carl and Clara, didn't you?"

"I did." Rose looked anything but happy about admitting it.

"But that was before the beggar took out her garden."

"The sheriff is right, Frankie," Myrtle told her.

That earned her a pointed look and a sharp-tongued response. "Well, you can tell Caroline that when he puts a bullet through her head. I'm sure she'll be comforted." Frankie snorted. "Dead, but comforted."

Myrtle grunted, focused on the sheriff. "Frankie's got a point, Harry."

"He won't be shooting Caroline, and we'll get him for wrecking Rose's garden," the sheriff promised. "But not here or now. Let's let him get down the road a piece—on the other side of the cemetery."

"You're having a deputy intercept him?" Rose asked.

"Course." The sheriff nodded. "But not a word about it from any of you until—"

"After the funeral," Rose finished for him seemingly satisfied. "Thanks, Harry."

It's the right thing to do," he said. "Nobody has the right to go around damaging someone else's property. Not in Even."

Martin Easton was going to jail.

Christine let out a breath she hadn't realized she'd held, and lowered her hand at her chest, willing her pounding heart to settle down. "Yes!" She smiled, grateful for the unexpected justice.

And the gift. At least Martin's whereabouts for the rest of the day were clear.

There was another up side to his intrusion and taking out Rose's garden. In the future, Christine would bet Rose had no more problems with funeral flowers from Frankie or Myrtle.

A woman who'd lend you her gun wasn't likely to make you look like a fool—or to deliberately provoke you.

Even did have its ways… and its charm.

Chapter 10

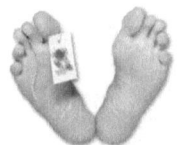

Jackson retrieved Christine from the safe room. On the way down the stairs, he said, "I guess you saw the garden incident unfold on the monitors."

"I did," she admitted. "Sorry about Rose's garden."

"It was worth it. I think the locals took her in today. She's one of them now."

"There is that." Christine smiled at his back. "And Martin is going to jail."

"Figured that would make your day."

"It did." No sense in lying about it.

The aroma of food cooking wafted to her before hitting the bottom stair rung. "Something smells good."

"Matthew's making dinner," Jackson paused to wait for her. "You're in for a treat."

So they expected her to stay here, at least, through dinner. "What's he cooking?"

"Chicken, I think. Whatever it is, it'll be good," Jackson said. "It always is."

In the kitchen, Matthew stood at the stove, stirring a huge pot.

He glanced back at them. "There you are, Caroline. I'll bet you're starved."

"I am always starved, and that smells great." Her stomach had been growling for the past hour.

"It's chicken and mushroom gumbo. Seafood is a little scarce here. They truck it in once a week on Monday, so we eat it on Monday." He grinned. "Rose says I'm picky, and she's right. I like my food fresh."

"Jackson says you're a good cook."

Matthew lifted a brow at her. "I do all right."

"Thank you for inviting me to dinner."

That set him back on heels. Surprise flashed through his eyes, and he quickly masked it. The little muscles at the outer corners of his eyes twitched.

"If you didn't, that's fine," she said, wishing she hadn't presumed. "Actually, I should use this time of knowing where Martin is to clear out."

"Clear out?" Jackson frowned. "No."

"Absolutely not," Matthew said. "I'm sorry, Caroline, but you misread me."

"You were surprised, and that's fine. Really."

"I was surprised, but at the invitation remark, not at you being here. I figured you'd be staying with us a while—protection from Martin."

"Oh, I see." She had the grace to blush, feeling a little over-whelmed. She could count on one hand the number of people who had willingly gone out of their way to protect her, and that included those being paid to do so after her parents' deaths. "I appreciate the hospitality truly, but I've caused enough trouble already. It's best that I go." How she'd pick up on Caro knowing them and stay safe from Martin she didn't know… yet. But Martin would seek revenge, and she couldn't be responsible for him seeking it against them.

"You have to stay." Jackson moved to face her. "The sheriff will cut Martin loose tomorrow at the latest. You know he'll come for you."

"That's my problem," she countered. "Making it your problem isn't right."

Jackson's phone beeped. He pulled it from his jeans pocket.

It wasn't the same phone he'd used earlier. Christine noted it, and wondered why he carried two. She knew why she did, but why would Jackson?

"I'd better step outside to take this," he said. "This discussion isn't over—and don't you go anywhere, Caroline. Promise me."

Why it mattered to him, she couldn't imagine. "Okay."

SATISFIED SHE'D STAY PUT, Jackson stepped outside and off the porch, making his way to the big oak. He accepted the call. "Hello."

"Jackson, my boy, it's me."

Miss Emily. "Have you learned anything?" The sun slid behind a cloud, slanting over the lawn and Martin Easton's tire ruts.

"Dr. Goodman won't be reachable for at least two days. Maybe three," she said, more than a little flustered. "It appears communing isn't communion over there. He's isolated himself on a mountain with no phone service and has to hike down to get to where a phone will work. That's after somebody hikes up there to tell him to come down and call."

A solid three days. Maybe longer. "What about Darby?" She kept a tight rein on everything at the Park. She'd know what was going on with Caroline.

"Darby has checked all the records and talked to the employees. There's nothing about Caroline leaving us, Jackson. Not a record one, and Speckles says he hasn't driven her to the gate. She should be here. Darby was stunned to discover she wasn't." That flustered Miss Emily. "I don't need to remind you how rare it is for anything to stun Darby."

"No, ma'am, you don't." Speckles was the ancient carriage driver who hauled people from place to place inside the Park. If anyone wanted to know anyone's whereabouts, usually they checked first with Speckles. "Well, at least we know where Caroline is, if not why she's here. She's standing in Rose's kitchen right now," he said. "The woman has a healthy appreciation for food."

"Must be the company. Dr. Goodman has been concerned about her paltry appetite."

She'd just told Matthew she was always starved. Strange. A pair of cardinals flitted from the big oak over to a magnolia tree. "Did Darby say anything about Caroline's mental condition? Knowing what to say or not say to her would sure help."

"She still doesn't know any of you?"

"No, ma'am. She doesn't."

"Are you certain she isn't pretending, Jackson? Desperate people can be very good deceivers."

"She's not pretending." Admitting it stung. "She looked at me like she'd never seen me in her life, Miss Emily. No doubt about it."

"How unexpected. Darby said she's been doing so well. We don't have the notes of her last session with Dr. Goodman, but Darby reviewed all the others. Caroline seemed to be well-adjusted and stable. Actually, she's been going through a little rebellious stage."

"What kind of rebellious stage?"

"It's common with abuse victims. She's asserting her control over her life." Miss Emily was smiling at that; Jackson could hear it in her tone. "It's all about choice."

Made sense. It was liberating to make your own choices about your own life after being denied the right. "So Darby found nothing in the notes or any insight to offer about Caroline's memory loss?"

"I'm afraid not, which means, Lester is right," Miss Emily said. "I did as you suggested and spoke to him. He feels it's best to bring Caroline back to the Park right away—so the medical staff can talk with her and see what's going on."

And how would Caroline react to that suggestion? Jackson wondered but couldn't predict. She might be okay with it, or refuse to go. Odds were fifty-fifty. "I'll do what I can."

"I'm afraid you don't understand, my boy." Miss Emily paused, then added, steel resolve in her tone. "You get her here before she does us damage. We'll care for her, of course, but our top priority is to first secure the residents. Lucas is pretty upset that she's there and not one person on the entire security team had a clue she departed the Park. He's already putting new procedures in place."

It was a command performance. Whether Caroline wanted to go with Jackson or not, she would be returning to Sampson Park. "So if she says she doesn't want to go…?" He shifted uneasily. "She doesn't know us, Miss Emily."

"Charm her. If that doesn't work, then get creative," Miss Emily said. "I don't care how you get her here, Jackson, just do it." She softened her tone. "You do understand the critical nature of this situation, don't you?"

"Yes, ma'am, I do." It wasn't his understanding that concerned him. Would Caroline understand? Highly unlikely, and he wasn't free to explain, which means he would have to insist. So much for her warm smiles and the amusement that lit up her eyes. He sighed, already missing both. "We'll travel tonight."

"Excellent. I'll tell Lester. Speckles will meet you at the gate and alert Lucas. I expect after this he's going to make life difficult for everyone for a while, especially the guards."

"Yes, ma'am." Jackson would bank on it. Lucas was a dedicated security chief and devoted to the residents. He'd be furious—not in anger, but in fear—Caroline had left and no one knew it.

"See you then," Miss Emily said. "Drive safe and keep me apprised of any developments."

"Yes, ma'am." Stowing the phone, Jackson did a mental shift. *Now how exactly could he explain this development to Caroline?*

The possibility of driving all the way to the Park with her in the trunk held no appeal.

Chapter 11

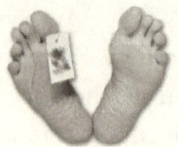

"If she refuses," Matthew told Jackson, "you can always stuff her in the trunk."

"I thought of that, but—"

Rose laid an exasperated sigh on her beloved that he'd be remembering for months. "What's wrong with you two?" She glared at her husband and then at Jackson.

"What?" Jackson shrugged, propped a foot against the oak's trunk behind him. "Miss Emily said Caroline had to go." He dropped his voice even though they'd come outside under the shade tree to be certain Caroline didn't overhear them. "Critical to the residents, she said."

Rose parked her hands on her hips. "You do not stuff a woman who's been abused like Caroline was into the trunk of a car, Jackson Lee Grant." She swerved her gaze to Matthew. "You should know better. Sounds to me as if you've been spending too much time with Lester."

Lester was loved by all three of them, but he'd been Rose's neighbor in Biloxi, Mississippi: A senior, insomniac who often forgot his pants and got arrested. Every time Rose had to bail him out, she had to use her grocery money to do it, which meant she'd be stuck eating peanut butter sandwiches for a week. She finally bought him some boxers with money printed on them to help him remember, and because his briefs were getting ratty anyway. But she knew as well as Jackson that had been a ruse and a trust test. Lester was as sharp as a tack. His logic was twisted, but his mind worked fine using Lester-logic. This, putting Caroline in the trunk, in Rose's opinion, was Lester-logic.

"It was a hypothetical, honey," Matthew assured Rose. "*If* Caroline refused to go willingly..."

"I see. A hypothetical." She frowned deeper and held it to be sure they both felt it full-force and effect. "And has it occurred to either of you Einsteins that Jackson drives a truck." She lifted her arms; her hands, palm up. "No trunk."

"I wasn't serious, Rose," Matthew insisted, an amused lift at the corner of his mouth.

"I'm glad to hear it. We have enough to worry about without Lester-logic invading your brain."

Jackson planted a hand against the tree. "Has it occurred to you she might not be willing to go, Rose?"

"Why would she refuse?"

Rose was confused? Seriously? He checked his sister again, and she was indeed confused. "Gee, I don't know." Jackson resisted the urge to roll his eyes. "She doesn't know any of us. We're wanting to haul her to another state for an undisclosed reason when all she remembers is Martin and his thugs. Your driving today scared five years off her, taking out the azaleas and the trash can and nearly mowing down a mailbox. Then you threaten to shoot Martin with the sheriff's gun."

"I don't think you'll win with that one." Matthew nudged him. "Just saying."

Jackson gave Matthew that one, but soldiered on. "All that, Rose. Well, I can't think of a single reason she wouldn't be eager to jump all over taking a trip with us."

"I did not take out the azaleas." Rose hiked her chin. "Just almost. Seeing her gun print under her t-shirt scared me." Rose worried her lower lip with her teeth. "But you do have a point.

Maybe she wouldn't feel as threatened if she were traveling with just you."

Matthew agreed. "Not so outnumbered. Yeah, that might help."

Rose latched onto the idea. "We don't have to be there for the associates' meeting for a couple days. You and she go now and get her head examined. " Rose looked contrite over that unfortunate remark. "You know what I mean."

"Rose and I will follow in a couple days." Matthew nodded.

"She might be more open to going under those conditions." Jackson did what he should have done coming out of the gate. His sister wouldn't be happy with anything except following her own thoughts on disclosure. It was the abuse thing. She'd had some bad foster parent experiences along with the good ones, and she took serious exception to any kind of force being exerted against anyone or anything. "How do you think we should handle disclosure?"

"Tell her the truth."

That Jackson hadn't expected. "All of it?"

"Of course not. That would just put her in more jeopardy," Rose said. "And us. We don't know if she's stable, though I haven't seen anything to make me think she isn't."

"You mean, aside from her not remembering us or being here?" Matthew said.

"Well, there's that," Rose reluctantly agreed. "But she handled the flower crisis just fine, and she didn't shoot Martin Easton on sight today. That took a lot of stability *and* self-discipline, considering."

Jackson couldn't fault Rose's thinking there.

Matthew rubbed at his neck. "Maybe just tell her about bringing her here at Christmas then taking her down to Sampson Park. Skip the whole Dixie side-trip and do not mention Mr. Perini or the legal precautions taken there. If you have to get into that, I'd wait and do it at the Park."

"That would minimize the possibility of her going to an outsider on anything." Less risky for the group. Jackson straightened up. "We all agree then?"

Matthew nodded. Rose hesitated. "Give me a minute. I'm factoring in the fact that she's packing."

"What kind of gun is it? Do you know?"

Rose looked at Matthew. "A 1911. Nearly certain it's a .45."

"Serious weapon," Jackson said, half-surprised. If she could rack it, she was stronger than she looked.

"Very serious weapon." Rose agreed. "I say you should tell her what you must to get her to go, but not so much you shake her up. If she gets worried about us and our motives, she might see you as just another Martin. That happens and she'll do her best to give us all the slip, head underground, and disappear."

Spending months looking for her held less appeal than the trunk. Jackson grimaced. No one in the group would be happy with that scenario. "She could skip out. Miss Emily said she was going through a rebellious stage. Making her own choices."

Caroline walked out the door and onto the porch. She stopped at the stairs down to the lawn and raised her voice to carry over to them. "Is this a private conversation or may I join you?"

"Don't blow this, Jackson," Rose warned, speaking softly so Caroline wouldn't hear. "They'll have your head."

They would. And then some. Jackson walked back toward the porch. "We're just coming in."

"We've got to go check on supper," Rose said. She and Matthew walked past Caroline and went inside.

Jackson stopped closer. "Let's talk a minute, Caroline."

"Something is wrong. It's written all over your face." Her eyes stretched wide and she gasped. "Oh, no. Martin got away from the deputy, didn't he?"

"Actually, he did. Harry called a few minutes ago." That disclosure put her on edge. Now, unfortunately, Jackson had to knock her over the cliff. "But that's not what I want to talk to you about."

"I knew that's why y'all came out here to talk. So I wouldn't hear." She blinked rapidly, hunched her shoulders, preparing to fight or take flight. "I—I have to go." She turned to leave.

Jackson snagged her arm. "Go where?"

"Away," she said, trying to free her arm from his clasp, but he held fast. She stopped tugging and stared at him, calmed her voice. "You've got to let go of me, Jackson. Martin will come back here. You, Rose and Matthew will all be in danger. It's me he wants. If I'm no longer here, he will leave to come after me and all of you will be safe."

Jackson continued his hold but gentled it, and his voice. "If he returns here, we'll handle it. Here, you're safe. Out there alone, not so much."

"That's why you had the private session? To decide whether I should stay or go?" Suspicion filled her eyes and his non-response confirmed it. "Why didn't you tell me? I should have been in on the discussion. He wants to kill me."

Jackson was losing her. He had to turn things around. "You might not realize it, but we know you don't remember us or being here, Caroline. We don't know why you don't remember, and that's okay. The less said about that, the better."

"You don't want to know what happened to me?"

"Of course, I care what happened to you. I only meant it's for professionals to sort out who are trained to find answers the right way." Was he telling her too much, too little? How would she respond to being told her memory had failed her? Was she already aware of it? "Honestly, we're not sure what to tell you or what might be…"

Suspicion and her accusatory demeanor fell to understanding. "Too much?"

She'd gotten a grip on them that wasn't horrific. Jackson nodded, confirming it. "We came out here to talk because we didn't want you to be afraid or to not feel safe. Martin might come here but you have nothing to fear from him, okay?"

"Okay." She believed Jackson, and looked torn, as if she wanted to explain something to him but changed her mind, opting not to say anything.

"Can we discuss what I want to discuss now?" he asked.

"Oh, no. I know that tone." Her hand at the soft hollow of her throat, spanning her collarbones, she moved toward the nearest rocker. "I think I'd better sit down for this."

She expected the worst. Jackson wished he could reassure her, but if he did and then dropped the truth on her, she'd never again believe a word that came out of his mouth.

Years ago, Lester and Rose had told him, once trust is broken, it's broken. Things can never go back to the way they were or be the same. With a lot of work, trust might be patched, but there would always be a crack where doubt seeped in and gnawed at the marrow of your bones. "Yeah, you probably should."

Chapter 12

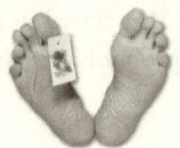

The urge to wring her hands burned in Christine.

She laced them in her lap to keep from mangling them. She'd never believed she was the hand-wringing type, but after the day they'd had, and now learning that Martin was still on the loose... Well, not wringing them required conscious effort and challenging discipline.

Jackson's expression didn't help. His square jaw was tight, teeth near cracking, his eyes guarded, and if his words got any stiffer, they could make the trip from his mouth, across the little table between them and over to her all on their own. Strange, because when he'd stood behind Martin in the chapel, Jackson had seemed alert but loose, ready for whatever happened. Now, he seemed board-stiff and extremely uncomfortable. She played the hunch. "This isn't about Martin, is it?"

"Only indirectly," Jackson admitted, choosing his words carefully. "It's more about you."

Seriously worried, she decided. For her and for his family. "I've already told you I'm going. I realize that my being here puts you all in danger."

Jackson braced his hands on his knees and leaned forward. "That's not it."

"Then what is it?"

He didn't answer, studied his shoes and her feet.

Christine refused to prod him. Clearly, he was deciding exactly what he wanted to say and how he wanted to say it. The least she could do was to give him time to work through it.

"I told you. We know you don't remember us, or being here," he said, his voice just above a whisper. He lifted his gaze to look into her eyes. "But we all remember you."

Her heartbeat again sped up, thudding deep. They knew she wasn't Caro. Having no idea what was safe to say that wouldn't cost her their help in finding her sister, she stayed quiet.

"I can't do this, Caroline," he finally said. "I thought I could, but I can't."

"What can't you do?" What was *this*?

He didn't answer that question, either. He rubbed the back of his neck and shifted on his seat. "Look, I don't know what's happened to you, or why you can't remember us. I don't know if you know. But you trusted me once, and I protected you. We all did. So I'm asking you to trust me again."

He feared freaking her out, or damaging her. Her insides twisted. They thought she was fragile, that maybe she'd snapped. Rebelling inside—*Christine Branch did not do fragile or snap*—she somehow managed to keep her mouth shut and her voice civil. "Trust you on what?"

Jackson blew out a sharp breath. "I need to take you somewhere, and I want you to come with me without asking questions."

She could do that. Relieved, she started to say so, but he lifted a staying hand.

"No, I need to say this." He softened his voice. "I'm a chef, not a doctor, and I don't want to do anything that could hurt you. I—we —think you've been hurt enough." He let her see his concern and uncertainty. "Anything I say could be the wrong thing, you know what I mean? To me, those are unacceptable risks." He gazed off toward the large oak, its shadows melting on the lawn under the weak setting sun. "But I need to go and you need to come with me. So will you trust me, Caroline?"

Christine didn't know what to say. They didn't know she wasn't Caro. They thought she'd had some sort of breakdown and were really worried about harming her. Warmth settled in her chest. The kid gloves were to protect her not them. "I know you said no questions, but may I ask where is it you want to take me?"

He nodded, then looked her straight in the eye. "Back to Sampson Park."

Christine nearly fell out of her rocker. She'd been searching for Sampson Park since Caro mentioned it on Christmas and she had found nothing on it. Her techie friends had also failed. Between them, they'd concluded Sampson Park had to have been a euphemism or a code for some other place. Now, Jackson wanted to take her there?

Easy. Easy. She cautioned herself to tamp her reaction and not seem overly eager. Caro would naturally be uneasy and reluctant— because she didn't know any of them and didn't know the reason her memory had failed. "Am I allowed to ask why?"

He nodded. "Yes, but I hope you won't."

Because he might say the wrong thing and deepen her breakdown. Since August, twice Christine had wished for the luxury of a breakdown. Constantly under pressure from Martin and his thugs, worrying herself sick about Caro, Christine fleetingly had thought she needed the respite. But it was against her basic nature to give in to something like that. Both times, she convinced herself she couldn't afford the luxury—and seeing the impact a perceived breakdown had on Jackson had her sorry she ever had permitted the thought to cross her mind. "You have a good reason for taking me there?"

"I do."

She studied him for a long minute. Because he let her, she stopped rocking and focused on his unsettled gaze, more confident in her innate reaction. "I think you're a good man with a good heart, Jackson. I think, if Martin had tried anything today, you would have done your best to clean his clock. I don't remember you or Rose and Matthew. That has my head telling me I'd be crazy to go anywhere with you. But my heart and every instinct in my body says to trust you."

"You can trust me. You did before and you had no reason to regret it. You won't now, either."

She believed him. Of course, that was irrelevant, really. In their last conversation, Caroline was about to leave for Sampson Park with the chef. Jackson was a chef. So she had to have been about to leave Even with him. "I also think you're reluctant to tell me much because you're afraid I'm too fragile and not because you have nefarious plans for me. Am I right about that?"

He laced his hands on his bent knees. "Yes."

"Your intentions are good—for me, I mean. You don't intend to harm me?"

"Lord, no."

"And you know I'm armed and, if your intentions are not good and you should make such an attempt, I will shoot you."

He nodded a third time. "You'll have no reason to do that. I give you my word."

She leaned closer, dropped her voice, and looked up into his eyes. "Jackson, tell me. What's your word worth?"

He didn't blink, twitch or flinch, or evade. "To me, everything."

She waited but he didn't add anything. "Thank you." He'd asked for no questions but tolerated the ones she needed answered to ease her mind. Finally, she said what she intended to say all along. "All right, then. I'll trust you. I'll go with you to Sampson Park."

He clasped her hand seeming humble, but his palm felt clammy. "Thank you, Caroline."

So, she deduced, he was sincere but her trust had little to do with anything. She wasn't foolish enough to believe she actually had a choice. He would prefer her trust, but with or without it, he'd be taking her with him to this mysterious place.

Fortunately, they wanted the same thing. Barely able to contain her excitement, she lowered her gaze to the porch. Jackson knew Sampson Park, it was a real place, and he had taken Caro there.

And soon Christine would be one step closer to finding out what had happened to her sister.

Chapter 13

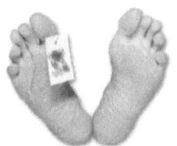

Standing in the safe room at Matthew's elbow, Rose faced the wall of monitors and focused on the screen filled with images of Jackson and Caroline, sitting on the front porch.

"Well, well." From his seat at the desk, Matthew looked back at his wife.

"What?" Rose stroked Matthew's neck. One thumb was hooked into the back pocket of her jeans.

"Jackson didn't tell her much of anything, and she agreed to go with him." A worried furrow creased Matthew's brow. "I've seen Jackson charm women, but this isn't how he went about it." Matthew squinted, narrowing his brows even more. "There's something wrong with this picture, Rose."

"Looks fine to me."

"The monitor is fine. I'm talking about the way they relate to each other. How could he trust her and she trust him? It's too fast."

"Short memory, love." Rose stroked his face. "Think back to the day we met…"

They'd been in New Orleans at Matthew's restaurant, Jameson Court. She'd faked her death and had come to him for a job. He'd given her one, fed her—she'd just been mugged—and he'd let her stay in the apartment above the restaurant. Since they both had suffered losses in Hurricane Katrina—he, his family, and she, everything she and Jackson owned—Matthew had also taken her in as his ally. Jackson was already in Dallas then, so she was on her own, and so was Matthew. "You even gave me an advance."

He nodded, the look in his eyes soft. "You wore sneakers. Every employee knew you'd wrecked your ankle being mugged, and they were still shocked I didn't require you to wear heels."

Rose smiled. "Fond memories." She planted a quick kiss to his lips. "And you do remember what it was like when we met."

"Of course." He smiled. "Best day of my life."

"Mine, too, which is why I know the way Jackson and Caroline relate is a good thing."

"It's the same way we were."

"Are."

"Are." He agreed. "But it seems somehow different for Jackson."

"Different but good." Rose scraped her lower lip with her teeth. "In fact, it seems to me everything is just fine." A little squeal of delight slipped out. "Caroline's going with her gut—and, I suspect by the way she watched his eyes, the twinkle."

"The twinkle?" Matthew looked back over his shoulder at Rose. Totally lost, he added, "You're going to have to explain that one to me."

"We've talked about it before," she said. Seeing his blank look, she indulged him. "In Dixie, Florida, when we left Paul Perini's funeral home the very first time."

"Ah, so that's what she was checking for when she asked what his word was worth. The twinkle." Matthew grinned. "You can't hold me responsible for forgetting, Rose. We had just been married in a funeral home."

"No, I was wrong. We talked about the twinkle after we died and left the crematorium. We already had married the second time, with our new lives, remember?"

"The morgue wedding."

She nodded. "That's it. You remember now?"

"I don't remember the twinkle," he said, then grinned. "The wedding, I definitely remember."

Rose sniffed. "We were both pretty emotional. Two funerals and two weddings inside a week." She grunted. "All that mob stuff swirling around us. We were a mess."

Matthew nodded. "Best days I'd had since the storm."

"Our wedding day?"

"Both of them."

Rose recalled both fondly. "I have to say, getting married while sitting on a gurney in the morgue isn't exactly a woman's dream wedding, but it was memorable. They both were."

Matthew agreed, then his smile faded. "I still don't really get the twinkle, babe."

"Look at Jackson's eyes." Rose tapped the screen. "He's crazy about her, and she knows it by..."

"The twinkle." Matthew smiled, pulled his wife close.

"Yes." Rose rolled her eyes. "Women never pay much attention to what a man says," she confessed. "The truth is always in the twinkle."

"So I had the twinkle?" he asked, clearly curious.

"From the first time you looked at me," she said, stroking his jaw. "You still do."

"Ah, you like the twinkle." Matthew hiked his eyebrows.

"I love the twinkle," she admitted. "And right now, it has me thinking you might be right."

"There's a first."

"It's not." She swatted at his shoulder.

"May I ask about what?" He dipped his chin. "It's rare for you to admit it. I don't want to miss my gloating opportunity."

"The baby."

He stilled. "Rose, I'm not ready for round thirty in the baby battles, okay?"

She persisted. "I was going to say that I think you were right this morning, and I was wrong. We should just do it." She lifted a shoulder. "With our crazy lives, if we wait until conditions are perfect, we'll be buried again childless."

"So you want to have a baby, then?"

"I've always wanted to have kids, I just debate the wisdom of doing it, considering our, um, special circumstances."

"Being dead and all."

Having rival mafia families gunning for you could make you apprehensive. Of course, thanks to Mr. Perini and his staging team, those families had witnessed firsthand Rose and Matthew's traffic accident deaths and their cremations. They'd seen the bodies. But if anyone from their old lives ever spotted them, all that nasty business could flare right back up again. "If we have to die and run again, it's far easier to do without little ones."

"True." Matthew paused to watch the monitor. "I thought about this today, too. Martin Easton showing up here made it impossible to not think about it."

"What did you think?"

He glanced back at her again. "That you were right. We need more time to see if things are going to work out for us here. It's only been a year, Rose. And I don't want our kids living in fear and having to start over, hoping they and we will be safe. I don't want us having to worry about that, either. Since Martin knows we're here, and he's sporting a grudge because we helped Caroline, we might have to move again."

"I so don't want to do that. We're just getting settled."

"I know." Matthew stroked small circles on her hip. "We'll see what Lester and Miss Emily say when we go to the Park for the associates' meeting."

"As much as I don't want to leave Even, if we must, then we must. Realistically, every parent worries about their child being safe, so I'm not sure that's as big a factor as we're making it."

"It's a huge factor in our case," Matthew said. "Every parent hasn't ticked off both the Marcello and the Adriano families."

Rose had witnessed a hit in a turf war. "And their assassins." An image of Lou Boudin filled her mind. Big, burly, and as mean as a snake coiled to strike. Imagine what he would do for a chance to snatch their child? Cold shivers raced up and down her backbone.

"I guess you're right. Giving ourselves a little more time to settle in is best."

"Ah, thank heaven for small mercies. We agree." His gratitude burned nearly as bright as his twinkle.

Rose pulled the phone from her jeans pocket and dialed.

"Who are you calling?"

"Hazel," Rose said, talking about Danny's wife down at the diner. "She's got Billy Joe and Dean helping her collect Christine's things from the motel."

"Glad you sent them along with her." Matthew nodded.

Hazel answered huffing. "Hey, Rose. Hold on a second." She paused a short beat, then said, "Billy Joe Baker, don't you dare touch Caroline's unmentionables. I'll be packing those myself. Get her shoes in there, boy. Didn't your mama ever tell you when you pack a suitcase, the shoes go on the bottom?"

Rose bit back a smile. "I just wanted to know how much longer before you get here with her things?"

"Give us fifteen minutes," Hazel said. "Oh, Dean wants to know if you want him to bring her car over to your place?"

Rose considered it. "Best not. That Martin devil is on the loose." If he found her car at the funeral home, there's no telling what he'd do. "Let's leave it somewhere neutral where it's easy to keep an eye on it."

"Danny says he'll keep it parked at the diner unmoved. It's under a big security light. Anybody messes with it, and we've got a straight shot from our bedroom window."

Martin hadn't seen Caroline in her car, leaving the diner. Maybe he didn't know what she'd been driving. He could assume her car was Danny's. "Here's hoping neither of you has to take that shot." Rose suspected Martin was out there somewhere, watching and waiting. He couldn't know for certain that Caroline was with them, but he had shown up for Carl Wooten's funeral, so he did suspect it. He'd be an idiot not to suspect she remained there.

Martin Easton was many things, but an idiot wasn't one of them.

"Billy Joe, don't you dare touch those either!" Hazel snorted.

"Let me go, Rose. The boy's rifling through Caroline's pajama drawer. I'm going to have to box his ears yet."

That boy was a man in his thirties and the size of a mountain, not that he'd dare to cross Hazel. Since his mother passed a year ago, he took most of his meals at the diner, and he had no taste for all burnt food.

Everyone in town knew not to mess with Hazel. She never got mad. She always got even.

Chapter 14

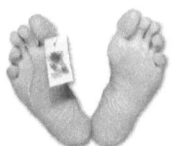

Hazel passed the suitcase to Rose. "It's pitiful, but that's all Caroline had with her."

"I suspect she travels light in case the jerk finds her and she has to leave everything behind."

"Danny figures the man's found her before. He says when she saw him, she was shocked."

"She was. It was awful, Hazel."

"Well, a woman's got to choose her battles, I always say. I tucked her wages and a little something extra in the corner of her suitcase." Hazel, ample, mid-fifties, and graying winked, then whispered, "Don't mention it, though. A woman can always use more pin money."

Hazel had a generous heart, helping Caroline with a fresh start somewhere else. Yet another confirmation that the decision to set up shop in Even and make it home had been a good one. Caroline was loaded, but no one in Even aside from Matthew, Rose and Jackson knew it. If anyone had, it would have been Hazel. She was wired into all things Even, though torn loyalties forbid her sometimes to share information. Like Frankie and Myrtle with the flowers.

Touched by her pin money for Caroline, Rose promised, "I won't say a word."

"Tell her we're going to miss her at the diner," Hazel said. "Especially the prayer breakfast boys. They just love her."

"We all do."

Hazel nodded, then got back into the passenger's seat of the car. Billy Joe Baker was driving. "Don't you be spewing gravel outta here, boy."

"I won't, Miss Hazel." He looked out the driver's window to Rose. "Figure Caroline's bugging out. You want Dean and me to escort her to the Interstate?"

With Martin on the loose, that probably wasn't a bad idea... "Jackson's got it covered, but thanks." Behind her, Jackson and Caroline walked out the door. "You go on and get Hazel home."

Danny was known to have an itchy trigger finger and, if Martin should go back to the diner, hopefully Hazel would keep her husband from exercising it. Course, she might exercise her own. Still, Danny was shorter on patience and Hazel always fired a warning shot.

Well, most of the time.

Okay, some of the time.

"Later, then." Billy Joe waved out the window, and Caroline stared at her suitcase in Rose's hand.

She walked over and passed the luggage to Jackson, then told Caroline, "Hazel brought your things. She says they're going to miss you at the diner. Especially the senior prayer breakfast group."

"That's sweet. They're good people."

"Yeah," Rose agreed, knowing they were grumpy as the dickens but on their best behavior when in the diner. They didn't much care for burnt food, either.

Jackson hugged his sister. "We'll see you in a few days."

Caroline's eyes widened.

"We have an associates' meeting," Rose said. That disclosure had surprised Jackson. "Funeral directors," she added.

"Oh, so that's what happens at Sampson Park."

Rose nodded. "For us, yes."

"I'll tell you about the Park on the way. We need to get going." Jackson guided Caroline toward his truck with a nudge to her back. "Be careful, sis." He planted a kiss on her cheek.

He didn't have to remind Rose to keep her wits. With Martin loose and in the vicinity, she was only too well aware of the risks. Wishing now she'd had Billy Joe escort them to the Interstate after all, Rose stepped back, away from Jackson's truck. "Drive safe."

Caroline crawled inside and settled in her seat. Jackson closed the door then walked around and got in on the driver's side. "Love you. I'll call when we get there," he told Rose, then shut the door and cranked the engine.

He took off down the drive, the gravel under his tires crunching, then pulled onto the road.

Rose watched them go, hugging her arms over her chest. There were twenty-one miles between their driveway and the Interstate. Most of the time, that was the perfect distance. It cut down on the chances of strangers cruising into Even by accident. But tonight, she worried. Each one of those miles carried added dangers.

When the truck rounded a curve and was out of sight, Rose turned for the porch.

Matthew stood on the top step, dangling his keys. "I'll come with you."

Not at all surprised he was worried, too, she smiled. "Love you, but that's not happening." Rose snatched the keys. "It's your turn to do the dishes."

"Love you, too, but I wasn't seeking permission." Matthew's jaw set as hard as if cast in concrete. "I'm coming, Rose."

"All right, then. But I'm driving." She was better at it, though there was no sense rubbing salt in that wound unless of course she had to do it to get her way.

"Okay, but not the hearse. It's too obvious," he said. "Take the Jag."

"Oh, you're letting me drive your Jag?" Rose grinned and hustled to it then slid into the driver's seat. "No backseat driving the whole way."

Matthew didn't smile, but he wanted to; the skin under his eyes crinkled. "I won't say a word."

Of course, he would. The Jag was his baby and he loved the car more than almost anything. He pampered it. Kept it parked and garaged out of the rain. He only drove it on special occasions. And he rarely permitted her to drive it without grumbling and constantly giving her instructions. If she so much as crossed a center line passing a car and pulled back into her own lane a millimeter too close, he'd hyperventilate.

Once or twice, she had to confess, she had gone a little road-crazy on purpose, testing the high-performance response time… and just to watch him squirm. She looked over at him. "I love being married to you."

His smile still turned her soft and mushy. "I love being married to you, too, honey, but don't even think about playing your mind games to get me riled up tonight."

"But soothing you is so much fun."

"You've got me there." He adjusted his seatbelt, clicked it into place.

"What kind of car does Martin drive?" She'd seen it but only noted his tires running over her plants.

"Black Lexus."

"Anything else you want to share?"

"He's gotten three speeding tickets in the last two weeks." Matthew had done a little research.

"So he's a lead foot." She knew how to outmaneuver a lead foot.

"Carl's funeral today went well," Matthew said, changing the subject.

"It did, thanks to Caroline." Rose glanced over. "That stunt Frankie and Myrtle pulled with the flowers made me a maniac."

"They're over it now."

"I'm glad. More of that kind of business, I do not need."

"That reminds me. Frankie called while you were talking to Hazel. She wants you to call her."

"Was something wrong?" She'd been nice after the funeral, when Martin had torn up Rose's garden. Maybe it was a guilty conscious. She and Myrtle should feel bad, messing around with Carl's funeral like that. They were supposed to be his friends.

"No." Matthew looked out the window to the thick trees lining the road. "She, Myrtle and Hazel want to have a tea to officially welcome you to Even."

That set Rose back on her heels. "But we've been here a year."

"Yes, but they didn't accept us into the Even family until today." Matthew glanced over. "Don't kick a gift horse in the mouth. We're going to need them."

She didn't like what the florists had done, but they'd made up for it after Martin trashed her garden. And Matthew did have a point. "You're right. We must never make an enemy on purpose," she finished the saying Mr. Perini had repeated to them a thousand times if not more during their comprehensive training. She pulled into the lane behind Jackson's truck. "A tea, huh?" Warmth flooded Rose. "That's kind of nice of them."

They chatted the next ten or so miles about everything and nothing. "Careful now," Matthew said. "We're coming up on Miller's curve."

A crossing that was notorious for wrecks and could be helpful to them in staging the deaths of special clients. "Got it," Rose said.

"If Martin's planning to ambush Caroline, it will be there." Matthew checked Rose's safety belt and then double-checked his own. "Back off a little, love. Give Jackson a bit more space."

"But if the jerk is there, I need to be close enough to intercede."

"I'd rather you not do it by running up Jackson's tailgate with my Jag, Rose."

She kept the gap between the Jag and Jackson's truck what it had been. Barry, Mr. Perini's sidekick in Dixie, had pushed her and Matthew hard on the driving obstacle course. Rose was more aggressive than Matthew, so Barry had taken her to the proverbial wall in the lessons.

Tall grass lined the lonely stretch of road. Miller's curve lay just beyond the north-south crossroad. The curve was sharp, a wicked angle. She eased up on the accelerator.

"Black Lexus. Two o'clock!" Matthew's voice boomed, startling her.

Jackson spotted the danger and accelerated. Rose punched the gas and the Jag took off like a shot. "Martin's going to ram them!"

"Lord, I hope Caroline doesn't shoot him," Matthew said. "Maybe she'll pop his tires."

Closing the gap, Rose whipped over, straddled the center line. "If she does shoot him, we are not doing his funeral." Another half-minute and he'd run Jackson off the road.

"Do something!" Matthew told her.

Rose slammed her foot down on the gas, ran up alongside Martin, and laid on the horn.

Surprised, he jerked left into the other lane. She cut harder, totally into the left lane, and he blocked her. Nosing toward him, she pushed him to let her back into her own lane. He kept pace, adjusting his speed to block her reentry. "Jerk."

"Car!" Matthew shouted. "Oncoming car!"

The headlights shone right in her eyes. Martin didn't slow down or back off, still blocking her. She assessed her options. The width of the soft shoulder to her left. She had one choice. Matthew would have a fit, but there was no help for it. She gauged the distance to avoid a T-bone.

"Don't do it, Rose." Matthew's tone proved he'd come to the same conclusion.

"Sorry, babe." Taking aim, she slammed into Martin's Lexus.

The Lexus spun then slid into the ditch, rocking on the uneven terrain. Finally, it stopped.

"Perfect. Did you see that? Textbook perfect." Rose checked her rearview then hit the brakes hard. She backed up and overshot him, then inched up to see inside Martin's car. "Can you see him? Is he alive?" He should be, if he was wearing his seatbelt, he shouldn't be injured. Maybe a little head tap on the steering wheel… unless his airbag deployed. But it shouldn't have.

"Yeah, he's moving. No airbag." Matthew rubbed his shoulder. "I think he's wearing the right side of my car. I told you not to do it, Rose."

"No choice. There wasn't another option." She patted Matthew's thigh. "Don't worry. Billy Joe will fix it up in no time."

Matthew glared at her. "I specifically told you not to intercede with my Jag, Rose Green."

"I know, honey, but—is Martin out of commission?" She had to get her beloved refocused. The sooner, the better.

He sighed. "I'll check." Matthew opened his door and drew a weapon from his back at the waist, then made his way over to the Lexus.

Its engine was off. Headlights still on. Thin ribbons of smoke seeped out from under its hood. Martin sat still, slumped over the steering wheel.

"Hey, jerk. Are you okay?" Matthew asked, approaching the door. "You've got some explaining to do, man. Why wouldn't you let us back into our lane? You trying to kill us?"

No answer. No movement. And no sign of weapons.

"He's unconscious," Matthew called to Rose then opened the Lexus's driver's door.

Martin Easton sat slumped over the steering wheel. He still didn't move. His arms hung loose, his hands open. No sign of a gun.

Matthew pressed his fingers to Martin's throat. "He has a pulse."

"Should we call 911?" Rose called out from the Jag.

"I'll handle it." Matthew rushed back to the car, pulled out his phone, and reported a speeder losing control and hitting the ditch just west of Miller's curve. He ended the call. "Dispatch is sending someone right out."

"I guess we should wait."

"Oh, yeah. We want to verify the man's either arrested for reckless driving or in an ambulance inbound for the hospital."

That was their assurance Jackson could get to Sampson Park with Caroline unimpeded. Rose's phone rang. She checked caller ID. "It's Jackson." She answered. "Hello."

"Don't you hello me." Anger shook his voice. "Are you crazy, sis?"

Where's the gratitude? "He was about to ram you. What did you want me to do? Ask him real nice not to do it?"

"You didn't have to sideswipe him with Matthew's Jag. Man, I know he's having a fit. How bad is she damaged?"

"The Jag will be fine. Minimal damage."

"Minimal damage?" Matthew's jaw dropped open. He clamped it shut, seething. He was absolutely livid. She lowered her voice to pull him away from his upset. "I couldn't let him follow you to the Park, Jackson." Hopefully, that remark would make both men pause to think. And they claimed women were emotional? She sniffed. Dealing with Jackson and Matthew at the same time could try the soul of a saint.

"You're not hurt, right?"

The question got her hackles up. "Not at all, and Matthew isn't either. Thank you so much for asking—after you asked about the condition of the car." He was as crazy about the Jag as her beloved. "I do know what I'm doing behind the wheel, Jackson."

"Why didn't you just shoot out his tires?"

"Well, Jackson, I could have done that. But it would have escalated the risks. He likely would have lost control, and—"

"Forget him, Daisy," Jackson cut in. "Taking out his tires would have spared the Jag and not risked your life and Matthew's."

Daisy? Rose stiffened, but reminded herself her brother was upset. He'd never slip and call her by her old name unless he was terrified. "Rose," she reminded him and winced. "Tell me Caroline didn't hear that."

"Not a worry."

If she had heard it, she'd probably just taken it as a sisterly endearment. Or so Rose hoped.

"Tell me why you wouldn't keep a safe distance and shoot out his tires."

Obviously, he'd been too upset to hear her loss of control rationale. Just as well. She'd prefer another tact. "Because it'd take Billy Joe a week to get a new set. I don't want Martin Easton nosing around in Even for a week—and neither do you."

Behind them, sirens pealed and red lights flashed atop two cars.

Rose checked the rearview, noted Matthew turned in his seat, looking back over his shoulder. "Police are arriving," he said.

She repeated that to Jackson. The two vehicles pulled up and parked behind them. The sirens stopped, but the lights continued flashing. A cop car and an ambulance. "Keep going, Jackson. Don't you even think about coming back here."

"What's all that racket?"

"We called 911. Well, Matthew did. It's their radios."

"Why did he do that?" Jackson sounded surprised. "Is Martin dead?"

"No. He took a little bump on the head. Just a little one," she said, hoping that proved right. "But big enough that the cops or the emergency medical team will detain him a while, checking him out. He'll refuse to go to the hospital, of course."

"Of course." Jackson's tone calmed. He understood the value of the detention. "Thanks, sis."

Much better. "You're welcome, brother dear. Now, put some miles between you and Even. Martin's resourceful, giving Harry's deputy the slip, and he is determined. That's not a healthy combination for anyone on the receiving end of his ire, especially Caroline."

"I will—if you'll promise me you won't do anything like ramming his car again. Good grief, Rose. I can't lose you, too."

Fear and pain stabbed her and squeezed her heart. Abandoned by their mother, never knowing their father… They'd only ever had each other. Some things even a grown man never forgot or got over. A grown woman, either. She cleared her throat. "Matthew and I were never in any real danger, Jackson. I promise. I just did a text-book maneuver Barry taught us at driving school. That's all."

She ignored Matthew's grunt and his glare.

"I'm not sure I believe you," Jackson said.

"It's the truth. Wait." She passed the phone to Matthew. "Tell him."

"It wasn't exactly—" Matthew started.

She cut him off and put a warning in her tone he couldn't miss. "Do it, Matthew. He's worrying."

Matthew took the phone. "Hey, Jackson. She's telling the truth, and we're fine. The only casualty is my Jag—which your sister will pay dearly for by cleaning the kitchen every day for the next three months."

She nodded, grateful it wouldn't be longer and he'd still cook. Matthew was a chef of the five-star restaurant variety. At least, he had been until the mob bombed Jameson Court, his restaurant in New Orleans. Still, she objected because her beloved expected her to and she didn't want to disappoint him. "Three whole months?" She grimaced. "That's harsh, honey."

He nodded a warning he wasn't in the mood to negotiate. If she pushed him, she'd lose.

Matthew had reached his limit. Accepting it, she nodded. "All right, then." It irked her to give in gracefully, but sparing Jackson worry was worth more than the fun of sparring with Matthew. Of course, if she hadn't eased Jackson's mind, Matthew would have done it. The men had been best friends since chef school. Knowing Matthew would do anything for her brother took the sting out of her being zapped with three months of kitchen duty just for doing what needed to be done. Family trumped cars in every case. When Matthew got over his snit, he'd agree. His whole life had always been about family. "Three months is reasonable."

A deputy appeared at the driver's window. Recognizing him relieved Rose, and she lowered the glass. "Evening, Punch."

Dean Hester's younger brother touched the brim of his hat. "Evening Rose. Matthew." Punch bent low and hung an arm on the window opening. "Y'all all right?"

"We're fine," Rose said. "Does that road hog still have a pulse?"

Punch nodded. "And a bad attitude." He shifted on his feet. "He says you ran him off the road."

"I was passing and he blocked me in the left lane. There was a car coming and he refused to let me in." She frowned. "He kept pace, Punch. The road hog tried his best to force us into a head-on collision."

A muscle ticked in Punch's jaw and his eyes narrowed, drawing his eyebrows into a pinch above the bridge of his nose. "Well, now. That's a whole different story than the one he's telling." Punch focused on Matthew. "Is that pretty much what happened?"

"Pretty much."

Punch took down a little more information then got sidetracked. Martin was on his cell phone, refusing medical attention and insisting Even Automotive get him a rental and send a tow-truck to pick up his Lexus.

Good luck with that. Rose bit back a grin. "We free to go?"

"Sure." Punch shared a longing look warning he'd like to go with them. "You folks did a nice job on Carl Wooten's funeral, by the way. His widow's been bragging on the matching flower pots. He'd have been pleased."

Her blue guest room drapes contribution. Caroline had pulled off a miracle. "Thanks, Punch."

He dropped his voice, bent deeper into the window. "This hothead in the Lexus is the same Martin who wrecked your garden, right?"

"And my blueberry bushes." She nodded. "He's threatening Caroline."

"Thought so. I like Caroline. From the first time, she remembered just how I like my coffee. Reminds me to eat something other than carbs, too."

"She's a wonder," Rose said. The woman had jumped into Even residents' lives with both feet.

"Well, no worries. I'll be hauling him in. Can't have a road hog endangering lives and wrecking property. Not in Even." Punch hitched his pants. "Doesn't much matter, really. Billy Joe Baker is not going to get out of bed to bring that man a car or tow his in, and it'd take Easton until tomorrow to walk all the way back to Even."

"It'd serve him right, but I think it'd be safer to know where he is and what he's doing." Rose sent Punch a level look.

"I'm with you on that." He straightened, stepped back from the window. "Have a good night."

"Thanks. Night, Punch." Rose drove on, and at the crossing after Miller's curve, she turned around and then headed home.

"Lord, I love small town life." Matthew smiled.

"Me, too." Rose glanced his way. "I'm guessing that *pretty much* of yours cost me another month of kitchen duty."

"Maybe two." Matthew sniffed, still stiff-jawed. "Two's reasonable."

It's just a little scrape, Matthew."

"A scrape?" He wiggled a finger. "Front to back, Rose. The whole side needs work. The whole side."

"I'm doing all that kitchen duty for a just cause and your nose is still out of joint?" She clicked her tongue to the roof of her mouth, then grimaced. "That's just not right."

"Not right?" He glared at her. "You better tread softly for a while, Miss Indy 500."

"Good grief." Rose blew out an exaggerated breath and drove on.

A wise woman knows when to hush and cut her losses.

Chapter 15

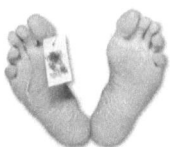

Christine sat silently, letting the truck eat up the miles and Jackson calm down. When he realized Rose was interceding and she side-swiped Martin's car, Jackson had been horrified.

That was easy to understand. If Caro had been in the Jag, Christine would have been horrified, too. After he'd talked with both Rose and Matthew, Jackson had been relieved but, if Christine lived to be a hundred, she would never forget the fear or the anguish in his voice when he told Rose he couldn't lose her, too.

The agony in those words struck a familiar chord. She'd felt it on learning her parents had been killed. Felt it again, and an over-whelming sense of loss, the Saturday after Christmas, when ten o'clock came and went and Caroline didn't call. She felt that same agony each and every silent Saturday. And a simple truth bore responsibility for it.

If Caro could, she would phone. That she hadn't meant she wasn't capable. Due to interception, injury or death, she couldn't call.

All bad. All the agonizing stuff of nightmares.

What he'd said flashed back to her. *Daisy...* Why had Jackson called Rose, Daisy? Christine considered asking him and decided against it, tucking that anomaly in her pocket. It could be nothing, but it could be something helpful or useful down the road.

"You okay?" Jackson glanced at her.

"The wreck shook me up a little," Christine admitted. "Takes my mind places that aren't good for me to go."

"Mine, too." He steadied himself. "It doesn't help that there's not much to look at out here."

"It's more than that, Jackson. I know Martin and how evil he is. I knew he'd come after anyone who helped me. I shouldn't have involved any of you."

"We helped you before," he reminded her. "We were already involved."

"Are you saying Martin might have found you and not me?" She hadn't once considered that.

"I don't know, but it's possible," Jackson said.

A chill rippled through her. "Why do you think it's possible?"

Jackson spared her a glance, gauging her mental state.

"I'm fine, Jackson." She forced a rise to her upper lip she hoped would pass for a smile of reassurance.

"Just checking." He hesitated then decided. "When I drove you out of Dallas and brought you here, our exit wasn't as clean as I hoped it would be."

"What do you mean?" Had Caro been threatened? Christine's heart beat faster.

"I tried to get you out under their radar. Steps were taken, but…" He paused, chanced a look to weigh the impact of his words, then continued. "His men located us on the outskirts of the city. There was a little scuffle, but I lost them."

He had deliberately downplayed the incident, still afraid of upsetting her. But if the event had been more significant and she had been in serious jeopardy, he'd be tense and stiff, and he wasn't. It had irritated him, but he hadn't considered the incident a serious complication. Further proof her instincts were on-target was that his voice sounded guarded but relatively normal.

So it was possible Martin had gone to Even with no idea Caroline was there until he had seen her. Why that made her feel better, she had no idea. But it did relieve a little of the guilt, if not all of it. They had been helping her sister. Christine's guilt was justified. "I should have done something differently. I shouldn't have further jeopardized the three of you."

Jackson shrugged. "Like I said, we were already in jeopardy."

His remark released a sneaking suspicion and the truth dawned on her. She took in a sharp breath. "Martin's been watching you since you returned to Dallas."

His knuckles went white on the steering wheel. "Pretty much. But it's definitely been no big deal."

It had been a huge deal. She knew; she'd lived with it every single day. "Jackson, I—I'm so sorry."

"No. Don't, Caroline. I made my choices, and I'm fine with them."

She'd turned his life upside down. What did you say to someone willing to put up with that for you? Anything, everything, was insufficient. "Thank you, Jackson."

He winked at her. "I made them work hard."

She chortled. "Me, too." She looked out the windshield and relaxed. Jackson would have done what he did for anyone. *Amazing.* Taking on the likes of Martin for someone else's benefit, he had to be a good man. Nothing nefarious about him, but plenty interesting. Intriguing. "Why do you take the risks?"

"Because they should be taken."

"Yes, but why do you? Lots of people know others are in trouble, yet few do something about it. Why do you?"

He paused a long minute. "It's not complicated. When I needed help, someone was there. An old man named Lester," Jackson said. "I could have been headed for serious trouble. Rose was busy working, keeping food on the table, and Lester was a neighbor. He stepped in."

"What did he do?"

"He taught me to fish, about faith, about compassion and how to change a tire." A wistful expression accompanied what were clearly good memories. "He also made me think about things I should have been thinking about and wasn't. Things like the sacrifices Rose was making to give me the best life she could, and how I could help her instead of getting into trouble."

Jackson admired Lester, and so did Christine. "Was Lester a relative?"

"No, not by blood." Jackson's expression turned tender. "But he was more a father to me than I've ever known. Still is."

"You love him."

"Oh, yeah."

"He sounds like a wonderful man."

"He is." Jackson chuckled. "Eccentric, and very strange at times, but he's an extraordinary man."

"So you helped me because, when you needed help, Lester helped you."

"Yep. That about covers it."

"Admirable." Christine settled in her seat and let her gaze wander to the tree-studded terrain. Not a building in sight, just the headlights of light traffic. She gazed up at the stars. She and Caro hadn't had a Lester in their lives. Lawyers and advisors, a guardian who was cold and distant but performed his duties to the letter. Still, they'd been provided for and monitored and no one had abused them. Jackson and Rose had survived so much more...

A couple hours of Interstate later, Jackson turned South and then East. The signs along the road were mostly for Tallahassee and Mobile. Jackson still hadn't said where Sampson Park was located, but it seemed pretty apparent it was somewhere along the Gulf Coast. Florida maybe, or Alabama. She had offered to drive for a while, but he had refused. He still watched the rearview mirror closely, if not constantly, so despite the all-night driving, he was staying alert in case of trouble.

Now, he glanced her way more frequently. "You okay?"

"Fine." She'd wanted to ask their destination's location but battled the temptation. He was taking her to Sampson Park. When she got there, she'd know. Until then, she could speculate but refrain from asking in a show of trust.

"Is there something you want or need to talk about?" he asked.

Daisy. Where's this park? "At some point, maybe, but not right now."

"Do you mind if I talk, or do you need quiet time?"

"Of course, talk." She liked talking with him. It kept her worries at bay.

He gripped the wheel with a loose hand. "The truth is, I'm still a little rattled. Rose scared the fool out of me, taking chances with her life."

"Me, too." Christine patted Jackson's forearm. "But I've been thinking about it. She really didn't seem out of control. Not for a second. You said she could drive anything with wheels and I have to agree that her maneuver seemed deliberate and measured."

"Thanks for sharing that. I couldn't see as well as you, watching through the mirror." Christine had turned around in her seat. "I don't remember a time when she didn't drive." He smiled.

Clearly he was reliving a fond memory. "What?"

"Oh, we were kids. Rose couldn't have been more than nine. Wait... Eight. She was eight, because we were both living with the Grassley family then. Most of the time, we were placed with different foster families." Jackson shifted and relaxed. "Anyway, Mr. Grassley loved his beer, and one night, he, shall we say, over-indulged."

"He was drunk."

"Falling down drunk," Jackson admitted. "He ran out of beer so he grabbed his car keys, bent on making a beer run. Mrs. Grassley couldn't stop him, and she couldn't drive, so she tells Rose and me to drive him so he doesn't get a DUI."

"She thought it was better for Rose, at eight, to drive without a license than for him to get a DUI?"

"Better odds of not getting a ticket at all." Jackson grinned. "Rose was so little she couldn't see over the dash so Mrs. Grassley propped a pillow on the seat under her. Then Rose couldn't reach the pedals."

"Oh-oh. I'm seeing this adventure going in a very bad direction."

"Actually, it's not bad."

"You're kidding me."

"No," Jackson assured her. "Mrs. Grassley told Rose to get her some rubber-bands. She used them to band chunks of wood to the pedals, so Rose could reach them. And off we went to the liquor store."

"Mr. Grassley rode with Rose driving?"

"To get his beer, and get Mrs. Grassley off his back, he'd have ridden with me driving."

Jackson was a couple years younger than Rose, so he'd been five, or at most six at the time. The irresponsible absurdity of the situation was totally inappropriate, but who would actually do something like that? Yet Jackson was deeply amused and laughing hard, recounting details of the ordeal.

Christine laughed with him until tears ran down her face. Jackson hadn't had an abundance of good memories to draw from, bless his heart. At least, not until Lester had come along. She loved Lester for being a good man and stepping up for Jackson and Rose. How different their lives might have been without him. "So Mr. Grassley got his beer, and you all got home in one piece."

"We did." Jackson smiled. "And Mrs. Grassley kept the wood banded to the pedals and a pillow in the backseat so Rose could take her anywhere she wanted to go."

"Mr. Grassley didn't take them off when he sobered up?"

Jackson dipped his chin. "Mr. Grassley never sobered up." He dropped his voice to a whisper. "I think Mrs. Grassley liked him better that way. He wasn't as grouchy."

"Rose was a gutsy kid, wasn't she?"

"She had to be." Gauging by his expression, Jackson resented that. "She did get stopped by a cop on a beer run once."

"Oh, no." Christine frowned. "What happened?"

"She told the cop there was no way she would let her baby brother ride with a drunk and took off. She wouldn't stop, so he called for backup to clear the way. That cop followed us all the way home, and…"

"He arrested her?" Christine was beside herself. On the one

hand, he had to keep her off the road, but on the other, Rose's argument had merit.

"No, he didn't arrest her. She was a pretty good driver by then. No violations, aside from the driving without a license. He warned her, though, to stop driving until she was old enough and got a license." Jackson smiled. "She promised not to drive except in emergencies."

"So what... Oh, wait. He issued her a written warning." When Jackson nodded, Christine gasped. "And that ended you two living with the Grassleys?"

"Unfortunately." Jackson spared her a glance. "They got the boot. No more foster parenting."

He passed a silver SUV, then moved back into the right lane. "We didn't have your typical family life with the Grassleys, and it wasn't by any stretch of the imagination ideal, but at least Rose and I had been together. We were devastated at going back into the system." Sadness settled in his eyes.

What being together had meant to him was evident in the timbre of his voice. Christine's heart suffered a fierce tug. "You lived with a lot of different families, didn't you?"

"We both did. But that was the last time we were placed together in the same home," he said. "We stayed in touch, and Rose came to see me as much as she could. When I got old enough, I'd go see her. Like I said, it wasn't as good for us as the Grassleys, but it worked out okay. Finally, Rose got set up on her own and she took over."

She'd gone and gotten Jackson. "So Rose became your mother and guardian as well as your sister."

"She always had been. Only mother or guardian I had—and that includes life before our birth mother abandoned us at the Piggly Wiggly. Later, we kind of adopted Lester."

"Your mother abandoned you at a grocery store?"

He nodded. "She gave us each a Grant half-dollar then went to park the car." Memories of that day had his jaw tight, his whole body stiff. "She never came back."

"Did something happen to her?"

"She abandoned us, Caroline." The betrayal of that burned in his eyes.

"That's awful."

"It was. We stood there, waiting for her until dark. Rose was sure she'd come back, but she never did."

"Never?"

"Never."

"And she wasn't hurt or killed or anything?"

"She was fine, just done with us. We never saw her again."

"I'm so sorry." Christine imagined how empty and scared they both must have been. "You were... how old?"

"Three."

"Rose must have been scared to death."

"At first. But the longer we stood there, the bleaker she became. She wouldn't let go of my hand. Kept telling me, 'Don't worry, Jackson. I've got you.' If she said it once that day, she said it a hundred times."

"Were you worried?"

"Not really. It was dark before someone in the store called the cops, and late at night when we were taken to the police station. They found our mother, but she refused to come back. Was I worried? No. Even before she dumped us, it was Rose who took care of me. I don't remember my birth mother doing a thing. Not saying she didn't. Just saying it was always Rose seeing what I needed, worrying about me, teaching me right from wrong."

"Mothering you?"

"Yes." He chewed at the inside of his cheek. "I wonder sometimes how Rose managed. When she came and got me, she was only sixteen. We had nothing, lived in a dive, and money was always tight. But not once did I put my head down without a pillow under it and a roof overhead, and I never dozed off feeling unloved." His voice went thick and he cleared his throat. "Looking back, I know Rose didn't have that luxury. Oh, she knew I loved her, but I can't say I did much to help her. She was so busy all the time, scrambling to provide for me and keep a roof over our heads. I didn't think about what she needed back then."

"She let you be a kid."

"She did, at great personal cost."

Christine swallowed a knot in her throat. No wonder Jackson and Matthew bowed to Rose's every wish and would rather cross a bed of hot coals than refuse her anything. "I understand now."

"What?"

"Why you were so afraid of losing her."

"You know exactly why," he said.

Her parents. "I wish I didn't," she said. "But I do." Awful as it was, hers had been a far smoother road than the one he and Rose had journeyed. Christine's parents had died not abandoned her and Caro. And they'd had money, were always well cared for. Never having to worry about rent or food or any physical need. Emotional needs were another matter, but she and Caro had never been separated. She admired Rose immensely. "Well, Rose did a lot right. You both turned out to be extraordinary people."

"I wouldn't say that." Jackson tapped the vent. "I would say, the day she came and got me, I made up my mind I'd never ask for anything else and I'd try to never do anything to bring a tear to her eye. No matter what."

"Which proves I'm right. You are extraordinary."

"We try to be ordinary but, like everyone else, we have our moments." He passed a Ford truck poking along, then signaled and moved back into the outside lane. His stomach growled. "We've got a couple more hours to ride. You hungry?"

So they were a couple hours from Sampson Park. "Perpetually hungry." She smiled. "I love to eat."

"Do you cook?"

"Not at all, but I have a healthy appreciation for good food."

"Music to a chef's ears." He smiled. "There's a diner about three miles up the road. We can have breakfast there, and I'll tell you a little about Sampson Park."

Finally! Christine's heart hammered. It took effort, but she kept her tone in check. This was too important for her to come across as overly eager. "Sounds great."

Thirty minutes later, they sat across from each other in the back booth at a bustling truck-stop type of diner, eating omelets stuffed with bacon, mushrooms, cheese and tomatoes, and fresh biscuits slathered with real butter.

"So," Christine attempted to clarify. "Miss Emily owns the Park and her adopted daughter, Darby, runs it?"

Jackson chewed and swallowed. "With a lot of help. Staff at the house, staff that works the ranch, in the village, the medical clinic and such. It's this whole little community."

Clearly, he was giving her details, hoping to trigger her memory. Of course, Christine had no memories to be triggered. "So why isn't it on any map?" she asked, adding strawberry jam to half of her biscuit. If she kept eating like this, she'd have to be rolled out of here.

"Can't figure why it would be on a map. It's private property."

"A privately owned park?"

He nodded. "Actually, it's a privately owned estate. Sampson Park is just its name. The only way you can get into it is by invitation —well, except for the village. But access to it is controlled, too."

Her and her techie friends' failure to find Sampson Park now made sense. "So what you're saying, is aside from associates' meetings and such, Miss Emily built and maintains the Park to help people like me?"

Again, he nodded. "To help all kinds of people start fresh."

"Wow." Christine was impressed. Never had it occurred to her to use her money for something like this. Considering Caro's position during her marriage to Martin, that shamed Christine. "Was Miss Emily… in a situation like Caro?"

Under the guise of chewing, Jackson didn't answer. By the time he swallowed, he'd thought over what he wanted to say. "In the Park by a footbridge, there's this enormous bronze statue. It explains everything." He spooned more jam on a half biscuit. "I'm sure you saw it when you were there—you can't talk to anyone in the Park until after you read it. I can't quote what it says, but the upshot is Sampson Park exists to aid people the rest of the world's given up on. Miss Emily never gives up on anybody."

Jackson's knife stilled mid-air and he studied her. "You still don't remember anything about it, do you?"

"I'm afraid not." Worried he'd stop talking, Christine added, "I'm trying to, though. What you're telling me is helpful but, so far, no images of from there are coming to my mind. That is why I'm asking so many questions."

"Looking for triggers."

She nodded.

"I'm sure not recalling makes you nervous, but you don't need to fret. An entire group of professionals are there, ready and willing to help," he said. "They figure out what you need to get right, and then provide it."

"That's reassuring." It was. She and Nell had worried about this very thing with Caro. "Like counselors?"

"And doctors, chaplains—whatever you need. If they aren't already there, Darby brings them in."

"How does Miss Emily fund all this?" Caro couldn't be the only person there. Not with the setup he was describing.

"I wondered that, too," he confessed. "You'd never know it, especially if you met her away from the Park like we did, but according to Lester, Miss Emily's always been richer than Caesar."

"She'd have to be to fund an undertaking on this scale." That set Christine to thinking. "So do I pay her to be there?"

"Nobody pays Miss Emily for anything." Jackson's glance slid to the wall and his eyes went unfocused. "The Park's a serene place. No phones or clocks, except for the one in the village square they need to conduct business. No televisions or computers—you know, all the things that are supposed to make life simpler but only keep people busier."

"Why no TV?" Christine popped the last bite of biscuit into her mouth.

"Unnecessary stress." Jackson dipped his chin. "When's the last time you saw anything good happening on the news?"

"I see your point." She frowned. "How many people are out there?"

"A couple hundred."

Surprise rippled through Christine. Sampson Park was indeed a community. "So when I left Martin, you took me there?"

"When we met, you had been in Dallas for a while. When you left, it was with me. We went to Rose's first. It was Christmas, and I wanted to see her and Matthew. Then you and I went on to the Park."

"I see." A hitch in his voice warned her he had left out something between Rose's and the Park. Had they gone somewhere else, to see someone else? Maybe to see Lester? Christine felt certain Jackson had deliberately omitted something, but she didn't dare ask what. Not with the elusive Sampson Park only hours away.

"Okay, enough about me. It's my turn to ask a couple questions... if that's okay."

She clenched her hand into a fist around the napkin in her lap. "Of course." He had been so open with her. How could she refuse?

Jackson put down his fork, picked up a tall glass of ice water. "Why were you in Even?"

His simple question ignited a war in Christine. She didn't want to lie to Jackson, but she didn't dare to tell him the truth. The only reason he—or Rose and Matthew, for that matter—was helping her was because they all believed she was Caro. If they realized she wasn't her sister, they'd jettison away from her so fast she'd drown in the backwash and her head would spin indefinitely. Christine would never find Sampson Park. She didn't even know Miss Emily's full name.

He took a long drink of water, set the chilled glass down on the table. It sweat a ring of water under it. "It's not a hard question, Caroline."

"For me, right this second, it's a more difficult one than you might think." She frowned, deciding to stick as close as she could to the truth. "It was on my phone bill."

"You didn't remember Even, either?"

She'd never heard of Even until Caro mentioned it; what was there to remember? She shook her head. "No."

Worry flickered through Jackson's eyes and his jaw settled in a grim expression. "And you don't know what happened to you that affected your memory?"

Christine paused and carefully chose her words. She wanted to be as accurate as possible. "I remember a Christmas phone call with my sister."

"You never mention her. Is she older or younger?"

"I'm older," she said. "Just a little bit." That was true, and a fair compromise.

"I remember that call," he said. "You were standing in Rose's backyard during it."

Caro had been. Christine had been on her ranchette in Dallas. *Walking a fine line here.* Left with zero wiggle room, she said nothing about it, but changed the subject. "So what happened after the call?"

"I took you to Sampson Park, and dropped you off with Miss Emily," he said. "We were being followed—Martin's people were only an hour or so behind us. I couldn't risk them catching us, especially not there. After I left you, I had to keep moving to throw them off our tracks."

Jackson had gone to so much trouble. "Where did you lead them?"

"New Orleans. Down in the French Quarter. I ditched them on Bourbon Street." He grinned. "Anybody can get lost on Bourbon Street."

She smiled. "Did you come back to Sampson Park then?"

"I normally spend as much time there as I can, but dropping you off was the last time I saw you until I walked into Danny's Diner to meet Rose."

Christine reached over and covered his hand. "That's a pity, Jackson Grant."

He didn't move his hand, and the look in his eyes warmed. "Why is that?"

"You're good company. I would have enjoyed more of it."

Caro had told Christine that Jackson would be perfect for her. Granted, an attraction was the last thing she needed, but who could resist this rare breed of a man? She examined her reaction to him and accepted defeat. Caro, had been right. Christine was seriously attracted to Jackson. Yet no one knew better that attraction loses its sparkle and fades. She respected him, though. And respect never fades. In their circumstances, that worried her more.

"I like your company, too." He smiled and held it.

Something inside Christine awakened. One second she liked and respected him. The next, he levied a full-out assault on her senses. Shocked by the intensity of her response to him, she pulled back her hand and drained her juice glass. *Lousy timing. The absolute worst.*

But this was the first time in a very long time a man had caught and held her interest for more than a couple hours. That was positive. The negative was she'd never been this attracted to anyone. With Jackson, you knew exactly where you stood. He didn't mince words or put on airs, and he certainly didn't engage in a personal pity party, though she honestly could have forgiven him if he had, considering his childhood. He was very matter-of-fact about the past, amazingly well-adjusted, and content in his skin. No overblown ego, and his genuine gratitude to Rose for her sacrifices held the appeal of a magnet.

Christine thought she might just love those things about him most of all, though they were the very things that also saddled her with strumming pangs of guilt. She had a low tolerance level for insincerity, was habitually short on patience and, okay, she admitted it, demanding. But after hearing about Jackson and Rose, and the paragon Miss Emily, Christine promised herself she would treat others with a little more compassion just in case they too had traveled a rough road.

"You're deep in thought over there." Jackson tilted his head. "Everything okay?"

She nodded, twisted her mouth then glanced at him. "I think you bring out the best in me."

"Aha, I appeal to your higher angels," he said. "Everybody says I have a knack for it." His lips twitched but he didn't crack a smile. "Rose used to say that all the time—like when she stubbed her toe and wanted to cuss but didn't because it'd be a bad example for me."

Honored to align with his sister on anything, Christine seriously debated putting Rose in for some prestigious woman of the year award. At eight, Rose Green had been more of an adult than most adults Christine had met in her life. "Yeah, my higher angels. That'll work."

Higher angels were far easier to admit to than the avalanche of conflicting emotions tumbling through her. They were in full-fledged riot. His life was an inspiring story—Rose's, too—but Christine had met inspiring people before and none them had affected her like this. This was... more.

She stiffened. *You'd better stick to higher angels. You're deceiving him. Regardless of your reasons, he deserves far better than you.*

Guilt shut this down as a flight of fancy. Resentment aided it.

Didn't it just figure? The first man who had inspired and captured her interest in ages and he was off-limits. And he cooked, too.

A memory of the kitchen drawer full of take-out menus on the ranchette mocked her. Jackson lived and worked in Dallas. She might even have eaten something he'd cooked.

Chapter 16

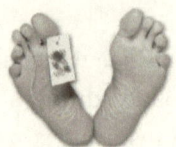

March 22nd
Sampson Park, Florida

"Just how big is this place?" Christine asked Jackson. She'd been looking at fencing for what seemed like miles.

"I'm not sure exactly. It's sizable." He turned into the entrance, an unassuming paved road that ended in a relatively small parking lot.

Only a half-dozen cars occupied slots. If hundreds worked and lived here, where were all their cars?

Broad arches spanned an entrance, a funneling walkway that dead-ended at the door of a two-story brick building. Christine scanned but no signage identified the property as Sampson Park or anything else. Decorative concrete barriers and metal fencing stretched from the building through the thick trees flanking it. Most government properties, including courts, didn't have barriers as substantial. That signaled Miss Emily took security seriously, which probably made people like Caro feel safe here. No doubt, that had been Miss Emily's objective. "Where do the staff and residents park?"

"There're several lots on the outer perimeter." Jackson motioned with a tilt of his head back to a branch opening off the right side of the main road. "The closest one to here is through there."

Christine had mistaken it for a footpath. It curved out of sight beyond the far side of the building.

The front door opened. A man in his thirties with dark hair, wearing a crisp uniform, came outside. His smile was open and genuine. "Hey, Jackson." He extended his hand. "It's good to see you, man. It's been a while."

They shook and Jackson returned the open smile. From their posturing, these two had known each other for some time and were friendly. Christine hung back, hoping he wouldn't be suspicious or blow her Caro cover. Security types were trained observers. They noticed little details and behavioral nuances others didn't. She trembled, afraid she was finally here and her chance to get inside would evaporate.

"Lucas, glad to see you, too." Jackson nodded. "You remember Caroline."

"Of course." Lucas nodded at her. "Welcome home, Caroline."

Caro had been here. His greeting squashed any lingering doubts. Hope beating at her chest, Christine prayed she'd soon know what had happened to her sister. She smiled, more nervous than she'd been on releasing her first software program. "Thank you, Lucas."

Strange clopping noises caught her ear. She looked toward the sound, through the building's front window and beyond to a window on the back of the building. A door on the far wall opened into a courtyard with a metal gate that spilled into the Park.

The clopping grew louder. Two horses pulling a carriage paused near the inner gate. A spry old man with wild white hair shooting out in every direction from under his top hat, sat atop the carriage. Dressed in a livery uniform with shiny buttons, he stretched his neck, looking their way. Jackson hadn't mentioned him or the carriage.

"Ah, your ride's here. Let's get you guys cleared so you can get going," Lucas said. "Miss Emily and Darby are waiting for you at the manor house. They're excited to have you both back with us."

Lucas led the way, and Christine followed Jackson into the Security office. It was a wide room with two doors on the far end and a staircase up to the second story. Security cameras were embedded into the ceiling and upper corners of the walls. A row of sleek chairs lined the wall, and a narrow marble counter ran the long length of the room. Lucas walked around its end, reached underneath, and pulled out a clipboard. Behind him, rows of fabric-lined baskets fitted into the wall.

He grabbed a pen and glanced down at the clipboard. "Any electronics? Mobile phones, iPads or iPods, computers, laptops or tablets? Anything like that?"

"No." Jackson said.

"No." Christine added. So this is why Jackson had asked her to lock their phones in the truck's glovebox after he'd called Rose to let her know of their arrival. The no-phones policy could explain Caro's silence. If she hadn't known she'd have to surrender her phone, she couldn't have warned Christine…

Lucas marked the paper. "Jackson, I'll need your watch."

He took it off then passed it over.

Lucas pulled a basket from the top row in the wall and placed the watch in it.

"Wallets, licenses—anything like that on you?"

He wanted her purse? She'd be stuck here with nothing, including any ID or a way to call for help? Wary, Christine shot Jackson an uneasy look.

"It's okay." He seemed sincere. The look in his eyes reminded her she had agreed to trust him.

Still wary, Christine weighed her options. She honestly had none. If she wanted to enter the Park, she had to leave her stuff. She snagged the shoulder strap then placed her handbag on the countertop. "There's a loaded gun in my bag, Lucas. The carry permit is in my wallet. Thought I better mention it."

"Thank you." He removed the weapon, then the bullets.

"Can I take it in with me?"

Lucas paused to look at her. "Once the doc clears you to have it, sure. Just tell Speckles you've been cleared and he'll bring it to you. Or you can have any member of the security team contact me and I'll drop it off."

He'd lost her. "Speckles?"

"The carriage driver," Jackson said. "He's Speckles."

Looking more worried, Lucas grabbed a second basket and placed the weapon into it. "If you have money and you want to keep it with you, that's fine. You don't need it—you just sign for anything you want or need in the village." His expression softened. "Having cash makes some feel more comfortable, so it's allowed."

Jackson spotted her growing edginess. "People come here under a lot of different circumstances. Some had to leave everything behind, and some had nothing to leave. That's why everything is provided."

"Oh." His explanation made sense, and he had said more or less the same thing at the diner. Still, that kind of generosity was a little hard to wrap the mind around.

Lucas didn't frown but his lips thinned. He was uncomfortable because she didn't remember any of this. He didn't mention a word about it, and Jackson hadn't spoken to him privately, which meant everyone at Sampson Park must think she'd had some kind of breakdown that triggered her memory failure.

They could only have gotten that idea from Jackson or maybe Rose or Matthew. Christine wondered. Would that be helpful to her or cumbersome?

Everyone could walk on eggshells around her to keep from saying or doing the wrong thing and sending her sliding over the edge. That could make finding out anything about Caro from them more difficult. Christine would have to think on how to turn that into a positive. If they thought telling her things might help her... That would work. Of course, Christine could end the kid-glove treatment of her at any time just by admitting the truth. The pangs of guilt about withholding her identity were growing stronger and more frequent.

Christine's natural inclination leaned toward confessing she wasn't Caro. Normally, she would do that. But to put her only lead on Caro at risk? No, she'd just have to bear the guilt of not being honest—at least, for now. They could close the gate and forbid her from entering the Park, and then what would she do? This was it. She couldn't tell them anything.

"Jackson," Lucas said. "It's been awhile, so I better run a quick rules refresher to keep you out of trouble."

"Thanks." Jackson smiled.

Lucas's refresher was for Christine's benefit, not Jackson's. He took the extra effort of doing it for Jackson's benefit to diminish pressure on her and to spare her any discomfort. Kind of him, and of Jackson to accept it. It poked at the independent woman in her, but the compassion in the act was touching.

Lucas reached under the counter and pulled out a map. "Before you go into the village, or anywhere other than to the manor house, walk over to this footbridge. There's a huge bronze statue near the foot of it. Read what is written on it." He marked the map with a little X. "After you read it, if you like, you can interact with the other residents. Do not interact with any of them until then."

"Except at the manor house," Christine repeated for clarity.

"Correct." Lucas nodded.

"You'll like the statue." Jackson looked at her. "Wait, Lucas. She doesn't understand why." He paused a second, then said. "You never know what someone else is facing. We all have our demons. Before you talk to anyone, you need to understand some things so you do no harm."

"I see." She nodded. "Thank you for explaining, Jackson."

"Course." He motioned to Lucas to continue.

"This area is off limits." Lucas drew a circle around a clump of trees, started to say something more but evidently decided against it. He shifted on his feet. "The rest of the Park is yours to enjoy."

"Seems easy enough." Christine smiled. "Thanks, Lucas."

His cheeks flushed. "These rules are for your protection and everyone else's. If you want to leave the Park, have Speckles drive you to the gate. He makes himself available twenty-four seven. You're free to leave any time you choose, but no one leaves without letting us know." His voice was firm, but his expression gentle. "We're responsible for the safety of everyone here, which means we need to know who is here and who isn't. No-notice departures trigger all kinds of alarms and inconveniences everyone in the Park."

Christine pointed to the off-limit area on the map. "What is that place?"

"Just marsh and woods, but it has lots of wildlife. Snakes and gators, bobcats and bears. That kind of thing." Seeing tension in her response, Lucas grinned. "We call it Miss Emily's private reserve."

Jackson tapped the counter. "Residents are free to roam, except for the woods there. Non-residents can only come into the village to visit the shops. They're not allowed anywhere else."

Christine frowned. "Martin can come to the village?"

"No," Lucas said. "Martin Easton is banned. He can't come within five-hundred feet of the Park's perimeter fence without being arrested."

"What if he does anyway? He's not much for following other people's rules." Christine had the restraining orders to prove it.

"He'll be arrested or otherwise detained," Lucas said with no emotion in his voice. "Whatever it takes, the team will assure any threat he might pose is neutralized long before anything reaches you or your cottage, Caroline. You have nothing to worry about. You're safe here."

Her mouth went dry. "What about the men who work for him?"

"We're aware of the investigators he hired, and the thugs," Lucas said. "They're on the banned list, too."

Wow. They hadn't been kidding about taking security seriously. "Thank you for easing my mind."

"That's a privilege." Compassion laced his smile.

"Speckles is getting itchy out there." Jackson tilted his head to where the spindly-legged man stood waiting. "I'm surprised he hasn't retired already. Last visit, he said he was about ready."

Lucas laughed. "Speckles has been about ready at least a dozen years that I know of. He'll never retire. He loves his horses and driving that carriage. It's what keeps him going."

Christine listened with one ear but her thoughts turned inward. Caro had a cottage here and stringent security protecting her. She must have been beside herself, so relieved to finally feel safe. Jackson had given her that by bringing her here, and Lucas had maintained the respite and kept her safe. Christine came awfully close to weeping. She rarely permitted herself to cry, but her eyes burned, the back of her nose, too, and tears thickened her throat. After years of Martin the Miserable and his abuse, how much feeling safe and protected must have meant to Caro. Christine thanked Lucas for the blessing he and his security team had been for her sister in the only way she could—she smiled.

He smiled back. "Any questions?"

Too unsure of her voice to speak, Christine gave him a negative nod.

"Appreciate it, Lucas," Jackson said, then guided Christine through the back door, into the courtyard, then through the gate into Sampson Park.

Speckles held open the carriage door. "Miss Caroline!" He gave her a toothy grin. "Welcome home."

He liked her. His eyes sparkled and lit up from the bottoms. "Thank you, Speckles. How are you?"

"Fiddle fit, thank you." He motioned for her and Jackson to get into the carriage. "And if it ain't Jackson Grant himself." Speckles sniffed. "A body could start to think he'd been forgotten, seldom as you been around here lately."

"I'm sorry." Jackson looked genuinely contrite. "I've been hamstrung in Dallas."

He hadn't wanted Martin's men to follow him to the Park, Christine decided. That's why he hadn't been back here.

"Well, I'm glad you're here now—and that you ain't dead."

"There is that bit of good news." Smiling, Jackson sat down on the seat beside a surprised Christine. When Speckles shut the door, Jackson turned to Christine. "You're surprised. Why?"

She whispered, "He's glad you aren't *dead*?"

"It's nothing. Just his way of shaming me for not visiting more often."

"Oh, I see." She bit a grin from her lip. "He's clearly fond of you, or I'd be worried."

"No need for that," Jackson quickly reassured her. "We're all family here."

Another attitude Miss Emily fostered, Christine suspected. She hadn't yet met the woman, but Christine admired all she'd already learned about her.

Speckles climbed up and settled in, and soon the carriage began moving.

Glancing out the window, Christine tried seeing the Park through Caro's eyes. On arriving here, she had to be a tangled emotional mess. *Nervous. Safe. Guarded and worried. Protected. Anxious. Nurtured. Excited.*

The gauntlet continued, and Christine worked through her projections one at a time. When she had, she imagined Caro on the other side of the building, entering the Park. It would take time to process all she'd been through, but she had to have seen this as her chance for a fresh start. A chance to create a new life that was hers to do with as she pleased. It didn't take much imagination to grasp how much power that generated in a woman who had lived as oppressed as Caro had been for such a long time. Heady power.

The rolling green grounds stretched out in long spans. At the edge of a little lake, a white gazebo offered shade from the bright sun. Gorgeous flowers, planted in fragrant patches, dotted the lawn, and the profusion of color repeated in lush bushes bearing heavy blossoms. The pace here had her relaxing. Slow and easy; the sense, tranquil and calm.

Christine looked at Jackson, whose thigh rested near hers on the seat. "I get it now."

"Get what?"

"Why Miss Emily banned all the gadgets." He hiked an eyebrow and she added, "So you shed outside interference and just absorb the calm. She's created a sanctuary, a serene and peaceful escape."

"Strikes me that way." Jackson smiled. "You like it here."

"So far." A little girl stood on the bank of the lake, fishing. Her teddy bear was on the ground beside her. It had a fishing pole, too.

"I love it here." He took in a deep breath and gazed out the window. "As soon as I walk through the gate, I feel peaceful." He glanced back to Christine. "It took me a while to recognize it as peace. I used to just say, the world's a million miles away."

Used to. "So what do you say now, about the outside world?"

He searched her eyes. "It's a lifetime away."

She wasn't sure she understood the distinction, but from the change in his voice, Jackson understood the difference well. "Miss Emily should franchise this place. Of course, few could afford to take on all the expenses."

Jackson's smile faded, and he looked away.

Odd reaction. "Did I say something wrong?"

"No, not at all." He said it, but clearly didn't mean it.

What should Christine make of that?

Swinging his gaze back to her, Jackson changed the subject. "The manor house is right over there, through those trees." He pointed through the window on his side of the carriage. "Watch. You'll be able to see it right about…now."

Beyond the thick copse of ancient oaks, a three-story house came into view. "Oh, it's a Victorian. I love Victorian houses." Christine placed a hand on his arm. "Jackson, look at that turret. I've always wanted a turret. Wouldn't that be an amazing reading retreat?"

"You like books."

"I love books." She leaned closer and confessed in a conspiratorial whisper. "I'm an armchair adventurer."

He smiled. "You'll love the house, then. It's stuffed with antiques and historical items. Miss Emily has a fondness for both. Part of it is like a B & B for invited, short-term guests, and part is her and Darby's private residence. Business is restricted to the third floor so—"

"Her residents aren't affected." Christine waited for his nod. "Her special guests stay here."

"Those closest to Miss Emily," he amended. "There are lots of other places to stay in the village, including a motel. Most stay there at first, but a few stay in the manor house with Miss Emily and Darby."

"Like your Lester?"

"Definitely." Jackson chuckled. "When he's here, Miss Emily keeps him on a short leash so she can watch him. Lester is one of the finest men I've ever known, but he bends really low on the eccentric side. That's fine with Miss Emily, so long as it doesn't upset the residents. She takes strong exception to anything that upsets the residents, unless it's essential to them healing."

"Jackson, are all the people who come here sick?"

He twisted his mouth. "More like broken."

And Miss Emily gives them the time and space and resources to mend and heal. That was it. Christine loved the woman she'd yet to meet. "First Rose and now Miss Emily. Do you ignite the appeal to higher angels in all the women in your life?" Compared to the two paragons, Christine felt like a slug.

Jackson snorted. "Miss Emily's been at this a lot longer than she's known me. She's a saint in my book."

Christine smiled. "So how did you meet her?"

"Through Rose," he said. "Miss Emily kind of adopted us both."

"Big heart, huh?"

"Definitely," he said. "But don't cross her."

"I find it difficult to believe she'd get mean."

"You'd be wrong—and if you cross her, you have to fight her and everybody else." He drew out that *everybody*, giving it a great deal of emphasis.

"I see." The protective instincts Miss Emily aroused in others ran incredibly deep. "Big battle on your hands, eh?"

He chuckled. "Oh, yeah."

Heartening but also disheartening. Fierce competition from admirable women in Jackson's life—and none of them were lying to him.

Christine had to stop this. Let go of this illogical attraction before it got out of hand. It could only lead to an impossible relationship. She couldn't compete for a place in his life and, in her precarious position, that she even considered wanting to was absurd.

She lowered her lids and glanced at him. Her heart leapt. Unfortunately, emotions weren't logical.

Grimacing, she nailed her resolve. She'd have to work at it.

The horses slowed their clopping in a circular drive in front of the manor house, and the carriage stopped. A minute later, the door opened. "The manor," Speckles shouted, though he stood not three feet from them.

They stepped out, and Speckles tugged at Jackson's t-shirt sleeve. "Miss Emily and Darby's holding tea for you two." Speckles squinted. "Bring me a couple of those tea cookies she favors. The ones with the pecans in 'em that's rolled in powdered sugar."

"Speckles, you can have all the cookies you want. Just tell Ned or Mr. Jenkins you want them, and they'll bake you your own batch. "

"Don't you be telling me to ask no chef nor that snooty Jenkins neither for cookies." The old man grumbled. "I ain't asking 'em for nothing. Jenkins runs this house, sure enough, but that stiff-backed reprobate don't run me. We both been here better than twenty-five years, Jackson Grant. You know we don't geehaw."

"Are you still at odds with Mr. Jenkins for calling Buttercup a hag?"

"He ain't apologized to either of us, so you'd be right about that." Speckles raised his chin so high you could park a teacup on it.

The man was probably ninety pounds soaking wet and rickety enough to blow over in a stiff breeze, but a ton of indignant outrage surrounded him.

His face scrunched up in wrinkles. "I don't care who you are, there's two things a grown man just don't do. That's strut himself around, and insult a man's horse or his woman." He ticked them off on his arthritic fingers.

"I'll bring you the cookies." Jackson gave Speckles' sleeve a pat, then walked on up the sidewalk to the front porch.

Christine grinned. "I take it Buttercup is his horse—or is she a woman?" With a man named Speckles, who dressed like he'd stepped out of a history book, a woman named Buttercup wasn't out of the realm of possibility.

"Buttercup is the horse."

Why that made Christine feel better, she had no idea. "I noticed she outranked the woman. He mentioned the horse first."

Jackson laughed. "It's best not to dwell on those kind of things too much unless you want to land in the middle of the Speckles-Mr. Jenkins' feud."

"Got it." She looked up at Jackson. "Speckles is a force unto himself."

"They both are."

The big wooden door swung open and a tall, proper gentleman wearing a charcoal gray suit answered. *Stiff back, and wrinkle free. Had to be Mr. Jenkins.* "Welcome home, Jackson," he said.

"Thank you, Mr. Jenkins." Jackson nodded, his eyes lighting up. "You remember Caroline."

He focused on her and a strange look passed through his eyes. It was gone so quickly Christine wasn't sure she hadn't imagined it. Disquieted, she forced herself to smile. "Hello, Mr. Jenkins."

His eyes narrowed, and he studied her intensely. It took everything Christine could do to not squirm.

Finally, he inclined his head briefly, then gazed back at Jackson. "Misses Emily and Darby are in the downstairs parlor."

Jackson led the way, and Christine looked back over her shoulder, deafeningly loud alarms ringing inside her. Mr. Jenkins stood stiff and still, staring at her, his expression as blank as a painter's empty canvas. Every nerve in her body revolted. Had he somehow known she wasn't Caro? "Is Mr. Jenkins upset about something?" she asked Jackson.

"We were talking to Speckles. It's likely his feathers are a bit ruffled, though Mr. Jenkins would never mention it."

Christine hoped that was the reason. "Out of curiosity, how long has this feud been going on?"

"Years and years. It was in full swing when I first came here."

"Jackson!" A small, ample woman with a round face, sparkling eyes, and graying hair styled sweetly to frame her face rushed out from the parlor and enveloped Jackson in a hug. "Bend down, my boy. I'm a wee bit shorter than you."

Miss Emily.

Jackson bent and lifted her off her feet, swung her around, sending her skirt swirling. "Oh, it's good to see you, Miss Emily."

Wrapped in the bear hug, she giggled like a school girl, though she had to be well into her seventies. "Put me down, you rascal, so I can greet Caroline."

"Yes, ma'am." He lowered her feet to the floor and held on until sure she was steady on her feet.

She took the two steps to Caroline and hugged her hard. "Oh my dear, Caro. I am so glad you're back home." Miss Emily pulled back, her hands firm on Christine's shoulders. "I've been extremely worried about you, what with Martin pulling stunts out there." She hugged her again quickly.

Miss Emily called Caroline, Caro. Her hug was fierce, and the emotion in her voice about worrying and Caro being back and about Martin... She'd taken Caro under her wing in a big way. Considering that a good sign, Christine hugged her back, grateful and amazed, her eyes again stinging. Not since before her parents' passing had she felt so welcome... as if she belonged. The saddest part in that was, until that moment, she hadn't consciously understood the value of what she'd been missing.

Oh... Oh, no. Miss Emily was welcoming Caro home, which meant Caro had been here, but she probably wasn't at Sampson Park anymore. Where would she have gone? She had to be here. Of course, she was here. Wasn't she?

Miss Emily backed up a step and cupped Christine's face. "Now, Jackson's told us you're having a few forgetful moments. Don't you worry about a thing. You'll be right as rain in no time." She looked back behind her. "Darby will help."

Christine let her gaze follow to a woman in her late twenties, early thirties with long silky blond hair and a tan hat with the brim folded back. She smiled. "Hi, Caroline."

"Darby," Jackson whispered to confirm.

"Hi, Darby." Christine nodded.

Miss Emily looped their arms. "Come in and have tea. Darby, pour for us, dear heart." Miss Emily patted Christine's hand. "Nothing in life reveals solutions like a good cup of tea."

Christine could have disputed her on that, but she didn't dare. Instinctively, she had the strongest urge to do nothing to upset Miss Emily. Jackson had warned her no one upset Miss Emily on purpose, and no one else would tolerate anyone upsetting her.

And that was, most likely, Miss Emily's secret weapon.

She loved her opposition into surrender.

Chapter 17

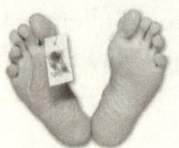

Some men might not feel comfortable, sitting in a parlor full of antiques with three women, sipping tea, but Jackson loved it. It gave him a chance to watch Caroline interact with Miss Emily and Darby. So far, he'd had a rough time gauging where her head was; sometimes she seemed tender and fragile, sometimes scared witless, and sometimes amazingly cool and calm and competent, like with Frankie and Myrtle's sabotaging the flowers at Carl Wooten's funeral.

Caroline didn't seem much like the woman he'd brought to the Park at Christmas, but three months at Sampson Park made for lots of changes in people in far worse shape than she'd been back then. Something basic was significantly different about her. People healed and relaxed, became less afraid and guarded or less fractured, but they usually didn't change at the core. She had. He couldn't put his finger on exactly what had changed, but something…deep. Maybe Darby or Miss Emily could enlighten him.

Darby refilled their cups for the third time and the women conversed, their tones light and chatty, and they laughed often. Caroline, included. She seemed totally comfortable and at ease with the others. He wouldn't have expected that, if he hadn't witnessed it. Typically, abuse victims who had been isolated for a long time took longer to reintegrate. Nell, Caroline's counselor in Dallas, said sometimes victims never trusted others enough again to let them get emotionally close. And the longer the abuse went on, the harder it was for victims to lower their protective shields, open up to others and permit them into the victim's inner circle.

Apparently, Miss Emily and Darby bypassed that issue with Caroline. Spotting the cookies Speckles favored on a tiered tray reminded Jackson of his promise, and he stood up. "I'm going to see if Ned has more tea cookies in the kitchen."

"There's plenty here, my boy."

"They're for Speckles."

"Ah, I see." She frowned. "Why he refuses to end this ridiculous feud, I have no idea."

Jackson's eyes twinkled. "You know exactly why."

Miss Emily rolled her eyes back in her head. "Mr. Jenkins is never going to apologize, especially to a horse." She fretted over that, glanced at Christine. "He says he didn't do anything wrong and Speckles knows it."

"It's a pickle," Caroline said.

Darby grunted. "If Mr. Jenkins says he didn't do anything wrong, then he didn't."

"Staunch defense." Caroline sipped at her steaming tea.

"If Speckles says he did, then I expect he did." Miss Emily sniffed.

"And an equally staunch counter-defense." Caroline took another sip.

"My best advice is for all of us to stay out it," Jackson said. "They own it, and only they can settle it."

Miss Emily's eyes narrowed. "You sound like Lester."

"Thank you for that compliment, Miss Emily." Jackson smiled. "I'll be right back." He moved toward the parlor door, heading for the kitchen.

"So, my dear," he heard Miss Emily say, turning her attention to

Caroline. "Why don't you tell us what you remember and what's happened to you?"

Glancing back, Jackson watched Caroline break into a cold sweat.

IN THE KITCHEN, Jackson stood across the counter from the chef, Ned, a fiftyish brute of a man well over six-feet tall with broad shoulders and heavy scars marring his forearms and neck. Ned was busy filling a wax-lined white box with tea cookies.

Mr. Jenkins entered and warned Jackson, "You'd better get back in there. They're giving the girl the third degree, and she looks like she's about to faint or declare war. I'm not sure which she'll do, but neither will end well for her."

Surprise rippled through Jackson. "Why would they do that?"

Mr. Jenkins stared at him. "I'm sure I don't know." He lifted a hand. "Go, Jackson. I'll get the cookies for you."

"They're for Speckles," he warned Mr. Jenkins, determined not to be perceived as choosing sides in the feud.

"I'm aware of that. Just keep it to yourself and don't tell that bag of bones I touched them."

Jackson narrowed his eyes. "You're not going to spit on them or anything, are you?"

"Jackson Lee Grant." Mr. Jenkins pulled himself up to his full height and sneered. "You well know that I do not spit."

Ned muffled a snort with a cough.

"Course not. Sorry." Before he could get into more trouble, Jackson rushed back to the parlor.

Caroline was gone. "Did you run her off?"

"Of course not." Miss Emily shot him a frown. "She's in the powder room."

"Ah." She was cooling off, Jackson figured. "Well, what do you think?" Hopefully, they had some insight to share on what had happened to her or her memory. He glanced at Darby, who shrugged, then shifted his attention to Miss Emily.

"She doesn't know spit about either one of us, or about her time here. That's a fact." Miss Emily worried her bottom lip, dragged her teeth over it. "I honestly don't know what to think, Jackson. She sounds fine, looks fine, acts fine, but she doesn't know spit."

"What's Dr. Rossi say?" Dr. Laura Rossi ran the medical clinic for the Park, and Jackson had no doubt Darby had discussed Caroline with her.

"Not much," Darby said. "She is at a disadvantage. She's met Caroline in the village, but she's never seen her as a patient, so she doesn't have a baseline frame of reference. And, for some reason, Chaplain Goodman has his session files with Caroline password protected." Darby frowned. "I've had the best hackers in the business working on breaking into them since you called, but so far they haven't been successful. I can't explain why. They do say they are close."

"You think the answer to what's happened to her memory is in those files?"

"I'm hoping so." Darby poured herself another cup of tea from the delicate pot. "But I'm not counting on it." She sent Jackson a knowing look. "Chaplain Goodman wigs out about privacy. Quite often, the only records that exist on his sessions are in his head."

Understandable. He'd been the pastor at a mega church until his wife left him and filed for divorce. He'd lost her, his kids, and his church. Natural, to be private after going through something like that. Jackson sat down and folded his knees, then braced his arms on them. "Has he called in yet?"

"Not yet." Miss Emily answered. "He's still communing. They say it might be another day or two."

"Did anything unusual happen here that spurred her to leave the Park?"

"So far as we can tell, not a thing," Miss Emily said. "Lucas checked everything. Her cottage is undisturbed and in good order. The people in the village said she seemed fine. No one knew she was gone. Everything appears to be business as usual."

"Perplexing." Jackson sighed.

"Confounding. We couldn't determine exactly when she'd left or how she did it without been seen on a single monitor, which has Lucas in an uproar, as you can well imagine." Miss Emily turned thoughtful. "Clearly, we have to keep her here until we hear from Dr. Goodman."

"Easy enough to explain, with the associates' meeting just two days away."

Miss Emily nodded. "We'll put her back in her cottage and monitor. Maybe being at home will trigger her memory."

"Maybe so." Jackson hoped something did. "If you'll tell me her favorite places, I'll take her to them. Something here is bound to spark her recall."

"That's a great idea, Jackson." Darby agreed. "Meantime, I'll see if we can speed up those records and get Chaplain Goodman to call home."

"You'll spend a lot of time with her, of course," Miss Emily said. "She's probably feeling very much like a fish out of water. That kind of uneasiness doesn't encourage her to remember anything." She shifted to look at him. "You haven't slept since leaving Dallas, I expect.

"No ma'am. There's been no time."

"I understand. Abigale's got your room ready and waiting for you."

Abigale was on the housekeeping staff. "Great." Miss Emily had no idea how much having a home to come to meant to Jackson. Or to Rose. "First chance, I think I'll give Nell a call and see if she has any advice."

"Caroline's therapist in Dallas?" He nodded and Darby grimaced. "Good luck with that. She never responded to our record's requests. We sent three. Could you ask her for them?"

"I will, for whatever it's worth. She might have purged them. She's a little paranoid about releasing any information," Jackson said. Dr. Nell Richmond had counseled Caroline from the time she left Martin until Jackson had taken her out of Dallas. She'd brought Caroline to Jackson for help.

"Her input could be helpful," Miss Emily said. "I wonder. Did Caroline have memory lapses during her time in Dallas?"

"None were mentioned to me." Jackson rubbed at his neck. "I'll have to ask."

"Well, learn what you can, my boy, but be careful not to reveal too much," Miss Emily said. "With all the associates coming in, we'll be a target-rich environment."

It was hush-hush, but the sixty associates had agreed to franchise operations. Final discussions and the formal vote was the reason for the meeting. "I will do my best."

Caroline returned, looking a little pale, and Jackson stood up. "Ready to go home?"

"Home?" She looked confused.

"To your home here, my dear," Miss Emily said. "Your cottage."

"Oh... right. Yes. Yes, I'm ready," Caroline stammered. "Thanks for the tea and the conversation, Miss Emily. You, too, Darby."

"Our pleasure, my dear."

As they departed, Mr. Jenkins stood waiting beside the front door. He passed Jackson a white box.

"Thanks." Jackson said.

With a curt nod, Mr. Jenkins stepped back and opened the door. Its hinges creaked, clearly annoying him. They walked outside, and the door closed behind them.

Speckles stood waiting at the foot of the sidewalk in the circular drive, holding open the carriage door. Jackson passed him the box. "We need to make a pit-stop by the footbridge."

"What for?"

"Lucas said. Part of the refresher course," Jackson explained. "Then to Caroline's cottage."

"All righty, then." Speckles tucked the box in the crook of his arm and swallowed, his mouth clearly watering. "Thanks for remembering my cookies."

Jackson nodded, then climbed inside and took his seat beside Caroline.

She dropped her voice so she wouldn't be overheard. "Why didn't you tell him Mr. Jenkins—?"

"Shh!" Jackson shushed her. "Speckles hears that and he'll squash them under the carriage wheels."

"Or feed them to Buttercup." Christine grunted. "I know, I know. It's best to stay out of the feud."

Jackson wholeheartedly agreed. "Exactly."

Chapter 18

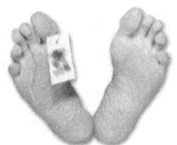

At the footbridge, Christine squinted past the hot afternoon sun, up at the bronze statue. "I don't know what I expected, but this isn't it," she told Jackson, who stood to her left. "It must be eight-feet tall and an arm-span wide."

"A little over that," he said. "I guess Darby wanted to be sure no one could miss it."

"It's highly unlikely anyone could miss this." Christine shifted a little so the monument blocked the stark sun, then read the words...

LIFE SHAPES AND DEFINES US. When experiences are positive, we embrace them. When they are not, we bury them, shutter, and become whole. But little shuttered remains shuttered. Past secrets surface and torment. We try but fail to break free, and being imprisoned steals our present and future.

Some so tortured seek traditional help, gain new insights and wisdom, and successfully put the past to rest. Some die never realizing their potential, robbed of their destinies and peace. Others cobble together a life, but remain haunted by their pasts and their unrealized dreams.

And still there are others. Those deemed helpless and hopeless, condemned to stumble forever through their darkest night.

These are the lost souls. Abandoned and forgotten by all to remain lost with their misery. Or so it was…but it is no more.

An ordinary woman refused to forget the Lost. Though it cost her mightily, she welcomed them here, met their challenges and her own, and she discovered an extraordinary thing:

Pasts may be horrific. Trials may be incredibly risky and dangerous and outcomes riddled with uncertainties, but with faith all things are possible, and with God no one is ever truly lost, without hope or help, or forgotten.

Embracing that discovery, she became a bridge between the Lost and these truths. That revealed another truth:

We are all someone's bridge.

And that is the secret of secrets at Sampson Park.

CHRISTINE BLEW OUT A LONG, slow breath. "Beautiful."

"Gives me chills, every time," Jackson said.

"Darby did this, talking about Miss Emily, didn't she?" Christine could almost hear Darby's voice, as if she were speaking the words chiseled into the bronze's flat face.

Jackson nodded. "But truthfully, it could have been written by just about everyone here." He shrugged. "Everybody feels the same way about her."

Miss Emily had built this Park as a refuge. Her refuge, then opened it to others. "What happened to her, Jackson?"

"I can't say. You'll need to ask her, though don't expect her to tell you. She might, but then again, she might not."

"Well, whatever she had to endure to dream all this, I know one thing for certain. She's using her life to make a difference. Her Park has changed lives." Christine had been here for hours, not days or months, and she was certain she'd never be the same.

"Thousands of lives." Jackson's eyes shone overly bright.

He wasn't kidding about being emotionally moved by the bronze. Of course, only those dead as doornails, wouldn't be moved. But for someone broken… powerful. Christine sniffed.

"Ready?"

She nodded, still too caught up in her thoughts of standing

where Caro had once stood, reading the words she'd read. "How long do most people stay here?"

"As long as they like." Jackson waited for her to get into the carriage. When he was settled in, he added, "Some stay a couple months. Some stay forever."

Christine thought about that. Buttercup whinnied, and Speckles made a clicking noise—her signal to go. He headed toward a rise. "Is that where the cottage is?"

"The village," Jackson said. "There's a fork in the road ahead. Your cottage is that way."

"Ah." Christine relaxed, a little lost in her own thoughts. The absence of computers and modern conveniences like electricity would drive her crazy in a couple days, much less forever. She'd starve to death without take-out and a microwave. And yet there was something special about the stillness here. The quiet. Shutting out the busy-ness and noise of everyday life outside the Park made a person inside it more introspective.

Maybe it wasn't really that different here. Maybe their thoughts talk to people all the time. Maybe they can't hear themselves think over the barrage of noise in their lives. Overstimulation could do that.

Here, the noise level dropped. One could hear. Think. Wonder. Christine had thought more about her life in the last few hours than in the last five years. Whether that turned out to be a blessing or a curse remained to seen.

They followed the fork in the road and headed down a row of cottages painted in pastel colors. Speckles halted in front of a pale pink one trimmed in white. A low picket fence surrounded it, and it had a wide front porch with an inviting swing. Its seat was full of soft cushy pillows.

"You planted a lot of flowers," Jackson said. "I don't remember them being here before. And I like all those pillows on the swing."

Christine killed air plants. If not for her service, every green thing in her house would be gasping its last breath or dead. Caro had the green thumb.

Jackson stepped down from the carriage to the ground, then

extended his hand. She took it, and stood beside him at the foot of the walk to the porch.

"Pretty, ain't it?" Speckles said.

"It looks like a postcard," Christine admitted.

Speckles grunted. "It looks like a home."

She had to agree.

"Thanks for the ride, Speckles." Jackson nodded.

"Thanks for the cookies." The old man gave Jackson a toothy grin. Sprinkles of powdered sugar marred his livery jacket and caught the sun.

Speckles had snitched cookies on the way. Christine loved that.

"Ready to go inside?" Jackson asked but didn't move, clearly leaving the call to her on whether or not she needed more time.

She nodded, only half-holding her breath.

Chapter 19

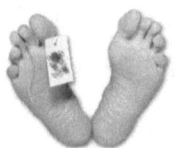

From first glance, the cottage enchanted Christine.

The front door opened into a living room dominated by a plush sofa and a rocking recliner. Both held lots of little pillows in bright, light colors. The living room abutted an eat-in kitchen with an intimate table for two. Christine walked through, noting the appliances were high end, the stove was gas and the fridge was electric! She smiled. Apparently, Miss Emily had drawn the line on some modern conveniences to make sure residents were able to cook and didn't starve.

Jackson cracked open the fridge door. "Fully stocked." He lifted a package of chicken breasts. "Why don't you explore the rest of the place and I'll rustle us up some dinner." He grinned. "I'm sure you're starved. It's been a couple hours since you've eaten."

Her stomach growled. "Are you sure you're not reading my mind, or something? How do you know what I'm thinking and feeling, and that I'm hungry?"

"I can't explain it," he admitted. "Hasn't happened to me before, but I just know."

Attuned. That pleased and frightened her. Did he just know she wasn't Caro, too?

She left Jackson in the kitchen. The sounds of banging pots followed her back into the living room and on into a wide hallway. A bath stood tucked into the center of the house, and a large bedroom on the back. It was decorated in soothing colors. Sea green and cream. Caro's favorites. Touches of her were everywhere. That comforted Christine.

She paused at the window to look outside. Close, in Caro's yard, more flowers and flowering shrubs, and beyond her lawn, row upon row of something growing… an enormous garden. It had to be a community garden, it stretched far beyond the cottage's lot lines. Caro probably loved working in it. She'd had a mini-garden at home, and a micro-garden on her balcony in New York.

Looking up, Christine glanced up to the underside of a wide deck. Stairs led down from it to the ground, ending at small stone patio. *What was up there?*

An unnoticed door opposite the bath snagged her eye. It opened to a narrow staircase. She climbed the stairs. The top landing emptied into a single large room, full of windows all across the back of the cottage. The lighting was fantastic, and the room was filled with canvases and paints. A radio sat on a canvas-draped tabletop. *Caro, breaking the rules?* The radio was contraband. Lucas would have a fit if he knew it was there.

And Caro had returned to painting.

Shocked, Christine's jaw dropped loose. So far as she knew, Caro hadn't touched a brush that wasn't of the basting variety since marrying Martin. A cluster of six easels stood on the far end, facing the front of the cottage. They were separated in groups of three. Christine moved to examine the canvases placed on them.

The first three paintings were timid, angry, and monotone. The remaining three were stunning landscapes that exploded with color.

A flood of unexpected tears threatened. Caro, Christine realized, was healing.

An easel set apart and unnoticed caught her eye. She moved in front of it, recognized it as a self-portrait, then examined it. Her hair was red, not blonde, and chopped short, more sawed-off than styled. Most interesting was her jaw. Sharp angles and hard planes, it appeared rock-hard. In case the viewer missed that telling sign, she'd accentuated another indicator they couldn't miss: her raised fist.

Dark and bold letters left her message permanently etched on the bottom right. "Victory."

Overcome, a sob shuddered through Christine and tears of gratitude slid down her face.

Caro had reclaimed herself, and her life.

HALF AN HOUR LATER, Jackson bellowed. "Caroline, dinner!"

Having had a really good cry, Christine hauled herself out of the lone chair on the upper deck outside Caro's studio. She locked the sliding door behind her and headed down the stairs, stopping at the bathroom to splash her face.

She drenched her cheeks with cool water at the sink, then blotted her face dry. Her eyes were a little red and her skin splotchy, but not too bad.

"Caroline!"

"Coming." She finished up and then went to the kitchen.

On seeing the table set, she gasped. "You're kidding me."

"Pour the wine," Jackson said, still at the stove.

He'd found a frilly apron and put it on over his black t-shirt and jeans. Took a confident man to pull off wearing a frilly apron. She smiled and filled two glasses. "Anything else?"

"No, we're ready." He filled their plates, then brought them to the table.

The spicy smells awakened her senses. "Mmm, glazed chicken, fire-roasted tomatoes, shaved petite squash and porcini mushrooms." She identified the items. "You did all this while I was upstairs? Wow, Jackson. It looks terrific and smells even better."

He flushed. "It's no big deal. I'm a chef, remember?"

"Maybe not to you, but I can't cook. It's huge to me." She sat down and they began to eat. From the first forkful she had to resist the urge to mumble, "I'm in love."

"Everything okay?" he asked.

"Terrific." She motioned with the tines of her fork. "I love these mushrooms."

"I'll make a note of it."

"Do you bake, too? If so," she grinned, "I love brownies."

He laughed. "I'll note that, too."

The implication he'd cook for her again had her ecstatic. "Any time you need a taste tester, I'm up for the job, Jackson." She smiled. "You're very good."

"Rose paused her college education to send me to chef's school," he said, as if that explained in all. "That's what we always called it."

"You wanted her to never regret it."

"Honestly, I wanted her to be proud of me." He lifted a shoulder. "Rose hates to cook. Matthew spares her most of the time, unless he's frosted about something."

"I don't like it, either."

"Darby said you cook all the time."

Caro. Not her. Caro did that. "Only when I'm seriously stressed. Otherwise, I hate it."

"I see." Jackson grinned, keeping it light. "I'll remember. If I ever see you reaching for a pot or pan, I'll know you reaching your limit is on the near horizon."

She chuckled. Had anyone before cared enough about her stress levels to note what triggered them? If so, she couldn't remember it.

They talked about everything and little nothings, cleaned up the kitchen, and then settled into the front porch swing. Normal night sounds—an owl softly hooting, the faint strains of a guitar, frogs croaking—broke the silence.

Christine parked a hand over her tummy. "I'm stuffed and sleepy now."

"We drove through the night. I'd be worried if you weren't ready to sleep a while."

"When I was on the deck upstairs, I saw a lot of activity in the village. It looks as if they're preparing for some kind of festivities."

Jackson stretched out a lazy arm, draped it atop the back of the swing. "Little Independence Day."

"In March?" Christine slumped back, clutched a pillow to her chest. "But that's in July."

"Little Independence Day," he repeated. "It's a Park holiday, celebrated third only to Christmas and Easter."

Christine puzzled on it, decided she was too tired and groggy to guess, and just asked. "What's Little Independence Day about?"

"It's a big deal in the Park. People openly declaring themselves free from their pasts. They do all kinds of things."

"So everyone here is hiding from a Martin?"

"Or someone like him. *Something* like him. There are all kinds of people here, with all kinds of problems. A couple doors down, you've got a Vet suffering PTSD. He only comes out at night, and he doesn't talk to anyone except the kid next door. She's always outside with her teddy bear."

"What's wrong with her?"

"Her dad died and she can't accept it." He swallowed hard, empathy in his eyes. "She'd already lost her mother. So she just keeps waiting for her dad to get home."

"Oh, that's awful." Heartbreaking and awful.

"It is. Everyone here came with an awful story, Caroline. Most replace it with a better story."

The work being done at Sampson Park was more than noble. It was amazing.

They swung in the porch swing in silence. After a time, the conversation replayed in Christine's mind, and she asked, "Jackson?"

"Mmm?"

Whether or not he'd answer her, she had no idea. But she had to ask. "Who are you hiding from?"

He glanced over at her, the moonlight casting shadows on her chin. "A relative witnessed a mob hit," he said. "I'm collateral damage."

"What does that mean?"

He curled his fingers against her shoulder. "I'm not in hiding, but I'm not really free to roam at will, either."

Christine let her head fall against his shoulder. "It's complicated."

"Yeah, sometimes. Fortunately, I live a simple life so it's not a big problem."

"I'm glad." She covered a yawn and just couldn't hold her eyes open another second. "I hate the thought of you having problems, Jackson."

Lying to him, and continuing to lie to him, rankled her more and more.

"I feel the same way about you." He cocked his head and pressed his cheek against her crown. "You're falling asleep," he said. "Best get some rest and I best get back."

"Back to where?" Panic set into her stomach. "Where are you going?"

"To the manor house," he said.

"Ah, you're one of those special guests, then."

"I have my own room." His tone teased, but there was a real joy in it, too.

"Well, aren't you special?" She laughed. "Actually, don't answer that. You are special, and I'm feeling a little inferior at the moment. I'm not used to it."

"Why?"

"Honestly?"

He nodded.

This was it. The moment of truth. "Because you are special…"

"And…?"

"And you're surrounded by all these iconic women in your life, and I'm just… every day average."

"There's nothing every day or average about you, Caroline."

"Really?"

"Really." Jackson touched her face.

Her mouth went dry. "You don't really know me, Jackson." That was truth. "Right now, I don't really know me."

"I know what I see," he said, his mouth inches from her face, his breath warming her skin. "And what I feel when I'm with you."

"Don't kiss me." Her tone didn't support her words. "With everything going on—it's just the wrong time."

"Sorry. I have to." His apology sounded sincere. "There's no guarantee I'll be lucky enough for a second chance." He closed the distance, fingertips to her face, brought his mouth to hers, and kissed her lips.

A long minute later, he pulled back and looked down into her eyes. He must have liked what he saw; he smiled. "But you can bet I'm going to hope there's a second, and a third chance."

She smiled back, unable to restrain herself. "Is that Lester-logic? About second chances?"

He nodded then stood. "I'll pick you up at noon tomorrow. There's someplace I want to take you."

"Where?"

"It's a surprise."

"How should I dress?"

"However you like, but remember it's hot."

"So it's outside?"

He laughed. "You're cagy, and I'm not saying another word. See you tomorrow." He took off down the sidewalk.

Speckles was nowhere in sight, so it appeared Jackson intended to walk back to the manor house.

Unable not to be elated and excited, Christine went inside and turned her focus onto her sister. She turned the cottage's contents upside down and inside out, seeking clues. *What, in addition to returning to her painting, had Caro done while here? How long had it been since she'd left? Where could she have gone, and where was she now?*

And throughout her search, Christine recalled and relived every second of time with Jackson, igniting a tumultuous mixture of elation and dread. She pulled open the last dresser drawer, carefully rifled through the contents. Things between them *would* go wrong. The second he discovered her true identity, he'd cease trusting her, and that would be the end of something special and really, really good. Finding nothing helpful in the contents, she shoved the drawer shut.

Two hours later, Christine had worked through the entire cottage, searching even the folds of the towels stacked in the bathroom's linen closet. *Empty. Not a single clue.* And she still hadn't resolved what to do about Jackson.

If she had any sense, she'd steer clear of the man. Yet that wasn't what she wanted to do. Typically, reaching that conclusion would settle the issue for her. It didn't this time. Not with him. Steering clear would be smart, but did she have to continue to struggle to do only things deemed smart?

You're picking a bad time to not be smart.

True, but she'd never felt like this. Never been totally engaged or giddy over a man. Not even as a teen. Outside of business, she'd never been eager to hear what one had to say or hung onto his every word and recalled his words and actions over and over again in her mind. And never had she ever lived and relived a kiss. So the timing wasn't great. So their circumstances left a lot to be desired. So what? Why couldn't she, just for once in her life, follow her heart?

While you're lying to him? Don't be ridiculous.

Her conscience trotted back out in full force, and she had no comeback for it. It was right and she was wrong—and when she checked the bedroom and the kitchen for a second time and she hadn't found a thing that could tell her where her sister might be, she accepted it.

Tension had pain streaking through her temples. They started pounding. No sleep, high anxiety at locating and coming to Sampson Park, being afraid of someone recognizing the truth about her, experiencing everything that had happened since she'd looked out Danny's Diner's front window yesterday morning and had seen Martin the Miserable standing across the street—all of it conspired and slammed her into the proverbial wall. It was time to pack it in and rest. "Tomorrow's another day, Scarlett." Things had to get brighter. Better. The tension had to ratchet down.

Christine took a quick shower, pulled on a pair of black yoga pants and a t-shirt with *Strong* emblazoned across the chest in red, and then crawled into bed, so exhausted she couldn't think beyond the immediate. *Caro. Where are you?*

Sampson Park, this cottage, was perfect for her sister. Once here, how could she bear to leave? If Christine were guessing, she'd bet Caro would have to blasted out of the Park. Yet according to Miss Emily and Darby, she had been gone for an undisclosed length of time. Even with all their Security, there was neither a record of her leaving nor an incident reported of any event prompting her to leave.

Maybe she hadn't left...

That seemed more likely, and raised three questions:

Was Caro still here somewhere, just not at her cottage?

Why would Caro leave her cottage?

And if she did leave the cottage but not the Park, *where* would she go?

Christine didn't know, but she hoped for answers to her questions by the end of her outing with Jackson.

Chapter 20

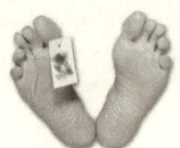

Jackson slept like the dead.

He awakened and cranked open an eye. It took a second to remember where he was; in his room at Miss Emily's. The bright room alerted him he'd slept longer than expected. He checked the clock on the bedside stand, groaned and tossed back the covers. Residents weren't allowed to have clocks, but the manor house guests had a different purpose here and required them.

If he hustled, he could take a quick shower before the 9:00 o'clock meeting on Caroline. When he'd walked back last night, Mr. Jenkins had informed Jackson of it. No way could he make time for breakfast, too.

His stomach growling and craving a cup of coffee, he showered then dressed in jeans and a pale yellow shirt. Having trouble shaking off the urge to sleep longer, he headed to the conference room.

Miss Emily was already seated at the head of the table. "Good morning, Jackson."

"Am I late?"

"No, my boy. You're fine." She motioned to a seat at her right.

Jackson sat down, and nodded to Darby and the blonde bombshell, Dr. Laura Rossi. Close to his age, she'd shown some interest in him on his last visit, and it was flattering. Laura Rossi was a beautiful and brilliant woman. Unfortunately, her all science and no spirit philosophy just didn't do it for him.

Mr. Jenkins placed a cup of coffee before Jackson, then a moment later, he returned with a plate of two blueberry muffins.

Jackson smiled and mumbled, "Thanks, Mr. Jenkins."

"Get that down," he whispered. "You need to be sharp for this."

Great. Jackson lifted his cup, and asked, "Are we waiting for Reginald?" He was Miss Emily's financial manager and normally present for all collaborative meetings.

"No," Miss Emily said. "He won't be joining us this morning. Away on assignment."

"Thank heaven for small mercies." That came from Darby. She and Reginald constantly butted heads and always had.

"I didn't bring the others in either, though I had a slim hope Dr. Goodman would join us by phone."

"That would have been helpful," Laura Rossi said. "He knows Caroline best."

"It is what it is," Miss Emily said. "Darby, did you get Caroline's records to Laura yesterday?"

"I did—all we have, anyway," Darby said. "And Dr. Rossi reviewed them last night." Darby looked to Laura to disclose her findings.

"Such as they are, I reviewed the records," she said. "Unfortunately, Chaplain Goodman doesn't record much in his notes, and they included nothing from their last session at all. So we have no insight into Caroline's state of mind at that time."

Miss Emily huffed. "Well, what did he say?"

"'Doing well. Good progress. No nightmares since our last session. Maybe they've ended?' And—my personal favorite—" She referred to her notes for an exact quote. "'She's not talking today. Sat silently through the whole session.'"

Darby frowned. "But that is significant, Laura."

"The session was a complete waste of time," she countered. "Chaplain Goodman should have insisted she talk," she said, refusing to call him Dr. Goodman. "No one can counsel someone who refuses to converse."

"Darby is right. That session was significant." Miss Emily folded her hands together atop the gleaming wooden table. "You're forgetting, Dr. Rossi, that Caroline had no choice in what she did or when she did it. For years, Martin Easton dictated her every action. She ate, slept and talked when he said for her to, and if she refused to comply, he beat and berated her." Miss Emily tilted her head. "Do you see the power Caroline exerted in coming for a session and refusing to talk?" Miss Emily's eyes shone bright and she smiled. "Caro was putting Dr. Goodman on notice."

Laura Rossi looked surprised then contrite. "She would do what she wanted when she wanted."

"Exactly." Darby looked happy.

Miss Emily nodded. "And she would refuse to do anything she didn't want to do—like talk."

Dr. Rossi grunted, then sighed. "In that case, I must agree. She's exhibiting excellent non-verbal progress."

"Sounds like a good thing to me." Jackson motioned for a refill.

Miss Emily agreed. "But I have to say, I am deeply concerned about her memory issue. Lucas insists no event noted by him or anyone on his team spurred it. Caro clearly doesn't remember any of us or her time at the Park." Her gaze swiveled to Jackson. "Did she react to anything at the cottage?"

"Nothing," he said. "It was as if she was seeing everything and meeting everyone for the first time—Mr. Jenkins, her next-door neighbors, Millie and Ruddy. Same thing at Rose's."

Worry clouded Miss Emily's eyes. "And we still have no idea what happened to her to cause this."

Darby lifted a hand. "How could we? We didn't even know she'd gone." That grated at Darby. Her snarl signaled she found that fact extremely unacceptable. "Lucas has personally reviewed all the sign-outs and he's run through the security tapes multiple times. There's just nothing showing any incident or her leaving the Park."

"Well, I trust he's still investigating and tightening procedures, considering she showed up in Even and apparently spent at least a week there." Miss Emily sat back in her chair. "We can't know what to do for her until we hear from Dr. Goodman. I guess, until we gather more information, we'll have to fly blind and take our cues from her."

Darby shifted on her seat, clearly uneasy about that.

Jackson looked at Dr. Rossi. "So do I need to treat her with kid gloves, or what?"

"I lack sufficient information to make that determination." She looked at Miss Emily. "I'm sorry, but I'm not comfortable making a call with nothing to speak of to go on."

"Not a problem, Dr. Rossi," Miss Emily said. "I understand your position completely." Miss Emily smiled and turned to Jackson. "At this time, the best any of us can do is to take our prompts from Caro." Miss Emily stroked her chin. "Until we understand the etiology of her memory loss, we must be cautious to first do no harm."

"What does that mean?" Jackson asked. "Exactly."

"In practical terms, it means, don't challenge her, just support her, and go where she leads."

"That's what Dr. Goodman would suggest. I just know it." Darby nodded. "So she stays comfortable. Comfortable people reveal more of what's going on inside them."

Miss Emily agreed. "Jackson, have you asked Caro what happened?"

He swallowed a sip of coffee. "I have, but she's fuzzy on the details, and I didn't push her for information. It just felt wrong."

"Good instincts, my boy." Tapping her lips, Miss Emily weighed what he told her. "And a strong signal you'd better give her a reason to stay put."

"What kind of reason?" he asked.

"The kind that makes her comfortable. We can't have her trying to leave until we better know what's going on. Make her want to stay, Jackson. That's vital to us all."

"Especially with all the associates coming in." Darby agreed with her mother. "Any attempt for her departure could cause significant challenges to the rest of us, Jackson."

"Whatever happened was probably traumatic," Dr. Rossi said. "I suspect she's blocking the incident because it was so bad—at least, in her eyes. But eventually, I suspect the inciting incident will surface. Maybe over time and not all at once, but things that manifest with this level of significance—memory loss is not a small thing—rarely stay suppressed. When she's ready to recall, she'll remember. Whether awake or in dreams or flashbacks—they'll find a way to her awareness she can accept."

"So she'll tell us?" Jackson asked.

"Her revealing the incident to others is dicey and could go either way, but odds are highly likely she will remember it."

Jackson sent Miss Emily a level look. "I'm not a doctor or a shrink, and no offense, Dr. Rossi…"

"Go ahead, Jackson," she said. "You've spent a lot more time with her than me."

"What you're saying sounds logical and it might be typical, but it doesn't feel right to me. Not in her case."

Miss Emily didn't discount Jackson's opinion. "What does feel right?"

"From what I've witnessed and Caroline's said, it's not that she's burying or suppressing, or whatever Dr. Rossi called it. It's more like she just doesn't remember." He paused to really think.

"What is it, my boy?" Miss Emily asked.

"Reviewing her behavior," he said. "Caroline strikes me as fully capable of dealing with an incident. She's calm during crises. At Rose's, the town florists pulled a stunt and delivered over a thousand flowers for their first funeral. They were loose, not arranged. Caroline was the calm and steady one. She jumped in, watched a couple videos on arranging flowers, and did them."

"Arranging flowers is not traumatic." Dr. Rossi lifted a hand. "And Caroline wasn't directly impacted by the consequences."

"That's true," Jackson conceded. "But Rose, Matthew and I were upset. Caroline was methodical. She immediately sought a solution to the problem, determined a strategy for solving it, then acted on the strategy."

"Logical response," Dr. Rossi admitted.

"She didn't want Rose upset," Jackson said. "So I can't see Caroline blocking something out to avoid it. That's just not her. She'd look for a solution and act on it."

"Dr. Rossi?" Miss Emily looked to her.

"Her reaction on the flowers indicates her conflict or crisis resolution skills and suggests a distinct and logical pattern of addressing issues. But to know for certain, we'd need more incident data for comparison."

Darby tilted her head. "This isn't my area of expertise, but I've reviewed a lot of records and materials here."

"What do you think, Darby?" Miss Emily asked.

"I think when people are in crisis, or confronted with a problem, their reaction is largely instinctive, so they fall back on familiar responses. Caroline would do what comes naturally to Caroline. She doesn't stop to think it through, she just faces the problem the way she always faces problems," Darby said. "I've seen it over and again in the records."

Miss Emily looked to Jackson. "Does that feel more like what happened?"

"It does. Yes, ma'am."

"Dr. Rossi, what else could cause Caroline's issue?"

"All kinds of things. From shock to fear, or a physical injury."

"Like a healthy smack in the head? We've seen that happen before," Miss Emily said. "Has Caro been injured?"

"I can't say for sure," Jackson said. "We saw no signs of any and she didn't mention an injury. But with Martin's thugs…"

"So she's talking to you otherwise," Darby said, probing.

"Oh, yeah," Jackson responded. "About all kinds of things."

Miss Emily and Darby shared a look Jackson couldn't interpret. They had some suspicions or something they weren't sharing, though he couldn't guess its nature.

"Well," Miss Emily said. "Watch her, Jackson, and do what you must to keep her here until we get some answers."

Mr. Jenkins refilled Jackson's cup. "There is another possibility."

"What?" Jackson asked.

All eyes trained on Mr. Jenkins. He hesitated, then looked at Miss Emily. "Sorry, I shouldn't have interfered."

"Good grief, Mr. Jenkins. Caroline bonded with you more than anyone else in the Park. If you have any insight or an idea to add, voice it. We're floundering here."

"It's just that I couldn't help but notice yesterday she is different."

"That happens with healing," Dr. Rossi said.

"Of course, Dr. Rossi." He deferred to her expertise. "But, unless healing includes growing a foot of hair in two weeks, or I'm mistaken and she wore a wig yesterday, there is a physical-change issue."

"Mr. Jenkins is right." Darby gasped. "About two weeks ago. I saw Caroline in the village and her hair had been cut short and dyed red. I'd forgotten."

"Yes, ma'am." Mr. Jenkins nodded.

"But her blond hair is lovely. Why would she do that?" Miss Emily asked.

Mr. Jenkins answered. "She said at tea she liked her hair short because it was cooler and that she'd gone red because nobody messes with redheads. They've got tempers and fight back. People try to walk all over blondes. She also said she intended to keep her hair red the rest of her life."

"Yet it's long and blonde now," Jackson said. "This doesn't make sense."

"Changing one's hair color is not difficult, Jackson. Once, I dyed mine a different color every day for a week." Miss Emily sniffed. "But length is a different matter. Caro wasn't wearing a wig yesterday. I can spot a wig at fifty paces."

Jackson cringed. Miss Emily couldn't see well across a room and refused to wear glasses. But when they'd kissed, Jackson had stroked Caroline's head. "It wasn't a wig."

"Are you sure?" Darby asked. "Some wigs are very good. And extensions could account for the length."

"It wasn't a wig," he insisted.

Darby hiked an eyebrow. "Are you sure? Some even have the scalps."

Jackson frowned. "My hands were all over her head and I'm telling you, it wasn't a wig, Darby."

Darby grinned and held out her hand to her mother. "Pay up."

"I didn't bring my purse." She grumbled. "I'll have to owe you."

They'd bet on him touching Caroline's head? Jackson frowned and held it so they wouldn't miss it. Heat crept up his neck and burned his ears.

Mr. Jenkins' expression soured. "You're all missing the point. It wasn't a wig two weeks ago—short and red—and it wasn't one yesterday—long and blond. That's the point. Hair simply does not grow fast enough for hers to be as long as is less than two weeks after she sawed it off short in her studio."

"Sawed it off?" Concern elevated Jackson's voice. "What upset her into doing that?"

Mr. Jenkins countered. "She wasn't at all upset. It was part of her reclaiming her personal power."

"What?"

"Martin insisted on the long hair. He took her personal power to choose for herself. She hacked off her hair to reclaim it and choose for herself."

"I see," Jackson said, instinctively looking at Miss Emily. "So what does this mean—symbolic gesture aside?"

Miss Emily shot Mr. Jenkins a sober look, then turned a cool gaze on Jackson. "It means you definitely must keep a close watch on her and keep her here. Whatever it takes." She signaled an end to her explanation by swiveling her focus to Darby. "You get on the phone with our communing chaplain and tell those people there that I want a phone call from him by nightfall or I'm going to send a plane with instructions to retrieve him from that mountain with or without his consent."

Miss Emily moved on to Dr. Rossi. "You talk to some of the residents and see if anyone recalls anything odd in Caroline's behavior before she went missing. Get Speckles to help you."

The meeting ended and everyone started to rise. Miss Emily called out, "Jackson, one more thing."

"Yes, ma'am."

"Did you talk to Dr. Richmond?"

Unaccustomed to hearing the woman addressed as anything other than Dr. Nell, it took him a second to slot her. *Caroline's Dallas counselor.* "Not yet. By the time I walked back to the house last night, it was too late to disturb Darby for a phone or to call Nell, and I slept in this morning."

"Understandable, considering your lack of sleep the last two days. You still look a bit worn, my boy. But do handle the call as soon as possible. Dr. Richmond knows Caroline best."

"I still need a phone."

"See Darby about that."

"As soon as we're done here."

A squeal pealed through the air and into the conference room. Jackson jumped to his feet.

"Easy." Miss Emily held up a staying hand. "Everything is fine."

"Doesn't sound fine." Jackson started for the door. A woman had squealed.

"It just means Lester's here." Miss Emily smiled.

Confusion fell to certainty. "Ah, he's back to forgetting his pants." Jackson understood perfectly.

"Yes, and that squeal was Abigail's."

"I'll go remind him he can't parade around in his briefs—before Abigail has a heart attack."

"He pulls this trick every single time I hire a new housekeeper." Miss Emily sighed indulgently, tilted her head and lifted her teacup. "It's his trust issue, rearing its ugly head."

It was. Lester had pulled that stunt with Rose for months. Every time he checked the mailbox in his underwear and got himself arrested, Rose would go down to the station and bail him out of jail. Money was so tight for her back then, she'd have to eat peanut butter sandwiches for a week. Finally, she'd tried a creative solution that slowed Lester down. "He's going to pull his trust tests. That's just Lester. But you might try giving him boxers with money printed on them." Lester liked money. And it turned out he had a lot of it. Course, Rose and Jackson hadn't known that then.

"I remember." Miss Emily's eyes twinkled.

Jackson shrugged. "Worked for Rose."

"Wonderful idea," Miss Emily whispered in a conspiratorial tone. "I'll stock up and tell the staff if they see Lester in his shorts not to react. Just pull a pair of boxers from the stack of stock and give them to him. That should nip this brief business in the bud." She planted a kiss to Jackson's neck. "Thank you, dear boy."

Jackson smiled. "My pleasure."

As Jackson walked past, Mr. Jenkins told Miss Emily he'd be away for a couple hours. He had an errand to run in the village.

He didn't meet her eyes when saying it, and Jackson had a strange feeling in his stomach. Jenkins would die before hurting Miss Emily or Darby. He'd been a father to Darby, and she doted on him. So this mysterious errand couldn't have anything to do with them. Jenkins would just say what the errand was. Yet something he felt might not be in their best interests sat stuck in the man's craw. And, whether or not he and Caroline had bonded, because of his comments about Caroline's hair, Jackson thought whatever was stuck might just be about her.

Now what was the man up to?

Conflicted, protective feelings rumbled through Jackson. He didn't know what Mr. Jenkins had in mind, but if he intended to walk to the village in this heat—no way would he ride with Speckles because of the feud—his errand had to be significant.

That put Jackson on edge. And made him determined to find out.

Chapter 21

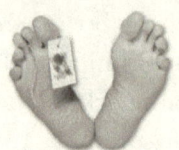

Jackson got an issue phone from Darby, then retreated to his room to phone Dr. Nell.

The call rolled over into her voice mail. After the beep, he left a message. "Nell, it's Jackson. I'm out of pocket, but I need to talk to you about C. B." Not knowing who might overhear the message, he avoided using Caroline's name. "There's been a development. I'll phone again this evening. Don't call me back on this number."

He hoped Nell followed those instructions. If not, he'd have to burn the issue phone and go to Darby for another one.

Stowing the phone in his dresser drawer, he headed downstairs. Mr. Jenkins and Lester stood talking quietly near the front door, and then Mr. Jenkins departed. It was good he'd been delayed, not that it would take much effort to follow him closely enough to see where he went. Mr. Jenkins was getting up there in years, and he was dressed in his typical suit and tie, which meant he'd be scorching hot and slow moving on his walk to the village. The bulge in his pocket confirmed it: a bottle of water.

"Jackson!" Lester spotted him and his delight had his leathery face crinkling. "Spitwads and fudgesicles." He hurried toward the stairs. "It's good to see you, son."

Jackson grinned and hustled down to the foot of the stairs. He hugged Lester hard. "How are you doing, Lester?"

"I'm good." He pulled back and clapped Jackson's shoulder. "Better now that I can see you with my own eyes."

"I've missed you, too."

"Is all well in Dallas?"

"No complaints." Jackson inquired about Lester, his health, and how long he'd be staying at the Park, then he worked around to asking about Mr. Jenkins. "He's being awfully secretive this morning."

"He's got a meeting." Lester dropped his voice low. "Not that it'll do any good, but if you see fireworks coming from Caroline's cottage, you'll know things didn't work out like the woman hoped." Lester shook his head. "She ought to have the good sense to leave other people's business to 'em but apparently even with what's happened to her, she ain't."

"Miss Emily says she's reclaiming her personal power." That had stunned Jackson. He hadn't picked up on any signs she felt she'd lost it. "What exactly is she doing in this meeting with Mr. Jenkins?"

"I ain't sure exactly. But whatever it is, it's bound to blow up in her face."

"I'm supposed to meet her at noon." Jackson grimaced. "Guess I'd better get there a little early."

"I'd say soonest might be smartest, son." Lester shrugged. "I'd come as backup, but I'm kind of eager to watch the fireworks."

The fireworks weren't scheduled until dusk—for Little Independence Day.

"Not those fireworks," Lester dropped his voice. "The fireworks at Caroline's."

That worried Jackson. "Everybody knows she's got this memory thing going on. Surely Mr. Jenkins won't risk pushing her. That could cause—"

Lester snorted. "Since when does Jenkins not push everyone on everything?"

Jackson's gaze collided with Lester's, and he nodded. "I'd better get over there."

"Like I said, son. Soonest."

Jackson rushed out the door.

Chapter 22

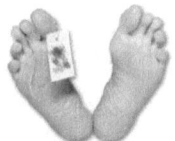

Christine set the table with a fine white cloth and Caro's best dishes. When she put the fresh flowers in the table's center, she dared to hope this whole idea didn't create such a mess it made her an outcast.

It was actually her conversation at dawn with a little girl a few cottages down that sparked the idea and had her extending the invitations. Well, actually the conversation was with the girl's teddy bear, Miss Dixie. The bear talked. The child, Gracie, did not.

If Christine could pull this off, she hoped it would have the same effect in the Park as her arranging the flowers had had at Rose's. If it failed, well, she was busted.

Somewhere in the rounds today, she had to work up the courage to tell Jackson the truth. Once she'd accepted the decision and it settled in, she realized how afraid of it she had become. Jackson mattered. She hadn't expected him to; men rarely did, considering most were after her money and could care less about her, the woman. But Jackson was different. Important enough that she didn't want to lose him.

Whether or not she was falling in love with him, it was too soon to tell. But she sure had fallen in like.

She pulled a white box from the kitchen counter and opened it. The tea cookies Speckles favored were inside, lined up in pretty rows. Ned, Miss Emily's chef, had graciously provided them with a warning to not execute her plan. He was trying to look out for her, and when she explained her intentions, his horror warned her of the risks she was taking, but she decided to go ahead anyway. She needed an in here so people trusted her. And it had to be a good in, because as soon as she confessed the truth to Jackson, all of them were apt to line up to bounce her right out of Sampson Park on her foolish elbow.

She set a tiered tray onto the table, then placed the cookies on it. *Don't think too much. Just do it, and pray for the best.*

The teakettle whistled. She moved to it and poured steaming hot water into the teapot. Her hand shook and she spilled it, then mopped up the splash with a dishcloth.

A knock sounded at the door.

She opened it and her smile faded. A red-faced Mr. Jenkins stood there. "Oh my gosh. Are you okay?"

"I'm fine. It's a bit warm out this morning."

"It's a scorcher." She guided him into the cottage and he sat down on the living room chair nearest the door. "Did you walk all the way here from the manor house?"

He nodded, too winded to talk.

"Mr. Jenkins." She retrieved a cool cloth from the bath, then returned and mopped at his face. "You're lucky you didn't get heatstroke. Take off your coat."

"I will not." He reached up and stilled her hand, his voice as stiff as his back. "Stop fussing. I'm fine. I just need a moment."

She'd invaded his space. He liked it, but he didn't want to like it, and he didn't want to like her. "I'm sorry, if I offended you," she said softly. "I was worried."

"You're compassionate," he said stiffly. "Thoughtful, but totally unnecessary."

Mr. Jenkins was comfortable in his role as caretaker, but not in one where he was being cared for by another. Christine understood that. She'd been in that position most of her adult life.

"So what was this mysterious note you sent me?" he asked.

"Let me get you some water." She stalled. "You're probably dehydrated."

She grabbed a chilled bottle of water and wiped down the outside so it wouldn't be wet, unscrewed the cap and then passed it to him. His face was still as red as the strawberries in the garden out back. "Drink."

He took several long swallows. Rested a second, then swallowed again.

Five minutes elapsed, then ten. "Your color is getting back to normal."

He shot her a steady look. "I'm fine. You're delaying."

She was, and she couldn't deny it. Fortunately, a rap sounded at the door. "I need a favor, Mr. Jenkins."

"What is it?"

"I need for you to promise me you won't lose your temper and storm out until you hear all of the conversation."

A strange look crossed his face. As if she'd confirmed something he had suspected. "Very well."

"Thank you." She opened the door.

Speckles walked in and saw Mr. Jenkins sitting there. "Oh, hell no," he said then turned on Christine. "I told you I'd come and drink your tea, but you didn't say nothing about *him* being here."

"Speckles," she insisted. "You gave me your word."

His internal battle raged, and Mr. Jenkins had a sour look on his face that proved he was seriously considering tossing out his promise, too.

"Come in and sit down," Christine told Speckles. "I've got cookies."

"Them tea cookies with the pecans?" He squinted at her.

She nodded. "Rolled in powdered sugar. Ned made them special."

He snorted, shuffled a wide berth around Mr. Jenkins and sat in the chair farthest from him.

Getting them to the table would take an act of Congress, so she filled tea cups and little plates with the cookies and delivered them to the men.

"Thank you." Mr. Jenkins said, his voice stiff and cool.

"Thanks." Speckles reached for a cookie and popped it into his mouth.

Christine retrieved napkins. "Now I know you two have a feud going, and far be it from me to interfere. I like a good feud as well as the next woman."

"What is your point?" Mr. Jenkins said.

She looked at him, then at Speckles. "I think a good feud requires a good cause, otherwise it's just a squabble."

"Insulting a man's horse is a good cause," Speckles said, then grumbled. "Ain't no squabble."

Mr. Jenkins frowned. "I did not insult your horse, you old fool."

"You called Buttercup a hag," Speckles shot back. "If that ain't an insult, I don't know what is."

"I most certainly did not call her a *hag*," Mr. Jenkins said. "I said she was a fine nag, which I daresay, she certainly is."

Speckles looked pole-axed. "A fine *nag*? Not a *hag*?" He sounded doubtful. "Is that a fact?" He chewed and swallowed. "You ain't just saying that to end this feud, right?"

Mr. Jenkins stilled and glared at Speckles.

"A fine nag." Speckles rubbed at the back of his neck. "Hmm, well, that there kind of changes things, don't it? A fine nag." Speckles looked at Christine. "I guess I'll have me another cup of tea, then."

"As will I." Mr. Jenkins extended his cup.

Sweet peace. Christine smiled, and refilled their cups. "As soon as I heard Mr. Jenkins' accent, I suspected this had all been a misunderstanding. I'm so glad it was and you two have resolved the matter."

Mr. Jenkins' eyebrow lifted but neither man said another word about the confusion. They chatted for a few minutes, then Mr. Jenkins announced he needed to get busy.

"Full schedule?" Christine asked.

"Um, yes." He turned to Speckles. "Would you have time to

take me back to the manor house? I walked down, but in this heat, I don't think I dare to walk back."

"Be happy to." Speckles stood up.

So did Mr. Jenkins. When Speckles cleared the front door, Mr. Jenkins paused and looked at Christine. "At some point in the near future, you and I have to chat," he whispered.

To chew her out for bringing him here under false pretenses? Uncertain, Christine asked. "About what?" No way did she want to worry about this non-stop between now and then.

"About who you really are," he said softly, his tone flat and even, matching the look in his eyes. "You look like Caroline, but you are not."

Christine felt her blood drain to her feet.

"I'm convinced you mean none here any harm or I'd expose you immediately and remove you myself. Should I prove to be wrong about this, I warn you, there is nothing I will not do to protect them, and that includes Jackson."

The moment of reckoning had come more quickly than she'd expected, and from a surprising source. Denial would be just plain stupid. "You're not wrong, Mr. Jenkins. But I swear to you, I'd never harm anyone here. Never."

"Very well." He looked her straight in the eye. "Because you've ended this feud and you're too similar to Caroline not to be her sister, I'm going to trust you. But if at any moment I come to regret it, I will kill you." No drama, only truth in his tone. "Are we clear?"

He meant it. Every word. She nodded, too shaken to speak.

"Good. We have an understanding, then. Thank you for your hospitality. Good day." He walked out the door, and pulled it closed behind him.

At the window, her hand at her pounding chest, she watched Mr. Jenkins climb into the carriage and Speckles close its door. He stroked Buttercup, then climbed up top. Grabbing the reins, Speckles headed back toward the manor house.

Something rustled outside the cottage window.

Christine looked toward the sound, at the bushes to the left of the porch. The leaves shook, but she didn't see anything. Must have been a little breeze, or a squirrel. During the night, they'd nearly scared her to death, running across the roof.

Still uneasy and emotionally torn, she turned to tidying up. Had her plan been a success or a failure?

Honestly, it was hard to say. She'd ended one feud, but clearly had started another—or the potential for one, between her and a too-sharp Mr. Jenkins. Still, he hadn't exposed her, and he had taken a leap of faith and trusted her. Why? Only he knew. But she was grateful for the reprieve; she needed time to find the truth.

What had given her away? Why had he recognized she wasn't Caro when none of the others had?

That didn't make sense.

Regardless, it made her telling Jackson the truth more urgent. That set her to shaking again and had the bottom of her stomach dropping out.

Jackson might not be as accepting as Mr. Jenkins. He might expose her and boot her out of the Park and out of his life for good.

Which worried her more, she didn't want to think about. Not now. But it ripped the option of further delay right off the proverbial table. She had to tell him today. And she would—after she found out every scrap she could about Caro… just in case Jackson did show her the gate.

JACKSON KEPT his back flat against the cottage's lap-siding and didn't so much as breathe until Caroline left the window. Then he made his way to the community garden behind the row of cottages, and snitched a long, cold drink from the water-hose.

She'd taken a whale of a risk, bringing Mr. Jenkins and Speckles under her roof at the same time. Jackson filled his hand with cool water and splashed his heated face. But it'd worked. So Speckles had heard an insult when Mr. Jenkins had been complimenting Buttercup, and for that they'd been feuding for years. Who knew?

It'd taken Caroline to set things straight.

She had a knack for that. Jackson splashed his face again, then a third time. Finally, he felt a little cooler. For calming ruffled feathers and smoothing the waters—when she set out to do it. Course, she could stir them up just as fast, too. He looped the hose and hung it back on its holder, nailed to a post, then turned off the water spigot. And she hadn't been above using Speckles' love for tea cookies to do it.

A smart man would remember that manipulation.

Jackson plucked a ripe berry from a lush bush. And what had Jenkins been whispering to her right before he'd left? The little girl down the block had chosen just that time to begin strumming her guitar—serenading her teddy bear on her front lawn. All Jackson had been able to make out was Mr. Jenkins saying, *convinced you mean them no harm* and then Caroline swearing she'd never do anything to hurt anyone here. Jackson had risked a glimpse, and she'd looked scared. He had been half-a-second from interceding, but then the guitar strumming had stopped and he'd heard Jenkins thanking Caroline for her hospitality. So whatever they had been discussing couldn't have been that bad.

Jackson popped the berry in his mouth and savored the explosion of flavor. Nothing as good as a ripe berry right off the vine. Except maybe a tomato. He walked over to the tomato plants and saw one about neck-high loaded with cherry tomatoes. Plucking a palm full, he went back to the water-hose to rinse them, and Mr. Jenkins' comments about Caroline's hair at the meeting this morning came rushing back.

Mr. Jenkins didn't believe Caroline was Caroline.

Worry worms slithered through Jackson, and he paused chewing. What if Mr. Jenkins was right? What if Caroline's memory loss wasn't memory loss?

What if the woman stealing Jackson's heart really wasn't Caroline?

Chapter 23

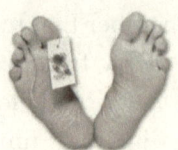

Jackson met Christine at exactly noon. "Should I bring water or anything?" she asked, recalling how the heat had affected Mr. Jenkins.

"No, we're good." He stepped back rather than inside.

Christine had changed into a soft yellow sundress and sandals, and pulled her hair up into a knot to get it off her neck. A lightweight skimmer was draped over her arm, to wear to keep from getting too much sun.

She stepped off the porch and followed Jackson down the walk. "So do I get to know where we're going?"

"To the village." He fell into step beside her. "Little Independence Day doesn't start until tomorrow, but there's a pre-festival going on today during the decorating."

"That sounds like fun. So what is it like?"

"You'll see." He smiled at her, but it oddly didn't touch his eyes.

They walked down the row of cottages to a small wooden footbridge, aptly called Little Bridge, then crossed over. The village lay nestled just beyond a line of trees on a rise.

"You're awfully quiet," Christine said. Had something happened?

"Just enjoying the calm." He said hello to a couple walking back from the village. When they were out of earshot, he added, "I don't get much of that at home."

"I know what you mean." Her life had been anything but calm for the past eight months. Dogged by Martin's henchmen. Worried sick and hunting for Caroline. "It feels good to not be looking back over your shoulder all the time."

His relaxed expression faded. "You felt you had to keep watch here?"

She didn't want to lie, but she wasn't ready to admit she hadn't been here. Still, she steeled herself, she would tell him the truth today. Later...today. "Look, Jackson. The kids are singing."

The village bustled. A cluster of shops circled a town square that consisted of a fountain and a clock. The shops, like the cottages, were painted in pastels, and most had awnings that draped over sidewalks to provide shade. A general store, jewelry shop, Corner Drugs, and Candle Shoppe. A shoe store and clothes shop resided at the far end.

"I love this," Christine said, pausing at the jewelry store. Distinct designs. All handmade. "Beautiful."

"Your neighbor makes all that," Jackson said.

"Really?" Christine had no idea. "Which one?"

"Jenny." When he realized that didn't ring a bell, he added, "Gracie's aunt. The little girl with the guitar and the teddy bear is Gracie. I forget her bear's name."

Recognition lit. "Miss Dixie," Christine said. "The bear and I have chatted. Gracie doesn't talk to me."

"She doesn't talk to anyone. But she hums," Jackson said. "She can talk. She just chooses not to do it. How about a snow-cone?"

"Sounds good."

"What's your flavor?" He stopped beside the stand.

"Banana. Or something red."

"Two bananas." He told the vendor, a young girl in her teens wearing shorts a t-shirt and a baseball cap pulled low over her eyes.

The machine ground and the teen spread syrup onto the shaved ice, then passed the cones.

"Do I need to sign?" he asked.

"I've got it, Jackson."

"Thanks," he said, then passed a cone to Christine.

She smiled her thanks.

They meandered around and ended up back near the kids' chorus, then stopped and finished their cones while listening to the kids sing. The group performed three more songs, then shuffled off the elevated risers in formation. A large group of adults replaced them.

"They're going to sing, too?" Christine asked.

Jackson nodded.

And they did sing, lifting their beautiful voices harmoniously on complex songs of gratitude and hope. Sweet and haunting, the melodious sounds filled the square and floated beyond. The emotional performances sent chills up Christine's spine, lifted the fine hair on her arms and neck. When they finished, she applauded enthusiastically, realizing tears stung her eyes and blurred her vision.

"They moved you."

She sniffed. "They did." She looked at Jackson. "Inspired."

His glance softened. "They always get to me, too. Miss Emily says they have the voices of angels."

Christine grunted. "That's exactly what went through my mind." She tossed her snow-cone paper into a trash drum. "Boy, I wish I could sing like that."

"You can't?"

"No. My voice is more of the screeching cat variety."

"Mine's like frogs." Jackson chuckled. "Guess we'd best leave it to them."

"Definitely."

They walked on, leaving the village, and entering a stretch of open land that looked like a big public park. People sitting on blankets, playing horseshoes and baseball dotted the expanse. Jackson skirted them and headed toward a cluster of old oaks. Some were bent and twisted with huge limbs close the ground.

He took a seat on a limb. "Ah, the shade feels good."

"It does." She sat beside him. "Isn't this the forbidden area?"

"It's a bit further in, down the path," he assured her. "We're okay here."

She scanned and saw the path in question about twenty yards away.

Jackson eyed the tree and then scooted backward into a fork. "Ah, that's better."

Christine laughed. "It looks like a chair."

"It's a great place to snooze." He grinned. "I've caught twenty winks in this spot more times than I can recall."

"Do all the village shops decorate everything up like they are now for Little Independence Day?"

"Oh, yeah. They're still working on it today. Tomorrow, everything you see will be decked out."

"I get why outsiders would come to the village for this. It's magical."

He frowned. "Outsiders can't come into the Park on Little Independence Day." He rested back against the tree and let his eyes flutter closed. "It's strictly for residents."

"Oh, I misunderstood." Christine said, then fell silent.

The late afternoon sun slanted across the stretch of lawn. Someone on the ball diamond started cheering, and others joined in. Horseshoes clacked against metal posts. Men, women and kids played together. And it seemed everyone got along and had a good time.

Peaceful. Serene. She glanced at Jackson. He'd dozed off.

The heat, little sleep in the previous few days, and the relaxed atmosphere had conspired against him. Deciding to leave him to it, Christine went for a walk—and headed toward the forbidden path.

It wasn't that she intended to deliberately break the rules. It was that she had to check as many places as possible for Caro, and there'd be no better time to check this place than now.

With every step, her guilt increased. She shouldn't be here. She shouldn't be putting off the inevitable, lying to Jackson. *A lie by omission is still a lie.* Something was definitely up with him today. He was more reserved and distant—not that anyone else would realize it, but when you've basked in his warmth and it's withdrawn, you definitely know the difference. Christine knew the difference.

Had Mr. Jenkins revealed her secret anyway? Had he told Jackson she wasn't Caroline?

She wouldn't bet a nickel either way. He'd meant what he'd said about her causing anyone harm.

Don't do this. Don't.

Walking up the wooded path, she stopped suddenly. The words sounded as clearly in her mind as if someone had spoken them. Instinctively, she made a U-turn on the path and headed right back to the tree.

The sun dipped lower still and, before she returned to her seat on the limb beside Jackson's, twilight settled in.

"Where have you been?" he asked, opening only his eyes.

"I walked a little."

"You didn't go—"

"Oh, no. Just a little way on the path, but not into the forbidden area." It was time. She'd put this off as long as she dared. Moving closer to him, she cleared her throat. She'd tell him, but she couldn't look into his eyes when she did it. "Jackson, there's something I have to tell you." She dug deep for courage and met his gaze, but now too many shadows fell across his face. She couldn't read him. Whether he was calm or in turmoil, she had no idea. "It's important."

"Oh-oh. I'm not going to like this, am I?"

"It's doubtful."

"Are you going to break my heart, Caroline?"

Christine faltered. "Can I break your heart?" she asked. "What I mean is, do I matter enough to you to be able to break your heart?"

"I think you do," he said. "And I think you know you do."

Her heart squeezed until her whole chest hurt. "I never want to break your heart, Jackson. Doing that, well, it would break mine. Just so you know." He started to say something, but she lifted a hand to stop him. "But the something I have to tell you…"

A loud, high-pitched siren like the ones used to signal tornado warnings at home ripped through the quiet.

People dropped what they were doing, ran, scattering in all directions.

"What's happening?" she asked. High-powered perimeter lights swept the grounds, fanned in every direction.

Jackson scrambled off the tree. Grabbed her hand. "Come on!"

"What is it?" she asked, running alongside him.

"A breach!"

Chapter 24

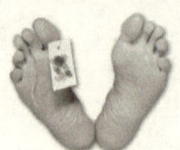

Someone had gained unauthorized entry into the Park.

Martin! Dread flooded Christine. People ran all around her, carrying balls and gloves and horseshoes. Parents carried their smaller kids, the kid's balloons bobbing overhead, anchored by strings circling their wrists. Teens ran in small packs, their faces pale, sickening fear in their eyes. "Where are we running to?"

"The cottage." Jackson spotted a boy about six who had fallen onto the grass and scooped him up. His parents were a few strides ahead and hadn't yet noted he lagged behind. Jackson sped past the father, then handed him his son. "He took a spill."

"Thanks, Jackson."

He nodded and looked back over his shoulder for Christine. She caught up with him. "When security activates the sirens, you head home," he said. "It's the most efficient way for the team to account for everyone quickly."

By the time they reached the row of cottages, Christine had a stitch in her side. She kept running, straight through to Caro's cottage. Minutes later, Christine climbed the steps then collapsed on the front porch swing, hot and winded and huffing.

Jackson scooped her up and hauled her inside. "We can't be

outside until Security signals the all-clear." He deposited her on the sofa.

She crumpled back against the cushions. "Every muscle in my body is bellowing at me."

"It's a pretty good run from the path to the cottages. With the heat, you're probably a little dehydrated." He moved to the kitchen and returned with a bottle of water. "Drink."

She took it. "Thanks."

He nodded. "Do you mind if I forage? I'm starving."

"Not at all," she said, not yet able to muster the energy to move. If her head would stop swimming, she'd feel a whole lot better. "You can bury me after you eat."

"You'll live." He grinned. "But, baby, you have got to start walking more or running or something."

"I did walk the treadmill every day—except Sunday… and when I got too busy."

"How often was that?"

"Exactly? I'm not sure."

"Roughly?"

"Three, maybe four days a week."

"So you walked four days a week? Or you got too busy to walk four times a week?"

"I guess I walked twice a week." She'd become a slug.

"How do you look so good, doing so little?" he asked. "You have a healthy appetite."

She looked good? That helped revive her. "Great metabolism, I guess."

Jackson pulled out pots and pans and began dicing vegetables and braising meat. The smells enticed her into breathing more deeply. "Whatever you're making smells good." Her arm draped over her forehead. She lifted it to expose one eye and peeked out at him. "Maybe you can wait to bury me after we eat."

"Sure thing." Jackson didn't miss a beat. "Can't expect a woman to face eternity on an empty stomach."

They'd just finished eating braised beef and vegetables and cleaning up the kitchen when a knock came at the door.

Standing in the kitchen, Christine started to answer it, but Jackson stopped her. "I'll get it." Jackson opened the door. Two men from the security team stood on the porch.

"Hey, Jackson," one of the men said. "You and Caroline okay?"

"We're fine," Jackson said. "What's going on?"

"Perimeter breach." He glanced at Caroline. "Everything's good with you?"

She nodded. Had there been other breaches? Had Caroline been through them? Or would this be new and strange and scary to her, too? "Did you find the person?"

"Not yet." He didn't look happy about having to admit that. "Stay inside until you hear the all-clear."

"Thanks," Jackson said, then shut the door.

Weak all over, Christine leaned heavily against the cabinet near the sink.

"What is it?"

"I'm worried." She looked up at him, fear burning her insides fire-hot. "The perimeter breach… It could be Martin." And here she stood unarmed, her weapon in her purse, secured in a bin inside the building near the Park entrance.

Jackson moved closer to her and held his arms open.

She walked into them and, when he closed his arms around her, she rested her head against his chest. The steady beating of his heart calmed her. "Aren't you worried that it could be Martin?"

"Not really." Jackson stroked her hair. "There's nothing to lead him here. He was detained in Even until we were long gone from there."

Jackson was right. She hadn't thought, just reacted in fear. She rewarded him by rearing back and smiling up him. "That makes sense."

"I'm a sensible man." He smiled and pecked a quick kiss to her lips. He guided her to the sofa and they sat down.

"Do these breaches happen often?"

"Rarely." Jackson shrugged. "Village visitors know about Little Independence Day and once in a while they get curious about the festivities. Probably some teenagers just wanting to see what's going on."

"It's possible," she agreed. "But if everyone here is here because they have bad trouble outside the Park, I wouldn't assume it."

"Oh, no one assumes anything. That's why we're under lockdown." Jackson sat back and stretched out his legs, crossing them at the ankle. "Lucas is excellent at his job. If he weren't, Miss Emily wouldn't tolerate him."

Christine sat with her back against the arm of the sofa and they talked about everything and nothing. Jackson fascinated her. He exhibited no fronts, no airs, no pretense or party faces, and no monumental ego. The man had been real and genuine and... perfectly comfortable with himself and others. As at home with the formal Mr. Jenkins as with the eccentric Speckles. "So how does a Dallas chef wind up playing white knight to an abused woman and bringing her all the way here?"

He smiled. "I got lucky."

Cagy response. She called him on it. "You've been acting differently all day today. Have I done something, or made you uncomfortable?"

The surprise in his expression proved he hadn't expected her to be blunt and just ask. "I don't know, Caroline. Have you?"

Her instincts had been right. Something was off. "Let's skip the dancing around. Just say what's on your mind, Jackson."

"Okay." He nodded and sat up straight, then leaned forward and braced his arms on his knees. "At the tree, you said you had something you wanted to tell me I wouldn't like." He grimaced. "Heartbreak was involved."

Two short siren blasts rent the air.

Startled, Christine jumped, a hand to her throat. "What's that?"

"The all-clear." Jackson said. "The Park is secure again."

She breathed easier. "Oh, that's good. So they've caught the intruder, then."

"It wasn't Martin," Jackson said to ease her mind. "If it had been him, Lucas would have had someone come and tell you." Jackson walked to the front door and looked outside. "No additional security guards have been posted. It definitely wasn't Martin." He made his way back to the sofa and sat down. "Now, tell me what you have to tell me. I've been trying to be patient but my mind is spinning with possibilities. Put me out of my misery."

She wished she could. "I'm afraid what I have to say is going to make you more miserable, and I really don't want to do that."

"So you've realized I'm crazy about you and you don't feel the same about me. Is that it?"

He was crazy about her? Her emotions rioted. "No, I'm kind of crazy about you, too."

"Thank God." He clasped her hand. "Then tell me. Whatever this heart-breaker is, we'll work it out."

She'd lied to him, to his family, his surrogate family. And she still hadn't found Caro. Did she dare tell him the truth?

Looking at him, she didn't dare not to—and if she didn't, Mr. Jenkins would. Hearing this from someone else would be ten times worse.

He could shun her. Boot her out. He would definitely be angry. Would he get over it, or would she lose him?

"Out with it, Caroline."

"Okay." She swallowed hard, blinked fast. "Jackson, I'm not who you think I am."

His jaw clamped down, his expression faded, and shields slid down to guard his eyes. "Who are you?"

Chapter 25

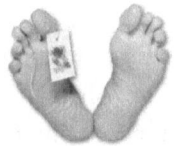

"My name is Christine Branch." She stiffened, unable to see a way this ended well. "Caroline is my sister. My twin sister, actually." She paused to try to gauge his response, but noted no change. Was that a good sign or a bad one?

"When Caro left Martin and came to Dallas, she was so broken, Jackson. Just terrified of him and what he would do." Christine took in a breath, shuttering the memory of her sister bruised and battered. "She needed time and the space to heal. Of course, Martin wouldn't give her that. Not twenty-four hours after she arrived, he had goons outside my ranchette, trying to intimidate her."

Christine couldn't sit any longer. Jackson hadn't said a word. Not a word. That couldn't be good, but at least he wasn't hauling her to the Park exit by the scruff of her neck. "I concocted this plan, Operation Switch and Bait."

He raised an eyebrow. "Do you mean Bait and Switch?"

"No, we had to switch identities first, and then I had to act as bait, to keep Martin away from her," she explained. "I became Caro and she became me. Martin knew better than to mess with me. The objective was to give Caro that time and space she needed and, on that front, the operation was successful. Caro worked with a counselor in Dallas and, I hoped, she would divorce Martin—which she did do, though it took her a while—while I convinced Martin and his henchmen I was Caroline and kept them busy chasing me."

She paused for breath and to glance at Jackson, but other than that one brow lift and question, he buried his reaction. *Definitely not good.* Her insides knotted and she paced, front door to the far end of the sofa. "That went on for months and months. Then Martin showed up at the ranchette, and Caro got fired up. She was sick of it and of him. As me, she stood up to him—at least, according to Nell—Dr. Nell Richmond, her counselor. As soon as Caro booted Martin off the ranchette—again, according to Nell—Caro realized he'd come after me to get to her. That hadn't occurred to her before then, and I certainly wasn't going to point it out." Flustered, Christine shook her hands. "The bottom line was she figured then he would hurt us both. Hurting either of us would hurt her. And we both deserved our lives back."

Christine paused to collect her thoughts and tried to calm down. Her heart strummed like a revved race-car's engine. She inhaled three deep breaths, then checked Jackson again. He hadn't moved. His face was still without expression, though he followed her every move with his eyes. How he was responding to her confession internally only God knew. Before she'd started talking, he'd seemed about to boil over. What she was saying couldn't be making things any better.

Clueless and without any insight, she went on. "Then Caro called me on Christmas. She was with you at Rose's. I know that now, though I didn't then. All she told me was that a chef from Dallas was helping her. In Even, I figured out you were the chef helping her. Thank you for that, Jackson."

No response.

Totally neutral. Dangerously neutral. "She also told me she was leaving Even within the hour for Sampson Park." Christine tilted her head. "I spent weeks looking for it but couldn't find anything. When you told me it was a private estate, that's when I discovered why I hadn't been able to find it." Christine paced the path of fifteen steps to give him time to process what she'd said. With any luck, it would also give him some perspective. "That was the last time I talked with her." Christine's nose burned, and tears threatened. "Caro stopped calling. Every Saturday, I wake up hoping I'll hear from her, and I pray so hard she will call and say she's okay, but... she hasn't."

A fist-sized knot lodged in Christine's throat. It took her a second to get it down so she could talk again. "I didn't know what to do about her being missing. Martin's people were still dogging my heels so I didn't think he had Caro—though I wondered if maybe he did and he was still hounding me to keep me from being certain he had her. That could've gone either way." She lifted a hand. "I'd flip back and forth on it, sometimes a hundred times a day. I still do."

A chill slithered through her body. She shook it off. "I had one lead. Caro had been in Even, Georgia. So I finally accepted she wasn't going to call, and if I wanted to know what had happened to her, I had to find her. I worried I'd lead Martin to her, but that was a risk I had to take. What I know for fact is that if Caro could have called, she would have. So I went to Even to find her."

Christine plucked up a pillow on the far end of the sofa and squeezed it to her chest. "I got a job at Danny's Diner to come into contact with as many residents as possible. But for eight days, no one I asked knew Caroline or had ever heard of her." And every negative response had pushed Christine a little deeper into the despair of ever finding her. "I have to say, I was losing hope. But then you and Rose showed up and I looked through the window and saw Martin standing across the street."

Choking tears and fear had Christine's throat thick and the back of her nose burning like fire. She swallowed hard, cleared her throat. "I didn't know what to do. Then Rose told Billy Joe Baker that Martin was my abusive ex. To know that, she had to have known Caro. And you said you'd protected me before..." Christine pursed her lips, blew out a short burst of air. "I guess, that's it. You've been there for the rest."

Pausing in front of him, she forced herself not to curl her hands into fists. "Jackson, please. Say something."

He looked up at her. She'd hurt him; pain and betrayal burned in his eyes.

"I didn't intend to deceive you. Really, I didn't. It's just that I was Caro all those months and I had to keep being her to give her time to get away and to look for her. I was afraid to not be her. I didn't expect you to come along and, when you did, and Rose—you knew Caro. If I'd told you I wasn't her, I feared I'd lose my one chance to find her."

Waiting. Calm. Still. And silent.

Why wouldn't he say anything? Good grief. "Jackson, I know us connecting on a personal level complicated everything. Under the circumstances, I didn't want more complications, but it just happened. You happened. I didn't really get a choice. My head said, don't get personal. My heart said, the minute we met, it was already personal." A tear trickled down her cheek. She pretended it wasn't there. "Maybe this combustion type attraction happens to you all the time, but it was a first for me. I didn't expect to feel this way. Who could have expected to? I didn't know anyone could feel this way."

Watchful but silent. Still nothing. No reaction. Not a sound.

Fear of his reaction fell to anger that he had no reaction. Enough was enough. She'd stood here and faced the music, fessing up—and she'd poured her heart out, and he says nothing? That was just wrong. "I know you're ticked off at me, but it's only fair to at least acknowledge what I've said." She frowned. "Just so you know, I'm getting pretty ticked-off myself. You better say something, Jackson."

A muscle tic started throbbing in his jaw. "You should have told me, Christine."

That's it? All this, and that's all he's got to say?

"When? At the funeral home when everything was in an uproar about Carl Wooten's flowers? On the way to Sampson Park—a place I'd failed to find a single mention of on my own? Would you have brought me here anyway? I doubt it." She shrugged. "When exactly should I have told you, Jackson? In my shoes, when would you have told me?"

"You should have trusted me."

"I didn't have the luxury of trusting you. I didn't even know you." She calmed her voice. "But I do trust you now." She met his skeptical look with a firm one. "I do, or I wouldn't be telling you anything."

He folded his arms across his chest. "Why now?" He frowned. "You've acted deliberately since Caroline arrived in Dallas. "So why did you pick now to tell me?"

She could say Mr. Jenkins knew the truth and she wanted to tell Jackson herself first. That was true, but it was actually a secondary reason, and probably best kept to herself. "Because I know you now and I trust you, and because we're here and I still can't find my sister. And honestly, because I'm scared. Really scared she's running and in danger." Christine revealed the primary reason for her revelation. "She's not cut out for it. If she had been, I wouldn't have had to switch lives with her in the first place."

"Maybe she wasn't cut out for it then, but clearly she is now or she'd be here." Jackson sat back. "Caroline told me she had a sister —when I was bringing her here. She didn't tell me you were twins or that you had been posing as her, or about your Operation Switch and Bait. You could have been killed, Christine. What were you thinking, taking on those kinds of risks?"

"I was thinking I had to help protect my sister from a monster."

"You're lucky you didn't wake up dead."

"I won't lie and say there weren't hairy moments where I feared exactly that would happen. There were." Jackson was angry. Upset. Maybe even furious. But he was still totally in control. How could he do that? Sitting where he was, she'd be screaming like a banshee. Something was definitely off. "Caroline didn't tell you anything about Operation Switch and Bait."

Jackson shook his head, confirming it. "On the way down, we made a pit-stop and an attorney took care of all her legal needs."

"Legal needs?" Christine asked.

"She wanted to make some arrangements, in case she had to start over fresh with a new identity."

Christine stilled. Not liking where her mind was going at all. "So you were attracted to her from the start?"

"Good grief, no. I wasn't at all attracted to her." He shot Christine a look that showed how far off-base that assumption had been. "That's exactly why I thought I was losing my mind at the diner in Even. I took one look at you, and it was like being zapped by a thunderbolt. I should have known right then you weren't the same woman."

A thunderbolt. That sounded pretty good. Oh... *Oh wait.* Christine went statue-still. "Are you saying you knew all along I wasn't Caroline?"

"I *should* have known it, I said." He rubbed at his neck. "I guess I knew it, but I didn't really know I knew it... until yesterday." He reasoned through it all, then added, "You look alike but your personalities are different. You don't react the way she would."

"Is that what gave me away?"

"My reaction to you is what gave you away," he said. "But your reactions made me think to recognize it." He paused. "Something else entirely gave me proof."

"What?"

"Your kiss." He looked up at her. "I spent a lot of time with your sister and not once did I feel even a twinge of attraction much less the desire to kiss her. Yet with you, it was kiss you or drown. I wouldn't make it unless I kissed you. That's when I knew for fact you weren't Caroline."

His disclosure explained a lot. "So that's why you were acting differently today."

He nodded. "Ticked off at you for lying. Trying to figure out why you'd lie to me. Whether you were faking having feelings for me for some other purpose. Hurt because you weren't telling me the truth and frankly shocked you were good and pulling it off to the point that even with doubts, I was falling for you. That grated on me something fierce. But mostly I didn't know who you were or why you were faking being Caroline."

She sat down beside him and risked stroking his face. "I lied. I lacked trust. I hurt you and I was hurting, too. But I have never, not once, faked my feelings for you, Jackson."

He just looked at her. "You sure I'm not the means to an end and that's it?"

"I'm sure." She worried her lower lip, studied his reaction. "You believe me but you're still furious with me, aren't you?"

"I am, but I get it."

Surprise rippled through her. "You do?"

He nodded. "We do what we have to do to protect those we love. Sometimes those ways are ones we expect, and sometimes they're not."

"Jackson?"

"What?"

"I'm sorry I hurt you." She leaned closer and kissed his lips.

A long minute later, she released him and met his gaze. "You kissed me back, so I'm guessing you'll forgive me."

"Eventually," he admitted. "Provided we live long enough."

"You say that as if we're in danger." When he didn't dispute her, she went serious. "Are we in danger here?"

"Yeah, we are." He stared off at the wall, near the front door.

"From who?"

"Everybody," he confessed, and hauled himself to his feet. "You stay put. I'll be back to get you for the Little Independence Day celebration tomorrow." His eyes narrowed. "Don't leave the cottage until then."

"Why are you worried? Why are we in danger from everyone?" She lifted her arms. "I thought Sampson Park was a safe haven."

"It is," he said. "But only for invited guests."

She stilled. "That doesn't include me."

"Let me work through this." He opened the door. "I need expert advice."

"What kind of expert advice?"

"Lester's." Jackson shut the door.

It echoed a hollow *wham*.

Chapter 26

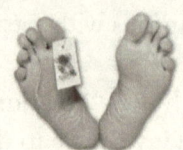

Jackson rushed into the manor house, but didn't see Lester. In the kitchen, he spotted Ned at the stove, stirring something in a large pot. "Have you seen Lester?"

"Not lately." Ned rubbed his fingertips, sprinkling in salt. Fresh minced garlic smelled strong, wafting in the rising steam.

Jackson spun around to continue his search and collided with Mr. Jenkins. "Sorry."

"Come with me," he said, his voice calm and stiff.

In silence, Mr. Jenkins led Jackson out the front door and across the moonlit lawn to the gazebo by the lake. It stood empty, confusing Jackson. "Lester's not here. Why—?"

"Sit down, Jackson." Mr. Jenkins pointed to the slatted seat running along the gazebo's inner perimeter. "You've just left Caroline, correct?"

Bewildered, Jackson nodded.

"Did you figure it out yourself, or did she tell you?" he asked.

Sticky hot, Jackson didn't want to touch that question with a ten-foot pole. "Excuse me?"

"Your hearing isn't impaired." Mr. Jenkins frowned. "Don't

make me repeat myself, and don't play games with me, Jackson. Not about this."

He frowned. The gig was definitely up. "I knew it."

"When?"

He looked into the man's eyes. They were deadly serious. "When I kissed her."

"Really?" His brows shot up on his forehead. "Not before then?"

"Not for sure," Jackson hedged, then confessed. "But I had strong suspicions."

"So she didn't tell you the truth."

"Actually, she did." He shifted on his seat and repeated the upshot of what Christine had told him. "I should have known from the minute I first saw her."

"Why?"

"I wasn't at all attracted to Caroline, but Christine…"

Awareness rippled through Mr. Jenkins' eyes and across his stern face. "You love her?"

Jackson shrugged. "I'm not sure what love looks like, Mr. Jenkins, much less what it feels like. But she gets to me."

"Relationships have been built on far less and endured." Mr. Jenkins took two steps, then turned and took two more steps back toward Jackson. "I take it you are looking for Lester to tell him about her and to discuss what to do."

Jackson nodded. "That was my thought."

"In a word, don't." Mr. Jenkins advised.

"Why not?" If anyone knew how to handle this sticky wicket, it'd be Lester.

"Because she's not one of us. If you tell Lester, he'll certainly tell Miss Emily. He has no choice. And neither will she. The committee will be convened and—"

Seeing where this was going, Jackson cut in. "I can't not tell them, Mr. Jenkins."

"Think, Jackson," he whispered on a rush. "You know the rules here. The moment you say anything to any of them, you will be in the same jeopardy she is in."

The truth hit Jackson. "You knew she wasn't Caroline, too."

"Of course. I knew it immediately, though I did have an advantage over you." He hiked his chin. "Caroline and I have had tea most afternoons since shortly after her arrival. She confided many things to me, including all about her sister and their Operation Switch and Bait."

"Why did she do that?"

"So I would charge her phone battery."

"She had a phone—in the Park?" Jackson couldn't keep his surprise to himself.

Mr. Jenkins nodded. "On arrival, she had two. One she left with Lucas and her special phone, she smuggled into the Park. Before her arrival, she had used it for the sole purpose of contacting her sister, and she needed the battery charged to phone and let Christine know she was safe."

"You did it?" Jackson stood up, stunned.

"I brought it back to the manor house to charge and, eventually, I did charge it. But when I returned it to her, she tried to use it and the phone didn't work."

"Course not," Jackson said. "Lucas's scramblers."

"His what?" Mr. Jenkins looked confused.

"There are security scramblers in the Park, to keep phones from working anywhere except at the manor house."

"I wasn't aware of that," Mr. Jenkins said. "We—Caroline and I —supposed the phone was somehow damaged. She was very distressed at not being able to phone Christine."

"Christine has been worried out of her mind, too." Snakes coiled in Jackson's stomach. "So if you know all this, then Miss Emily... already knows?" Jackson couldn't imagine a scenario where Mr. Jenkins hadn't told her. Yet at the conference meeting this morning, she hadn't said a word or even hinted at having other information...

"I know you don't expect me to answer that."

Jackson was doomed either way. "You told her. Miss Emily knows it all." Jackson gained his feet, worried. "Why didn't she warn me?"

"I'm sure she had her reasons. She always does." Mr. Jenkins rubbed at the back of his neck. "Perhaps it was a trust test."

"If so, I failed." Jackson let out a resigned sigh. "What am I going to do?"

"You do have a dilemma," Mr. Jenkins said. "Christine is an outsider, and you brought her here."

"But I thought she was Caroline."

"I know." He shrugged. "But you know what you thought won't matter. The rules are the rules for a reason. The safety of everyone here depends on them. If she'd come to Sampson Park as herself, as Caroline's sister, that would have been one thing. But to impersonate Caroline?" Mr. Jenkins shook his head. "The committee will not ignore that infraction—and Miss Emily will have no choice but to inform it."

Dread dragged through Jackson. The whole committee would be calling for their heads, Christine's and his. Worse, the associates had been arriving all day, and they'd weigh in as well. Jackson sought a way out, but there just wasn't one. "They're going to kill us."

"Or make you wish they had." Mr. Jenkins tilted his head. "Now, where is Caroline—the real one?"

"How would I know?" Jackson asked. "I told you, when Caroline ended Operation Switch and Bait, Christine stayed Caroline to go to Even to find her. She hasn't. Neither have I."

Worry clouded Mr. Jenkins' expression.

Disappointment slid through Jackson. "I take it you don't know where she is either."

Mr. Jenkins nodded that he didn't. "Martin?"

"It's possible, but my gut says no. He wouldn't have stayed on Christine. My guess is, if he had her, he would make the two of them disappear."

"Most likely, you're right." Mr. Jenkins sigh heaved his shoulders. "One day she was here, then she wasn't."

"She couldn't just vanish."

He frowned. "She did."

Jackson rubbed his forehead. "So what do I do now?"

Mr. Jenkins rubbed his jaw, his gaze distant and unfocused. "Nothing."

"Nothing?" Of all the answers he could have been given, that one he never saw coming. "I can't do nothing. Deceive Lester and Miss Emily? Rose and Matthew?" Jackson grunted. "They have arrived, right?"

Mr. Jenkins nodded. "Earlier this evening."

"Rose is going to be so ticked off."

"Will she?" Mr. Jenkins looked thoughtful.

"If she has to die and move again, she'll be furious." Jackson knew that for fact. "She's still assembling her team in Even."

Mr. Jenkins tapped a fingertip to his lips. "But she sideswiped Martin in Matthew's Jag to run interference for you, didn't she?"

Jackson nodded, unsure where he was going with this. "Yes."

His eyes narrowed, bunching his thick brows between them. "Knowing you and Christine were coming to Sampson Park."

"Well, yes, and no. Rose thought it was me and Caroline. Then, I thought so, too."

"But Rose aided you in getting the woman here."

Jackson picked up on Mr. Jenkins line of thought. "Matthew, too, but we can't mention that. No sense dragging them into trouble with me."

"I have an idea." Mr. Jenkins seemed far less troubled. "You go on back to the manor house and grab some sleep. You look worn out."

"I am, but who can sleep now—with all this—?"

"Rest, Jackson."

"Then what?"

"Leave it to me," Mr. Jenkins said. "Tomorrow, you pick up Christine and go to the Little Independence Day celebration as planned."

"What are you going to do?"

"It's best you don't know…" Mr. Jenkins took off back toward the manor house.

Jackson wanted to argue, but good sense won out. What he didn't know, he couldn't tell… or be forced to admit. "Thanks," he called out, hoping he wasn't making the biggest mistake of his life.

CHRISTINE DRAGGED herself out of bed and put on a pot of coffee. If she could hook up to an IV, she'd stand a chance of feeling human today. Since she couldn't, she'd pull herself together as best she could and be grateful for whatever she got.

After Jackson had left the cottage last night, she'd pulled on black slacks and a t-shirt and then searched the Park for Caro until dawn. She'd been tempted to head straight back to the forbidden area, but it'd be just her luck that Lucas had alarms all over it. She didn't want to risk tripping them and sending the whole Park into another chaotic lock-down. ·

She'd walked the banks of the lake, the little bridge to the village. She'd hiked all the way out to the ranch, but couldn't search it thoroughly. If she'd gotten the animals stirred up, the people in the bunkhouse, if not the main house, would have come running, probably armed.

On the way back, she'd hung close to the edge of the woods. Small wildlife she couldn't see but heard scurried around, and she prayed hard she didn't stumble over any snakes or alligators. Jackson claimed both and more were natural to the area.

By the time she made it back to the cottage, the sky was threatening pink. She warned herself not to cut the time that close again; she could have easily been spotted. People here got out of bed early. As it was, she'd had a near-miss encounter with a man watering in the community garden.

Finally, the coffee was ready. She poured a cup full, and went onto the porch to drink it. Squinting up at the sun, she checked the shadows under the giant agapanthus near the street. It was about eleven o'clock. Not having a watch wasn't so bad, once you figured out how to gauge time.

Her stomach rumbled.

Back inside, she refilled her cup from the pot, wishing she'd brought a few of the pastries home with her from the village yester-day. Instead, she slapped together a peanut butter sandwich, certain Jackson would have a stroke at her eating habits.

Dropping onto a seat at the table, she grunted. Forbidden or not, she was going to check out that secret area. It was the only place left to look for Caro. What was the worst that could happen?

More awake and alert, she topped off her cup and then took a steaming sip. Jackson—the whole bunch of them—would be ticked off. Lucas wouldn't be pleased, either. If she had to, she could always tell them all the truth. Now that Jackson knew it, a confession wouldn't be the end of the world. So they'd be upset. Deceiving people did that. But if she'd concluded Caro wasn't in the Park and she explained… really, how bad could it get? It wasn't like they'd kill her or anything.

She finished her sandwich and went for cup four, feeling a lot more energetic. Hoping the feeling didn't fizzle before the festivities began, she showered and tossed opened the closet, looking for some-thing appropriate to wear.

A sea-green sundress caught her eye. If her hair were still red, she would have looked right past the dress but, as a blonde, the dress would be a good look for her. She put on the flowing dress and a pair of strappy sandals, then pinched her cheeks—which the heat would have flaming within minutes of stepping outside—then swiped on a little lip gloss. Twisting her hair up into a knot to get it off her neck, she snapped in a barrette to hold it in place.

A mirror check surprised her. She looked like Caro.

Her heart hitched and Christine squeezed her eyes shut. "I will find you. Whatever it takes, I will find you."

Chapter 27

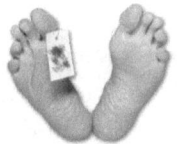

In the village, people filled the street, milling from vendor to vendor. From strings looping their wrists, kids and many adults, floated balloons, munched on funnel cakes and cotton candy.

A group of seniors sat at a table in the shade, laughing and chatting. Some ate shrimp stew and some enjoyed thick slices of apple pie topped with homemade ice-cream. Beyond them, a barrel Christine had seen yesterday and wondered what it was for, now held a tabletop. Four white-haired men, including Speckles, sat in rockers around it, playing checkers and sipping at what looked like mugs of ice-cold beer.

All the sidewalks were shaded with fabric awnings, giving the vendors who had set up tables in front of their stores respite from the blazing sun. Huge bows had been tied to everything stationary, the ribbon ends left long to dance in the breeze created by foot-pumped fans being pedaled by teens. Large metal washtubs and bins lined the outer walk, filled with sodas and mason jars of tea resting on beds of crushed ice. In the middle of the street near the big clock, a cluster of residents sat seated, playing musical instruments. From fiddles to trumpets to flutes. Beyond them, others coupled and danced to the music. Others danced alone, and when some took a break, still others joined in, and kept the music and the dancing going.

"This is great." Christine smiled at Jackson. "It reminds me of the old-time ice-cream socials."

"I can't say I've been to an ice-cream social," he said.

"We had them at church, when I was a kid. In-gatherings, they called them. Everyone would bring a casserole and play games, and of course, make home-made ice-cream."

"If I'd known that, I'd have spent more time at church. Rose was always dragging me to services at one or the other. She thought attending church would keep me out of trouble."

"Did it?"

"Mostly, worrying what she'd do to me if I got in trouble kept me out of trouble." He grinned. "She took me to Sunday School nearly every week."

Something in his voice warned Christine there was more to the story. "But…"

"But I'd go in the front door then sneak out the back, find a tree, and take a snooze."

"Jackson." The reprimand was only half-hearted. "You didn't get caught?"

"I did." He nodded. "I woke up and the preacher was sitting beside me on the grass."

She tried not to laugh. "What did he say?"

"He asked me what I was doing there."

"What did you tell him?"

"I said I was having myself a talk with God."

"And he believed you?"

"Seemed to." Jackson grunted. "Actually, Pastor Brown was a wise one. He said sometimes he liked to get off by himself and talk to God, too. It was easier to hear what He had to say when a body could get to the quiet." Jackson dipped his head. "Pastor Brown had a harping wife and four daughters."

She laughed hard. "Not much quiet in his world, I expect."

"I expect not." Jackson grinned. "The thing is, we sat there a long time and never said a word. Then, he let out this big sigh, and said, 'Ah, that's much better.' He thanked me for sharing my quiet with him, went inside, and gave his sermon."

"What did you do?"

"I followed him," Jackson said. "I had been quiet and listened but I couldn't hear what God said, so I figured I'd go listen to what He told Pastor Brown."

"How did that work out?"

"Well, we met under that tree for quiet talks with God the rest of the time I went to that church and I never missed a sermon, so I guess it worked out pretty good."

Christine smiled. "God does work in mysterious ways."

Jackson slanted her an amused look. "Don't He though?"

A pungent smell wafted to her. She followed it and saw the biggest pots she'd ever seen. Burners burned, open flames beneath them. "What are they cooking?"

Jackson sniffed. "Shrimp—likely corn on the cob and new pota-toes, too—or maybe crawfish."

"Spicy smell."

"Spicy taste, too." He grabbed her hand. "Let's have some."

They walked over to one of the plywood tables covered in butcher paper. People stood around it, filling plates from a mound of food that had been dumped in its center. Jackson filled two plates, then looked over at her. "What kind of sauce do you want?"

The squirt bottles, she surmised. One was red, the other white. "What's the difference?"

"One sets your mouth on fire and the other doesn't."

"The non-fire one, please."

He grabbed the white and squirted some on her plate, then on his own. "Good call," he whispered. "The seafood is spicy enough on its own. Grab us some drinks and let's find a shade tree."

She snagged some napkins and two mason jars full of tea from a bin and they walked away from the fray, beyond the horseshoe game, to the tree where Jackson had caught twenty winks in its forked limb.

Christine sat down on the grass and lowered her plate in front of her.

"Not afraid you'll mess up your dress?" When she nodded she wasn't afraid, Jackson sat down beside her. "You look pretty wearing it, I have to say."

"Thank you." He looked really good to her, too. Jeans and a sky-blue shirt that made his eyes look amazing. "If you'd ever seen me try to balance a plate on my knees, you'd know why I'm on the ground."

"It's easier to peel the shrimp not doing a balance act."

"I'd be wearing them." She shelled one, dragged it through the sauce, then popped it into her mouth. Flavor excited her taste buds. "Mmm, good."

"You make fast work of shelling. You've done this before."

"I have," she admitted. "Though this sauce is new to me."

"Remoulade," he said. "Mayo, Creole mustard, horseradish, pickle juice, a little Tabasco and garlic. This was made yesterday."

"How do you know that?"

"The flavors have had time to mingle and marry." He took a bite of corn. "Takes at least half a day to get that blend."

They ate and talked about all kinds of things. Everything except Caro. When they finished their meal, Christine eased into Jackson's tree-fork and leaned back. Her all-night jaunt through the Park, the warm breeze and her full tummy conspired. "I could take a nap right here with zero guilt."

"Go ahead," Jackson said. "I'll try my hand at a game of horseshoes."

"Have you played before?"

"No, but how hard can it be?"

Famous last words. Smiling, Christine rested back against the tree-fork and settled in. Just as she dozed off, Jackson came back over to her. "I didn't fare so well at horseshoes. It's harder than it looks. I'm going to give baseball a shot." He pointed further away, to a baseball diamond.

She cranked open an eye. "Sounds good."

He headed in that direction and, hearing voices coming from behind her, she sat up. People were walking down the path—to and from the forbidden area! It must be okay to go there on Little Independence Day. Seizing her chance, she scooted off the rough limb and headed down the path.

A couple coming toward her passed, then a man walking alone. Both returning from...whatever was ahead of her. Flowering crepe myrtles lined the path and huge bunches of blooming wisteria wound through the trees. Christine walked on, beyond a bend, and came to an abrupt stop.

A cemetery?

She'd asked what was in the forbidden area and Lucas had said nothing. Wildlife, and that was it. Miss Emily's private reserve.

It didn't look like nothing to Christine. Dozens and dozens of headstones lay in uniform rows. Two stones had white cloths draped over them. She slowed her pace and walked down the rows, reading the names. *Miss Emily, Darby, Lester, Daisy Grant, Mark Jensen...* Wait. Christine stopped. Jackson Grant had called Rose *Daisy* on the phone—just after his sister had rammed Matthew's Jag into Martin's Lexus. This couldn't be a coincidence. Christine slowly moved on. *Jenkins, Speckles, Abigail ...*

Christine's mouth went dry. Her hand shook. She lifted the edge of the nearest headstone covered in cloth. *Caroline Branch Easton.*

"Jackson!" Christine screamed, and kept screaming.

IN RIGHT FIELD, Jackson heard someone running toward him and turned toward the sound. "Mr. Jenkins?" Why would the unflappable Mr. Jenkins be running, looking scared to death?

"Come. Now! It's Chr... Caro... *her!*"

Jackson dropped the glove and followed, running full speed toward the tree where he'd left Christine. "What happened?"

Flustered and red-faced, Mr. Jenkins' voice filled with dread and regret. "Infernal woman went into the forbidden area."

"Oh, no." Jackson muttered under his breath. "What did she see?"

"What do you think? She saw everything—including Caroline's headstone!"

"God help us." Jackson ran full out, found Christine sitting on the ground with her knees drawn up close to her body, her arms curled around her knees, and slumped over, crying her heart out near Caroline's headstone.

He stopped running, and walked up behind her.

"I called you." Christine looked up at him, pain ravaging her face. "But you didn't come."

"I didn't hear you." He sat down beside her. "But I'm here now."

"She's dead, Jackson." Stricken by grief, Christine touched the cold stone. "Caroline is dead."

He softened his voice, noted Mr. Jenkins keeping watch on the path. "There are stones for Miss Emily and Darby, too."

"And Lester and Mr. Jenkins," she said, sniffing. "But I've seen and talked to them. Not Caroline."

"It's okay, Christine."

"Okay?" She looked ready to murder him. "I'm sitting at my sister's grave—my only relative in the whole world, Jackson —and you're telling me it's okay?" He touched her arm and she flung his fingertips away from her. "No. No, it is not okay."

"You had tea with Miss Emily and Darby. Did they look dead to you?"

Christine stilled. She had, and Mr. Jenkins, too. "So what is this? Is everyone in Sampson Park dead?" She couldn't begin to wrap her mind around this.

In a sense, yes, they are," he said.

"What?" The horror of that response would be with him all the days of his life.

"Symbolically," he explained. "They're dead symbolically."

"I don't understand."

His expression closed. "And I'm not at liberty to explain."

"Don't you dare tell me that." She pointed to Caroline's stone. "Her name being etched into that stone entitles me to an explanation and I want it. Is my sister dead or alive?"

"I'm really not sure."

"Those are not the words I want to hear, Jackson Grant. But... why aren't you upset?"

"I am upset. How could I see you like this and not be upset?"

"You're not making a spitting bit of sense." Christine couldn't stop the flow of tears from starting up again. "Caroline is my sister. I've given up my life to protect her. If she's dead, then I failed. I'm devastated—and if you at all cared for me, you'd know that and you'd be devastated, too."

"Christine, don't." Jackson cupped her chin and turned her head, pressing her to look into his eyes. "Death is relative—at least, it is here. Even if Caroline is dead, she's not dead."

"What?" Crazy. Her puzzlement cued him flawlessly. To her, he sounded crazy.

"People die here all the time, for all kinds of reasons. Some die and then come here. Some die after they're here—mostly so they can keep breathing. I don't know where Caroline is, so I don't know if she's dead or alive, but I'd bank money that wherever she is, and dead or alive, she's breathing just fine."

Christine's eyes narrowed and she let that disclosure sink in. "The funeral homes. Symbolic deaths. Faked deaths... Is this about fresh starts?"

He nodded. "Sometimes to live, ya gotta die."

"To get away from others trying to hurt you, or to shed the past that's killing you inside." Christine tore her gaze from the headstone, riveted Jackson. "Is that it? This is about healing?"

He hesitated. "I can't say another word about any of this. I can't. We've got to get out of here. If anyone found out I told you as much as I have, well, it wouldn't be good for either of us."

"Too late." Lester stepped out from behind an oak. "You're right, Jackson. It wouldn't be good—and it isn't."

Others joined Lester. Miss Emily. Darby. Dr. Rossi. Mr. Jenkins. Lucas. Rose and Matthew. "Oh, boy."

"Indeed." Miss Emily frowned. "Lucas, please place these two under house arrest."

"Miss Emily!" Jackson stood up and pulled Christine to her feet. "You're putting us in jail?"

"House arrest." Lester's frown deepened. "You deserve worse, son."

He was serious. Jackson swiveled his gaze to his sister. "Rose?"

"Sorry." She raised her hands. "You deserve exactly what you get. You know the rules, Jackson Lee Grant. Every action causes a reaction."

Miss Emily grunted. "You're not going to jail, my boy. You either, Christine," she said, revealing she knew the truth. "Until the committee decides what to do with you, I'm sequestering you in the cottages. Lucas, take Christine to her cottage and put Jackson in the blue one next door to it." She turned her gaze back to Jackson. "Don't mess with me on this. Either of you. Stay put and follow orders until the committee's decision is made." Looking at Jackson, she sniffed. "I can't believe you put us all in jeopardy, Jackson."

"She's Caroline's sister and Caroline is missing. She's been terrified," he said, attempting to explain.

"So why didn't you tell us that? Why didn't either of you?" Miss Emily swiped at the air. "Never mind. Whatever the reason, you've made us all vulnerable."

"It's all my fault." Christine let her gaze slide from Miss Emily to the other end of the line at Rose and Matthew. "Jackson thought I was Caroline. When we got here, he had no idea—"

"Enough!" Miss Emily lifted a staying hand. "Lucas, take them."

"Speckles," Lucas called out.

"You'll have to walk back with them," Miss Emily said to Lucas. "I need Speckles myself."

Ashamed, Christine glanced at the row of graves, not at all sure she and Jackson wouldn't soon have stones beside them. Real ones.

Chapter 28

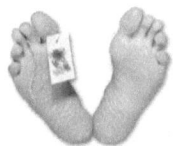

For hours, Christine paced the cottage floor. She couldn't stand this. Fear and doubt and all the uncertainty of what the committee would do to them was making her crazy.

She'd already taken two showers, changed into exercise pants and a soft t-shirt and now she was replaying every word and glance and questioning every nuance of the entire exchange with the others in the forbidden area. Until the cemetery ordeal, she had been relaxed here and had felt safe. Now she felt like a prisoner. She *was* a prisoner.

And that emitted an entirely different feel to Sampson Park.

Fed up with her own thoughts, she grabbed a bowl of walnuts from the kitchen, set them on a little table beside the side window in the living room that faced Jackson's cottage, then lifted the window open. She tossed a nut at his window. It pinged against the glass.

She waited but Jackson didn't appear. She tossed another walnut. And then another.

On the fifth walnut that hit the glass, he appeared—and got smacked right in the head with number six.

"Yeow!" He jerked backward, grabbing his forehead. "Christine? What are you doing?"

"Sorry," she said, hoping he and not the entire neighborhood would hear her. "I wanted to apologize again. This is all my fault, Jackson."

"It's okay. I told you, I understand. To protect the people we love, we do expected and unexpected things. I've done it myself."

She hiked a hip and sat on the windowsill. "I don't understand something."

"What's that?" He noted her sitting and mirrored her in his own window.

"When you went to play baseball, I saw people coming and going down the path into the forbidden area. I figured they were allowed there because of the holiday."

"Well, that explains that." He reached behind him and grabbed a can of cola. "I wondered why you'd deliberately do something you knew was off-limits. Course, when I mentioned that to Lucas, he informed me of your midnight jaunt."

"Jaunt? What midnight jaunt?" No one had followed her. She'd bet on that.

"You scouted half the park between the time I left you and daylight, Christine."

She couldn't deny it. Not that there was any reason to deny anything now. "I was looking for Caro."

"Figured that." He cracked the walnut and pulled the nut from the shell. "So did Lucas."

"Does he know where she is?"

"If so, he didn't tell me." Jackson shrugged. "Not that he would tell me anything now. My credibility is kind of shot around here."

He sounded sorry about that, and guilt pounded into Christine. "I'm taking full responsibility. Surely the committee will let you go. I'm going to do everything I can to restore your reputation, Jackson."

"You can't. I broke the trust," he said. "Not about you, but in what I told you at the cemetery. I knew better when I did it, but you were so upset. I couldn't stand seeing you like that."

She had been devastated. "Seeing Caro's headstone was quite a shock."

"I'm sure it was." He popped the nut into his mouth and slowly chewed. "You know, Caroline told me on the way here she wished we could meet. She thought we'd be perfect for each other."

Christine nodded. "She told me that too—when I talked to her on Christmas."

"I think she might have been right." Jackson sobered. "I've seen plenty of women upset, but none of them did to me what seeing you in tears did. Man…"

"For what it's worth, I think she was right, too." Christine dropped her voice. "I don't have a ton of experience with relationships, but I understand all the fuss about them a lot better now." She twisted, rested her back against the window-frame. "Have you had serious relationships?"

"A couple I thought were serious. Well, pretty serious." He chewed a nut then swallowed. "But something was missing. I didn't know what."

"I didn't think I wanted one. Probably because of my parents," she said. "When they died, I hurt so bad for so long… I never wanted to care that much about anyone else ever again. Well, except for Caro. But then I already loved her because, well, that's what sisters do."

"I know what you mean. Rose was the rock—even when our mother was there. She wasn't much on mothering. If it weren't for Rose… she's always loved me. I've always loved her, too. But to risk falling for a woman who could or would do what our mother did? That wasn't happening."

"I'm right there with you. People say if you fear being hurt so much you refuse to love, then you've blown your chance at it without trying. I say those people have never loved and lost or they wouldn't spout off to other people like that."

"So you could never love me?" Jackson asked.

"It's a scary thought. To risk it, I mean. But the truth is, I—I wouldn't object to finding out," she hedged. "Would you risk it?"

He hesitated a long time. "I think you—we—might be worth the risks."

Unable not to, she smiled. "I hope we get the chance." *House arrest.* Good grief, who knew what that meant? "How long do you think they'll keep us here?"

"No telling." Jackson frowned. "It's a serious offense and they won't take it lightly. That much, I do know."

Christine swallowed hard. "But they won't really kill us, will they? I mean dead in the permanently dead sense."

"If they feel they must to protect the Park and those in it, I think they would." Jackson's sigh carried to her. "Actually, I know they would."

That was not the answer she'd wanted, but it was the truth as he saw it, and he knew these people a lot better than she did. "I'm thinking about the words written on the bronze at the foot of the bridge. The ones about Miss Emily." Christine let the words replay in her mind. "I think that woman would kill us to keep the people here safe."

"No doubt." He agreed. "She died herself to start this place. Then died again to protect it."

Christine tried not to gasp. "If she'd do it to herself…"

"Exactly." Jackson looked desolate. "We don't stand a chance."

They fell silent for a long moment, stewing in their own thoughts.

"Jackson?"

"Mmm?"

"I really am sorry."

"I know, honey. Me, too."

"What are you sorry for?" she asked. "All you did was help a desperate woman find safety and try to protect another you thought had lost her mind. Well, her memory."

"I'd like the chance to see where things go for us," he admitted. "I think it could be… special. I know for fact it's rare."

"Me, too." She straightened. "I'm not going to give up on us. I'm just not. After all we've been through, we deserve a chance— and that's just what I'm going to tell that committee."

"Um, I don't think we'll get to do much telling. I think we'll be mostly listening."

"Then I'll hope for that, too." She fell silent and stared at the sky. "The sun will be coming up soon."

"We'd better call it a night then. See you at sundown?" he asked.

She smiled. "Your window or mine?"

"Uh, both."

"Works for me. Sundown, then."

Chapter 29

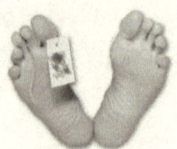

At sundown, Christine heard something ping at the window.

She rushed around the little table, went to the window, and opened it wide. "Hi." Just looking at him left her breathless.

He held a rope in his hand. "Catch the end of this." He tossed the rope to her. Something heavy and metal slid off and landed on her foot. "Ouch!"

"Sorry," he said. "It's a pulley. Put it back on the rope."

"Why?"

"So I can send you over some food." He told her how to rig the ropes and then attached a heavy pillowcase. "Pull."

She fed the rope, hand over hand, until she could reach the pillowcase. "Hey, take-out! This is awesome, Jackson."

He laughed. "I figure your body has had all the junk food it can take."

"I am about out of peanut butter."

He scrunched his face, twisting his lips.

"So what's in here?" She peeked inside the white case.

"Chinese." He shrugged. "I had a lot of time on my hands and little to do, so I cooked."

"I love Chinese." She smiled and inhaled. "Sesame chicken, spring rolls, fried rice and vegetables. It's the mother-lode!"

He laughed deeper. "No fortune cookie. Sorry."

"Would it be rude to eat while we talk?" She was starved.

"No, I waited for you, so we could eat together."

By moonlight instead of candlelight, they had an intimate dinner. He, in his window, and she in hers. And they shared good conversation. Life, death and the universe conversation about things that matter. And about little, everyday nothings that didn't matter at all.

"Jackson, I'm surprised you haven't been snatched up by a dozen women. You cook, you understand people and what's important in life, and you have a great sense of humor and a huge heart."

He blushed a little and a reluctant smile curved his lips. "If you keep this up, I'm going to have a big head, too."

"Facts don't inflate the ego. Just flattery. I don't do flattery." She grinned. "Did you make dessert?"

"Depends."

"On what?"

"On whether or not you'll share that bottle of wine I saw in your fridge."

"Of course, I will." She set her plate aside and crawled down from the window. On retrieving the wine from the fridge, she sent it to him in the pillowcase over the rope pulley. "There you go."

"I need the corkscrew."

"I'll have to find one. Send the case back." She rummaged through three drawers and then located it. Back at the window, she slipped it into the waiting case then sent it to him.

"Thanks." He brought the case inside his window so she couldn't see what he was putting inside, then attached it to the rope and sent the case back to her. "Your reward."

She opened it and saw her favorite. "You made me brownies?"

"I did."

Tender, she tilted her head. She'd mentioned that to him once. The first time they'd gone into the village. Once, and he had remembered it. "Thank you, Jackson." Biting into the brownie, she murmured. "Oh, that's good."

"Glad you like it."

He had no idea. "Jackson, I'm a connoisseur on brownies. Wine? What I know about it would fill a thimble. But I know brownies. They're my turf."

"So how do mine stack up against the competition?"

"Seriously?"

"Yeah, be totally honest," he said. "I've been perfecting the recipe for a while now."

This was important to him. "How long a while?"

"Two years, so far." He flipped a hand waving the questions away. "Just tell me how you like it—and no sparing my feelings."

"Straight up," she said, "these are the best brownies I've ever had in my mouth. On five continents, bar none."

"Score." He smiled. "I'm seriously thinking about marketing them."

"You definitely should. I could probably keep you in business all by myself. Course I'd weigh nine hundred pounds and exist in a permanent diabetic coma, but it'd mostly be worth it."

"We really need to have a serious talk about your health habits. Here you are doing everything you can to make me fall in love with you and I know better than to let myself do it."

"Why?" Who knew what tangent he'd zoom off on now?

"You don't eat right, you don't exercise—hooked up with you, I'd be a widower really young." He frowned at her. "For the record, I think I'd be ticked-off if you died and left me, Christine."

"Well, I guess after all I've already cost you, that would be an awful thing to do—to make you a really young widower, I mean."

"Glad you agree. We'll work on it all together. I could do more myself on that front." He tilted his head. "So what's on your top-ten list of things to do in your life?"

"I'll answer, but you have to answer, too."

"Why not? We have until dawn."

They did. And they both knew they'd talk until the very last minute before sunrise.

AT DUSK, the committee broke discussions for the second night and Miss Emily and Lester disappeared.

"Where are they off to in such a hurry?" Rose asked Mr. Jenkins.

He cleared his throat. The entire household was upended and edgy due to this business with Christine and Jackson. "I couldn't say for sure."

"But you have your suspicions," Matthew suggested. Rose elbowed him, and he rubbed his ribs. "What? He does have suspicions. Look at his face."

Mr. Jenkins lowered his voice. "If one wanted to find out, I'd suggest one begin looking on cottage row."

"Cottage row?" Rose gasped. "That's where Jackson and Christine are sequestered, isn't it?"

"Why, yes, Rose." Mr. Jenkins nodded. "I believe it is."

He knew darned well it was. "Where's Darby?"

"I can't say."

She was on cottage row, too.

"Is everyone there?" Matthew asked before Rose could.

"Is everyone where?" Mr. Jenkins gave Matthew a blank look. "I have no idea what either of you are talking about."

"Come on, Matthew." Rose headed for the door. "Hurry."

Mr. Jenkins opened it just in time. They headed toward the footbridge in a full run.

Satisfied, Mr. Jenkins watched them go. He should man the manor house while the others were gone... He should, but he wanted to see what was going on for himself. "Oh, why not?"

Mr. Jenkins walked out the door, then eased it shut.

ROSE STOPPED three cottages down from Christine's. "Matthew, look." Rose stared at the dozens of lawn chairs lined up across the front yard between Jackson and Christine's cottages. Right in the center of them sat Miss Emily and Lester. A huge bowl of popcorn rested in her lap.

"Miss Emily?" Rose moved around to look at her. "What are y'all doing out here?"

"Shhhh!"

Half the people seated shushed Rose at once.

Miss Emily motioned for Rose and Matthew to sit down.

They dropped onto the lawn. "Why are we out here?" Rose asked again in a whisper.

"We're watching."

Lester nodded. "It's like our own personal movie at an open-air theater."

"What are we watching?" Rose craned her neck but couldn't see much beyond the lawn chairs in front of her and the lush tree limbs beyond them.

"Wait. Any second now," Lester said.

A creak filled the air.

The whispers ceased. "Here we go. Weeee!" Miss Emily grinned.

Rose felt as confused as Matthew looked.

A tomato went flying from Christine's window to Jackson's. It splatted against the glass.

His window shot up. "Did you really just throw a tomato at my window?"

"I didn't want to break the glass," she said. "I ran out of walnuts last night."

"Well, I can't throw those back. I ate them."

"Did you make popcorn?" Christine sniffed the air.

"No, why?"

"I smell popcorn."

"Probably the kid next door," Jackson said. "Half the people around don't bother with air-conditioning."

"I don't know how they can stand the heat. Even at night, it's just plain hot."

"It's all in what you're used to," Jackson said. "The trees help shade."

They helped conceal, too. Long, thick limbs, lush leaves provided a barrier. From their perspective, Christine and Jackson couldn't see their audience. But, when the breeze stirred the limbs, the audience could catch glimpses of them. It was a cross between gathering around the radio to listen to the broadcast and an outdoor play.

Miss Emily and a slew of others, munching on corn kernels from big paper buckets, let out a collective sigh.

"Jackson, I've been thinking."

Muffled groans surrounded Rose. "What's wrong with that?" Rose whispered to Miss Emily.

A woman from the village store answered. "Every time Christine says that, you need to worry."

"What's she talking about?"

Miss Emily answered. "It's a tell for our Christine," she explained. "If you'd been here last night, you'd understand."

Rose had no clue what Miss Emily had meant, and no clue anyone had been out here, eavesdropping last night. "You were all here then, too?"

"There weren't as many of us," Lester said. "But word's gotten around. By tomorrow night, I expect we'll be spilling into the street."

This was their entertainment? Rose shot Matthew a quizzical look that he responded to with a half-hearted shrug.

"What are you thinking?" Jackson asked Christine.

"I knew he'd ask. I just knew it." The woman beside Rose nudged her. "He's a dream, that one."

Christine hesitated, but finally answered. "If they're going to kill us, maybe we should at least try to get away."

"Don't even go there, Christine," he said. "I love these people and this place. I've already hurt them enough. If they want me dead, I'll be dead, but I won't betray them again."

"That's... noble," she said. "Nuts, but noble." A pause, then she added. "I think if I were dead, I'd still miss you, Jackson."

"I know I'd miss you." He grunted. "You're a chef's dream. You love food and you aren't afraid to show it."

"Is that the only reason you'd miss me?" she asked.

Rose was stunned. The militant woman who'd so bravely taken on Martin and his thugs sounded soft and vulnerable. Almost fragile. Of course, she thought the odds were high she was going to die. Rose well knew, unfortunately from personal experience, how vulnerable that could make one feel. *Lost... Helpless. Hopeless.*

"Of course not." Jackson pulled out the rope. "You ready?"

"I am."

He tossed it and they quickly set up the pulley system between their windows.

"What's that for?" Rose asked.

"He sends her food on it," Lester whispered.

"Chinese last night," a woman Rose didn't recognize said. "I can't wait to see what he's cooked her tonight. Been wondering what it'd be all day."

Lester and half the rest of the people sitting on the lawn sniffed.

"Mexican."

"Tai."

"No, it's Mexican," Lester said. "I got a five that says it's Mexican. Any takers?"

"I'll take that bet."

They waited for official word.

"Mexican," Jackson finally said. "Enchiladas, refried beans and my version of the amazingly sinful burrito—all calories removed, of course."

"You're so thoughtful." Christine laughed.

"Smells really good," Matthew mumbled.

"Wish I had the recipe." A woman tapped on Rose's shoulder. "Down the road sometime, will you get the recipe for me?"

"Sure."

"Shhh!"

Rose rolled her eyes. Jackson and Christine ate and chatted. "So," Rose whispered to Miss Emily, "why are we out here watching them like we're at the movies?"

"To see what they're saying, of course."

"Of course." Rose looked at Matthew and hiked a shoulder. "I have no idea why."

"Entertainment?" he suggested.

Lester let out a huff. "We're watching them fall in love. Now if you two don't hush, we're going to have to ask to you to leave the show."

The show? Whoa! Rose's eyes stretched wide. "Jackson's falling in love?"

"Where you been, girl?" Lester groaned. "Jackson's been in love."

Stunned, Rose looked at Miss Emily, who nodded her agreement. "He just don't know it yet."

"You're kidding me." Rose couldn't believe it. Finally, Jackson had found his *the one*?

"It's all right, hon. Don't fret," Miss Emily said. "Christine don't know it yet, either."

"But we all do." Lester grinned.

"Yeah." Miss Emily let out a shuddery, wistful sigh. "I sure hope we don't have to kill them." She took a bite of popcorn.

Lester worried at his lower lip. "At least, not before they figure it out."

Rose's jaw fell open. She looked at Matthew. "Are they serious?" She mouthed the words for fear of being drop-kicked off the lawn.

He nodded and mouthed back, "I'm afraid so."

"Last night, we did bucket lists and things we love," Christine told Jackson.

"And hate," Jackson interjected.

"That's right. We did things we hate, too." She paused to chew. "Tonight, let's do fun things."

"Um, that's a little problematic for me," Jackson said. "I haven't had a whole lot of time for fun things."

"Me, either. I've been too busy trying to find my feet. Developing software is extremely competitive. Everything changes so fast." Christine paused, then added, "Being at the Park already had made me think about that, but our current... uncertainty... has me thinking it's a huge mistake to tell myself there's always tomorrow and later. We might not have either."

"I wouldn't bet a nickel either way," he said. "I'm guilty of tomorrow and later, too—and of after."

"After?"

"Yeah, you know. I'll get to that *after* I get out of my apartment and into a house. Or *after* I get my brownie recipe perfected and my product onto the market."

"There is nothing that needs doing to your brownies, Jackson. I told you, I've eaten brownies across five continents. Yours are as perfect as they can get this side of heaven."

"Five continents, eh? Wow, thanks." He sounded moved by the compliment. "Now that I think about it, maybe doing fun things has nothing to do with tomorrow or later or after and everything to do with us feeling like we don't deserve to have fun."

"Bingo," Miss Emily whispered.

Lester hushed her with a hand to her forearm.

Rose's heart felt squeezed. Why would Jackson feel he didn't deserve to have fun?

"Maybe so," Christine said. "After my parents died, I thought I really had to do something stellar with my life or I'd be letting them down."

"You had to be their legacy," Jackson said. "I've always felt that way about Rose. She made a lot of sacrifices for me—to give me a decent life, I mean. I'm ashamed to say it, but then I didn't realize how many. Looking back, I know there were times she went to bed hungry to feed me." His voice choked. He cleared his throat. "I know she did."

"She's oldest, and she loves you, Jackson," Christine said. "It's like with me and Caro—though I'm just a few minutes older and Rose has a couple years on you. Still, when it was just us against the world… there's nothing I wouldn't have done for her, and I'm sure Rose felt the same about you. Probably still does. She wants the best for you—even if that means she has to do without."

Rose couldn't stop the tears filling her eyes from spilling.

Matthew eased an arm around her shoulder and pulled her close to his side.

"I know," Jackson said. "Who can take time for fun when someone they love has done that for them. Every minute has to count. You have to be worth it."

"Mmm," Christine paused. "So they don't regret their sacrifices?"

"Well, yeah."

"I can't speak for Rose, but I don't want Caroline feeling like that. I want her to smell every rose in life and all their leaves and stems. I want her to know I think she's worth it." Christine halted. "Oh, Jackson. Oh, no."

"What?"

"I did the same thing." She sounded horrified.

Everyone in the chairs and seated on the ground, including Rose, leaned forward, riveted to Christine in her window and Jackson in his, shifting to see between the limbs and leaves semi-blocking their view.

"What same thing?" Jackson asked.

"I think we've really messed up, Jackson."

"Clearly, or we wouldn't be under house arrest."

"No, I mean in our other lives. I've been so busy making every minute count, I never really thought this whole fun thing through before. Have you?"

"I thought I had, which is why I always put fun off until later. But maybe not. Where are you going with this?"

"Rose loves you. My parents loved me," Christine said. "It's so simple and I totally missed it."

"I'm still missing it."

"They love us, Jackson. And I'll bet if they knew we turned our backs on having fun, it would break their hearts. They wanted all good things for us, including fun. Joy makes life worth living, right?"

"We have joy. In our work."

"What about joy in others? What about being content and joyful just for the sake of being alive and breathing and being healthy and, well, just being?"

Miss Emily inhaled a sharp breath. Lester squeezed her arm. Rose waited to hear Jackson's response, not daring to breathe. She wanted her brother happy. Like Christine said. Not feeling guilty and denying himself joy or fun. If she'd had any idea that he felt this way... The truth hit her. She looked back at Miss Emily. "You knew."

Miss Emily winked.

Finally, Jackson answered. "Humph. I'm seeing all this a little differently now," he said. "Serious perspective shift."

"Me, too."

"I think Rose would be heartbroken."

"And worried," Christine said. "My folks, too."

Jackson's voice firmed. "Well, we need to change."

"Agreed."

Miss Emily raised a pumped fist. "Yes!"

Lester grinned.

So did Matthew.

Rose clasped a hand over her heart. Deeply moved, she couldn't speak.

"Okay, then," Christine said. "Let's list five fun things we would most like to do. If we live through this, we'll do them. If not, well, at least we'll know what they are."

"No, we'll do them together either way," Jackson insisted. "We'll really do them or we'll do them in our minds, right here from our windows."

"Now that's romantic." Miss Emily sighed. "Isn't that romantic, Lester?"

"Yeah, there's a real sweetest to it. I like that."

Rose laid a snide glare on Lester. "Is that why you're fighting so hard in committee to kill them?"

Lester snorted. "One thing ain't got nothing to do with the other, Rosie girl—and you know it."

"Shhh!"

"Last warning, Rose." Miss Emily said softly. "Now hush. They're getting to the good part."

"There's something else in that pillowcase," Jackson said.

"Brownies?" The hope in Christine's voice was clear to all listening.

"No, no dessert tonight, I'm afraid."

"If we don't kill them, Lester, we need to help the man get those brownies of his to market," Miss Emily whispered.

"No need to be nagging," Lester whispered back to her. "I already started on that this morning."

"My taste buds want to declare war at no dessert, but my blood sugar thanks you for the reprieve." Christine checked the pillowcase and pulled out a bunch of daisies. "Oh, you sent me flowers. They're beautiful, Jackson."

"You like them." He smiled. "You know, for a rich woman with everything, you're easy to please."

"Money doesn't make you happy. Oh, it's been a blessing not to have to scrape by or worry about rent and paying bills. But I think if I had to choose, I'd choose a life with a man who brought me flowers he picked from my yard over one with buckets full of money any day."

"Picked up on that, did you?"

"Uh-huh. The flowerbed by the kitchen window is looking a little bare."

"I tried to get a few from different places, but I wanted a decent bunch. Hard, when you can't leave the property. Millie, next door on the other side of you, has a slew of them. I don't know what she's doing to her flowers, but they're thicker than thieves."

"I saw that. She's got a green thumb," Christine said. "It's a gift."

Millie, sitting two chairs down from Rose, whispered to the man sitting beyond her. "He likes my flowers." She glowed. "See, Ruddy? I told you people appreciate having pretty flowers to look at."

"Yes, dear."

Wise man to not argue, in Rose's opinion. No way would he win in this crowd.

"I love them," Christine told Jackson. "Thank you."

"You're welcome." A long minute passed, then another. "Um, Christine?"

"Yeah?"

"What you said… about what you'd rather have. You were kidding, right?"

"No. I meant every word." Her voice went soft. "Having money doesn't insulate you from problems, Jackson. It just changes the nature of them. You have a whole different set of problems." She stopped, then started again. "You can't buy someone caring for you from their heart. Worrying about you, cooking healthy food for you, or doing thoughtful things like remembering you love brownies and making them for you just because they want to do it. And you can't pay someone to be thoughtful and pick you flowers just because. Those things come from the heart and they create moments, Jackson. Money can't compete with moments from the heart. It can't even come close."

"That's beautiful," Rose whispered. "She's head over heels crazy about him." A tear slipped from Rose's eye. "I just love her."

Matthew grinned. "You love her for loving him?"

"Yeah, I do."

"Me, too." Matthew said.

Lester pulled out a hanky.

"Lester, don't you dare honk your nose." Miss Emily warned him with a wagging finger. "They'll hear you."

"Wasn't gonna honk." He reached over to Miss Emily and dabbed a tear from her eye. "You sprung a little leak."

Rose took that tenderness as a good sign for Jackson and Christine's future.

"For goodness' sake, Mr. Jenkins."

Rose looked back, and her jaw dropped. Mr. Jenkins was rubbing at his eyes, too, with the hem of Abigail's sleeve."

Mr. Jenkins? The staid and stiff, Mr. Jenkins? Rose's heart lifted. Jackson's future looked… well, like he'd have a future. Maybe.

Between Miss Emily, Lester and Mr. Jenkins, they held a lot of influence with the committee. Not all of it, but a lot of it.

"Stop fretting." Matthew slipped her hand into his. "This will all work out fine."

Rose frowned at her husband. "The last time someone told me that, I ended up in a burn box inside a crematorium."

"A crematorium?" Millie gasped. "Holy smoke! Did you hear that, Ruddy?"

"We all heard it, Millie. Everybody knows they had special circumstances. Hush, now so we can hear." That came from someone in back near the street that Rose couldn't see. Their ranks on the lawn had swelled to nearly twice as many as when she'd sat down.

Rose bit her lip. She hadn't meant to say that about the crematorium, much less to say it loud enough for anyone to hear. It just kind of popped out.

Matthew sent her a level look to knock-off complaining. "We lived, Rose."

"Barely." That was no lie. "I had stinky singed hair for months —and don't you dare say I could've shaved my head."

Millie frowned at Matthew. "You actually told her that?"

"I only said it was her choice and she *could* shave her head." Seeing he was losing favor, he added, "I'd love her even if she was bald."

Rose elbowed him. "Quit trying to score brownie points."

"Shhh!" The crowd collectively complained.

At the window, Christine stilled. "What was that noise?"

"I don't know," Jackson said. "Probably nothing. I'll go check."

Panic erupted and forty or so of those nothings scrambled to get out of the line of sight from Jackson's front porch, huddling behind trees, diving under bushes, behind rain barrels.

Rose and Matthew watched for Miss Emily and Lester, to be sure they didn't get run over. Miss Emily tripped over a water cooler and did a respectable tumble roll right back to her feet.

"Impressive," Matthew said.

It was impressive… and the reason for all this hit Rose like a tomato to the window. "Those sly rascals…"

"Who?" Matthew asked, not tracking her.

"You'll see."

Chapter 30

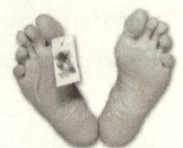

March 31st

Christine sat at the window and stared across to Jackson. "It's been a week. How much longer are they going to make us stay like this?"

"I don't know."

How could he not know? He'd been here often. "Are you telling me you've never seen anyone else in the Park under house arrest?"

"Actually, I haven't." He lifted a hand. "I didn't even know there was a jail until they threatened to throw us in it."

"Maybe there isn't one. I didn't see one, and you haven't seen it."

"No, there is a jail. Lucas never makes false claims when it comes to Park security." Jackson twisted in the window to stretch out a bit. "I've been thinking about it. The jail has to be out by the ranch."

"I don't think so. There's just three buildings out there. The main house, a barn, and a bunkhouse."

"How do you know that?"

"My midnight jaunt, looking for Caro," Christine reminded him.

"Right." Jackson sighed. "The jail could be to the west of the ranch. That area changes a lot. They're always building something and tearing down something else over there."

"Why?"

"Giving people what they need." Jackson caught himself. "But we shouldn't be talking about that."

"What's the harm? We can't leave here, and it looks like they're in no hurry to make up their minds about what they're going to do with us."

Jackson stayed silent.

That made Christine think. "Character is what you do when no one is looking." She grumbled and groused. "You're right, okay? You're right."

"Or maybe it's on the other side of the village, but I can't see Lucas putting a jail that close to the perimeter." Jackson speculated a little more. "The perfect place would be under the security building. That might be where it is."

"Enough about the jail. If they sentence us to it," Christine said, "we'll know exactly where it is. Until then, it doesn't much matter."

"I guess, it doesn't."

"Jackson, the more I think, the sorrier I am I got you into all this. When the committee calls for us, I am going to take full responsibility for deceiving you, and Rose and Matthew, to get here." Christine couldn't believe anyone on the committee wouldn't understand. This had been her only option. Her one chance to find Caro. Surely they would all see she'd had to deceive Jackson and seize the chance. "Maybe then they'll let you go." She didn't hold out much hope for herself. As an outsider, was she held to a higher or lower standard?

"I appreciate the thought, but nothing you say will make much difference. I did what I did, and I knew better than to do it. The thing is, this isn't about you or me. Not really. It's about everybody." He stopped, his voice trailing. "We've been through all this. As an insider, you protect the Park and the people in it. Period."

"Because we're all somebody's bridge." Christine let that roll through her mind. "Bridge in life and death." She groaned. "Why didn't I think of that before, when I read the bronze?"

"What are you talking about?"

"The bronze statue. The secret of secrets. We're all somebody's bridge."

"Yeah?"

"In life, we help bridge the gap. In death, we bridge the gap. If we're not there to bridge the gap…"

"It's not bridged." Jackson groaned. "Wow, I should have figured that out a long time ago."

"Now, I'm not just worried, I'm panicking."

"Why?"

"Before I left Dallas, I made this video and wrote this letter."

"Okay."

"I left it with Caroline's counselor."

"Dr. Nell Richmond, yeah. So?"

"I told her if I didn't contact her on or before the 31st, to deliver them both on the first."

"To whom?"

"An attorney." Christine cringed. "I retained him to look for Caroline and me and told him to start looking in Even."

"What?"

"Don't shout, Jackson. You'll wake up the neighbors." She deliberately lowered her voice. "I didn't know anything then, if you'll recall. And I figured if I didn't find Caro and get back to Dallas before the 31st, that it'd be because Martin or his goons had killed one or both of us."

"So you retained the lawyer to look for you or Caro."

Christine nodded. "Whether or not he will, I don't know. He hand-selects his clients. But he's got an amazing reputation for helping people who really need it, and I figured, if it came to pass, we'd really need it."

"Nell called me," Jackson admitted.

"You know Nell Richmond?" Christine's surprise was evident. Her voice cracked.

"She put Caroline and me in touch. Nell is the reason I brought Caro to the Park."

"So Nell works with everyone here?"

"No, she knows nothing about Sampson Park—and she never will. There's a Dallas group that helps people in trouble. She knows the people in it."

"You said she phoned you," Christine reminded him. "About what?"

"I don't know. I called her back but got her voice mail. Then all this happened and I haven't connected with her yet."

Disappointed there'd be no information coming from that venue, Christine cringed. Jackson wasn't going to like her adding to the list of their crimes, but she had no choice. "We have to tell someone, Jackson. Before Nell passes on that video and letter to the lawyer."

"But there is nothing in it to bring him here to look for either of you. What's the risk?"

"This isn't just any lawyer. If he does take the case, he's ruthless and relentless. There isn't a rock he won't flip over twice." Christine tried to impress upon Jackson the urgency to reveal this to Miss Emily. "With all the secrets hidden here, he could create a lot of problems. And what about Rose? He's going to start looking there. Everyone in Even was at Carl Wooten's funeral and they all saw me at the diner. That'll take the lawyer straight to Rose and Matthew. We can't just let that happen."

"No, we can't," Jackson agreed. "Rose loves Even. If she has to move, she's going to be spitting mad."

"Maybe we better skip Rose," Christine said. "She can't stop this. We need to tell Miss Emily."

"We have to tell them both," he countered. "But be warned. It won't help us or our case."

"I know that," Christine said. "But we have to protect the others, Jackson. It's the right thing to do."

"I'll summon security."

"How?"

"The bell-pull, remember? Everybody has one. You tug it twice for security."

"At two in the morning?" She gauged the time by the positioning of the stars. "Maybe we should wait until dawn. I can end this problem with a simple phone call, and I can't see Nell trying to contact the lawyer before dawn."

"No, we need to take care of it now. There's too much at risk."

Christine felt an emotional blast that nearly knocked her from the window. All she'd wanted was out of here so she could continue her search for Caro. Now, she feared she wouldn't be coming back and that her time with Jackson and their nightly talks were coming to an abrupt end. "Jackson, wait!" she cried out. "I—I…"

He smiled at her. "I know, Christine. Me, too."

A man appeared in the yard between their windows. His white hair caught the moonlight. "Speckles, is that you?" Christine asked.

"Yep, sure is." He nodded. "Nice night, ain't it?"

Christine didn't know what to say. It'd been days and days since they'd seen anyone else.

"What are you doing here?" Jackson asked.

"You summoned me, didn't you?"

"I didn't," Jackson said.

"Oh?" Speckles looked totally confused. "I thought…" he looked back over his shoulder, beyond the trees and then jerked back around to face them.

"I was about to, though," Jackson said. "We need to talk to Miss Emily."

"Well now, ain't that convenient?" His shrill voice elevated. "The committee's wanting to talk to you two, too." He swerved his wild gaze between them. "Don't linger. Mr. Perini's in a foul mood."

"What's wrong with him?" Jackson asked, halting Speckles' retreat.

"Mostly, he's fired up that Caroline's still missing and Martin Easton's swearing he don't know where she is."

"Caroline?" Christine stiffened. "Who's Mr. Perini?"

"Part of the family," Jackson said. "He's very protective. If

Martin knows what's good for him, he will not mess with Mr. Perini."

"What's he likely to do?"

"He's claimed Caroline just like he did Rose and me," Jackson said softly. "Nobody messes with his family."

Christine stilled. "You're not saying…"

"I'm saying, nobody messes with his family. That's all of us."

Speckles straightened his back. "I don't think now's a good time for you two to be jawing and keeping the committee waiting. They'll all be in a foul mood. Best step it up and get to the carriage."

Christine and Jackson shut their windows and exited their cottages. Jackson helped her into the carriage and when he took his seat and Speckles closed the door, Jackson kissed her.

"For luck," he said.

"We need a lot of it." She kissed him back, then kissed him again. "And that last one was just for me.

Nervous tension high-jacked her attempt at humor.

She debated telling him her discovery. He did need to know it, and it would probably be better to learn it now from her. "Jackson," she said softly. "I have a confession."

"Another one?" He looked troubled, not that she could blame him.

"This is different, but I think you should know it."

"Okay."

"Remember the night I smelled the popcorn?"

He draped his arm over her shoulder, pulled her closer to him on the seat. "Yes."

"I had the feeling we were being watched."

"Uh-huh."

"We were."

"What?" He looked from the window down into her upturned face.

"I saw them—with a mirror."

"Saw who?"

"I couldn't make out their faces, but there were a handful of people sitting in lawn chairs, facing the trees, between our cottages."

"Guarding us?" he asked.

"I guess. But the next night, there were more of them."

"Because we were talking at the windows, they figured we were going to try to escape or something?"

"I don't know why they were there," she said, though she'd spent a lot of time speculating. "But every night, there were more of them."

"They were eavesdropping on us?" He sounded horrified.

She couldn't blame him. They had gotten really personal. But she couldn't blame them, either. "I'm not sure our voices would carry that far."

"In that quiet? They'd carry for miles." He let out a healthy grunt. "I can't believe they would do this."

She stroked his shoulder, gave him a soothing pat. She'd had more time to think about this. "What we do impacts them directly, Jackson." She looked at him. "They're afraid."

That took the air out of his tires. "You're probably right."

"We shouldn't mention that we know, I don't think."

"With everything else, I doubt we'll have the chance. But if the occasion arises, I'll be taking it. We agreed to house arrest, and we—"

"Broke their trust," she said. "We have nothing to complain about no matter why they were there."

Jackson worked through that, then said, "I'm having a hard time reconciling the spitfire who took on Martin and his men with the understanding woman you are now."

"I know. Sometimes, I'm having trouble figuring myself out, too."

"This place changes you."

It did. But she couldn't be dishonest with him anymore. "Being cared for by a man you care for changes you more."

He smiled. "I totally get that."

The carriage stopped. Speckles opened the door, then stood back and announced, "The manor house."

The bottom fell out of Christine's stomach. The time to pay the piper had arrived.

Chapter 31

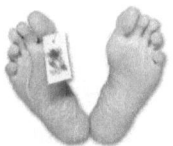

At the foot of the stairs, Mr. Jenkins stepped aside. "Go directly to the conference room," he told Jackson and Christine. "Do not speak to anyone, and do not stop anywhere between here and there."

Jackson nodded.

"Mr. Jenkins?" Christine couldn't resist. "Is there any word on Caroline?"

He looked right through her as if she hadn't even spoken to him.

Jackson tugged her hand and began climbing the steps.

The conference room didn't look at all like it usually did. The large table in its center had been removed. Now a long, narrow table had been placed at one end. A row of chairs had been placed behind it. Seats for the committee members. Two chairs stood in front, in the center of the room, facing the table. Ten feet behind them, thirty or so folding chairs stood empty and waiting.

They're allowing spectators? Jackson swallowed hard.

"Your seat is on the left," Abigail said to Christine. "Jackson, you take the other one."

They sat down and Abigail exited the room.

"This setting seems pretty formal." Christine swerved her gaze to Jackson. "Have you seen these type of proceedings before?"

Jackson shook his head that he had not, and shot her a worry-laced glance telling her he wished he weren't seeing them now.

The committee entered the conference room single file: Rose, who looked torn between being furious and scared to death, followed by Matthew, Darby, Mr. Perini, Lester, and then Miss Emily. Dr. Rossi left an empty seat next to Miss Emily. The committee members sat down.

A man about to enter the room stopped outside the door. Jackson couldn't see his face, but he did glimpse that the man was tall and wearing a dark suit. Who could that be? Jackson wondered, but Lester claimed everyone's attention with a gavel tap that echoed through Jackson's soul.

"Due to the late hour, and the attorney being delayed," Lester said with a glance at the doorway. It now stood empty. "We'll forget the formalities and just get on with this business." He looked to Jackson, then Christine. "You know your crimes well enough. So do we. If you have anything you'd like the committee to consider, now's the time to let us know it."

Christine raised her hand.

"What, Christine?"

She started to stand. A hand at her shoulder kept her in her seat. She looked back over her shoulder and saw Lucas. "Sorry," she said, then faced the committee. "I have to tell you two things. Well, maybe three."

"Spit 'em out, girl." Lester said, his voice gruff.

"When Jackson brought me here, he didn't know I wasn't Caroline."

"We know that already," Lester said. "Anything else?"

That blew her huge defense of him. "The wrongs done are all on me," she said. "All of them. Did you know that, Lester?"

"Actually, they ain't," Lester said. "Facts are facts, and Jackson played his part, too."

"I did," Jackson said.

"You ain't been recognized to speak, son. Zip it." Lester turned his gaze back to Christine. "What else you got?"

"I need to make a phone call," she said.

The whole committee gasped.

"A PHONE CALL?" Lester's jaw dropped. "That is not happening, girl."

"Wait, please." Christine went on to tell them about the video and letter, how if Nell didn't hear from her on the 31st, she'd be delivering those items to an attorney whose involvement could be problematic for all of them.

"Why did you wait until the 31st to tell us this?"

"There are no calendars at the cottage." Christine's face heated. "I didn't realize the 31st was today until tonight. I realize the deadline has expired, but if I phone Nell right away, I'm certain I can stop this."

Lester looked up and down the table, then just stared at Christine. "No phones allowed at the Park."

Christine had to convince them. "I understand that, but this call is critical, Lester. Not to me, to all of you."

That got their attention. Now they all glared at her, looking ready to pounce. "Explain yourself."

"When I delivered that package to Nell—Dr. Nell Richmond—I didn't know about any of you or what you did here. I didn't even know where here was until I got here myself. If I had known, of course, I wouldn't do what I did." Christine squeezed her eyes shut, then reopened them. "If you'll just let me call Nell, I can stop this and there won't be any threat to any of you."

The man glimpsed outside the door earlier walked in. Christine didn't recognize him, but since no one appeared surprised to see him, she figured they all knew his identity and why he was there. He was huge, distant and stern and intimidating.

He turned a cold gaze on her. "I'm afraid it's too late for that, Christine."

That comment set off a flurry of worried whispers and more than a few groans.

The imposing man took his seat at the center of the table next to Miss Emily. "Lester, we need a short recess," he said. "Lucas, get them out of here."

Lucas led Christine and Jackson to an adjoining ante-room full of antiques. A sofa, two chairs—no windows and the one door. They'd negated any means of escape.

"I'll be back for you." Lucas closed the door and locked them in.

Christine swallowed hard. "Jackson, who is that man?"

"Dex?" Jackson sat down on the sofa.

She nodded. "Dex?"

"Dexter Devlin. He's a lawyer."

"Oh my gosh." Christine grabbed the sides her head, certain her brain was going to explode. "Oh, my. What have I done?"

"What's wrong? Dex is a decent guy. He's helped a lot of people here—including Caroline and me," Jackson said, reacting to Christine's upset. "Christine, what is wrong with you?"

She paled, her skin losing all its color. "Dexter Devlin is the lawyer I told Nell to contact. He knows it all."

Jackson cocked his head. "Why isn't that a good thing? It strikes me as the best possible news. The information is contained."

"No, Jackson. If he already knows it, then it means Nell contacted him early!" Christine dropped her voice. "How can we possibly convince them she hasn't contacted anyone else?"

"Ah, I see." Confusion fled Jackson's expression. He actually looked almost relaxed.

She sat here having heart failure and he was relaxed? "Do you understand what I've said, Jackson?"

"I do."

Lucas entered. "They're ready for you."

Scared stiff, Christine took a steadying breath. Her goose was as good as cooked. Probably Jackson's too. What about Caroline? Would she be missing forever? And now what about Nell? This bunch had the reach—*Dexter Devlin, for pity's sake*. Would the committee use all this against Nell?

Christine let resignation slide through her. If the committee deemed it in its best interests, it would…

ROSE INTERCEPTED Jackson in the hallway. Her face was pasty, dark smudges circled her eyes, and her lips seemed fixed, thin and drawn tight. "What have you done, Jackson?" she spat in a stage whisper.

"He can't speak, right, Lucas?" Christine looked from Rose to the head of security walking behind them.

"He cannot," Lucas said, and his expression said if Jackson did, Lucas might just shoot him.

Rose growled, deep and throaty. "I've been fighting, begging and pleading with them to spare your lives for a solid week. You *knew* she wasn't Caroline and you didn't tell anyone—not even me?"

Lucas stepped between them. "Sorry, Rose. We have to get in there."

She glared at her brother, then entered the room and took her seat next to Matthew.

Jackson hadn't said a word, but even if permitted to speak, what could he say? His jaw was tight enough to crack and the pain in his eyes at having hurt his sister scalded Christine.

"I'm sorry," she whispered for the fortieth time.

He didn't so much as glance at her. She couldn't blame him for that. For anything, really. She'd been so bent on finding Caro, Christine hadn't given a single thought to what her actions could do to Jackson. To Rose or Matthew, or anyone else. She sat down in her same seat and Jackson sat beside her, focusing directly on the committee members.

Lester tapped the gavel, but it was Dexter Devlin who spoke. "The committee has now reviewed your video, Christine, and read your letter to me."

She waited for him to continue, but he didn't. The silence in the room stretched, taut and tense and discomforting. "May I speak, Mr. Devlin?" she said, unable to bear the silence another second.

He didn't answer, just stared at her.

"Briefly," Lester said.

"I didn't know about any of you. I only knew my sister was

missing and the odds were good I'd be killed trying to find her." Christine wanted to stop there but she had to admit the whole truth. It would complete her humiliation, but it could spare Jackson their retribution. Well, some of it. "Once I got here, everything changed." She'd belonged. "But this was my only lead on Caroline. I was terrified to say anything then. I was afraid I'd been removed and… I had nowhere else to look."

Christine's voice thinned. She paused, hoping by some miracle something infused it with strength. "If it were your sister missing, your only blood relative, would any of you have done anything different?"

That came out sounding a little more belligerent than she intended, but she wouldn't apologize for it. If they were willing to kill her and Jackson for their transgressions, they would certainly do worse themselves. Well, at least as bad.

"I'm going to take exception to that, young lady." Mr. Perini stood up, flung his hat down on the table. "Serious exception."

"Why?" Christine asked. "How could I offend you? I don't even know you."

"I am Paul Perini," he said. "I've taken enormous risks to help Rose and Matthew and your sister. We all have. So don't you dare take that tone with us."

Of course, they had. "I'm sorry, Mr. Perini." Christine said and meant it. "I am aware that while I was pretending to be Caroline and drawing fire from Martin and his thugs, all of you, including Jackson, were keeping Caroline safe."

"We were." He nodded.

"Jackson tried to put my fears for Caro to rest. He told me everyone here would die to keep her safe."

"Of course," Mr. Perini said. "She's family."

But Christine was not. "This is all so frustrating."

"What is?" Dex asked.

"Everything." Christine never resented being an outsider more than at that moment. "I'm here and I still don't know where my sister is. I've gotten Jackson and myself into all this trouble, and the whole bunch of you are scared to death—I'm not sure why. It seems counterproductive to be sidelined while Caro is still out there, maybe fighting for her life. She's not a fighter," Christine warned them. "She never has been. And she's not like any of you. If she had been…"

"She'd have taken on Martin and his thugs herself," Lester said. "We know all that, Christine. We know now you were telling the truth about things, and your video and letter to Dex confirms that things are what you said they were."

"Not to mention the retainer check," Rose said. "Nobody writes a check like that unless they're desperate."

Miss Emily nodded. "Thank God it was to Dex."

Lester slid them both a warning to hold their peace, then looked back at Christine. "Why was it to Dex?"

"He's the best." Christine shrugged.

"That's it?" Dex asked. "No one referred or recommended me? Nell Richmond didn't suggest me?"

"No," Christine said. "I don't know if Nell had ever heard your name before my video and letter." Christine paused, but clearly the committee members were waiting for more, so she gave it to them. "I needed someone I could trust."

Dex snorted. "You didn't know you could trust me."

"Not personally, but there are thousands of people on the Internet who trust you implicitly. Case studies, opinion essays, news articles. I should have recognized you, but you don't much look like your photographs. I'm thinking now that's intentional."

"I prefer a certain amount of anonymity," he admitted. "And you still haven't told us why you trusted me. We've never met, Christine. Someone had to send you to me."

"No, we haven't met, but no one sent me to you. I told you, I researched you. I wanted the best." Christine worried her lower lip with her teeth. "When I read your pleadings on the Mason case—"

"The New York Mason case or the one in Sacramento?" he asked.

"Neither," she said, frowning at him for baiting her. "It was the Florida case. When I read the pleadings, I knew you were the one. Oh, everyone says how great you are, and that you've got the sharpest legal mind maybe ever, but this was about my sister's life and maybe mine, and something was missing. So I kept researching you. I found what was missing in the Mason case."

"What did you find?" Lester asked.

"Heart." She hated admitting this aloud, but there was no help for it. "Here was a woman—June Mason—who clearly was as guilty as guilty gets, and yet you took her case and, by the time you were done, we loved her. No devices, no tricks, no manipulating the truth."

"Heart." Miss Emily said. "That's our Dex."

"I believe her," Matthew said.

"Me, too," Mr. Perini agreed, though he seemed a little put out at having to say so. "Not that believing her cures our ails."

Jackson broke his silence. "What exactly are your ails, Mr. Perini? Not with me. I know exactly what they are with me. I mean with Christine."

Matthew looked to Rose. Miss Emily to Lester. Mr. Perini to Darby, and Darby to Dex. He frowned. "We know what to do with you, Jackson. We don't know what to do with Christine."

She lifted a hand. "Why do you have to do anything with me?"

Dexter folded his hands on the tabletop. "The people here survive because they're all invested. Everyone has a lot to lose. That vested interest makes the survival of one another as important to each of them as their own. It takes all to have all here."

"The code keeps them all safe," Jackson said. "I broke the code, telling you anything. Even by bringing you here, since I didn't verify you were who you claimed you were. That's on me."

Christine frowned, looked at Mr. Perini. "Am I not at least a little bit of an insider here because I'm Caro's sister? She came to Sampson Park not knowing anyone, and you call her family."

"She didn't deceive us." Mr. Perini shot back. "Though I'm giving you props for taking the heat of being her for all those months. We know Martin's as mean as a snake. His henchmen, too. We don't doubt your courage or your devotion to your sister, Christine. Neither is in question nor our issue."

"I won't disagree about Martin or his men, though one of them was half-decent. He gave me a note warning me Martin was about to kill me, or to order them to and he'd do it. But he did give me a heads up."

"You believed him?" Lester asked.

Christine's expression turned deadpan flat. "Wouldn't you?"

"I reckon I would."

"So what is your issue?"

"It's simple," Lester said, lifting his arms. "You got nothing invested and nothing to lose."

"Nothing to lose?" Christine huffed, thoroughly ticked off. "What about Caroline? You took her in, sheltered her, protected her, right?"

No one answered.

"Right?" Christine elevated her voice.

"Yes," Miss Emily said.

"Well, I have to tell you, I'm insulted. You people don't know anything about me. Oh, I have no doubt Mr. Devlin has had scores of people digging to find every scrap of information out there, but someone glossed over everything that matters. Otherwise, I wouldn't be in this fix and neither would Jackson." Christine sat down and looked person to person down the row of the committee members. "You say I have nothing to lose. Nothing invested. But you're wrong."

"Christine, yelling and hurling insults at them might not be the best tact—"

"I'm telling the truth," she told Jackson, then looked back to the members. "I owe you. For what you did for Caroline, I'll owe you forever." Christine swallowed hard. "That's a matter of personal integrity. My integrity might not mean a thing to you because of the way I handled this situation, but it means everything to me. I would die before betraying a single one of you." She sat back down. "Wise or foolish, that's on me. But don't tell me I have nothing invested. That's just not true."

Jackson reached for Christine's hand. She slipped hers inside and he gently squeezed. Grateful for his support, she held on tight. Only God knew how this would proceed from here. She probably shouldn't have yelled or told them they were wrong quite so force-fully, but good grief…

Silence settled over the committee.

Lester noticed their clasped hands. He whispered something to Miss Emily, and within seconds, they were all looking at their hands. Christine tried to remove hers from Jackson's, but he held on tight. "No," he said. "No."

"This really isn't the right time for defiance," she said softly. At least, she had his support.

Miss Emily stood up. "We need a recess, Lester."

"But we just had—"

Miss Emily parked her hand on her hip. "Now, Lester."

"All righty, then." Lester whacked the gavel.

Lucas stepped forward between Jackson and Christine and motioned for them to rise.

Back to the parlor where they'd be sequestered. Christine didn't bother to complain.

"Could be worse," Jackson muttered.

And probably would be before it was all done.

Visions of the little cemetery in the forbidden area flashed through her mind.

Chapter 32

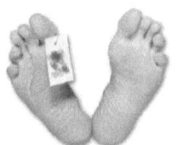

Jackson stood at the parlor window. His hands clasped behind his back, he looked outside.

Christine left the sofa and joined him, glanced out. "What are all those people doing?" They strolled around the lake, sat under the Gazebo and on the lawn, stretching from the road to the lake. More ambled toward the manor house along the road to the village. "Half the village has to be out there."

"Or more." Jackson spared Christine a glance. "You need to be prepared. It appears the committee intends to make an example of us."

Christine groaned, beside herself. How could she make this better? "I'm so sorry, Jackson. I know you don't want to hear it, but I feel awful about all this."

He reached back and covered her hand on his arm. Gave it a gentle squeeze.

An hour later, they still sat on the little sofa, waiting.

Nearly two hours later, Lucas finally unlocked the door and swung it open. "The committee is ready for you."

At the heavy wooden door to the conference room, Christine's step faltered. The empty seats behind them had grown to rows seven deep that stretched wall to wall, and all had been filled with Park residents. Most of the faces she recognized from Little Independence Day events, but a few she couldn't place. And one wearing a gray hoodie and sunglasses Christine didn't recall having seen before now. Was the woman intentionally shielding her face?

Bent low, she whispered something to Millie, who lived in the cottage next door to Caroline's. Christine studied the others. Some looked grim and some nervous, blinking furiously. They were all somber. If there had been any doubt about the seriousness of these proceedings, one look at this group would have been all the proof anyone needed to know it.

Jackson guided Christine to her seat with a hand at her back. When they were seated, the committee filed in and returned to their seats.

Lester tapped the gavel and the reverential murmurs of the villagers ceased. The room stilled, seeming almost breathless.

Miss Emily, not Lester, stood and spoke. "During the recess, many of you made your views known to the committee. We appreciate your opinions and suggestions. The decisions made here today impact your futures as well as ours, and we're acutely aware of it, which is why we summoned you and solicited your input. Thank you for taking the time to join us." Miss Emily sat down.

"Well," Lester said to Jackson and Christine. "We have ourselves a dilemma. Seems the people of the Park want you two to live. Yet that doesn't resolve our issue of personal investment." Lester's eyes narrowed on Christine. "Being Caroline's sister and owing us ain't enough, Christine. It's a start, meaningful to us, but it ain't enough for us to stake our lives on." He swiveled his gaze to Jackson. "Several residents believe there's a reasonable solution to this quandary. Frankly, Jackson, the problem ain't with you. You've been with us long enough to have as much mud on your boots as the rest of us. The problem's with you, Christine."

She opened her mouth to speak and Lester lifted a staying hand, warning her to keep quiet.

"The committee feels the solution the residents proposed is reasonable, but it also wants to assure itself that implementing it won't be opening a can of worms. Avoiding discord is essential to the well-being of many here."

"That's enough explaining, Lester," Miss Emily said. "Ask him."

Lester nodded. "Jackson, you ever kissed this woman?" He nodded at Christine.

"Yes, but not lately."

That grumbling response created a lot of little chuckles and muffled coughs.

"May we ask why?"

"I guess you may ask, Lester, since you're responsible. We've been under house arrest. Her in one cottage and me in one next door."

"Did you not eat meals together?"

"We did. More or less," Jackson said. "Her in her window, and me in mine."

Obviously the committee members hadn't been in the lawn chairs between their cottages or they'd know that. With the mirror, Christine had only been able to see them from the knees down, so she couldn't be sure. But that question from Lester kind of sealed it.

Lester grunted. "And the whole time you've been under house arrest, you never visited her cottage, nor her yours?"

"No." Jackson lifted his hands. "We were under house arrest."

"Did it occur to you to meet at the property line between the two cottages?" That, from Dex.

"Actually, it didn't." Jackson frowned. "Not until now."

That had the residents giggling and not bothering to muffle with fake coughs.

"Figured you were in enough trouble already, eh?" Miss Emily said.

"Caused enough trouble is more like it," Jackson clarified. "And house arrest means house, not property lines, right?"

"Technically, no," Lester said.

Jackson grunted. "We weren't told that."

Millie's Ruddy spoke out. "Put it to 'em, Lester. If they agree to our proposal, we'll be satisfied."

Christine looked back at him. The woman in the gray hoodie turned her head. What was Ruddy talking about?

"You all agree?" Lester asked the spectators. "You'll be satisfied?"

The residents responded in unison.

Lester looked at Emily. "That good enough or do you want to poll them individually?"

"I'd say their response was unanimous," Miss Emily said. "If anyone disagrees, please say so now."

Silence.

Christine's nerves strummed. Whatever this proposal the residents had concocted was, it couldn't be good.

"Well, all righty, then." Lester let his roaming gaze settle back on Jackson and Christine. "Our issue, as we've told you, is that Christine doesn't have a sufficient amount of skin in the game. The residents don't want either of you dead, *if* it can be avoided, so that's left the committee in a dilemma."

Lester paused to sip water. "During the recess, the residents came up with an idea that would have Christine deeply invested in Sampson Park and in all who reside in it. With their approval, which you just witnessed, we're going to recommend it to you." Lester studied Jackson and then Christine. "If you agree, you'll forfeit the $2,000,000 retainer to Dex as a penalty, and we'll consider this incident in the past."

"That's a steep penalty," Christine said.

"You've committed steep offenses," Lester countered.

The spectators mumbled their agreement.

"Yes, but I still won't know what happened to Caroline. I need that money to find her."

"You don't need money or anything else to find Caroline." Dexter Devlin said. "We've got her covered."

Christine pushed. "Do I have your word on that, Mr. Devlin?"

"I just said it." He frowned. "You said you trust me because I have heart, Christine. Prove it."

She studied him a long second. "Fine."

"So is that it?" Jackson lifted a hand. "You take Christine's money and it's over?"

"Not exactly, Jackson." Lester stilled. "You have to do your part."

"Which is…what?"

Lester lifted his chin. "You've got to marry her."

"What?"

"What?"

Jackson and Christine responded simultaneously, then stared at each other.

"Lester." Miss Emily rolled her gaze and stood up. "A little context," she said to Jackson. "As your wife, Christine would have a huge personal investment. The residents and the committee could rest assured of her allegiance because it wouldn't be just our futures at stake, but her own and yours." Miss Emily lifted a hand. "The question is whether or not you two are willing to marry. Now, we don't expect an immediate response. A decision of this magnitude requires thoughtful consideration. We will give you a little time to weigh the matter and discuss it."

"Are you really demanding this?" Jackson said. "Lester, I'm fond of Christine but marriage? It's too soon."

"It's barely soon enough," he countered.

Something in his tone changed everything. "What do you mean?" Jackson asked.

"The perimeter breach wasn't teenagers. It was Martin."

"Martin!" Christine gasped, shot a look back over her shoulder at Lucas. "Martin? And you didn't tell me?"

"You were never in jeopardy."

"Martin." Lester nodded. "He's apparently hooked up with some of our old enemies from New Orleans." The look in Lester's eyes warned Jackson the enemies that came to mind were the right ones. "You know they've been trying to get in here for years."

"Martin Branch hired the mob?" Jackson couldn't believe it. He looked at Miss Emily. This news had to terrify her, since she'd once been married to the mob boss Marcello, and to terrify Rose, who had witnessed a hit on that family's son by a rival family.

"Oh, no." Rose groaned. "Does this mean Matthew and I have to die again?"

Christine sure hoped not but Jackson looked worried. Rose loved it in Even and she'd just been taken in by the locals.

"Depends," Lester said. "On what these two decide to do."

"I don't understand," Christine said.

"If you're one of us, we'll deal with Martin. Our old enemy goes dormant again. If you ain't one of us, Rose and Matthew have to leave Even and start over for their own protection. You compromised them in their current location."

Torn between crying and screaming, Christine did neither. "I'm sorry, Rose. Matthew."

Rose squeezed her eyes shut, then opened them. "Me, too."

"So here's the bottom line," Lester said. "As of right now, you're engaged. You have six months to marry. If you choose not to, then that's it. If you do, life goes on. You'll return to your cottages and not interact with other residents until you decide and execute your decisions."

"Six months' house arrest?" Jackson grunted. "Lester, that's not reasonable."

"It's extremely reasonable. You'll both be breathing."

Christine couldn't believe this. They were as serious as a heart attack, but out of their ever-loving minds. Stay within the four walls of the cottage for six months? "What about my business?"

"No computers or electronics in the Park," Lester reminded her. "But Dex will have someone take over during your absence and keep the business going."

"Someone well qualified, Christine," Dex assured her. "You've no need to worry."

"No need to worry? I've poured my life into my business. Do you realize how long six months is in my technology world?"

"Your business is the least of your worries," Lester reminded her. "If you forfeit your life, you forfeit all of it, including your business. Now that's worth considering."

Chills rippled through her body. She stiffened.

"Your business is in good hands," Dex assured her. "You have my word."

"What about me?" Jackson asked. "My restaurant…?"

Lester snarled. "Your restaurant is covered."

Christine asked, "You own your own restaurant?"

"I was working on it."

That he thought that dream was now dead was clear. More guilt swamped Christine, heaping onto the old. She'd cost him everything, cost herself everything. "I'm sorry."

"Please, stop saying that." Jackson turned to face her. "I know, okay? I'm sorry, too, but done is done and being sorry isn't going to change things. So just stop saying it. Please."

It was all she could do not to say it again. He was so upset, and the blame truly was all on her. Riding the edge, she felt certain if she said it again, he'd pop a cork. Not that it wouldn't be warranted, but being in such close proximity during that explosion was just plain stupid. "What about Caroline?" Christine asked Lester. "Will you be looking for her? I have to know what's happened to her."

"Dex told you we had her covered. Leave Caroline to us." Mr. Perini and not Lester answered.

She opened her mouth to insist on details. Surely they had a plan for finding her sister. But face-to-face, the committee looked out of patience, and innately Christine feared anything she said would just turn them further against her. Caro could suffer as a result. Mr. Perini had claimed Caro as family. They wouldn't turn a blind eye to her. Not with their rabid security and fierce protective attitudes about family.

"Is that it, then?" Jackson asked.

"That's it." Lester nodded.

Jackson stood up, looked back at Lucas. "You'll be escorting us back, I guess."

Lucas stepped forward, though he didn't seem comfortable with it. "No choice."

"Yeah." Jackson looked at Christine. "Let's go."

Christine stood up, more than ready to be off the hot seat. It'd take time to process all this, but already she knew she had only two ways out of this place: Married to Jackson, or toes up in a body bag.

Chapter 33

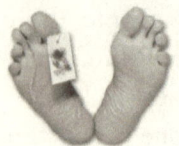

Just after sundown, Christine lifted her cottage window. A bowl of walnuts had been placed on the little table to her left. Who'd put them there? She had no idea. Someone had also restocked the pantry and filled the fridge with bottles of the flavored water she favored.

She pulled a walnut from the bowl, but hesitated. Odds were slim Jackson would come to his window. He had to be ready to wring her neck. But if they didn't try to work past this, at the end of six months…

She tossed the walnut.

No response. After waiting a few minutes, she tried again.

Still no response. But she caught a whiff on the breeze. *Popcorn?*

Leaning out the window, she looked but didn't see feet or lawn chairs. Whether that was a good or bad sign, she didn't know. She went to the vanity and dug through the cosmetics, looking for the little mirror but it was gone.

Disappointment sank into her like sharp talons. The committee knew about the mirror and the walnuts, too. She should consider herself lucky, she supposed, they hadn't taken her out right there in the conference room.

Back at the window, she reached to grab another nut to try Jackson again. A tomato splatted against her shoulder.

"Jackson!" Her shoulder stinging, she glared across the opening.

"Sorry," he said, looking contrite. "I thought the window was closed."

"Give me a second." She held up a staying fingertip, grabbed a dishtowel and swiped the mess from her shoulder into the trash, washed up, changed her t-shirt, and then returned to the window.

Maybe she should wait until tomorrow to talk to him. Today really had not been a good day for either of them. But, she changed her mind, things couldn't get any worse. Today or tomorrow, what difference did it make? Unless they talked through some of this, there's no way either of them would get a wink of sleep.

She looked across the lawn to his window. "I'm back."

"Meet me at the property line," he told her. "Bring a chair—and wine."

She hesitated. "You still ticked-off at me?"

"I'm not ticked-off. I'm miffed," he admitted. "I get why you did what you did, but, dang, Christine, it's costing us everything."

No way was she saying she was sorry again. "Ticked-off, miffed. Same thing."

"Come to the property line," he said. "We've got to work together, or we're both sunk."

Valid point. Since she couldn't dispute it, she nodded, grabbed a chair and a bottle of wine from the kitchen. Did he want red or white? Unsure, she snagged one of each and a corkscrew, then headed out the front door. When she stepped off the porch, she half-expected to see the lawn chairs, but there were none. The villagers watching them must have lost its appeal since Christine had jeopardized their futures.

Shame and guilt hit her hard. The jeopardy hadn't been intentional, but, as the saying goes, the road to hell is paved with good intentions.

Skirting the hydrangeas, she rounded the corner of the cottage. Jackson had a little table straddling the property line. "Are you sure we're not violating any of their rules?" Christine wasn't opposed to breaking them if she had to, but she wanted to know she was doing it.

"We're good." Jackson pointed to little orange flags stuck in the ground. "I asked Lucas to mark the boundary line to be sure."

"They'd probably cut off our legs, or something."

"I don't think so." Jackson placed a white cloth on the table. "They planted the idea."

They had. Christine scooted her chair into place, then set the wine on the table. "I didn't know if you wanted red or white, so I brought both."

"That's good news. I thought, after today, you were planning on getting sloshed."

"I don't do sloshed, but if I did, today would be the day for it." She set the corkscrew beside the wine. "What are we eating?"

He turned to a slender second table behind him. "Pot roast, carrots and potatoes. And brownies for desert." He shrugged. "I figured you might need them."

Her favorite. Such a thoughtful gesture. Even more so since he was admittedly miffed. "Thank you, Jackson."

He filled their plates and set them on the table. "You look tense. Is it them keeping the money, or are you worried sick about Caroline?"

"The money's fine." Christine sighed. "But saying I should leave Caro to them?" Did she dare? "It was comforting to hear Mr. Perini say they considered her family, though. I'm ninety percent sure, there's nothing these people won't do for family."

"I'll vouch for that." He pointed with a nod. "Eat."

If Jackson believed them without any reservations… She didn't know them well enough, but she trusted Jackson and his judgment. "It smells really good." She lifted her fork. "I'm having to restrain myself to keep from going for dessert first."

He opened the red wine and filled two glasses. "Why?"

"Just in case…"

"Ah, you're also worried about the dead thing." Something in his expression shifted and eased.

She had to have imagined that easing. Jackson seemed a little surprised and maybe a tiny bit amused. Perhaps being faced with the prospect of losing everything had been too much? "Uh, yeah." She frowned. "Of course, I'm worried about the dead thing. Aren't you?"

"Concerned? Yes," he said. "Worried? No. Big difference."

The smell of popcorn faded and roast filled her. "How can you not be worried? I honestly don't know if I can swallow."

"I know them better. They love me, Christine," Jackson said. "You can and will swallow—for you or for me. I've been cooking since we got back. Show some appreciation."

Her stomach growled and she took a bite. The beef melted in her mouth, juicy and tender. "It's good."

"That's my secret ingredient." He offered her a hot French roll.

"Why not?" She took it. Slathered on butter. It was senseless to worry about carbs and weight when you were living on borrowed time. Around here, any meal could be your last. "I can't imagine them not searching for Caro."

"They've got every available resource looking for her. And this bunch has a lot of resources."

"How do you know that?"

Jackson sniffed. "I told you, I know them. They took her into their hearts. They'll do whatever to whomever wherever to find Caro and make sure she's safe."

That reassured Christine in ways nothing else had. "You truly believe that."

He swallowed. "I know it for fact."

She let out a shuddery sigh, took a bite of carrot. "Thanks for sharing your insight with me. I've been about to go crazy, worrying." She sipped at the wine. "How do you think Martin found Sampson Park?"

"My guess is the New Orleans bunch directed him to it."

"The mob knows about the Park?"

Jackson stilled. He hesitated for a long moment, his emotions rioting in his face. Fear he'd said too much, doubt and uncertainty, and what struck her as longing, though she must have misread that. "Are you going to marry me, Christine?"

She sputtered. "I—I don't know." He hadn't really asked, and if he had, she wasn't sure how she would respond.

"Well, if and when you do marry me, I'll answer that question. Until then, I won't."

He knew the answer but was afraid loose lips would sink his ship. "I didn't think… I'm sor—" She stopped herself just in time.

They ate in silence. When Christine finished, she set down her fork, and refilled her wine glass. They had to talk about this marriage thing. Otherwise, they'd sit here six months and still end up toe-tagged. "I never really thought about getting married," she said. "I know lots of women do. Some think about their wedding day from the time they can walk. I just wasn't one of them."

"So you're against marriage?"

"No, I just never saw myself doing it. I guess if I'd ever been crazy in love, then I would have thought about it, but—we talked about this, Jackson, remember?"

"I do. We'd lost loved ones and focused on making our lives stellar so we didn't have to feel guilty about living."

"Well, that's a little bald, but yeah." She set down her glass. "Have you ever thought about getting married?"

"Sure." He tilted his head. "Later."

Later. After. Tomorrow. She smiled. "So what are we going to do?"

"I don't know." He sat back. "I'll admit. Sometimes I do get lonesome, but I have a pretty good life."

"I think even married people get lonesome sometimes," she said.

"I expect so." He paused, his thoughts wandering. "But when I see Rose and Matthew together, it gets to me."

"How? Are you jealous of their relationship? Because I could get that. For all those years, it was you and Rose against the world, now Matthew…"

"No. No way. I love Matthew like a brother. What gets to me is how in sync they are. It's like, no matter what life throws at them, they can deal with it. Like the baby debate."

"The baby debate?" Christine was lost.

"Should they have a baby? Rose says yes, Matthew says no. Then Matthew says yes, and Rose says no. They have good reasons to be uneasy, to wait, to have one right now, if that's what they want, but they go back and forth, seemingly always landing on opposite sides of the debate."

Finally, Christine pegged Jackson's thinking. "So they oppose during the debate, but they remain together during and after it."

"Totally." He nodded. "Like two halves of a whole having an inward discussion out loud."

"Balancing each other out," Christine said, thoughtful. That kind of synergy was hard to imagine having with a man when you'd never experienced it. Yet, often she had found Jackson and she doing that. Probably not to the same extent—too many secrets on both sides—but relatable.

What would that be like without secrets? She imagined it. That kind of bond would be... well, kind of amazing. "I think it's good to have a partner, especially when life's hard."

"Yeah. And life can be really hard, you know?"

It could. Even when things were going well. Shared joy had its perks over celebrating victories alone. She nodded. "So you want that—a bond like Rose and Matthew have."

Jackson looked across the table. "Definitely," he said. "They drive each other nuts now and then, too."

"That's normal." Christine said. "I see it in all my married friends. Though, when whatever has them at odds is over, it's over, and they're right back to being close."

"Were your parents content together?" he asked. "I can't judge by mine, considering I never knew my dad and my mom took off."

"I think so, yeah." Christine dug deep into her memories. "They looked at each other sometimes, and when they'd talk, they'd lean toward each other, really listening." She grunted. "I do think they were content."

"Of course, some aren't married and are content with each other, too," Jackson said. "Like Miss Emily and Lester. Sometimes, they have an entire conversation with just a look." He smiled. "They give each other fits, too, but... I can't imagine one without the other."

"They rely on each other. That's what all this is about," Christine decided. She looked at Jackson, weighed and measured. "I think I could rely on you and be fine with it." Oh, no. She'd said that out loud! Her face heated. "But I totally get your hesitancy to rely on me."

"I'm not hesitant to rely on you." He stared at her a long second. "I do rely on you, Christine. If I didn't, we wouldn't be having this conversation."

"Oh." What did that mean? She didn't dare try to reason it out. It could be really good. Or not.

"Ready for your brownie?"

She smiled. "Always."

He passed her a large brownie.

Obviously, the man wasn't counting calories, or he thought she needed serious comforting after the trials of the day. The gray hoodie woman flashed through her mind. "Jackson, did you notice the woman sitting next to Millie today? She was wearing sunglasses and a grey hoodie."

He chewed and swallowed a bite of brownie. "I saw her. Well, kind of saw her. I never got a clear look at her face. Why?"

"I never saw her face either." Christine took another bite, savored the rich chocolate taste. "I think that might have been deliberate. Every time I looked back, she turned away."

"Mmm." He didn't put much in it. "Lots of people have quirks here. Probably nothing personal."

"Maybe. I can't imagine it has anything to do with us." Christine glanced to the left, at the garden. The plants were over-her-head tall, and thick. "Does the property line extend into the community garden?"

"Why?"

"Do you smell those tomatoes?" She sniffed. "I saw them before from the window."

"And I hit you with one." He looked contrite. "I really did think the window was closed."

"I got you with a walnut and you forgave me. I'll forgive you for the tomato." She smiled. "What I was going to say, is it was hard not to go snitch a couple tomatoes from the garden."

"They're there for the taking, but we can't go get them. Cottage property ends at that last flag."

It was at least six feet to the first row of tomato plants. "Who keeps up with the garden?"

"Everybody does a little. A guy a couple of cottages down works in it a lot right at dark. I've seen him from my bedroom window upstairs."

"His thumbs must be forest green. Those plants are enormous."

They chatted about the garden, about the horseshoe games on Little Independence Day, about their other lives in Dallas.

Then they sat silently. It wasn't a stilted kind of silence, it was comfortable. "I think we both spend too much time working in Dallas and too little time having fun."

"We discussed this," Jackson said.

"Yeah, but we didn't actually name fun things we'd like to do."

"We were going to, we just couldn't think of anything," Jackson told her. "Which is really sad, when you think about it."

"Do you dance?" she asked.

"A little. I'm no pro at it, but I enjoy a twirl now and then."

"I'd like to dance, I think." She paused, then added. "Yeah, I would. I think I would enjoy that."

"How about water-skiing?" He leaned toward her. "I've watched people do it, but I've never tried."

"I've watched a couple videos of it on YouTube. That's as close as I've gotten to it."

"We could learn that together, I guess."

"Preferably somewhere there are no sharks or alligators in the water."

"You're knocking out all the water in and around the State of Florida."

"And more."

"Are we striking out again on fun things?" she asked.

"Scraping bottom."

Christine drummed her fingers against the table. "When I was little, we went to this amusement park and I rode the rollercoaster. It was thrilling."

"You loved it thrilling, or it scared your socks off thrilling?"

"I rode it three times. Loved it."

"We could become rollercoaster connoisseurs."

"Maybe we need to think about this fun thing a little more." Christine yawned. "But I've about maxed out for today. My brain feels gauzy."

Jackson stood up. "We can tackle this tomorrow. Let's call it a night."

A NOISE inside the cottage awakened Christine from a dead sleep.

Her heart rate shot through the stratosphere. *Martin? Had he come back and found her?*

Surely not. Lucas and the security team had stopped Martin from entering the Park. Now they were on full-alert. If Martin tried to come back, he'd be met with maximum force. Even the arrogant idiot had to know it. No, he would come back; she didn't doubt it. But he'd seek a subtle way to do it.

She tossed back the covers and crept to the bedroom door, then stopped to listen.

Splat.

More curious than afraid now that she'd convinced herself she wouldn't have to face the man unarmed, she made her way downstairs and just missed being hit with a tomato to the face. It sailed by and splat against the back of the sofa. She flipped on the light. The floor was littered with them. She looked at the window. Saw yet another one zing by and hit a chair leg.

"Jackson! Knock it off." She rushed to the window.

He drew back. "The window was open?"

"Uh, yeah." She tiptoed through the tomatoes. It'd take her half an hour to clean up this mess.

"Oh." He grimaced. "I thought you were sleeping and I was trying to wake you."

"What for?" She grabbed a broom, mop and trash bin.

"I wanted to talk to you about something," he said.

"How many of these things did you throw, anyway?" She'd cleaned up half a dozen already.

"I don't know." He sighed. "Could you do that in a minute. I need your attention."

"I'm not sure you want my attention right now, Jackson Grant."

"It's important, Christine."

She glanced over. By his expression, this was important to him. She leaned the broom against the wall then returned to the window. "Okay, you have my attention. Did we break some other rule, or something?"

"No," he said, then repeated. "No, I couldn't sleep."

"Uh-huh." Her arms crossed her chest.

"So I've been thinking."

Two in the morning, and his not sleeping and thinking became something important she needed to address now? "Did you try a cup of warm milk?"

"I don't need warm milk to think, honey."

Testy. She squeezed her folded her arms closer against her body. "What do you need?"

He loosened his t-shirt at his neck. "I have an idea I want to talk over with you."

"Now?"

He nodded. "It's about this marriage thing."

This marriage thing. "I believe I need coffee for this. Give me a minute." She put on a pot then dragged a chair to the window.

To Jackson's credit, he waited until she was seated and had downed a few steamy sips from her cup before saying another word. "Okay, I'm ready now," she said.

"Okay." Seated on his windowsill, he asked, "What if we approach this marriage thing logically?"

Had they been illogical? "Explain."

"We're attracted, right?" He lifted his arms. "I mean, it's pretty obvious."

"I'll stipulate to that. We're attracted."

He looked pleased. "But we need to know if it's going to last. Marriage takes more than an attraction."

"Agreed, it does." She refilled her cup. This was going to be a two—maybe three—cup conversation. She needed to be fully awake.

"Make a list of what you want, Christine. I'll make one, too. Then, in the morning, we can go over them and see if we're even on the same planet."

"A list." She tapped a fingertip against her cup. It wasn't a bad idea. Surely they both knew what they wanted…

"Yeah. A brutally honest list."

"I'd like to disagree with you," she said. "About this and for splattering my floor with tomatoes. But it's a reasonable idea and makes sense."

He nodded. "I thought so. I mean, if we want different things and there's no way we're going to meet in the middle and be content, sitting here for six months isn't going to close the gaps, you know?"

She'd thought the same thing herself. "Okay."

"I'll make French toast for breakfast," he said.

Her heart skipped a little beat. He remembered she loved French toast. "Okay. Night, Jackson."

"Night, Christine." He smiled. "Oh, and I'm sorry about the…" He motioned, mimicking the tomato toss.

"Not a problem." She shut the window, in case he had any more important ideas that couldn't wait until morning, finished cleaning up the tomatoes, then grabbed a pen and pad and went back up to bed.

When she'd settled in, she stared at the blank page. What did she want in a husband?

Her mind flitted from thing to thing. *Respect. Faithfulness. Honesty.* She wrote them all down…and then scratched them out. Jackson gave her those things already; it was his nature.

She thought some more, of things she didn't want. Things that wrecked marriages. Wrote them down…and then scratched them off. Jackson had been abandoned. He'd never pull those stunts on her or anyone else.

The blank page mocked her.

He was probably over there lying in bed writing a book, and she was stuck staring at a blank page? Furiously, she began to write. Anything. Everything. All things.

Hours later, when she cleared all the clutter from her mind, dumped the kitchen sink onto the page and finished scratching out, she'd done it. Satisfied with the finished draft, she let out a content sigh, stretched over to the bedside table's lamp and turned off the light.

Her list was complete.

Chapter 34

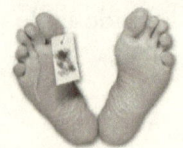

The smell of French toast wafted in the air.

Christine sat down at the table straddling the property line, hoping she looked at least a little better than she felt.

Jackson wore jeans and a lemon yellow t-shirt. Concern tensed his face. "Are you sick?"

"Hangover—I think."

"That's a stretch. You had less than two glasses of wine."

"Tell that to my head." It had been pounding since she got out of bed.

"Eat. You'll feel better."

Plying her body with carbs probably wasn't the smartest thing she could do, but he had gone to all the trouble of making her breakfast, and it did smell really good. She looked at the plate of French toast and sausage Jackson placed on the table. It looked great and smelled better. Her stomach growled. "Maybe just a little."

Jackson sat down. "Did you bring your list?"

She nodded. "But I want to change it," she said, then took another bite, chewed and swallowed. "Oh, Jackson. This is awesome."

"French toast is one of my specialties." He winked, then turned serious. "So what do you want to change on your list."

"I have to tell you, I'm really liking this whole food thing. Usually I live on take-out and delivery. I have a wonderful kitchen on the ranchette, but the less time I spend in it, the better I like it."

"So you're adding me doing the cooking to your list?"

"Why not? You're good at it and I definitely am not."

"I have a hard time seeing you not being good at anything you put your mind to."

"I'd rather not put my mind to cooking." Christine reached for another piece of French toast. "So what's on your list?" She tried to keep her voice light, but felt a catch in her stomach. Her mind had gone crazy with all the things that could be on it.

He reached to the table behind him and grabbed not one but two yellow-lined tablets.

Worry flooded her. "Two tablets? That's a lot of wants, Jackson."

"This is marriage. It's important and lasts forever." He set the tablets beside his plate.

If he did marry her, it wouldn't be for expediency's sake or even to live. Not with two tablets full of wants. That should be a good thing—he'd clearly put a lot of thought into it—but was it? The first page, which was all she could see, was packed. He'd even written in the margins. Her stomach twisted and her heart sank. Oh, this didn't bode well for her or for them. Who could measure up to so much stuff?

"I wrote for hours," he said.

"Hours?"

"Oh, yeah. The more I thought about it, the more things came to me." He polished off a link of sausage, then dabbed at the corner of his mouth with a napkin. "I read back through it several times, and it all seems very logical to me." He stilled, then risked a glance at her. "The problem is, relationships are messy. They're emotional and spiritual, too. And it occurred to me, logic isn't enough."

"What are you saying?"

"I want it all," he said softly. "And, if I can't have it all, I don't want any of it."

She stiffened. "Seriously?" They were going to kill them. He got that, so how could he make his wants so definitive? So black and white?

"Seriously." He nodded, lending weight to his response. "Marriage is… intimate. If you can't have it all, what you end up with is nothing except a lot of misery. With our histories, we've had plenty of that. We don't need to purposely add more."

She thought about it, then confessed. "I ended up in the same place as you, but I took a different route to get there." She sipped from her coffee. "Marriage is hard enough for people with it all. I can't imagine anyone being content with only part of what it takes to make it—and if I do it, I sincerely want to make it, Jackson."

He seemed relieved to hear that, and nodded. "We're on the same page there." He cut a piece of sausage and took a bite. "When I started dating, I went bat-crazy over this girl in History. She wanted no part of me, and I couldn't figure out why. I talked with Lester about it."

"Lester?"

Jackson nodded. "I told him I was in love with this girl but she didn't need me. I asked Lester what I could do."

"What did he say?"

"He said, 'When you find a woman and you want to be with her, you love things about her. Even annoying things. But a wise man never hungers for a woman because he needs her or she needs him.'"

"He's just knocked out half the relationships of the people I know."

"Exactly. Me, too." Jackson nodded. "So I wrote all this stuff down and then I remembered what Lester said. That made me think of you. You're smart, beautiful, gutsy and rich. You don't need me for anything. So, I wonder… What can I offer you that you don't have without me?"

That he was asking in earnest was clear. Did the man not see all his good qualities? "You might be surprised at all you bring to this table, Jackson. Aside from the food."

"Like what?"

Christine's hand shook. He had tomes over there and she had a single sheet of paper. She unfolded the yellow-lined page and passed it over. "My complete list."

Jackson took the sheet of paper, his hand not quite steady. He read it aloud. "I want you, Jackson."

"Me?" His expression changed from curious to stunned. "That's it?"

"That's my everything." She nodded. "You care for me, you understand me, you respect me, and you forgive me. You might be miffed, but you do forgive me." Certainty filled her voice, though his expression left a little room for doubt. "I think the clincher for me was when you came into the diner in Even. You spotted me and it was the first thing I saw in you."

"What did you see?"

"You had this amazing twinkle in your eyes. Like your sun and moon rose in me. It isn't there when you look at anyone else, not even Rose or Miss Emily." Christine had found that hard to believe. "Then, and every time since, when you look at me, I see the twinkle. It's mine." She swallowed hard. "I love that twinkle, Jackson."

"A twinkle." He grunted. "So what does it mean exactly?" he asked.

"Everything, to me. It says I'm… special to you. I matter. Is it love? I'm not sure, but if it isn't yet, it has enormous potential unlike anything I've ever known."

"So you're saying…?"

He wasn't going to comment. All that, and he still asked more questions. She got that. He had good reasons to have so little trust in relationships, as did she. But one of them had to take the leap or they'd both end up with nothing. "I'm saying, let's do this—unless I fall short on the wants on your list. Considering you've written volumes, I expect I will." That created an enormous amount of angst in her, especially after she'd put herself on the line and leapt. "I want you to be happy. Content and happy and—"

"You want me to have it all?"

She nodded. "And I want to have it all… with you."

He hiked an eyebrow. "So you're all in on us marrying? On everything?"

Just give it to him. You know what he's waiting to hear. Just do it. She tried, but at this point, she was so far out on the limb alone. She'd been brave, courageous even, but he had to climb part way out with her. He really did, or this would never work. "All in on everything. I am, yes."

A slow smile split his lips. "Okay, then."

"Not yet, okay. No, it's not okay yet." She wagged a finger at his tablets. "What is all that?"

"Just stuff it took me writing through to get to my bottom line."

Surprise and relief shot through her. "So that's not a laundry list of stuff I'll read and try to remember and never be able to live up to, so I have to feel I've failed you every day for the rest of our lives?"

"Good grief, no." He chuckled. Picking up the second tablet, he flipped to the last page, and held it up so she could read it. "Here's my list."

She couldn't believe her eyes. "You." One word. "You want me?"

"I love you, Christine." Jackson said softly. "All the rest of this was for me. But the truth is none of it matters. I love you. That's what matters. I want you."

Tears gathered in her eyes. "I love you, too, Jackson."

They stretched across the table, met in the middle and kissed.

Chapter 35

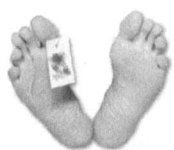

The garden came to life.

People popped up all along the rows of tomato plants, applauding, laughing, wiping away joyful tears.

Jackson stepped back and to the side of the table, pulled Christine close, he on his side of the line, she on hers. Miss Emily, Lester, Mr. Jenkins, Darby and Speckles—even Dexter Devlin—joined with dozens of villagers cheering.

"What is all this?" Christine asked, clearly as confused as Jackson.

"I think they've been watching us from the garden." Jackson's face heated.

Christine looked up into his downturned face. "I did smell popcorn again, and I was going to look for the chairs but my mirror was gone."

"Lester did this. They knew we were on to them, watching us through the trees from the front lawn. That's why Dex asked why we didn't meet at the property line. They set us up."

"Obviously. But why would they do that?"

"Good question." Jackson wanted to be angry. Outraged. But

looking into their joyful and excited faces, he couldn't work up the righteous indignation to be either. So instead, he bowed.

Christine laughed, curtsied, and gave them a royal wave.

Lester crossed the property line and shook Jackson's hand, clapped him on the shoulder. "Congratulations, my boy." He hugged Christine. "Welcome to the family."

"You planned all of this," she said. "Why?"

"Caroline knew Jackson was the one for you," Lester said. "She also knew neither of you would slow down working long enough to realize it. So we decided to intervene and give you the opportunity. Jackson, being Jackson, was predictable, and so are you. We figured you'd enter the forbidden zone, and that if you saw Caroline's tombstone, Jackson would move heaven and earth to comfort you."

"But that's entrapment?"

Lester shrugged. "Yeah, great isn't it?" He cackled. "It worked, too."

Shock pumped through Christine. "Are you saying all this with Martin was to get Jackson and I together?"

"Absolutely not," Miss Emily said. "Everything that happened with Martin Branch was real. Well, everything outside the Park."

The woman in the sunglasses and gray hoodie stepped from the garden over to them.

Christine's jaw fell loose. "Caroline!" Tears filled Christine's eyes and flowed down her face. "You're here. You're okay?" She crushed her sister in a hard hug, shaking from the adrenaline rush. "Oh, thank you, God. Thank you!" When she could bear to release her, she turned. "Jackson, it's Caroline!"

Caroline stood beside Christine. Her relief was so intense it had him blinking. His eyes shone overly bright. "I see her." He smiled. "Welcome back, Caro. You're a sight for sore eyes."

"Thanks." She smiled. "I have to say, you two put on quite a show."

Christine stilled. Her smile faded. "You've been watching us? All this time?"

"No," she quickly corrected her twin. "Just since the committee meeting—from the garden with the others."

"All of you spied on us?" Christine shot Jackson a feigned frown. "I'm stunned."

"Bosh. You both knew it," Lester said. "Unless your sniffer is on hiatus, you had to smell our popcorn."

No way did Christine want to go there. She looked at her sister. "Where have you been all this time?"

"At the ranch," she said.

"You've been in Dallas?"

"No, at the ranch here." She smiled. "Chaplain Goodman went on his trip, so I went on one of my own. I chose to spend time with the animals at the ranch, so I did it." She got a knowing look in her eyes. "Sometimes they're better company than people. I was having such a good time, I chose to stay a while longer, so Patches—he runs the ranch—set me up in the bunkhouse."

Christine planted her hands on her hips. "Did it occur to you I've been worried sick about you?"

"Well, of course, it did." Christine flipped back her hood and ran a hand through her short red hair. "There are no phones in the Park. What could I do?" Her mouth twisted to one side. "Honestly, Christine, I never thought it'd take you months to go to Even. I couldn't have expected that."

"I was afraid I'd lead Martin to you."

"That's what Dex said." Caro nodded. "Sorry about your worry, but we were certain you would get there. Since we needed the time to neutralize Martin, in case he did follow you here—" Caro shot Dexter Devlin a look of sheer gratitude "—we went with it."

"I was going crazy, not finding you here."

"I know. Lucas told me how you searched and searched. I am so sorry about that, but once I got here, I really couldn't reach you—no electronics in the Park—and I asked Mr. Jenkins nearly every day at tea about getting you a message, and he assured me all was well in hand. I had no idea you'd arrived until the committee meeting. I had to promise not to reveal myself."

"Not to reveal yourself?" Furious at that remark, Christine pinned Jackson with a shriveling glare.

"Wasn't me," he said, shrugging. "I didn't know it."

Christine wasn't at all happy with this revelation, and she intended to let somebody know it. "Who made you promise, Caro?" Christine had been half out of her mind with worry. And someone deliberately had kept the truth from her?

Miss Emily stepped forward. "She promised me."

"Miss Emily?" That admission knocked Christine back a full step, and then another. "Why would you do that?"

"You and Jackson needed a little more time to figure out what all of us already knew. So we gave it to you." She shifted on her feet. "We told you at committee, dear, to leave Caroline to us." She sniffed. "I'm a little disappointed that you didn't trust us to see to it she was fine."

"Trust you?" Christine bellowed. "You were threatening to kill Jackson and me unless we married."

Rose hugged Jackson. "The delay couldn't be helped, but I can't believe I missed the big reveal. So you love each other—and you finally know it." Rose beamed. "I'm so happy for you, Jackson. You too, Christine. I'm going to love having a sister."

"Thanks, sis." Jackson crossed his chest with his arms and nodded toward Christine. "I hope she calms down sometime in the next few years. She's pretty miffed."

"I'll see if I can help smooth the waters," Rose whispered, then turned to Christine. "The committee threatening to kill you is no reason to marry my brother, Christine."

She turned to her future sister-in-law. "I know that. But I couldn't find my missing sister if I was dead, now could I?"

A collective gasp rippled through the crowd.

Rose pinned Christine with a stare. "Is that why you agreed to marry Jackson?"

"Don't be ridiculous, Rose. I love Jackson. But I won't lie. I didn't want to die."

"Dying is a messy ordeal," Jackson said, "but it's not that bad."

Rose and half the others agreed with him. Christine couldn't believe her ears. "Not that bad? The end of life is not that bad? Are you serious?"

"Well, yeah." Jackson seemed confused. "You have to leave

everything you've got behind, but you get new identities, put down new roots. Some actually like it, having another chance for a new beginning."

The group agreed, and an earlier conversation with Jackson from the little cemetery came back. Christine stopped. "Dead isn't really dead—at least not here." She pivoted toward Miss Emily. "You weren't going to *really* kill us, were you?"

She stiffened. "What do you think?"

"What I thought was that you—the whole committee—was being literal, but now… Oh, dear Lord. You meant dead as in a fresh start." She shot a look to Jackson for confirmation and got only a flat look. "Rose?" Christine pivoted to her. "How many times have you been dead?"

"Um, three—so far. But it could soon be four," she said.

Matthew grunted. "Rose totally blew it the first time. Not the dying. She did that fine. Just the staying dead part."

"I needed practice."

"You said it could soon be four." Jackson's smile faded. "You're having to leave Even anyway?" When Rose shrugged, contrition filled Jackson. "I am so sorry, sis."

"It's not yet settled," Rose said. "Mr. Perini's thinking about retiring next spring. If he does, then Matthew and I might take over for him in Dixie." Her broad smile forecast her feeling that this specific move wouldn't be a bad thing.

Jackson's brow furrowed. "If Mr. Perini retires, where's he going?" He'd been in Dixie, Florida, for a lot of years.

"Here." Rose smiled. "He says he's always planned to move to Sampson Park permanently. He'd be free to help any associate anywhere in the wor… er, anywhere around who needs it. Wouldn't that be great?"

"If it's what he wants, it would," Jackson said. "Good for you and Matthew, too. He's got so many established contacts in Dixie."

"Including Barry." Rose was fond of Barry, Mr. Perini's assistant. "Matthew and I are excited at the prospect, though if it doesn't happen, that's fine, too."

"If the move comes to pass, what happens in Even?" Jackson asked.

"An associate would come in from Dallas to take over."

"Not me, right?" Jackson asked. "Christine and I—"

"Have no reason to die that we know of. Stay in Dallas. Live wherever you like," Rose said. "No, this is an associate… well, she's definitely down and dead there. But she could live a great life in Even."

The puzzle pieces fell into place for Christine, and she chided herself for it taking so long. This group had a franchise of funeral homes, for pity's sake. When one of the residents or someone new needed a fresh start, like Caro, they facilitated one.

After the mountains the group had moved to help Caro and everyone else, Christine saw the need for their services, but who could have expected to find anyone offering them? "So what about Martin and his henchmen?"

Dexter Devlin stepped forward, to Caroline's side. "The henchmen have returned to their former lives. Martin can no longer afford to employ them."

Christine's jaw dropped open and a gleam lit in her eye. "You took him down."

"We did," Dex said, smiling at Caro.

She looped her arm around his waist and laughed, hard and deep. "What Dex uncovers with forensic accounting is a sight to behold."

"So did Martin really hook up with the mob and breach the Park perimeter?" Jackson scanned and spotted Lucas in the group. "Was it him?"

"A group of teens wanting to see the Little Independence Day celebration," Lucas said. "We fudged a little to keep you and Christine anchored until we figured out what was going on with Caro."

Christine looked at her sister. "Wait. I'm confused… So Martin hasn't found Sampson Park?"

"Absolutely not." Caroline guffawed. "If he had, he'd be worse off than broke." She smiled. "Nobody messes with this family, Christine. Not without paying really steep consequences."

"All righty, then." Lester clapped his hands together. "Let's go people. We got a wedding to plan."

"Now?" Christine said.

"Naw, we got a few days. Chaplain Goodman is still on the mountain communing." Lester planted a kiss to her cheek. "Glad you made the cut, my girl. You'll be a good match for our Jackson."

Miss Emily elbowed Lester out of the way and hugged Christine. "I couldn't be happier. The sparks between you two is a sight to behold. I want my boy happy, Christine, and I want you happy, too." She glanced to see Caro, talking softly with Dex. "Sorry about the little delay in easing your mind about your sister," Miss Emily whispered. "Caro's exerting her authority, doing *only* what she chooses to do." Miss Emily dropped her voice a wee bit more. "It's her rebellious stage."

And they were all indulging her. Caro looked well and happy, and more confident. "She's wearing that authority thing well," Christine said. "Why is her hair still red? Do you know?"

"She says blondes get treated like doormats but nobody messes with redheads. No one is ever going to mess with her again. Not that any of us would tolerate anything of the sort. Especially Dex. She'll figure out that her hair color doesn't matter directly. That kind of insight comes from inside. Right now, she needs what she needs. And she needs the physical sign reminding her she can handle herself, you know?"

Pretty much what Mr. Jenkins had said. "I'd much rather see her strong and confident like this than scared to death like she was with Martin."

"That's a real killer, to be sure. But, honey, don't you give that sorry bit of baggage another thought. He will never touch her again. She's learned self-defense from Lucas, and to ride a horse and to shoot. Patches has been training her, and he says she's very good. She's motivated, is my take. But the best thing is she's worked closely with Dex and gotten back all her assets Martin had stolen from her. Now she knows she can because she has. I'll leave it for her to tell you. She's learned all kinds of tactics—not that Martin Easton will ever get close enough to her for her to need them. Point is, our Caro is not fragile or helpless anymore and *she* knows it. She's empowered and capable of dealing with anything Martin or anyone else throws her way." Miss Emily leaned close and dropped her voice so only Christine could hear. "Between you and me, Dex has made it his mission in life the past six months to see to it Martin's got nothing left to throw at our Caro." She sniffed. "If anything, I expect he's terrified of Caro now and of what she might do to him next. Those demons are in his own mind, of course. She's moved on."

Shock pumped through Christine. "Martin really is bankrupt?"

Miss Emily tilted her head. "Not bankrupt. He can live modestly, but let's just say, he'll have a hard time scraping together enough money to make anyone else miserable."

"That's a kindness to the world."

"We do what we can." Miss Emily nodded and again whispered with a twinkle in her eye. "I think our Caro is developing a fondness for our Dex."

"Caroline and Dexter Devlin?" Christine couldn't wrap her mind around that.

"They've worked together a great deal since Caro arrived, and Dex has spent more time here than away." Miss Emily chuckled. "He's definitely smitten, but he's taking things really slow. Caro needs time to heal and time being healed, if you know what I mean."

She did. Gratitude swelled and thickened Christine's voice. "Thank you, Miss Emily. For everything."

She cupped Christine's jaw. "We're all someone's bridge, sweet Christine." She glanced left and her mouth rounded in an O. "Lester, be mindful of that flower bed. Gracie's planted her some flower seeds there." He stepped in it, and she frowned. "Lead-footed man." She rushed to catch up to him.

Jackson circled Christine with an arm at her shoulder. "Pretty awesome family we have, isn't it?" He dropped a kiss to her jaw. "I love happy endings."

Christine's mind still whirled, but her heart was settled and sure. She nodded. These people were awesome and genuine. A few little questions remained, but they would sort out with time. When you knew the hearts of people, you didn't have to worry so much about their motives, and she was crystal clear on their hearts. *Be someone's bridge.*

By grace, she had become part of them, as had Jackson. Now all of these people were her bridge, and she would forever be theirs. *Her family.* "Especially when happy endings are really new beginnings."

"You still want to marry me, Christine?" Jackson turned serious, but the look in his eye proved the choice was hers to make. "I didn't realize you thought you were facing actual death. I thought you understood death is relative here. It was a surprise to hear... I love you, but I need to know... Do you still want to marry me?" he repeated. "No pressure."

"More than anything, Jackson." Christine tiptoed and kissed his lips.

READ on for a Sneak Peek at ***Down and Dead in Dixie***, the first novel in the Down and Dead, Inc. series...

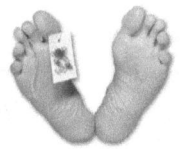

Dixie Prologue

DOWN AND DEAD IN DIXIE

Wednesday, October 22nd
Biloxi, Mississippi

If I'd known I was going to die today, I'd have worn more comfortable shoes.

I'm not fond of heels, but I have to wear them, and knee-length black dresses for my job. I'm a hostess at Biloxi, Mississippi's best four-star restaurant, *The Summer House,* and believe me, I'm not a whiner and I'm not complaining about the black dress. If I hadn't been wearing it, and I hadn't bumped into the garbage dumpster left behind after Hurricane Katrina, and my dress hadn't snagged on the rusty sucker (which probably had me flashing anyone caring to look), then the two jerks in the dark sedan who shot Edward Marcello dead on the street probably would have seen and shot me, too, and I'd have died then with him.

As it was, catching my hem was catching a break—odd for me, because my standard requirement to catch-a-break is to need both hands and a net to just miss out on any luck at all. I guess I was saving it all up for tonight.

So my dress snagged on the dumpster, I stepped back to keep it from ripping and hit a crack in the concrete. My heel sank and wedged in the crack—ruined my brand new shoe—I turned my ankle and went down hard, face first and kissed the dirt. Well, actually, I kissed the concrete. So I'm also sporting raspberry scrapes on my face, arm and knee. The ankle is shot.

That was *the fall* by Daisy Grant, Star Klutz (though usually I'm at least a little bit more graceful), which kept me from getting my chest blown open.

As it turns out, all I managed on the being murdered front was a short-term reprieve. Instead of dying on the street, I'll apparently die elsewhere. But at least I get to pick the spot the second time, and for an orphan who's been on her own since her sixteenth birthday (I'd maxed out on foster care and being forcibly separated from my only living relative, a baby brother, Jackson) getting to choose anything is pretty special. Even if it is something most people consider morbid like where you die.

Before you judge me, remember that this morning I had no idea I'd die at all. And I didn't bring this on myself. I was just leaving work and walking to my car, minding my own business and not bothering anyone. Now listen, I work, I pay taxes, and since Jackson moved to Dallas last year, I call and check on him at least three times a week. I feed stray cats because I can't stand the thought of anything being hungry (been there, done that, it sucked) and I don't even gripe about Lester, the old man in the apartment next door who stomps around at three in the morning—he's an insomniac; what's he *supposed* to do at 3:00 a.m.?

Lester forgets his pants half the time but I don't complain about that, either. Nobody's perfect. So he's forgetful; he can't help it. I just bought him some new boxers. His briefs were kind of ratty anyway, and he's pretty fond of dollar bills, so I figured he might remember to wear money-print boxers and, so far, it's working out. The cops haven't hauled him in for indecent exposure in almost two weeks— pretty harsh consequences for walking to the mailbox—and that means I haven't had to go bail him out in almost two weeks. That's progress, but it's all beside the point. The point is I'm a reasonably good person. I didn't ask for this fate twist. I didn't *want* my fate twisted, and I sure don't deserve it. Trust me, I've had a bellyful of that business already.

The thing is we don't always get what we deserve, do we? More often than not we get what other people, who might or might not be good people, shove in our faces. They make us choose either to suck it up and take whatever they dish out or to kick up dust. Unfortunately, I'm not much good at sucking it up, and when I kicked up dust this time, I didn't know who would be standing in the cloud.

Okay, I'll take the hit for that. I should've looked first and I didn't. I didn't, and done is done. Now I know, but now it's too late and there's no sense whining about something you can't change. All it does is make you sick inside and it doesn't fix a thing. The bottom line is this dust cloud won't settle . . . not so long as I'm breathing.

Some things you just never see coming. I mean, who could have expected something like this to happen at all, much less twice—in one day?

Yeah, if I'd known I was going to die today, I'd have worn more comfortable shoes.

Probably flats.

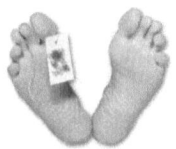

Dixie Chapter 1

DOWN AND DEAD IN DIXIE

"Miss Grant."

Clasping my shoe, I looked up at Detective Keller. In his mid-fifties, he stood leaning against the door-frame, a little stoop-shouldered and rumpled, though there wasn't a wrinkle in his white shirt or crease-pressed slacks—definitely married to sport those kind of creases—and ruffled his gray, thinning hair. Parted just above his ear, it swept over his reddened pate. The expression on his face was suck-lemon bitter, warning me the coming news was suck-lemon bad.

"The shoes are a total loss," I said, deliberately delaying so I had time to prepare myself for hearing it. Keller was a seasoned detective and if he dreaded telling me, the news had to be the kind that knocks you to your knees and keeps you on them for the duration. "The whole heel cracked off." I flicked it with a fingertip. It swung, dangling by a jagged piece of leather.

"Your ankle doesn't look much better," he said, glancing down at it. "Sure you don't want to run over to the hospital for x-rays? It could be broken, bruising up so bad so quick. Hard to tell with all the swelling."

It was swollen and black-and-blue and it hurt like the dickens.

So did my arm and knee, and the scrape on my face burned like fire, but I had to choose: x-rays or groceries; I couldn't afford both. Being kind of fond of eating regularly, I chose groceries. "It's okay. But the shoes really tick me off. I worked double shifts for two weeks to buy them." Tonight was the first shift I'd worn them, and adding insult to injury, they pinched and gave me blisters.

He nodded seeming genuinely empathetic and walked into the cramped office doing double duty as an interview room. With a muffled grunt, he sat down across from me at the scarred table. "Miss Grant, I hate to say this, but right now, you've got a lot bigger problems than your shoes."

I lowered my throbbing foot to the floor. "You've identified those men." I'd pulled two photos from a grouping in no time flat and told the officer, *These are the shooters.*

"Yes, we have," Keller said with a tense sigh. He seemed to age right before my eyes. "You don't know who Edward Marcello is, do you?"

"He's the guy who got shot, right?" I was nearly certain Keller had given me the same name earlier by the dumpster at the scene. "Isn't he a local businessman?" Used cars. Pawn shops—something like that. I'd definitely heard his name, but I couldn't recall where. I was still pretty shaken up. Seeing someone mowed down on purpose . . . well, it's not something an everyday-average woman like me sees, you know?

"Miss Grant . . . Daisy," Keller said, softening his voice. "Edward Marcello is Victor Marcello's only son."

"Okay." This *should* mean something to me. I knew it should, but I stumbled, lost and blindly seeking. Understandable under the best of circumstances, and these couldn't in any manner qualify as the best. I'd only lived in Biloxi for a little over a year. Jackson and I had been in New Orleans when Hurricane Katrina hit and we'd been evacuated to Houston. It didn't suit either of us. Jackson got a job in Dallas through Craig Parker, a friend he had made at chef's school, and that left me at loose ends. Nothing to keep me in Houston, so I came to Biloxi. It was struggling for normalcy but the scars from Hurricane Katrina ran as deep here as in New Orleans. That storm turned everything on its ear. Years now, and the whole gulf coast still seemed pretty much a mess. "What's your point?"

"Victor is the head of the Marcello family. Edward was being groomed to take over." Keller talked slowly, as if I was dimwitted. "Don't you watch the news?"

"I don't have a TV. Well, I did have one until last Christmas Eve when some jerk ransacked my apartment and stole it. But I gave up cable months before then—I needed new tires—and we only get one local channel." Lester complains about the thirty-year-old programming on it, but I'm not sure of what we even get. Honestly, I hadn't turned the TV on after daybreak for a couple months before the set was stolen and I have no idea what local programming is on at night. I work three to eleven six days a week and pull extra shifts anytime I can get them. One day, I'm going to buy me a house. I've never had one of my own—a real home, I mean, and I've always wanted one. It's a big dream, and big dreams take hard work. Who has time for TV?

"Organized crime." Keller leaned forward and laced his hands on the tabletop. The lines in his face deepened. "You have heard the term before, right?"

"Of course, but what does it have—" The bottom dropped out of my stomach. "Edward's murder was a mob hit?" Oh, man. This I did not need. This no one needed.

Keller nodded. "The two men you identified are Lou Boudin and Tony Adriano. They're members of the Adriano family."

"More mob people?" I couldn't believe it. A bad situation just nose-dived straight into the bowels of hell.

"Rival mob families," Keller said, a quiver in his deep voice. "Boudin is a suspected hit man. Tony is higher up on the family food chain. Third in line to take over the Adriano family."

"Oh, no." What had I done? I'd fingered the mob on a family turf-war hit? This situation ranked a lot worse than just kicking up a little dust. I'd kicked up a whole storm. What was I going to do? "Forget it," I told Keller, and reached for my handbag on the floor beside me. "I—I've been thinking and I'm not at all sure those two men were the shooters."

My hand shook so hard I dropped the strap and had to stretch again for my purse. I hauled it into my lap, reached into my wallet and grabbed my Grant half-dollar. It'd soothed me through hard times since I was six, and just rubbing its shiny gold surface now helped calm my insides down to a bellowing roar. Any comfort beyond that was hopeless. "Actually, I'm sure now I was mistaken."

Keller pinched his lips together. "A short while ago, you were sure it was them. *Definitely sure,* I believe, were your exact words."

They had been. A lump lodged in my throat. I couldn't swallow it so I croaked around it. "Adrenaline. You know how it is. Terror messes with your mind." I palmed the coin, stood up and checked my watch. "Look, we were shorthanded tonight and I've been on my feet since before noon. I—I don't know who I saw. I'm not even sure the car was a sedan. Really."

"Miss Grant . . . Daisy, sit down." Detective Keller waited until I did, then closed the door. "I don't want to be overheard, and I'll deny having said anything I'm about to tell you. You understand me?"

The inside scoop. *Definitely worse than suck-lemon bad.* Bracing, I nodded.

"It's too late to change your mind."

"I'm not changing my mind," I lied. "I was a little tied up falling and wrecking my shoes and hitting the concrete." I lightly rubbed the burning raspberry scrape on my face. "Edward was across the street and it was dark. I didn't have a clear look, you know?" I had seen perfectly. Edward had stood right under a streetlight, but I didn't want any part of this situation.

No doubt my denial would supremely tick off Edward's dad, Victor. Ticking off the head honcho of a mob family could *not* be a good thing. But ticking off the Marcellos *and* the Adrianos had to be even worse. This mess absolutely called for ignorance and distance. Lots and lots of distance.

Worried and more than a little annoyed, Keller frowned. "You don't get it, Daisy. These families have connections everywhere, including inside this police station. If it took five minutes for Victor Marcello *and* the Adrianos to find out you'd identified

Boudin and Tony as Edward's shooters, I'd be shocked. Honestly, they probably heard it within fifteen seconds of the words leaving your mouth."

Fear and dread slammed into me. Acid churned in my stomach and the irritating smell of pine cleaner intensified, making me nauseated. "Well, what am I supposed to do?" Before Keller could say anything, I held up a finger. "Don't tell me to testify and every-thing will be fine, because I really am not that stupid. If I talk, Boudin and the Adrianos will want me dead to shut me up. If I don't talk, Victor Marcello will want me dead to punish me. Either way, I'm dead, Keller."

"Either way, you're in jeopardy, but we've got a plan," he said, trying to stave off the hysterics hinted at in my shrill voice. "The FBI is on board because of the organized crime ties. I talked with a friend of mine, Special Agent Ted Johnson. He's deeply concerned about your safety."

"I'm not feeling too confident about it myself." I swiped at a dust smudge on my dress at the thigh and anger rose with the sting on my skin. "If you and Johnson know these jokers are mob members, then why are they still on the loose?

Keller looked me straight in the eye. "Because every time we nail them, the evidence disappears or the witnesses do, or else they end up dead before the trial."

I slumped back in my seat. *Daisy Grant's death warrants numbers two and three, right there.* Boudin or Adriano or Victor Marcello—one of them would do the deed. No way around it. This was the mob honcho's son, no less. The Marcellos and Adrianos obviously were already rivals, but now the Adrianos had declared war. Murder isn't a subtle hostility that passes unnoticed. And, lucky me, I don't have to mess with one mob family. No, not me. I have to tick-off two of them—at the same time.

"Don't panic, okay?" Keller glanced back at the door. His eyes darted and his hand shook. He wasn't happy to be stuck in the middle of this mess, either. "Like I told you, we've got a plan."

I grunted. "No offense, Detective, but if all your witnesses are missing in action or dead before trial, I'd say, your plans aren't working out very well." I squeezed my Grant coin. "Have these families killed cops, too, or just witnesses?"

My question irked him and stung his pride, but he chose to ignore it. "Special Agent Johnson is coming to get you. He'll hold you in protective custody until—"

"Protective custody?" Keller had to be kidding. "I can't do protective custody. I have to work or I don't eat. Understand? I can't hide out—and from what you've said, there is nowhere to hide, anyway." Some plan. They might as well paint a bulls-eye on my forehead.

"You'll be safe with Johnson," Keller said, then softened his voice. "Miss Grant, I know this is hard. You've built yourself a life and it hasn't been easy, being on your own. But if you were my own daughter, I'd be making this same suggestion, okay?"

"What suggestion?" I hadn't heard any suggestion.

"You need to enter the Federal Witness Security Program. It was created for witnesses needing protection. Organized crime, drug traffickers, terrorists. You'll get a new identity and be relocated — everything you need to start fresh somewhere else." He talked fast, then added, "Johnson's setting it all up with the U.S. Marshals."

New identity? Moving? Starting fresh? "No." I couldn't believe it. "You can't just kick my whole life to the curb like it's a piece of trash. I won't let you do it."

"You need to run."

I need to run. "Why am I being treated like the criminal here? If you guys would do your job, then I wouldn't be in prison—and don't think just because your Witness Security Program doesn't have walls it isn't a prison because it is."

"I *am* doing my job, okay?" Keller stood up, leaned toward me over the table. "Listen to me, Daisy. This is serious."

"No joke." He did think I was stupid.

"I didn't mean it like that," he said, and had the grace to flush. "It's just . . . well, you have no idea what these people are capable of doing."

"They're going to kill me, Keller. That clear enough?" I frowned at him. "I'm not stupid, and I'd appreciate it if you'd stop treating me like I am."

"I didn't intend..." He sighed and gave up. "I'm sorry," he said, and then started again. "Your best shot is protective custody and then to go straight into witness security. Seriously."

"No, that's what's best for your friend, Johnson. He needs a witness. I don't need any of this."

"Okay, look. Johnson does need you. Without you, he has no case. But you need him and his protection, too."

I'd end up dead like his other witnesses. "I don't believe this." I stood up then hobbled a short path alongside the table, dragging my cracked heel. "My life isn't much compared to most, I'll admit. But it is mine. I've made it from scratch by myself, and I want to keep it. What you're suggesting isn't fair, and I'm not catching a whiff of justice in any of this. I lose everything, Keller. How can a witness losing everything be right?"

"Who says it's right? Or fair? Or just, for that matter?" Keller raked a hand through his hair. Its tips spiked and caught the light. "It's not any of those things. But this isn't a lip-service warning to get you to testify, okay?" He cut to the chase. "If you enter the program, at least you'll have a life."

"Will I?" Always looking over my shoulder. Expecting them to find me every second of every day. What kind of life is that? None. And—I gasped, looked at Keller. "What about Jackson?" I asked.

Lost, Keller cocked his head. "Is he your boyfriend?"

"He's my baby brother," I said. "Well, he's not a baby. He's only two years younger than me, but if I did your witness security thing, I'd never see him again, right? Or is that just how it is in the movies?"

"No, I'm afraid that's how it is in real life." Regret scratched through Keller's voice, turned his tone gruff. "You wouldn't be able to have any contact whatsoever with Jackson or anyone else currently in your life."

No Jackson. No bailing out Lester. Alone. Totally and completely alone. Again. Everything in me rebelled. "No. Thank you, but no. I won't do it." My knees threatened to give out and the pain shooting through my ankle had me seeing stars. I stopped and leaned against the chair. "I—I can't..."

Keller stood up, stuffed his hands in his pants pockets. "You don't have any choice."

Something in his eyes scared me in a way I hadn't been scared since I was six and Mom gave me the two Grant coins then dumped Jackson and me out of the car at the front door of the Piggly Wiggly. She went to park her car and never came back. "Why not?"

Keller looked at my neck. He tried but couldn't meet my eyes. "Because if you don't agree to witness security and protective custody, you're going to be held here anyway—as a person of interest in Edward Marcello's homicide."

Shock pumped through my body. I planted my hands on my hips and glared at him. "You're gonna arrest me?"

"Technically, no." He blinked hard. "We can hold you forty-eight hours without arresting you."

Oh, no. Two mob families and a professional hitman after me and I'm taken prisoner by cops in a police station full of moles. *Great. Anything else? Through now, or do You think I need a couple more body slams?*

"Daisy, I don't want to do this. But if we cut you loose, you'll be dead in an hour." Keller motioned outside. "We can't protect you out there."

Too rattled to care about manners, I snorted. "You can't protect me in here, either."

He frowned, then stilled. "Your odds in here are a lot better."

I stared at Keller a long minute. My highly-honed BS detector swore he was being straight with me. At least he wasn't one of the moles. But his being straight about this also meant he'd been straight about my odds. Stay or go, it was just a matter of time before one of them got to me and I started my toe-tag stint. While being off my feet sounded really good, being laid out on a slab in the morgue held no appeal. What I needed was a plan. *My* plan.

My success record might not be great, but I had kept myself and Jackson alive and out of trouble. Their witnesses were all dead. I couldn't do worse. So the time had come to shift tactics. "Well." I sucked in a sharp breath. "I guess that's it, then."

"You agree to protective custody and witness security?" Keller sounded surprised.

"You said it yourself. I don't have any choice. If I somehow managed to elude them, they'd go after Jackson, and I can't have that." My eyes burned and I blinked hard, clenched the half-dollar until it dented my palm. "But I have to at least tell him good-bye. I'm —" I swallowed hard to get the crack out of my voice "—I'm all he's got."

"I'm sorry, Daisy." Keller said and meant it; the truth shone in his eyes. He might not be alone now but he had been. I saw it in the lines grooving down his face. "We can arrange a final conversation with Jackson. It'll have to be on the phone, though. We can't risk a face-to-face meeting."

"No. It'd put him in too much jeopardy. A phone call will have to do." I sniffed, looked down at the scuffed tile floor. "If you'll excuse me, Detective, I need a minute alone." I shuddered and crossed my chest with my arms. "Where is the ladies' room?"

He seemed torn. Surely he wouldn't refuse me even restroom privileges to preserve my dignity. "Detective?"

"Right this way."

He led me down a short dimly lit hallway, took a right and then pointed. "Second door," he said, stopping. His shoe squeaked on the worn white floor. "I'll wait for you right here."

"Thanks." He truly was afraid the families would kill me even in police headquarters. *Not good. So majorly not good.*

I went in and closed the door behind me. Two stalls. Both empty and painted a garish blue. One window—small but I could fit through it in a pinch. And two sinks with the crooked silver pipes sticking out underneath. I limped over, still wearing my cracked-heel shoe. Forget going barefoot in a public restroom. I'd seen a bacteria-and-germ segment on *Oprah* . . . or was it on the Health Channel? Whatever. Even restrooms that looked clean were infested. I took a closer look at the window. If I got out, Keller would likely have someone outside waiting to snag me the second my feet hit the ground. But even if he didn't, where could I go? Home?

Not bloody likely. I didn't even have my car here; I'd ridden in with Keller. That should have warned me, right there. Normally, it would have. But I don't see people blown wide-open everyday, you know? Edward Marcello's death rattled me; I admit it. I didn't think.

"Miss Grant, you okay?" Keller called to me through the door.

Nice of him to worry. Sweet, actually. Not that I was crazy enough to think he really was worried about me. He wanted to nail his case. That's what Keller was about. Special Agent Johnson, too. Not me. I provided the means to an end. That's it. They were all about the case. Likely had been trying to nail both of the mob families for years.

"I'm fine. Thank you." I turned on the tap and tried to think through this witness security program business. Never see Jackson again? *Ever?* I couldn't do it. I wouldn't. Because I really was about to cry and I didn't want to humiliate myself by blubbering like an idiot, I washed my face and then ripped off some paper towels and patted my skin dry in front of the mirror above the sink. My hair had fallen out of its neat chignon and shot out in blonde streaks in all directions. I plunked street grime out of it, tread lightly over a sore spot, and knew I'd be fighting embedded sidewalk grit for a week. Dabbing the streaked mascara from my face, I avoided the raspberry but nicked its edge anyway. Pain seared my jaw. Cringing, I glimpsed the ceiling in the mirror. Those big tiles . . .

One of my old foster parents, Mr. Venier, had crawled all over the ceiling in the attic once. He hid pot up above those big tiles, too. I looked at these tiles more closely.

The police couldn't protect me. The FBI or U.S. Marshals couldn't, either. I had to protect me. And I needed to buy a little time to figure out how to do it.

I opened the window and left it cracked. Inside the first stall, I stood on the stool then lifted the ceiling tile and slid it aside. I walked up the sides of the stall like I'd seen Bear Grylls walk up sheer-faced cliffs back when I'd had a TV and watched it. Scaling the wall looked easier than it was, especially with a bad ankle. Pain shot through my foot and up my leg. The whole mess throbbed. By the time I hoisted myself up into the dead space and straddled the rafters, I was in a cold sweat and my muscles burned so badly I shook like somebody half-frozen. Biting my lip to keep from groaning, I slid the tile back into its slot.

"Miss Grant?" Keller's voice carried up to me. "Miss Grant?"

I didn't dare answer. Crawling on hands and knees across and down the wooden beams, I made it to the other side of the building. Lifting the corner of a tile, I peeked down.

Keller was going nuts; he'd discovered I was gone, and he and half the force were looking for me, inside and outside the police station.

A younger man with a flat nose and short brown hair wearing a black suit and a bad attitude hooked up with Keller near the door. "Are you sure they didn't take her?"

"No, I'm not sure, Johnson." Keller shouted back. "I wasn't in the john with her. I was in the hallway. I'm not Superman. I can't see through walls, okay?"

"But the window was open, so they could've taken her," Johnson pushed.

"Yeah, the window was open." Johnson whipped out his phone and barked orders into it.

Special Agent Ted Johnson. The FBI guy Keller had said was coming for me. I hunkered down and stayed put. Once the dust settled, I could get out of here, get some money, and then get out of Biloxi.

They'll just hunt you down, Daisy. You know they will...

They would. Fear blew up inside me crowding into so much space I could barely breathe. Doubt crept in and took up the rest. Could I do anything to protect myself better than Keller and Johnson could protect me? They had training, I didn't. They had a track record—a bad one, yeah, but they did know what hadn't worked. I knew nothing.

You can't afford this kind of thinking, Daisy...

I couldn't. So okay, I wasn't formally trained, and I didn't have their kind of track record, and I didn't know what hadn't worked. And—just to not delude myself, rationalizing my situation—I was scared spit-less, which isn't the best condition to be in when you're making life-and-death decisions. The cops, FBI, and Victor Marcello wanted me alive to testify. Lou Boudin and Tony Adriano wanted me dead so I couldn't testify. Both groups would undoubtedly go to *any* lengths to get what they wanted. That left me with no choice but to be willing to go to *any* lengths to get what I wanted.

Well, I thought. I do have one thing the families, the police, the FBI and the U.S. Marshals lack, and it's nothing to sneeze at. Actually, it could be pretty powerful—and on several occasions in the past, it had been powerful enough to save my backside. I have a personal, vested interest in the outcome of this situation that is bigger and stronger and runs deeper than their interest or investment— singularly or even combined.

This is *my* life on the proverbial chopping block, and I want to survive to live it.

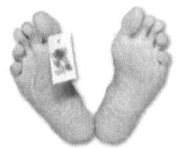

Dixie Chapter 2

DOWN AND DEAD IN DIXIE

The hustle inside the police station dulled to a quiet roar, and then fell to silence.

Except for a skeleton crew left to man the station, the cops on duty had hit the streets, looking for me. Between the underside of the roof and the backside of the musty ceiling, I'd crawled all over the building, rafter to rafter, and while my tights and skirt were now in about as good a shape as my once-white shirt and torn-up shoe, I had finally pegged a way out of the station—the side exit door I now watched through a hiked corner of ceiling tile.

Problem was the keypad on the wall beside the door. It had a four-digit code; I'd counted the beeps. But until now, I hadn't been in position to see the numbers the officers exiting the building punched into it. Straddling two wooden beams like a contortionist on crack, I had a clear view and only hoped my left hipbone held out. The constant pain in it had me dripping sweat and seeing spots, but I didn't dare move. The exit had been fairly active. It wouldn't be long...

A uniformed officer approached the door, lifted a hand to the keypad and tapped in the numbers. *Three, seven, three, seven.* The door opened, and he walked outside.

I waited a couple minutes, then slid back the tile just enough to drop down to the floor. I landed with a thud. My ankle gave out, and I crashed on my butt. Grunting and groaning, I scrambled to my feet. To me the racket sounded like a small explosion, but no one entered the hallway so I guess the real uproar was inside my head. I punched in the code and shoved the door hard.

Seconds later, the night swallowed me. I ran two blocks on the battered ankle with pain screeching up my leg before I slowed down, then standing on the side of the dark road, I wondered. *What do I do now?* I had my mobile phone, but the police would be monitoring it —I'd given Keller the number, for crying out loud.

Near a streetlamp, I twisted my wrist to check my watch. Finally, it caught the light—3:20 a.m. I had no one to call. Nowhere to go. I'd heard the FBI guy, Johnson, tell Keller to put an APB out on my car, so retrieving it was out. The beach and Highway 90 intersected about 2 blocks south. It'd be dense with traffic and people even in the wee hours before dawn, but some of those people would be cops. I walked another block north and noticed headlights on the road. Glancing back, I watched an old clunker pass by and the driver hit the brakes.

Spinning around, I took off south. It wasn't a good idea to cut across lawns—people had gotten itchy trigger fingers since the hurricane because of looters—but better that possibility than—a man in a ski mask grabbed my shoulder.

I gasped and struck out. "Get off—"

"Spitwads and fudgesicles. Don't kill me, Daisy girl."

Mid-swing on a big roundhouse, the man's words penetrated my mind and I stilled, dropped my arm and relaxed my fist. Only one person said *spitwads and fudgesicles.* "Lester?"

He nodded. The ski mask tugged down over his head bobbed and the eye slit crept over his right eye. "Get in the car."

I hustled over and got in. When he slid onto the seat behind the wheel, I asked, "Lester, what are you doing here? Whose car is this — and why are you wearing a mask?"

He slapped at the gearshift with a bony hand and punched the accelerator. "You didn't come home tonight. I got worried. I was sort of waiting for you."

"There was some trouble outside of work."

He grunted. "There was some trouble at home, too."

"What kind of trouble?" Could be anything. *A raccoon in the garbage, teens hanging on the corner.* "And whose car is this?"

"Emily's," he said, talking about the elderly woman two apartments down from him.

"Emily's blind. Why does she need a car?" Did she even have a car? I couldn't recall ever seeing one, and this clunker, I wouldn't miss.

"She ain't blind. She's got cataracts," he corrected me.

"But they can fix cataracts."

"Yep, if you got surgery money. She ain't, and she ain't old enough for Medicare. She's keeping the car for when she gets her eyes back."

Money. Always money. I sighed inside and shifted the topic. "Well, what are you doing with her car?" It did smell musty and like mothballs. Like it'd been closed up a hunter's moon or two.

"I borrowed it after the two men left your apartment."

My heart jackknifed. "There were two men at my apartment?"

"Nope, not *at* it. *In* it." Lester braked for a red light then hooked a right on Highway 90 and passed by my bank.

"Pull in there." Wagging a fingertip, I added, "I need to withdraw some money from the ATM."

"They pretty much tore the place up, Daisy." Lester made the corner and then doubled back to the bank.

Violated to the bone, I swallowed a knot of outrage. "Cops?"

"Thugs," he countered. "I called your work to tell you, and Gilbert told me what had happened with the shooting and all." Lester heaved a sigh and pulled into the drive-thru. "Are you crazy, girl? Why did you call the cops?"

"When I called them, I didn't know who the victim was, okay?" I fished out my bank card and gave Lester my pin number. "Get the max they'll let me get."

He adjusted his mask then stepped in front of the camera,

inserted the card, and then punched in the first digit. "What's the number again?"

I repeated it, realizing how this would look to anyone watching —but maybe the false impression was a good thing. They'd think the unidentified masked man was forcing me to withdraw the money and give it to him. This could be helpful in the way of a plan—as soon as I came up with a solid one, anyway—and it wouldn't jeopardize Lester. He had a history of vacant rooms in his personal mansion of a head.

Lester got the money, the card, and then pulled away from the bank machine and its camera. "Here you go."

"Hang onto the card," I said, taking the receipt and money. "And head for another bank branch."

"You're cleaning out the account and getting out of Dodge, eh?" "No choice."

"None," he agreed. "There's another ATM just this side of the Ocean Springs bridge."

"Hit it." I stuffed the money into my wallet, then looked over at him. "Why are you wearing a ski mask?"

"I was coming to get you before you went home. The thugs are watching your place. Couldn't let you walk into that nasty business unaware."

"Thanks, Lester." Touched, I patted his arm and took a shot at diplomacy. "Didn't you think they'd consider your mask a little odd?"

"They surely would, if they saw it. But I waited until I was out of the neighborhood to put it on," he said, clearly proud of himself for his foresight and cunning.

"Ah." I didn't know a spitting bit more now than I had before I'd asked. "So if not to hide your identity from the thugs, then why are you wearing it?"

"I was coming to the jail to get you," he explained. "If I showed up like I was, it'd be awfully convenient for them to arrest me, and who'd bail me out? You were being held. I'd a had to rot and you'd a walked in on the thugs at your place."

"Oh." We drove under a streetlamp and it fanned light over his lap. Dollar-bill boxers. Vintage Lester. "Forgot your pants, huh?"

"I remembered 'em—honest, Daisy. But I was scared the thugs'd stop me if I went back to get 'em, so I just grabbed the mask at Emily's."

In some weird and twisted way, he and his actions made perfect sense. For Lester, that is—and if you didn't look too closely and wonder what Emily was doing with a ski mask or how Lester expected the cops to react when a man walked into headquarters wearing a ski mask and money-print boxers. Having enough trouble already, I was perfectly content not to look at all.

We hit three more bank branches, then headed to Gulfport and withdrew the maximum from the two branches there. Unfortunately there was a $250 limit between midnight and dawn everywhere except the casinos, so we made a second trip to one of them. In the parking lot, Lester stopped but he didn't seek an open slot.

"You're going to have to do this one inside Daisy. It ain't a good idea for me to walk in wearing this, you know?"

"I agree." My conscience was nagging at me. "You realize they're going to think you abducted me or something and forced me to use the ATM, right?"

"Course, I do." He tugged at the mask. "Get moving now. The machine is just inside the hallway to your right. Don't linger—I figure we're on borrowed time 'til you're spotted. That's the trouble with firing up half the county, girl. Can't hide in plain sight, you know?"

"I'm learning. This is new to me." I left the car and about two-thirds of the way to the door it dawned on me that this didn't seem new to Lester. Had he been hiding in plain sight? I wondered, but then that crawling-flesh feeling snagged me. You know, the kind of feeling you get when your internal radar has picked up on something you're not yet really aware of and it shoots off an alarm in your gut. My gut-alarm blared. So I turned right around and headed back to the car.

Lester hadn't even moved away from the curb yet; maybe his radar had gone haywire, too. I tugged open the creaky door, got in and slammed it shut. "Something's wrong. Go."

A black van a few slots down chose that moment to back out of its parking place and blocked the road. We were sitting ducks.

"This ain't good, Daisy girl." Lester whipped off his ski mask. His thin hair standing straight on end, he shot a frantic look into the rearview mirror.

I hunched down in the seat and looked around but didn't see a thing that didn't fit. Was it my imagination? Fear making me jump at shadows that just weren't there? Maybe it was...

The casino door I'd been about to enter slid open and a man walked out. "Oh, no." I ducked fast, huddling on the floorboard in the wedge between the dash and seat.

"Who is he?" Lester asked, picking up on my fear.

"Lou Boudin." My heart slammed into my backbone. "One of the shooters."

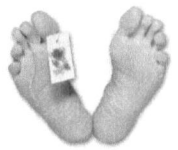

Dixie Chapter 3

DOWN AND DEAD IN DIXIE

Boudin didn't spot me. The black van moved, and Lester, bless him, took off normally to not draw notice. He pulled out on to Highway 90 and drove west. "Maybe you better start at the beginning," he said.

For the first time since I'd known him, all the lights were currently on in Lester's personal head-mansion. I spilled out the story and ended with, "What am I going to do?"

Lester pulled over at the harbor and parked facing the boat slips. "It's a sorry situation. Sorry situation." He tapped his blunt finger-tips on the steering wheel and then suddenly stopped. "Well, no help for it. Ain't but one thing you can do, Daisy girl."

"What?"

"Die."

Shock rippled through me. "I'm not ready to die."

"It's your only choice." Lester turned off the engine and killed the lights. "If Keller and Johnson don't get you killed, Marcello or Adriano will—and they'll all go after Jackson, too. Make no mistake about it."

I frowned. "This isn't exactly being helpful, Lester." He was right, of course, but what I needed was a solution not more worry heaped on the pile. It was plenty high already.

"Just making sure you got a realistic fix on your situation."

"Oh, I've got a realistic fix, all right. The question is what am I supposed to do about it? How can I keep Jackson safe and stay alive?"

"I told you. Ain't but one way." Lester shot her a sharp look. "To live, sometimes ya gotta die."

Bless his heart, he was trying to be helpful, but—

"Don't be looking at me like I got a half-baked brain. I ain't." He grunted and turned toward me on his seat. "If you're dead, and you ain't contacted Jackson, they'll leave him alone and you'll be safe. You'll have to stay away from him, though. They'll watch for contact."

Speaking from experience. Shocked, I swerved my gaze from the docked boats in the harbor back to Lester. "If I'm dead, I can't hardly hang around him or anybody else, Lester."

"That's right." He sighed. "Ain't what I'd a wanted for you, Daisy girl, but you got no other options."

We were on two different wave lengths. No surprise there, but he had something specific going on in his head and I didn't. Grasping for any straw, I asked, "What do you mean?"

He twisted and draped his arm over the steering wheel, then lifted a single crooked finger. "Beyond those boats is a big gulf. I suggest we get you lost in it."

"You want me to drown myself?" *No straw there. Definitely vacant rooms in his head-mansion, after all.*

"*Pretend* to drown," he amended then added, "Don't have to find a body if you're seen falling into the drink."

A plan to fake my death. Lights were on in there! "Okay, I drown. Then what?"

"Then you use some of the money to change your appearance and name, and you make your way over to Dixie, Florida. I got a friend runs a funeral home over there, Paul Perini. He can help you. Now, you head straight there and you tell him I sent you or he won't even talk to you."

A cold chill streaked up my spine. Lester wasn't at all vacant and apparently he never had been. He'd done this death-faking business before. Why had he had to die? Who was looking for him?

Safer not to ask, or to know. About to gag, I cracked open the window. The smell of salt water mingled with the pungent sting of mothballs. "So I go for a swim and drown."

"Nope. Ya gotta be seen and remembered. First, stash your cash and some dry clothes down the beach someplace safe. Then come back here and rent a boat. Any of the charters will do. Take the first one where a captain shows up. Go for a boat ride, hit the drink, and disappear. Then retrieve your cash and get to Paul Perini—no rental cars or public transportation, just in case. These types are awfully suspicious."

He meant the crime families, not the authorities. "Because maybe in their pasts, some of them have faked their deaths?" *Oh, let that not be the reason. Let it not.*

"Exactly." Lester glanced over. "Just get to Paul. He'll handle the rest." Lester looked out the window. "It'll be daylight in about an hour." He cleared his throat. "You got no time to waste."

Reaching over, I clasped Lester's bony hand. "If I do this, who's going to post your bond and get you out of jail?"

"I'll remember my pants, Daisy." His eyes watered. "It was handy, being ditzy. And a good way to get to know you and keep an eye out. Ain't safe for a kid your age nor right neither, having nobody."

I stilled. "It was a test. To see if I was getting close to you for a reason or just because."

He grinned. "That, too." He took in a deep shuddery breath and gave my hand a little squeeze. "Getting me a post card from Lily Nichols now and then would be nice. So I know you're all right."

I nodded, my throat thickening.

"There's somebody coming to that charter. Captain Dave's. See him?"

I did. "Thank you, Lester." I grabbed the door handle and looked back at him. "I'm going to miss you."

"I'll be fine, Daisy girl. Emily's here, and you'll drop me a note now and again. That's more than I've had most of my adult life." He motioned, his voice gruff. "Get going now—and rig the boat's radio so it takes the captain a spell to get in touch with anybody. He'll call for help as soon as you hit the water."

I looked back at Lester. "You never asked me if I could swim."

"You learned when you were nine and Jackson slipped off the bank of the creek. Figure if you swam good enough to save his hide, you can swim good enough to save your own."

A flood of emotion swamped me. "Lester," I swallowed hard, "I love you."

"I love you, too, Daisy girl."

I tried but couldn't make myself part with my cash. I bought a few things at a twenty-four hour boutique, stashed some clothes a mile down the beach then rushed back to the harbor.

The sky hadn't yet started brightening, but it wouldn't be long. Spotting a man working on the pier near a boat, I walked over. The slatted boards creaked under my feet, and the sounds of water slapped at the posts supporting them. "You have time for a short trip this morning?"

"Two hours long enough?" Stooped down and checking the ropes mooring his boat to the dock, he straightened up and looked over at me. "Rest of the day's already booked."

I smiled at him and double-checked the sign above his slip. "You're Captain Dave, right?"

He nodded. "Yes, ma'am."

"I'm not sure two hours will do the trick, but I'll take what I can get. I've had the night from hell, Captain." I dragged my fingertips over the raspberry scrape on my face. He'd remember the scrape. "A short trip can't hurt and it could help."

He spotted the scrape and then my bruised and swollen ankle. "No offense," he said, looking beyond my shoulder. "But I don't need no trouble." He glanced at my left hand, clearly checking for a wedding ring.

"Trouble is the last thing I need or want." I lifted my hand and wiggled my bare fingers. "There's no crazy husband or boyfriend. I fell in the parking lot at work. I'm local. A hostess at the Summer House." I offered him twice the fee his sign said he charged. "Sound okay?"

"It's too much." He grabbed the wad of cash. "But I'm short on rent money, so since you offered, I'm accepting."

I boarded the boat wearing a muddy-looking swimsuit as close to the color of the water as I could find. In my purse, I had stowed a floppy hat in the same dull shade of gray-green. Whether it'd really help me be harder to spot in the water or if that was just wishful thinking on my part, it was worth a shot. Of course, everything looked muted and gray at dawn. In the bright sunlight, the water could vary from blue to deep green. I should be back on shore by then. "Where should I sit?" I asked Captain Dave.

I hadn't even noticed the name of the boat. Odd for me. Normally I'd have looked for some kind of symbol in its name— *Survivor* or something to reassure me this was *the* boat I should take.

"Seat at the bow's probably best for you with that ankle."

Grateful it was closest, I sat down and looked back at the captain. He was about my age, tanned and leathery skin, black close- cut hair and a hint of a beer belly.

He coiled the last of the mooring rope onto the deck, then boarded. "So what's your name?"

I hesitated, considered lying to him, but then remembered I wanted him to think I'd drowned and everyone to conclude I was dead. "Daisy Grant."

He cranked the engine, eased away from the dock and out of the harbor. The light breeze felt good on my face. The smell of diesel didn't blend well with the gulf's salty tang and as the boat slipped away from the harbor and through the pass into open water, my stomach lurched. *Please don't let me throw up on his boat. Please.*

Captain Dave radioed the harbormaster, then made small talk with me and he kept talking until finally I told him what he wanted to know. Well, sort of. I told him what I wanted him to know, which was enough to tell the police who I was and to halt his questions so I had time to think. "I didn't just fall in the parking lot," I said. "Well, I did, but I fell because I saw a man on the street get shot. I've never seen anybody get shot before. Frankly, it's knocked me for a loop. I was on the way home, already dreading the nightmares, when I saw you at your boat. I thought maybe a quiet boat ride would help me relax. The water's soothing, you know?"

Surprise flickered over the captain's face. "Is he all right—the guy who got shot?"

"Only if he loved Jesus." I looked at the captain. "He's deader than dirt." I let my head loll back a long moment, then stood up and circled the deck. "I still can't believe it. I mean, who expects to leave work on a normal day and see something like that in the parking lot?"

"World's crazy these days. But that's really nuts." He grunted. "Sounds to me like you need a stiff drink. I would." Captain Dave's expression turned solemn. "Afraid all I've got on board is beer."

"A beer would be great." I hate beer. Don't just not like it, I hate it. But I needed a second of privacy to disable the radio. "I'll take the wheel."

"You know how to drive a boat?"

"Sure. My dad had one." I didn't like lying, but maybe I wasn't. He could have a boat. Course, I'd never know it since I have no idea who he is or what he has. And I had no idea how to drive a boat. But it couldn't be much different from driving a car. Besides, what could I hit? There wasn't a thing in sight moving but water. The boat passed another channel marker. I looked back to shore and pegged the lighthouse. If I aimed for it, I'd stay on target, swimming back.

The captain took the ladder down and disappeared below deck. I reached for the radio's wire but hesitated. Like me, he worked hard and worried about paying the rent. I couldn't destroy the wiring and cost him money. Compromising, I disconnected the cable and wedged it in place so he'd think it just had worked itself loose. Wave action could do that, couldn't it? Who knew? But any evidence of actual tampering would only arouse suspicion, and suspicion was the last thing I needed. Everyone—*absolutely everyone*—had to believe I was dead. For my sake and for Jackson's.

Dave returned with two beers.

I turned the wheel over to him, popped the top on the beer can, heard the little hiss, then sat down in the back of the boat. It was closer to the water than the seats at the bow, and more importantly, I sat at Dave's back. "I'm not much of a drinker, but after last night..." I took a swig. *Nasty!* I forced myself to swallow.

"Anywhere special you want to go?"

"No, just ride along the coast. Not too far out." I'm a lousy swimmer. With my bum ankle, I really wasn't sure how strong I'd be in the water or for how long, and I wasn't at all eager to make my fake death a real one.

He turned the boat and upended his beer can near a buoy.

There'd never be a better time.

I dropped off the back of the boat, released my beer can, jammed the muddy hat on my head and made for the buoy.

The boat kept going . . . and going . . . Hanging onto the buoy, using it as cover, Captain Dave got smaller and smaller. He wouldn't not notice my absence for much longer, and it wouldn't take forever for him to reconnect the radio. Soon he'd double back with reinforcements and the area would be swarming with people looking for me. I slung my purse strap over my shoulder, and swam hard for the shore.

My whole perspective shifted. In the water, the shore looked distant, and I couldn't see the lighthouse, but at least I could see land. If I could see it, I could eventually get to it.

Stay calm, Daisy. I stroked, smooth and easy. *The hardest part's over. You're dead.*

I did either the smartest or dumbest thing I've ever done. I hung out on a sandbar near the shore until after dark. The lighthouse was nowhere in sight, but the area was populated. I know, of course, sharks feed at dusk, but shark or bullet, I choose shark.

Once the sun set, the cool water felt cold. My arms and legs cramped every few minutes; they needed rest, and frankly, I didn't think my ankle would make it the last couple hundred yards without it. The distance might be two or three times more than it appeared. Being low to the water messed up my distance judgment.

I stood on the sand bar, my teeth chattering, rubbing the chill from my arms. The gulf temperature had come down from its summer high, but the weather had been warm so far, keeping the water warm, too. Still, the night breeze on wet skin felt cold and had a bitter bite, and when my goose bumps had goose bumps, all I could think about was getting to shore, getting dry and getting warm.

The burning desire stayed with me, and about a half hour after dark it occurred to me to float.

I rolled onto my back, my mouth so dry I was tempted to drink salt water, which even I knew would really kill me, and used my good leg to kick hard and the other to stay stable. I floated in the last of the way, and was never so happy in my life to scrape my backside on sand.

The beach might typically have been deserted, but a big group having a party littered it. I came out of the water downwind of them, blended in, weaving through the group, and skirted the volley-ball game and bright lights, then ambled toward the parking lot. So far I didn't recognize anything or anyone, which was a good thing, considering.

"You okay?" A tall guy with a winsome smile asked. His waxed chest looked smoother than mine. "You're limping."

I didn't want to talk to him. I didn't want to be remembered. "Fine, thanks," I said, ducking so the brim of my hat hid my face. I kept walking.

Figured. First decent guy to notice me since my breakup with Andy six months ago—not that I was attracted or could ever get past the smooth chest thing—but even if I was and could, I couldn't do squat to encourage him because I'm dead. In my new life, my luck was holding steady at lousy. Odd, but it seemed kind of comforting to be able to count on *something*.

The neon lights of a casino came into view. I headed toward them. It wasn't one in Biloxi. I drove by those all the time. Must have drifted west in the water. Gulfport maybe—I recognized a bank —yes, Gulfport. I really had drifted. Should have thought of the drift, but I hadn't. It was too far to walk to retrieve the clothes I'd stashed, but at least I'd kept my money with me.

There was something about stashing my purse and money that the woman in me just couldn't do. So I'd bought a waterproof bag, dumped my old purse in a trash drum and kept my cash with me. Now, I was grateful for the little female idiosyncrasy. I wasn't without clothes *and* flat broke.

Tour buses lined up in the casino's parking lot. I could catch a ride—no records. But where did I go?

I hung out at the edge of the beach until I stopped dripping water, shoved every strand of hair under my hat, then entered the casino to get some clothes. The stores were open around the clock. Approaching the first person I saw, I asked about the shops. She had no idea where they were located. Neither did the second person, or the couple that followed her.

A woman in uniform walked toward me. Not wanting to be seen or remembered, I tried skirting her, but she proved persistent. Running would have aroused more suspicion so I slumped and paused near a bank of slot machines.

Petite and in her forties, she intercepted me. "Why are you bothering our guests?"

"I'm not. I asked for directions," I said. "I didn't see you in your uniform or I'd have asked you." *Could she hear my heart thundering?* "Where are the shops?" Frowning, I lifted a hand. "Some jerk stole my clothes off the beach."

"He took your clothes and left your purse?" Her eyebrows shot up on her forehead.

"It was with me. Good thing, as it turns out."

She nodded. "Hotel won't cover items left unattended on the beach." Frowning her thoughts on their policy, she motioned. "All the stores are down the east corridor. You'll find everything you need. Guests get a discount, but only if you ask for it, so be sure you do."

"I will. Thanks." Letting her continue with the assumption I was staying at the hotel, I wound between banks of slot machines to the corridor and then stepped into the first clothing shop.

Within minutes, I walked out wearing a pair of jeans and a Crimson Tide t-shirt, sneakers and a red baseball cap. My next mission? Find a drug store.

A block down the street, I found a Walgreens. There, I bought a box of red hair dye and applied it in the restroom. The smell probably didn't make the employees happy, but I left the place tidy so they'd have no complaint other than the fumes.

As I left the store and stepped into the night, my stomach growled, demanding food. Considering hunger a good sign—for a while, I thought I'd never be able to eat again—I walked back to the casino and grabbed a burger and soft drink then exited out at the garage near the long row of tour buses.

Lester's warning to avoid rental cars and public transportation seemed like sound advice, but while his heart had been in the right place on sending me to his friend, Paul Perini, in Dixie, Florida, I couldn't actually go there. If something went wrong with my drowning death and push came to shove, Lester would know where I was hiding. I didn't want to burden him with the secret or to give anyone a reason to beat the information out of him. Dead is dead, until it isn't, you know? So, just in case, I didn't want to take any chances he or his friend, Paul Perini, would be hurt. And that meant I had to find somewhere to go. Somewhere away from Jackson and Dallas.

I ate the tangy burger while walking between the long rows of buses, gazing up their windshields to their destination headsigns. *Jacksonville . . . Dothan . . . Montgomery . . . New Orleans.*

I stopped, sipped at my soda. For a while, Jackson's friend in Dallas, Craig Parker, had worked with Mark Jensen in New Orleans. Mark had been in chef's school with Jackson and Craig. Unlike either of them, Mark had family money behind him. Going into chef's school, he already owned a restaurant in the French Quarter, Jameson Court. I could go there. Nothing connected Daisy Grant to Mark Jensen or Craig Parker, but Lester's Lily Nichols knowing Craig could help me get a job with Mark. Hey, maybe eventually I could somehow get a covert message to Jackson. Not right away, of course, but one day. . . The possibility brightened my mood.

The bus driver came up, dampening it. "Ready to leave already?" He checked his watch. "You've got another hour."

"Tapped out my gambling budget." Feigning a yawn, I asked, "Do you mind if I wait on the bus?" Standing exposed out in the open gave me the willies. "I'd love to grab a nap."

"You do look tired." He motioned to the open door. "Go ahead."

I got inside and walked to the very back. Hunching down, I begged my ankle to stop screaming its agony, closed my eyes, and took my first half-easy breath since witnessing Edward Marcello's murder.

Loving Down and Dead in Dixie?

Get the Book Now: Down and Dead in Dixie

How did Caroline get to Sampson Park?
Read ***Down and Dead in Even***, the second story Short Read in the Down and Dead, Inc. series.
The Beginning for Caroline...

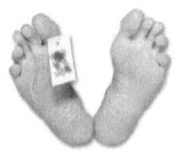

About the Author

Vicki Hinze is a *USA Today* bestselling author who has written nearly forty books, fiction and nonfiction, and hundreds of articles, published in as many as 63 countries. She's won a wide array of awards, including novels of the year in multiple genres. All of her novels include suspense, mystery and romance. The focus determines genre. Her works have been classified in nearly every genre except horror, with the majority being suspense, thriller, mystery and romance.

A Vice President for International Thriller Writers, Vicki also served as a consultant to the Board of Directors for Romance Writers of America and multiple other notable organizations. She is the former radio talk show host of *Everyday Woman*, and a columnist for Social In Global Network. Vicki was the first RWA PRO Mentor of the Year, and the recipient of RWA's National Service Award. She's recognized as an author and an educator by *Who's Who in the World*.

For early access to new releases and more, subscribe to the monthly newsletter at http://mad.ly/signups/82943/join

 facebook.com/vicki.hinze.author

 twitter.com/vickihinze

 pinterest.com/vickihinze

 bookbub.com/authors/vicki-hinze

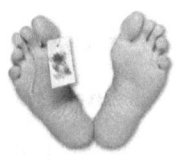

Also by Vicki Hinze

Clean Read or Inspirational:

S.A.S.S. Unit Series

Black Market Body Double | The Sparks Broker | The Mind Thief | Operation Stealing Christmas | S.A.S.S. Confidential

Breakdown Series

so many secrets | her deepest fear (Short Read)

Down and Dead, Inc. Series

Down and Dead in Dixie | Down and Dead in Even |

Down and Dead in Dallas

Shadow Watchers

(Crossroads Crisis Center related)

The Marked Star | The Marked Bride | Wed to Death: A Shadow Watchers Short

Crossroads Crisis Center Series

Forget Me Not | Deadly Ties | Not This Time

Inspirational

The Reunion Collection

Her Perfect Life | Mind Reader | Duplicity |

Lost, Inc.

Survive the Night | Christmas Countdown |

Torn Loyalties

Inspirational

General Audience:

War Games Series

Body Double | Double Vision | Double Dare | Smokescreen: Total Recall | Kill Zone

(out of print)

The Lady Duo

Lady Liberty | Lady Justice

Military

Shades of Gray | Acts of Honor | All Due Respect

Paranormal Romantic Suspense

Legend of the Mist | Maybe This Time

Seascape Novels

Beyond the Misty Shore | Upon a Mystic Tide |

Beside a Dreamswept Sea

Other

Girl Talk: Letters Between Friends | My Imperfect Valentine | Invitation to a Murder | Bulletproof | The Madonna Key (series co-creator) | Before the White Rose | Invidia

Multiple-Author Collections

Dangerous Desires | My Evil Valentine | Risky Brides | Smart Women and Dangerous Men | Christmas Heroes | Love is Murder | Cast of Characters | A Message from Cupid Seeing Fireworks

Nonfiction Books

In Case of Emergency: What You Need to Know When I Can't Tell You | One Way to Write a Novel | Writing in the Fast Lane | All About Writing to Sell |

Mistakes Writers Make and How-To Avoid Them

For a complete listing visit

http://vickihinze.com/books